'Had me laughing out loud in some places
and unable to tear my gaze from the drama
in others. Highly recommended'
Cass Green, author of *The Woman Next Door*

'A thrilling page-turner with a fresh, original heroine
at its heart . . . that dares to subject modern feminism
to a tough and timely cross-examination'
T.J. Emerson, author of *The Perfect Holiday*

'Exciting, contemporary, heartfelt and clever'
Greg Mosse, author of *Murder at Church Lodge*

'Plays with many themes and masterfully weaves
them into a narrative that is riveting, real and
raw . . . It is the book of the year for me'
Balvinder Sopal, actress

'Wisely and wittily leaps into the heart of friendships
made within rage, both how healing and harmful
they can be . . . an excellent, indulgent read'
Sabrina Mahfouz, author of *How You Might Know Me*

Nina Millns is an author, playwright and screenwriter whose debut novel, *Goddesses*, has been optioned for television. Her play *Service* won the ETPEP Playwriting Award and she has written the BBC Sounds series *Mortem* as well as her first play, *Delete*, and a *Doctor Who* International Women's Day audio special, *Turn of the Tides*.

Also by Nina Millns

FICTION
Goddesses

PLAYS
Delete
Service

SAY YOU'LL BE THERE

NINA MILLNS

**SIMON &
SCHUSTER**

London · New York · Amsterdam/Antwerp · Sydney/Melbourne · Toronto · New Delhi

First published in Great Britain by Simon & Schuster UK Ltd, 2025

1 3 5 7 9 10 8 6 4 2

Simon & Schuster UK Ltd
1st Floor, 222 Gray's Inn Road
London, WC1X 8HB

Simon & Schuster Australia, Sydney
Simon & Schuster India, New Delhi

www.simonandschuster.co.uk
www.simonandschuster.com.au
www.simonandschuster.co.in

The authorised representative in the EEA is Simon & Schuster Netherlands BV,
Herculesplein 96, 3584 AA Utrecht, Netherlands. info@simonandschuster.nl

Simon & Schuster strongly believes in freedom of expression and stands against
censorship in all its forms. For more information, visit BooksBelong.com

A CIP catalogue record for this book is available from the British Library

Paperback ISBN: 978-1-3985-1837-7
eBook ISBN: 978-1-3985-1836-0
Audio ISBN: 978-1-3985-1839-1

Typeset in the UK by M Rules
Printed and Bound in the UK using 100% Renewable Electricity at CPI Group (UK) Ltd

For the girls we once were

and the women we have become.

PROLOGUE

It took a month to find a day they could all do. And even then, it was a remote conversation. Online. Despite all three of them being in the same city, they had opted to talk via computer. And they were all relieved.

They were nervous in their different ways, but also in the same way. The way any form of reunion with people who have known you for so long engenders. The way it forces you to assess your own life in anticipation of others doing precisely that, looking around at your everyday situation, scrutinizing yourself in the mirror, and finding it all inevitably disappointing. A bit embarrassing. Not quite the success you'd expected you'd be by this point. Far from it in fact. And then the regret. Why put themselves through this? Why drag it all up again? Shine a light on all the wrinkly, dusty, bulgy parts? Why not just carry on, interacting with only those who were newer acquaintances? Who'd only ever known you to be disappointingly middle-aged from the start? Who didn't remember your smooth skin, lithe body, bright mind. Your potential.

Then came the defensiveness. Fuck them. If they're gonna be so judgemental then maybe they should think about their own sorry situation first. And actually, I'm very happy with my life, thanks. And if you've got a problem, you know what you can do with it. Then the self-righteousness followed by a desperate need to impress. Work's going amazingly well, actually. And I'm just happy, y'know? Good balance and all that. Just glad not to be a walking stereotype, free of labels. It's a breath of fresh air, actually …

It felt like a mistake now. Each of them wondering why they had agreed to this. Over the decades, they'd bumped into each other, mostly online, every now and then in person. It always started a bit overly enthusiastic, trying to outdo each other with how generous they were about the other person, how humble and self-effacing they were about themselves. No comparison, no competition. Eventually they'd fall into an almost comfortable familiarity. That's when the chat became quieter, less forced, monosyllabic at times, so much less needing to be said. Often there was a quip, a witty observation, a reference to an old in-joke followed by a giggle – a sound they had forgotten their bodies could make. Girly, young, involuntary. But there was also a moment where the distance, the miles covered without each other, made itself known. A slight misunderstanding, something patronizing, an insensitive comment that caused a gaping crevasse to open up between them, distance so vast and sudden they had no idea how to bridge it. And so they drifted apart once more. But then, once the smarting had eased, they'd see a comment or a like on their socials, maybe even a text message, and the little girl inside them got excited again. Because that was their old bestie, their first ever love.

And so, they gathered. Warily, wearily, hopefully.

Chairs were positioned. Backgrounds carefully curated. Make-up donned and tops chosen. Curious and expectant and defensive, they logged on.

'Hi.'

'Hey.'

'Hello.'

An awkward wave.

They scrutinized the details that might tell them something about the other's life now.

'It's you,' Tess said.

Arianna and Candace looked at each other briefly. One nodded.

'It is,' the other said.

It was a silly comment, but it did the trick. Because Tess was right. It *was* her. And her. The same ones, just older, weather-worn, and not the enemy she had built them up to be.

'You have books in your house,' Tess commented, pointing.

Arianna turned briefly.

'Yes. I do.'

'You have a picture of a sunflower.'

'Yep,' Candace confirmed. Then she looked down, building up the courage to begin. 'It seems a bit dramatic, all this,' she admitted. 'But ... she's gone. Dana's gone. And it's different this time.'

PART ONE

1997

DANA

'Wakey, wakey darlin'.'

Eileen crept into the room and opened the curtains halfway.

Dana stretched sleepily but kept her eyes closed. She heard the clink of a mug that she knew would be full of sweet milky tea, as her mum placed it on the bedside table, the rustle of the duvet as she snuggled in with Dana.

Dana felt her mum's bony body behind her and reached out for her arm, wrapped it around her. A whiff of her morning fag reached Dana's nostrils. It mingled with her shampoo and moisturizer smell, Timotei, Nivea, creating her unique aroma. But Eileen was soon moving again, giving her daughter a quick squeeze before getting up and pulling the curtains wide open, heading back to the kitchen. Dana groaned in protest as she sat up, reaching for her tea. Two neighbouring tower blocks leaned into view through her bedroom window, but there was enough sky visible from their fifth-floor home to brighten all the rooms in their impeccably kept flat.

She pulled her frizzy blonde hair into a bun, stretched her lanky limbs and did easy sums in her head. Something she did without realizing now. A habit that had formed back in primary school sometime, when she'd first been introduced to the rhythm of times tables. It calmed her, repeating the patterns, putting the numbers in order, balancing them out, finding the one, absolute correct answer. Finite, measurable. She took a few more sips of her tea and hauled herself out of her My Little Pony-themed bedding set, pulling the Minnie Mouse nightie down over her bum. Eileen sat waiting for her daughter to join her, second fag of the day already lit. She'd laid out a plate with pieces of white toast covered with margarine and Marmite on the kitchen table.

'Why'd you brush your hair out again?' Eileen reached over to touch Dana's hair. Dana ducked.

'Leave off, Mum.'

'People would kill to have curls like yours. Why d'you think I go hairdressers every other weekend to get my perm done? So's I look like you.'

Dana rolled her eyes, took a hungry bite of her toast.

'I'll get some gel from Auntie Naila. Show you how to scrunch it.'

Eileen watched her daughter through the curling smoke, her own piece of toast left untouched. Then she stubbed out her cigarette and blew the final puff of smoke out with force.

'Right. Shove off then.'

1997

ARIANNA

'Lend me twenny pee.'

Arianna turned to find a wide, round face in *her* face, thin Afro hair scraped into a tiny ponytail that stuck up vertically, and a hand thrust out, almost grazing her chin, palm upturned.

'Lend me twenny pee,' the girl demanded again.

Arianna clutched the pound coin in her pocket, the only money she had on her, which was meant to last her the whole day.

'I ain't got it,' she managed.

The girl studied Arianna closely.

'What you got?'

'I ain't got twenny pee for you,' Arianna replied levelly, trying to keep the tremble out of her voice.

Arianna braced herself for whatever came next. She kept her shoulders square but her gaze easy. Pony-Tail glared at her for what felt like ages, then she spun around and marched over to the next person.

'Oi, lend me twenny pee ...'

'Fuck off Shanice, why you always begging ...'

Arianna allowed herself a moment of relief. Maybe she'd actually make it to school before her first fight. None of the other kids had been interested in this mini-standoff and she made a mental note: Pony-Tail / Shanice was loud and in-your-face, but ultimately harmless.

She studied the groups of kids waiting for the number 14 bus to take them up the hill. Their school didn't have a uniform, but there was an unofficial dress code: black puffer jackets with an orange inner lining; baggy tracksuit bottoms or jeans with the bottoms pinched into pin-rolls; branded trainers carefully preserved and preferably with the tag still on; backpacks slung over one shoulder only, no socks in sight – ever; high-tops, curtains or a buzz-cut for the boys; hair scraped into tight buns or pony tails with the edges gelled down for the girls. Arianna was relieved to see not much had changed since she had last lived in this corner of Southwest London. But when she looked down, she was consumed with self-consciousness. Her trainers were three years old, her garms, bought in the shopping centre indoor market before she'd been sent Home and packed away until she returned, her hairstyle more of a statement than she now wanted to make.

She had woken up extra early to air out her old purple and turquoise shell suit, given her Reebok Pumps a wet-wipe and four lucky pumps each tongue. Then she'd scrunched gel into her curls, scraped them back into a half up, half down style with her fringe back-combed into a fan that rose from her fore-head and cascaded down the side of her face – all sprayed solid. The shell suit, the hairspray, the white musk perfume from The

Body Shop, all combined to make Arianna one highly flammable neon mass. But she was ready: London-ready.

Arianna tensed against the chill of the March morning, her neck retreating further into her jacket, her skin contracting in shock even after two weeks of being back. Her bones maintained the memory of the easy warmth that had defined her days for almost two years. She hardened herself, trying to shed the memory of the sun, the softness, the ease of that sweet era, and face her current situation head on. Like she had when her mum had told her she was being sent Home. And again, when she was told she was being brought back.

Arianna scanned the faces at the bus stop, hoping to find a familiar one. The schoolkids joked and shared music, hugged and leaned on each other, shoved and cussed each other out fondly. But beyond this group was another. Stiffer, stiller, more self-conscious, the girls from St Florian's – the private school halfway up the hill – stood in a tight huddle, keeping a safe distance from the larger horde while waiting for the same bus. Their fair hair was freshly brushed and hung natural and loose, free of product. Their blue blazers with the pink edging were pristine and their skirts were hitched high, exposing long, well-bred legs in woolly black tights. They chatted quietly among one another and hugged their musical instruments.

The 14 bus pulled up and the crowd of kids surged towards the door, engulfing an elderly lady who was also attempting to board.

'Oi! Back up you little hooligans. Show some respect.'

A small white boy who had shoved his way to the front

was suddenly gripped by the hood by a big black hand and pulled backwards.

'Get off me!' he protested.

Arianna turned to see an older girl, maybe even a sixth former, holding the boy and another smaller kid by the scruff of their necks. She towered over the lower-school kids.

'How you gonna mow down an old lady like that, Tony?' she chided as Tony continued to struggle in her grasp.

'Why you taking liberties Michelle?'

Michelle cut her eye at him.

'Watch it, Tony. Just cos you grew your first pube this weekend, don't mean you can back chat me.'

A roar of delight from the surrounding kids who fell about laughing as Tony turned bright red.

'Let her through. All of you.' Michelle's voice cut through.

The kids shuffled back, revealing the shaken old lady once again, who looked around bewildered, then boarded the bus.

The crowd surged forward. Arianna found herself carried along until she too passed across the threshold. She dropped her pound into the tray in front of the driver and got 80p in change, which she pocketed carefully. Then she let the wave sweep her up the stairs.

Arianna stood on the top aisle as the bus set off again, right beside the sign that said NO STANDING ON THE UPPER DECK. Next to her stood a Florian girl who was clinging onto her cello case and looking down at the floor. Pony-Tail / Shanice stood on her other side staring at Arianna.

'Escuse me. What school do you go to?' she asked loudly.

Arianna sniffed nonchalantly. 'Hallam.'

'Our school? What year you in?'

'Year eight.'

'How come I haven't seen you?'

'First day, innit.'

Shanice studied Arianna carefully. Arianna could see the various scenarios playing out in her head as she tried to place her.

'Did you get expelled? Is that why you're starting late?'

A few faces turned in interest.

'No,' Arianna replied.

'So how come you starting so late . . .'

'Why you asking about my business?' Arianna tried to sound assertive but not confrontational.

Shanice's curiosity got the better of her a second time. She took in Arianna's tight curls, her skin, still retaining the tan from back Home, the smattering of freckles on her nose and her dark eyes.

'Where you from?' she asked.

'Disraeli Road. You want my postcode an' all?' Arianna retorted.

'Are you Asian or half-caste?'

'Are you still up in my business?'

The upper deck had gone quiet. Inquisitive eyes took in every inch of her, the thickness of lip, the curve of her bum, the height of cheekbone.

'But where are your family from, though?' Shanice attempted once more.

'Shanice, man, allow her,' came a voice from somewhere further along the aisle.

A boy leaned over the other kids – a familiar face, finally. Chris R.P, his light afro curls freshly shorn into a high top, his right eyebrow shaved into stripes, his warm, wide brown eyes and freckled nose wrinkled in amusement. Arianna's face lit up.

Shanice looked from Chris back to Arianna. 'Do you know her?'

'Yeah, she's safe,' confirmed Chris.

'But how do you know her?' Shanice insisted.

Chris looked at Arianna, a knowing sparkle in his eye. 'She's my cousin, innit.'

There was a collective unclenching. Arianna had been placed. It was the perfect moniker – familiar enough to make her family, obscure enough to hold a myriad of potential biological connections – similar to many of their own large rambling families. Perhaps something in the eyes was the same, the freckles maybe.

Arianna smiled warmly at her old mate from primary school. They weren't cousins, but they'd known each other since they were four, had made animals out of playdoh together, played kiss chase and, once, when they were eight, he'd made a phone out of Lego and sung 'I just called to say I love you'.

'You back, yeah?' Chris offered.

'Yeah,' Arianna confirmed, smiling.

The bus lurched to a stop and everyone shoved their way off. Arianna stepped out and the ground felt a little more solid under her Reeboks.

1997

CANDACE

Candace was in a bad mood today. She'd woken up that way. End of. She walked into Registration, mumbling a *'SorryI'mlateMiss,'* and slumped into the seat Dana had kept free for her. Candace folded her arms on the desk, burying her head into them. Dana let her be, sitting quietly, loyally beside her while Candace seethed. Letting her ride it out. She knew her well enough not to ask. One sleepover at hers was enough for Dana to see Candace's home situation. And it was tough.

Science was first. They copied the water cycle down from their textbook, labelled it. Candace perked up then when she realized it was drawing and not writing. Her diagrams were impeccable, the spelling not so great. By the time they got to Maths, she was cussing Alan and John about their posh accents, mimicking the long words they had just used in History, grabbing Alan in a headlock until he turned purple – back on form. Maths was bollocks. The only thing worse was English. Because letters were worse than numbers. Fact. But Dana loved this shit – quietly, on the down-low. Candace leaned back in her chair and watched out of the corner of her eye as her friend transformed, going into some next zone where only the neat rows of numbers and symbols existed, working it out in her head with a focus that made her eyes blaze and her forehead crease, her brain working in a way Candace's never could. Sometimes Dana's hand shot up, then she'd answer a question before even John or Alan had figured it out. That was Candace's favourite. Under the table, she raised her middle finger at the white boys at the front. Dana was careful to keep her arms wide as she wrote, leaving space for Candace to copy.

'Why is Mr Austen's arse so wide? You reckon he's a batty boy?' Candace's dirty chuckle cut through Dana's daydreaming as they headed out for break time. Dana nudged her.

'Oi, you lot. Sponsor me.'

They turned to see Shanice striding over, holding out a clipboard and pen, her hair scraped so tightly into her tiny ponytail that her face looked permanently surprised. She shoved the clipboard in their faces.

'What's that?' Candace asked.

'It's my sponsorship form, innit,' Shanice explained.

'What's it for?'

'So you can sponsor me.'

'For what?'

'It's Comic Relief,' Shanice explained patiently.

Candace looked down at the three names scribbled on the form with a number and a pound sign next to them.

'Get that thing out my face, man.' Candace shoved the form away.

'It's for *Charitee,*' Shanice insisted. 'Look, Miss White's giving me two pound.'

'Two pound for what?'

'Sponsored silence.'

Candace turned back.

'*You're* gonna do a sponsored silence.'

'Yes. It's for the Africans.'

Candace burst out laughing. 'Get the fuck out of here with your scam money makin' ideas. What you chatting about, "*It's for the Africans?*" – I'm half African. Just give *me* the money.' Candace held her palm out, waiting for her *Charitee.*

'It's serious. It's Red Nose Day. You gotta wear the red nose and raise money for the kids in Africa.'

'And you're gonna do a sponsored silence.'

'Yes.'

'For how long?'

'All day.'

'If you manage to shut up the whole day, I'll give you fifty pound.'

Shanice's eyes lit up. 'Put it on the form!' she insisted.

'I ain't putting shit on your form cos you can't keep your mouth shut for two minutes. And anyway. You gotta sponsor us back.'

'Why, what you doing?' Shanice frowned. Dana also frowned.

Candace's mind raced. 'We're gonna do a dance routine. Tied together. As the Spice Girls.'

1997

TESS

Tess strode along the corridor, violin case slung over her shoulder as she headed to the lower foyer for lunch. Her mind still rung with the piece she had been practising, and she felt the resonance in her body too, her fingers still smarting from the strings. She hummed Bach's sonata under her breath and tested herself by walking in a rhythm that clashed with the complex melody in her head. For fun, she added the finger-work of an arpeggio and giggled as she faltered. Much harder than rubbing your belly and tapping your head at the same time.

She groaned as she reached the queue which still ran all the way down the stairs. She was twenty minutes late and had hoped it would have shortened by now. No such luck. She headed to the bottom of the staircase and her stomach sank as she passed Tony Gibbs, the little shit who bounced around the building head-butting and shoving, laughing and cussing. His absolute favourite pastime was to gob on the kids below him in the dinner queue. Only two weeks into the year, Tess had watched with horror as a phlegmy globule of spit had narrowly missed her and landed in the hair of the unassuming girl in front of her. And now she would have to spend the next fifteen minutes craning her neck up so that she could keep an eye on Tony at all times. Two more years until she'd be in upper school with the older kids, who had either grown out of gobbing on people or been expelled by then.

Chips and beans. Chips, pizza and beans. Beans and pizza. Pizza and chips. And pudding. Definitely pudding. Finally at the top of the line and mercifully free of spit, Tess took a tray and got her lunch. She clocked Joe and Andrew sitting in a huddle in the corner, the rest of the table empty. Andrew was wearing a polo jumper and slacks in muted earthy colours, his dark skin shining with cleanliness and good moisturizer; Joe, a mixed-race boy, whose natural loose curls had been allowed to grow out, his well-fitting understated green tracksuit only just passing as acceptable urban attire. Sensible shoes. They looked up in surprise at Tess's arrival.

'Hello,' she said. Joe and Andrew blushed immediately. Tess shrugged and started eating, until a clatter made them look up. The new girl placed her tray on the table, sat in the final empty chair and smiled briefly at Tess. Tess smiled briefly back, taking in the girl's shell suit, the hairspray and big earrings: a Rude Girl.

'Andrew, you peanut!' Tess looked up to see Tony and Shanice sitting on the table behind the boys, snickering.

'Joe, you Bounty!'

'Oi, you've got money. Sponsor me.'

The two boys flinched but said nothing. Tess waited for her turn, usually something along the lines of her being a coconut: brown on the outside, white on the inside. Her cheeks were already flushing and she stopped her hand from reaching up and pushing the round glasses further up her nose.

'Thass your Red Nose Day outfits sorted, innit: one's comin' as a peanut, the other's comin' as a Bounty. Easy.' Tony said. Shanice cackled.

'What you comin' as?' Shanice asked Tony.

'A pube,' someone shouted from another table. The surrounding tables guffawed.

Tony recovered quickly. 'I heard Gemma Haydon's gonna pierce her belly button with a compass.'

'Is it?'

'Yeah. She already got twenny-five quid sponsorship.'

'Twenny-five?'

'Yeah. Cos of all the blood.'

Tess sighed. Red Nose Day. Fuck. She'd have to think of something. Otherwise, she'd stand out for being the only one NOT in some kind of costume or doing something zany. Perhaps she could do a sponsored all-day violin-playing marathon? Could she tease her hair out into some kind of afro? Come as Angela Davis? Tess slumped. She might as well tattoo 'nerd' on her forehead and save herself the trouble.

'Oi, New Girl. What you saying?'

Tess felt a rush of relief as the focus moved to someone else. The new girl glanced over her shoulder.

'Are you safe or are you a bod?' Tony's annoying voice insisted. 'Are you a Bounty or a Curly Wurly?'

'I heard she got expelled and then got sent back to her country and then got expelled from there,' Tony continued.

'Thass why she's coming as a criminal for Red Nose. Straight up Triad gangster.'

Andrew and Joe glanced over at Arianna fearfully. Tess looked over with alarm. The new girl frowned but kept quiet.

'I already told you. Leave my cousin alone or I'll box you upside your face.' Tess looked around to see Chris R.P calling over from his table.

Tony raised a placatory hand and deferred to the older boy. 'Safe. Safe.'

ARIANNA

The smell made Arianna grimace. She could tell the meat had been defrosted and she knew that most of the contents of the crammed freezer had been there since before she'd *gone back Home*. She couldn't help but remember the trips to the market with Yiayia then, the negotiating of prices, the good-natured haggling, the fear and respect the hawkers had for her grandmother's keen eye, carrying the shopping back through the neighbourhood in the gentle warmth of mid-morning, before the sting of midday, her grandma's – Yiayia's – slower pace, stopping to talk to familiar faces – many of whom she was somehow related to; the peeling, sifting and washing, the chopping and seasoning; the ancient oven with its one temperature setting from which would emerge the best food Arianna had ever tasted, would ever taste. And the light. The bright mornings and the neighbour's cockerel crowing and Pappou's comfortable silences as he drove her to school. The uniform of every local school in Cyprus – a simple, girlish checked cotton dress and smart black shoes that her Yiayia made her polish every weekend.

She hadn't even known how to do her own hair. Her

eleven-year-old fingers had fumbled with the hairband every morning as her Yiayia hovered, threatening to take over and force her unruly curls into an old-fashioned French plait. So she learned quickly.

It hadn't taken long to establish herself at the top of the pecking order in the little school. A few tough retorts at the right moment in the local vernacular, a handstand contest, which she won easily, and suddenly she ruled – this new girl from London with her cool music and cooler dance moves. She had taken her new-found status seriously, ensuring that fairness and order prevailed in her realm. No one got away with bullying or leaving anyone out, and disputes were resolved with a carefully refereed hundred-metre sprint across the dusty playground. She would walk past the sleepy newsagents on the way home and pick up a chocolate bar to share with Yiayia and Pappou and the three of them would settle in for the evening to watch five-year-old episodes of *Neighbours*, which had only just arrived to the island, on one of their two channels.

Standing in this draughty London hallway now, the pull back Home was suddenly strong and devastating. She stood between two worlds, feeling the cold, the exhaustion of her first day at her new school. She'd tried so hard. Each interaction had been so carefully played out, meticulously delivered to establish herself in this ruthless new pecking order. And still she'd failed. No new friends. Just hours and hours of wary, penetrating stares and suspicious side-eyes.

It was still awkward at home. A re-learning of each other. A re-ordering of the family dynamics now that she was back.

She still wasn't sure why she had been sent back to Cyprus. A general sense of her mum not coping, but also that it would be good for her – to learn the language, to experience a simpler way of life; to help her Yiayia, come back fluent and dutiful and less of a burden, maybe. Arianna suspected that she'd been summoned back again because her mum had discovered that raising the two younger ones was almost impossible without her.

Cartoons were playing in the living room; little Theo was making his trains talk to each other. Lelia was sitting at the kitchen table struggling with some homework.

'Again,' her mum ordered loudly over her shoulder as she pulled a dish out of the oven with only a dishcloth for protection against its searing heat. She dropped the dish loudly on the counter when it began to burn her once again.

'Seven, fourteen, twenty ... twenty ... three?' Lelia wavered. Thankfully, Arianna's entrance took the focus off her for now.

Arianna took the crockery and cutlery to the table and yelled her brother's name. Lelia swiftly shut her maths book and replaced it with a plate. The two younger siblings tucked into the food enthusiastically. Her mum didn't have a plate of her own. Just like Yiayia, she cooked and then watched the others eat, maybe allowing herself a bite at the end, just a taste.

'You have homework?' she asked Arianna.

'Just this stupid English thing. We've got to learn a speech.'

'What speech?'

'Some Shakespeare speech she gave us. From Julius Caesar.'

'Good. You can learn a Greek one too.'

'I just said it's for English—'

'The Greeks invented speeches. And plays. You think there would be Shakespeare without Sophocles?'

Arianna sighed. The Greek book sat ready at the end of the table with a pencil and rubber next to it at all times. When Arianna or Lelia didn't look busy enough, they would be sent there to do Greek under their mum's scatty supervision.

'And I need you to sponsor me,' Arianna said.

'To what?'

'To sponsor me. For Red Nose Day.'

Her mum's face was already tightening. What new bullshit would this country throw at her now? What money was being demanded from her for what kind of British nonsense?

'Never mind. Look, just ... can I borrow some clothes?' Arianna asked.

1997

CANDACE

Candace slowed her steps until she was barely progressing down the street. She stuffed her hands deeper into her lime green Naf Naf gilet and turned the sound up on her Walkman. Queen Latifa spat the lyrics to 'Ladies First' – crisp and clear in her ears – and Candace rapped along, word for powerful word. She adjusted her baggy light blue denim dungarees. Her commitment to this new look, fresh from the East Coast, meant she was wearing one strap unfastened so that half of the top hung loose across her chest. It was a bit uncomfortable on her left tit, but she was rocking it.

She saw movement down the road. Her brother and his mate bounced out of the front door, already looking shifty as they headed in the other direction. Candace softened. Her patience had paid off. She picked up the pace and let herself in, straight up the stairs.

She reached under her bed and pulled out a small paper bag of 10p mix. Chewing noisily on a candy shrimp, Candace took the magazine from her rucksack and studied the cover. Queen L's face glowed confidently from it, a colourful Zulu hat perched proudly on her head, her skin flawless, her gaze warm and fierce. To her side, along the right of the cover, were two smaller figures, both wearing matching Kente Kufi hats with braids hanging down on either side. South London's very own Cookie Crew. Right there alongside the Queen. Candace tutted. That's who she should have gone as. It would have been perfect for Red Nose Day. But she'd said the Spice Girls, so now she'd have to figure out how to make that work. She pulled a few brightly coloured tops from her wardrobe, threw them on a pile to be considered later for her costume.

Then Candace threw herself onto the floor and pulled out the other stash under her bed: her pens, pencils and paper. With great care, she began to draw the women.

1997

TESS

Tess rode the bus home. It was almost empty. School had finished two hours ago and even the kids who'd stayed behind for detention had left before her. She was a bit frazzled now, her stomach growling loudly, but it was the only way she would have a chance of passing Grade 8. Mr Tamworth had noticed her talent last year and talked to her dad at parents' evening about extra classes just for her. There was always enough for good home-cooked food, second-hand books, but violin lessons were a bit of a stretch, so Linton had accepted.

Mr Tamworth. Tess contemplated his lanky build as she leaned back in her seat, his floppy hair and round glasses. She decided he looked a bit like a sexy Where's Wally.

She pulled out her English homework, a sheet in each hand. The first was a copy of Dr Martin Luther King's *I Have a Dream* speech, photocopied many times over until it was slightly askew, slightly out of focus, the photo that accompanied the text a little grainy, green-tinted. Something about his expression reminded her of her dad when he talked politics at a rally and a wave of affection flooded through her.

Miss Henderson had played a recording, muffled with age,

and Dr King's voice had boomed through the classroom. Tess had followed the rhythm of his speech, the long, drawn-out vowels that were almost a song, a hymn, an aria. The beat of the rule of three as he landed the final third that had caused the historic crowd to call out in response, in commitment to the movement, the slow rise to the final crescendo, the final roar from the audience: the ovation. Tess had realized her heart was beating harder, her breaths faster. But then Miss Henderson had stopped the recording and the back row had fallen into fits of giggles.

Tess folded the photocopy and slid it into her exercise book. She already knew what Linton would say if he saw they'd been studying Dr King. His lecture would last the whole of dinner, about how radical he had been, how watered down the curriculum had made his legacy, how all suggestion of fighting the very system that had enslaved his people and continued to oppress brown and black people across the world had been White Washed until he was almost unrecognizable as the radical activist he once was.

Tess looked at the other photocopy as the bus turned the corner onto her road. 'Friends, Romans, countrymen, lend me your ears.'

A safer dinner discussion. Tess scanned the speech, remembering what they'd been taught about iambic pentameter, counting out the syllables, noticing where it was broken on purpose. As she'd gathered her things to head to the next lesson, she'd noticed the new girl, Arianna, looking intently at the speech, her mouth forming the words silently. Her eyes were sparkling. They had locked gazes for a moment and

Tess had frozen, a half-smile on her face, before she turned and strode out.

Tess jumped off at her stop and climbed the three storeys to their council flat. The aroma of peppers and fish wafted out the window and made her stomach growl loudly.

She let herself into the warmth of the flat crammed with books and music, the lights glowing, a Burning Spear record playing loudly.

'Hello, Bilbo!'

'Hello, Samwise.'

Tess dropped her schoolbag and violin case in the tiny hallway and found her dad hunched over the cooker. His curly grey beard and short grey afro were beginning to grow out again, his glasses slightly steamed, his favourite slippers almost worn through. Linton reached out to the rack of spices just above him and chose a small jar, sprinkling it thoughtfully over the food. Around them shelves overflowed with condiments, ingredients, mugs, postcards and more books.

'Another day's quest done,' he pronounced as he lifted the wooden spoon up to her lips. She savoured the layers of flavour and the spicy aftertaste.

'Ten minutes,' he said, and gave her a peck on the forehead. Tess rushed up the narrow staircase and into the spare room. She sifted through a black bin bag full of summer clothes and found both of them – the leopard print scarf and the T-shirt that said *Savage* in pink writing across it – presents from her mum from the last two Christmases, both unworn, by Tess at least. In her room, Tess undressed, pulling on the T-shirt which smelled a bit musty but fitted okay. She experimented with the scarf, which was huge, more like an exotically patterned sarong. She tried it around her neck, her waist, attempted to tie it somehow in her hair. She pulled out her bun and tried shaking her hair out. It stood in a strange mushroom shape she wasn't sure what to do with. This was stupid. She looked stupid. Tess took off the outfit and chucked it on her bed, pulling her hair back into the scrunchy. She returned to the kitchen, arranging two plates on the little wooden table, either side of the flourishing pot of basil on the brightly coloured African-print tablecloth, a postcard-sized picture of Angela Davis tacked to the wall just above.

Linton served up the aromatic food and lowered himself into the other chair. 'Eat, beloved girl,' he said.

1997

DANA

Dana ran back to the HiFi and stopped the song. She pressed REWIND, counted in her head and then pressed PLAY. She caught it almost perfectly at the start of the song and they took up their starting positions again. They started strong, their moves synched almost perfectly. Candace wobbled in the middle but looked over to Dana and picked it up again. They finished with their solos: first Candace kneeled as Dana did the shuffle; then Dana took a knee as Candace did a sick running man. They stopped the tape and squealed with joy. They'd been practising all afternoon. Candace had already stayed over twice at Dana's, so Dana had come over after lunch and brought her nightie.

Candace's dad had sponsored her a fiver. Dana's mum had given her two quid and Auntie Naila had matched it.

'Right. Let's try it tied up and then after we can sort outfits,' Dana suggested.

They used one of Candace's dad's special-occasion ties to secure their wrists together and giggled as they had to shuffle over to the HiFi to press PLAY. They assumed their starting positions. But when the music started, they went in different directions and were yanked back by their wrists. They tried to pick it up again, but the same thing happened and they were soon yelling at each other, laughing and reaching to stop the tape.

'Dana, man!'

'What? That was you!'

'I went left!'

'So did I!'

There was a loud bang as the door was kicked open and a booted foot followed through. Another bang as the door hit the wall, denting it. And then a series of muted thumps as Dana's left side exploded with pain. They screamed. Dana felt her wrist being pulled violently as Candace leaped up.

'Nathan you fucking lunatic! Get out!'

'AAAAHAHAHAHA!' came her older brother's cackle, as he shot Candace once, twice at point blank range. She tried to wrestle the air gun from him with her free hand, but he easily shoved her off and took another shot at the ceiling.

'What's going on up there?' Candace's dad closed the front door and strode heavily up the stairs.

Dana felt Candace hastily untie their wrists, her hand falling to the floor, throbbing with pain. There was a scuffle, several thumps. More shouting. Banging. Then the front door slammed and all was quiet again.

'You okay?' Candace's dad's flustered face looked in from the doorway. They both nodded.

They got ready for bed in silence, Dana watching Candace carefully, tracking the pain and rage on her face. They lay there in silence for a long time. Dana was terrified and wanted to go home. Her side was still smarting where the bullet had hit her, her twisted wrist still pulsating with pain. She tried to even out her breaths, waited for her muscles to begin relaxing. Then she reached for Candace's hand and clasped it.

As they finally drifted into sleep, Dana remembered vaguely that they hadn't discussed their costumes.

1997

ARIANNA

She'd lifted the mattress, propped it up while everyone else was downstairs. She sifted through the first layer of bed sheets, then towels. Under it all was the treasure: a blue tie-dye wraparound skirt; brown leather platform boots; a green flannel boob tube; a box full of dangling earrings. Her mum's old clothes, relics from the 60s when she'd come over and re-invented herself as a hippie. Stuff she wouldn't have dared wear in Cyprus. Arianna pulled out a psychedelic-patterned halter-neck top and some orange flares. As she replaced the rest of the clothes, Arianna noticed a square of brown leather peeping out from the very bottom of the bed. She cleared everything from the top of the suitcase and unclicked the old-fashioned locks. Inside was a neatly packed collection of clothes, something for all seasons, a toiletry bag and a leather folder with official documents, all bearing her mum's name, including her Cypriot passport. All ready. Just in case.

Arianna closed the suitcase, covered it back over with the piles of clothing, towels and sheets. She repositioned the mat-tress and took the outfit into the bathroom. She rummaged around in the back of the cabinet until she found the tub of bleach. It was a year out of date. The faded label said it was for use on facial hair. She shook out her dark, almost-black curls, took a thick strand in between her fingers and started to work it in.

CANDACE

There were at least three Rachels, two Monicas, a Kate Moss, a Beckham and a Gallagher. There were bound to be some Destiny's Childs too. Definitely a Michael Jackson. Candace growled with frustration and chucked the hairbrush across the bathroom. Then she took a breath, retrieved it, starting again to try and emulate the hairstyle in the picture: two little mini buns on the top of her head with the rest of her curls left loose. She nailed it on the third go, the buns tied so tight, the top half of her face felt rigid. She was wearing her dungarees with both straps hanging loose this time, so the whole top of it was folded over, her lime-green vest top underneath and the thickest kicks she owned on her feet, the white Fila ones. She grabbed her dad's tie and headed out.

Dana was waiting in the usual spot, her hair worn loose, curlier. Was that mousse in it? As she got closer, Candace noticed the two little blonde buns at the top of her head. Then Dana turned around. Her face was covered in make-up way too dark for her skin. She looked like she'd been Tangoed and sunburned all at once. She was wearing her mum's platform heel boots, flare-cut jeans and a leopard print vest top.

'That ain't Baby Spice,' Candace said.

'Baby Spice? Why would I be Baby Spice?'

'Cos you're blonde. And white.'

'But my hair's curly. I'm obviously Scary.'

'*I'm* Scary.'

'No you're not.'

'Yeah, I am. That's the only one I can be.'

'No. You're Sporty Spice.'

'How am I Sporty Spice?'

'Cos you're sporty.' Dana shrugged. It was obvious.

Candace was at a loss. She scanned her friend's tanned face, her blue eyes looking at her so sincerely, the fair eyelashes blinking at her, two light circles surrounded by orangey-brown paint. Candace burst out laughing at the ridiculous state of them both, as kids wearing their clothes back to front, dressed as babies with huge, oversized dummies, sporting red noses tied with elastic on their noses or, in one case, sticking out from the side of their foreheads, streamed past.

'Come on,' she said, but Dana pulled Candace back. She took the tie from Candace's hand and tied their wrists together. Then, a little more awkwardly, they walked inside.

1997

TESS

She'd rushed to the safety of the music department, dodging Jimmy Savile and Princess Di on the way and an eclectic variety of cheap fancy dress interpretations, most of which she had to take a vague guess at. She got through violin practice feeling self-conscious. She'd never shown so much leg, so much midriff before. She'd never worn her hair loose. She adjusted her glasses nervously, wishing she'd brought her coat with her so she could cover up this whole ridiculous outfit.

The pips went and she rushed out. The foyer was already crowded with hungry kids. Everyone was even more hyper than usual, checking out each other's garms, trying to guess who they were meant to be, and abusing the red noses in a hundred different ways.

In the corner, a huddle of kids had gathered, looking down at something. Tess saw the new girl, Arianna, carry her tray of food towards the crowd. Two more girls from her year, a brown girl and a blonde tied to each other by the wrist, followed behind, peering over the huddle.

'Just do it.'

'Come on man.'

'Stab it. Go on.'

Gemma Haydon sat on a chair, the skin of her belly button pinched between two fingers, holding a compass in the other hand, the sharp end aimed at her belly. She gritted her teeth. The spike hovered. They waited, transfixed.

'Gemma man, hurry up. My chips are getting cold.'

Gemma braced herself again. Everyone held their breath. She pulled the sharp spike back an inch, ready to take a stab, but it remained there. Finally, she lowered the compass, defeated. The group groaned with disappointment.

'That was lame, man.'

'Gemma you pussy.'

'You ain't gettin' no money for that.'

'The Africans are gonna go hungry and it's all your fault.'

The group turned back into the foyer. Tess and the others stepped back. And then someone pointed a finger. The two kids next to him looked up and they too began laughing and pointing. Tess realized with horror they were pointing at her. And at Arianna. And also at the two girls standing next to them.

'What the ... ?'

'Oh my days.'

'I never saw so much leopard print. My eyes are burnin'!'

Tess looked at Arianna, then at the other two girls still tied together at the wrist. The curls, the animal print, the chunky footwear, the tight tops. And it dawned on her, at the same time as it dawned on them all.

The four Scary Spices stood stranded in the middle of the foyer as the whole of the lower school turned towards them, guffawing with delight.

'Oh thass scary.'
'Thass very scary.'
'Thass the *Scariest* shit I've ever seen!'

2022

CANDACE

She's gone. Dana's gone.

Candace looked pleadingly at her two old schoolfriends. She saw Arianna's face tighten.

'Again?' Arianna asked.

'This is different.' Candace said.

'How?' Tess pressed.

'Her number's not working—'

'Which one? I've got five—' Arianna interjected.

'And her emails. She's not on Facebook, socials . . .'

'I dunno, Cee. She's done this before—'

'No, she hasn't. Not like this—'

'We've been here before.'

'No, we haven't. If you look her up nothing comes up. Not even a picture. It's like she's completely . . . Like she never existed.'

Arianna sat back in her chair. 'Cee, man. We can't keep doing this. There's got to be a limit. Otherwise, if you keep bailing her out, she'll never learn to . . . She'll always think we'll be here to . . . I have to be careful, Cee.'

Tess watched Candace and Arianna glare at each other. She couldn't bear it. 'Have you called anyone?' she asked.

'I called you.'

'Anyone else.'

'Like who?'

'Her mum or ... the police.'

'I can't do that.'

'If you're that worried—'

'I can't do that,' Candace repeated.

'She'll turn up,' Arianna said. 'She always does, when it gets bad enough. When she needs money or somewhere to stay—'

'You're not listening. This is different. Please trust me.'

They both heard the tremble in Candace's voice.

'We do. That's why we're here,' Tess said. 'But you've got to give us something.'

Candace nodded, gathered herself. 'We ... haven't seen each other in a very long time, but we kind of ... keep in touch,' she explained.

'How?' Tess asked.

Candace swallowed. 'It's not easy to ... Every year – for the last eleven years – she calls. On the same day. She never misses it. She calls and she ... she doesn't say anything, but she stays on long enough to ... I know it's her. And I know why she's calling. Then she hangs up once she's sure. She didn't call this time. I waited. She always calls. Once a year. Something's wrong.'

Arianna and Tess waited for something more, but Candace remained quiet.

'That doesn't really make any sense,' Arianna said bluntly.

'How do you ... Why does she do that?' Tess pressed.

'She hasn't missed it since ... the very beginning.' Candace said.

'The very beginning?' Tess pleaded.

'From the very .... start.' Candace could hear how confusing her own explanation was.

'Okay,' Tess said. She knew better than to exchange glances with Arianna in front of Candace.

Candace huffed suddenly, with frustration. 'Look. It'll all ... come out soon. I promise. You'll understand what I'm trying to ... I just can't ... All I know is that it's different this time. Something's wrong. And I need you to help me track her down.'

'Maybe she doesn't want to be found,' Arianna suggested.

Tess nodded. 'You said it yourself: she's deleted everything. Photos, socials, any references to her. All gone. Maybe she did it all on purpose.'

Candace glared at them grimly. 'That's what I'm afraid of.'

1998

CANDACE

Candace was humming Whitney, basking in the huskiness of her own good voice, as she leaned gently on Dana's shoulder. It had been a busy day. A good day: the four of them had spent lunchtime creating a play called *A Day in The Life of a Chewing Gum*, then Arianna had taught them the Kid 'n Play dance move, and Tess had invented a secret language called Alamo, which all four of them were now fluent in.

'You're not even saying anything.' Shanice had said as she tried desperately to make sense of it. Finally, with frustration, she yelled, 'You sound like fucking spastics,' and pelted away when Candace stepped forward, ready to box her in her mouth. But their mood wouldn't be dampened today. It was Friday. They were done.

Tess and Arianna were waiting for them at the gate and no one was in a rush to get home.

'Come we go Burger King,' Arianna suggested.

'Ain't got no pees,' Candace replied.

'Let's go park then.'

'It's chaps,' Dana shivered. 'What about someone's house?'

Arianna shrugged. 'You can call my mum and ask her if you like, but I'm not.'

Dana turned to Tess. 'Let's go to your house!'

Tess panicked, blushed. 'I don't know if my dad …' she started uncertainly.

'Let's surprise him! I'm good with dads,' Dana pushed.

1998

TESS

She'd had a few friends from orchestra back at hers for extra rehearsals before, but she'd never had anyone from school over. The four of them climbed the concrete stairs in her block that smelled strongly of bleach, then Tess let them in the front door and called to Linton before he could call her one of their literary pet names.

'Hi, Dad, it's me. I've got some friends ...' The girls. Her friends. Over at hers.

He was in his reading chair, surrounded by shelves of paperbacks and clothed in corduroy, mercifully without that tatty blanket draped over him. The edges of his afro glinted as he turned – he'd used some water to neaten it up, thank god. Linton removed his reading glasses and stood, putting the book down as the girls stepped into the living room. Tess could see the title from where she was standing – *Trotsky* in big red letters – which meant the girls could too. She cringed.

Linton looked from Tess to the girls and back again. 'To what do I owe this pleasure?'

'Um, this is Arianna and Dana and that's Candace,' Tess said pleading with her eyes.

'Hello,' Dana said cheerily.

Linton raised his eyebrows at the girls, looked to Tess once more, then broke into a smile.

'I'm Linton, Tess's father. Not grandfather,' he quipped, patting his grey hair. 'Can you handle spicy food, girls?'

'Sure,' Candace replied, ignoring Dana's look of alarm.

'Then we'll get along fine. Dinner will be in an hour, and I hope you will stay and join us. In the meantime, why don't you head on upstairs, and I'll bring you some tea.'

Tess's gratitude turned suddenly to panic. Upstairs. Her room. Her sanctuary, her shrine. Tess had managed to keep herself aloof enough to glide through school with only the odd Coconut comment and critique of her appearance. She kept it moving, from rehearsal to class to private lesson to orchestra practice and didn't give anyone the opportunity to scrutinize her too closely. But now the girls were going to see her bedroom. It was strong ammunition to use against her and could seal her fate at school for years to come.

She led them up the stairs, past yet more shelves of books, including two copies of Linton's favourite classic, *Tess of the D'Urbervilles*, after which he'd named his daughter. She hesitated before stepping into her room. She tried to see it through their eyes: her old violin lying on the windowsill missing a string, a music stand in the corner crammed with sheet music, an ironic recorder and an array of percussion instruments scattered around. And then the posters. They covered every inch of wall and the entire ceiling. Mostly cut-outs from NME and Melody Maker blue-tacked with care, with the odd glossy Athena poster, which she received on birthdays. Kurt Cobain's heavily kohled eyes, Counting Crows standing in a moody cluster all in black in a field somewhere, The Levellers and R.E.M. and Crowded House. But mostly Bono. Bono and U2. Bono and The Edge back to back. Just Bono. Bono onstage singing passionately into the mic, a spotlight on him as he stood in a wide stride, black jeans and cowboy boots and colour-tinted sunglasses. Bono in a hat. Bono in shadow. Bono in close-up staring at her from six different angles, the lyrics to 'Bullet The Blue Sky' scribbled on scrap paper in his hand.

Tess watched Arianna, Dana and Candace take it all in and awaited their verdict. They said nothing for a long time. Then Dana turned to Tess.

'Cool.'

1998

ARIANNA

It was the best time she'd had since she'd moved back. For three perfect hours she'd hung out in the warmth of that cramped little haven and had her ears filled, her belly filled and her heart soothed. They had lain on the floor looking up at the posters, listening to song after song. Tess had brought over the tape sleeve so that they could follow the lyrics to 'Sunday Bloody Sunday', interrupting The Edge's solo to explain the story behind the song. The tragedy of that day in Northern Ireland. The injustice. The horror.

It had gotten a bit intense, so Candace wandered to Tess's bed where she found a book. 'Whass this?'

Tess blushed. 'Oh, Linton likes to leave inspiring books around for me to read when I've got some down time. He kind of scatters them about.'

Dana grabbed one from the other end of the bed and read. *'When I Dare to Be Powerful!'*

'Soledad Brother,' Arianna announced the title of another.

Candace held hers at arms-length. 'Who's Maya A ... Angel ... ou?'

'It's just ... Linton,' Tess explained. She started to gather the books, but Candace held onto hers defensively.

'You may shoot me with your words, you may cut me with your eyes—' Candace read aloud.

'Liberty,' Arianna exclaimed.

'You may kill me with your hatefulness, but still, like air, I'll rise.'

'Damn straight.'

Candace read the whole poem, delivering the final lines in a deep resonant voice, lifting her hand in a dramatic gesture as she promised, three times over, that she too would rise.

'Ladies! If you please,' called Linton from downstairs.

They all leaped up. Candace shoved past them to the door. 'Move man. Don't make me cut you with my eyes ...'

They sat gulping steaming bowls of food layered with flavours so different to anything from Arianna's home. It lined her stomach like a warm hug.

Dana's cheeks had turned bright red at the spice but when Candace persevered, so did she.

'Pepper soup,' Linton had explained. 'It's a Nigerian recipe, something I was taught to make by a lover long long ago.'

'Dad! That's disgusting!' Tess had protested, mortified. Candace choked on her mouthful. Linton let out a raucous chuckle. He asked about their families. Where they hailed from. Dana told him about her Irish nan. Candace tried to explain her Kenyan-Indian mix, her English parents. When Arianna had told him about living in Cyprus, his face lit up. An island girl, just like him. He talked of colonization, divide and conquer, something called The Diaspora, and the blessings of us all, brothers and sisters of the Empire, finding each other here, breaking bread together.

Tess had looked like she was going to die with embarrassment. Candace had asked for a second bowl.

They embraced, lingering in each other's arms, then Dana and Candace headed off. Arianna turned back on the threshold. She didn't have the words to thank Tess, so she waved half-heartedly. Tess smiled shyly back. The 93 bus carried her home as Arianna sang the words to 'Sunday Bloody Sunday' under her breath.

Al Green's voice drifted to her from the living room as she opened the door. Arianna blinked with surprise.

Dad.

She hurried in to find them all sitting on the sofa, Theo chuckling as Dad bounced him around, Lelia clinging on to one of Dad's arms, and Mum on the other side. Her smile changed to self-conscious guilt when Arianna walked in.

Dad put Theo down and stood up. He took two big strides and enveloped Arianna in his arms.

'My big girl. Look at you!' he exclaimed.

She took in his familiar smell, and tried to fight the relief, to remember she was angry, always low-key angry with him. But he didn't notice. Like he hadn't noticed how late she'd gotten home. And as he held her, she soon felt nothing but relief at having him back. She felt her insides unclench as she handed over the baton of responsibility for her mum, her younger siblings, once again – something she had been doing most of her thirteen years, stepping in and out of his big man-shoes as he came and went, as they became a single-parent family once more, and then not.

They listened to music, played with Theo and Lelia, like a proper family.

It was only once she was in bed that she remembered it all again. The joy of those hours in that other little family of two, Linton's magic soup. The lyrics to the song. The injustice of that moment in history. The violence it described. The way her dad just breezed in and expected them all to make way, step aside, transform into some happy family once again, rather than the desperate, stressed-out unit missing a key player that they had been just hours ago.

Arianna lay angry and tired and confused, a protest song beating a rhythm in her head, longing for a justice she didn't quite understand.

2022

ARIANNA

Arianna stared at her laptop for a long time, chewing the inside of her mouth. With an irritated sigh, she closed her eyes and opened out her arms, palms upwards, resting them on her knees. She waited for her mind to calm, until she felt the tingling in her limbs begin, the softening, the letting go. Then Arianna opened her eyes again and dropped her arms. She repositioned her laptop and continued typing.

She'd been in court all day and had paperwork to catch up on. She felt the weariness return to her body, to her very bones, and considered calling it a day, holding on to the remnants of serenity she had just attained, waking up extra early to finish it off before heading to court again tomorrow. But it was already going to be an early start, meeting with her client to prep and support her before heading into those halls of justice that had never intimidated her, because she saw right through it all from the start. So, she forged on, despite the dryness of her eyes, the ache in her shoulders, because thirty-three women were counting on her.

But her mind kept wandering back to Candace. The worry in her old friend's voice. Arianna sighed again. Every time.

Why did she let it get to her every time? It wasn't healthy. She'd told her as much. They had to let go. But Arianna found herself trying to remember the exact words. The timeline. The details that were the reason for concern. She caught herself about to type Dana's name into the search engine.

Maybe she should get some advice first before she jumped in with both feet, again. Not advice, Fellows, even Sponsors, couldn't give advice. That was the wrong word. Clarity? A sounding board? A check-in. A Share. Yes, that. A Share with a Fellow that may lead to some clarity about The Next Right Move from a Higher Guidance. But what to say? Nothing had actually happened. So why couldn't she stop thinking about Dana?

2022

CANDACE

Candace placed her phone on top of the Tupperware full of homemade falafels – Saffy's favourite. Then she picked it up again, checked the time once more. They needed milk. And bananas. She had left an empty carton and a banana skin on the kitchen counter yesterday: a visual reminder. She had planned to pop out at lunchtime, but instead she'd lost an hour, maybe more, worrying, searching old messages, old numbers, socials. A variety of nicknames and spellings. Dates. Anything that might give her a clue. And then she'd run out of time.

Saffy would be home soon. Within the next ten. Fifteen if she lingered a bit. And then Candace would get busy cooking up a storm, at the same time as giving Saffy her focus and attention, giving her space to do her homework, all the while making sure that Saffy was completely unaware of the shitstorm she was dealing with. That was the most important thing of all. Saffy wasn't to know a thing. They'd eat. They'd sit on their two-person sofa next to the kitchen area and read for an hour before TV time. Then her favourite bit, where the two of them sat in the darkness and just hung out. And then bedtime.

But what about the nutritious smoothie she wanted to make tomorrow morning?

And what about the figure she was sure she'd seen lurking, staring, at least twice this week?

Candace looked through the window with the view of the bank and stood, watching. She checked her phone one more time and decided. Throwing it in her bag, Candace stepped out of her houseboat. She locked the door behind her and stepped landward, walking along the short gangway onto the concrete quay and through the industrial park, her forehead wrinkled with worry.

TESS

Adrenaline pumped through her as Tess kept her hands steady, her eyes alert. Locked onto Callum as he raised the baton, counting the beats with his other hand, as the two drummers, facing each other on the immense stage, smashed out the rhythm at breakneck speed in complete synchronicity. It was impossible. But they were doing it, giving it everything, as she tried not to be distracted by such a remarkable feat, as she tried to keep counting bars along with Callum, along with the entire orchestra, all trying to keep their amazement in check, to remain professional and wait, suspended for the slight raising of the baton before it sliced downwards and they all played as one, perfectly on cue. The man at the very front of the huge stage jumped manically as they played, conducted the imaginary audience into a frenzy, waited for the pause when he'd bring the mic to his metallic mouth, speak his words with such passion, elation.

Yes. This was a moment. A full-circle moment. As her fingers flew over the strings and she manoeuvred the bow quick-time, double-time, tears sprang to her eyes. She breathed deeply, taking it in even as she worked. The piece rose to its crescendo, Callum's arms commanding it all, gesticulating, holding, directing, cueing, his hair now flopping around excitedly, a sheen of sweat covering his face. They followed, the drummers' hands and feet beating out complex rhythms at impossible speed, the man at the front shouting, jumping, leaping higher, the DJ lining up the final sample that would bring it all to its transcendent climax. The final note of the sample rang out across the Festival Hall. It reverberated a few seconds more, then they held the silence. And then it was complete. Callum dropped his hands, and they all awoke from their trance, as the man with the golden teeth, this legend of Drum and Bass, turned to the orchestra, an elated look on his face.

Callum suggested they take a short break. She knew better than to approach him at work, so Tess hovered among the other first violinists for a while, then headed offstage to the green room as the orchestra filed out. She reached into her bag and pulled out her phone. And soon she found herself searching, scrolling, sending out messages to people she hadn't spoken to in years. Anyone who had had any kind of connection with Dana. Who might know something that might bring her back.

1999

DANA

'IS IT JUST ME OR IS GARY BARLOW'S FOREHEAD GETTING BIGGER?'

The radio DJ's voice bellowed from the alarm clock as Dana was jolted from her sleep. She pressed the snooze button, then drew her arm back into the warmth of her duvet and drifted back into slumber. Five minutes later, it cut through her dreams again like a foghorn.

'WHAT DO MICHAEL JACKSON, JIMMY SAVILE AND BILL COSBY HAVE IN COMMON? I'LL GIVE YOU A CLUE. IT'S GOT SOMETHING TO DO WITH PETS ... FIND OUT AFTER THE BREAK!'

She slammed her hand down on the button again and groaned. She'd begged her mum for one of these for ages, then Uncle Don surprised her with it last week. But the reality of being woken up like this every weekday morning was verging on traumatic. She made a mental note to search for her old alarm clock after school.

Dana lingered for a moment longer, hoping that maybe this morning Mum would come in like she used to, place the mug of tea beside her, snuggle in. But that hadn't happened in a long time. The flat was quiet. And dark. She hauled herself out of bed and shivered, drawing her own curtains open and padding along the freshly hoovered hallway. Uncle Don's work boots and bag were slung on the mat by the front door. His dusty jacket hung up on the hooks above.

Dana switched the kettle on and leaned against the work surface, still sleepy, and cold now.

'What are you doing, love?'

Her mum walked in, wrapping her nightgown tight around herself. Dana could tell she was naked underneath.

'You can't stand about like that, love. Put some clothes on.'

Dana looked down at her Mini Mouse nightie. It was bobbled now and tighter, and it had ridden up her legs more than she had realized. She'd never had to worry about what she was wearing around the house before. She suddenly became aware she wasn't wearing any knickers. She pulled at the nightie and headed past her mum, back down the corridor, an uncomfortable feeling, worse than embarrassment, forming in her tummy.

A single, loud snore came from her mum's room as she passed by.

1999

CANDACE

'Miss White's starting girls' football on Wednesdays. You coming?'

Dana wrinkled her nose. 'Nah.'

'You're not coming football?'

She shrugged. 'I just can't be arsed with all that … sweating.'

Candace turned to her in surprise. They'd spent most evenings of the last two years at netball practice together. Dana, long and lanky from the very start, was goal shooter. Candace had claimed the bib with the big C on it for centre. They'd dodged and pivoted, caught and passed. And sweated. Lots.

She looked at Dana closely. 'What you done to your eyebrows?'

'Nothing,' Dana replied.

'Yes, you have. They're brown all of a sudden. And is that mascara? Since when do you put gel in your hair?'

Dana squirmed under Candace's scrutiny.

'Since now,' she returned.

Candace frowned and looked her up and down, checking

for any more changes. Dana folded her jacket tight over her so Candace couldn't see what top she was wearing.

'Is this cos that posh boy with the mop on his head said you could look like Claudia Schiffer if you made an effort? You know he was taking the piss?'

Dana glared at Candace. 'Yeah, well, you should try it sometime. You know, making an effort.' She turned and stomped off.

1999

ARIANNA

'Elke. Her name's Elke. What *is* that?' Tess exclaimed.

'Is it even a name?' Arianna said.

'It is in Germany, apparently,' Tess replied. 'She was in her pants and one of his John Coltrane T-shirts in the kitchen making coffee. First thing I saw this morning were her pasty bum cheeks.'

'That is unnecessary,' Arianna concluded.

'It put me off my Sugar Puffs.'

They clomped along the street in their biker boots, Tess wearing a second-hand cardigan with a CND badge pinned on it over her tie-dyed T-shirt and leggings, Arianna in a long grey skirt and black oversized jumper, both sporting twenty mini-braids in their hair which pulled their curls straight, parted severely in the middle. Tess was cultivating a dread-lock. They repeated Elke's name over and over in a variety of terrible accents.

Tess looked at Arianna pleadingly. 'Wanna stay over? We can watch *Twin Peaks*,' she suggested, trying to keep it light.

'Sure,' Arianna replied.

*

Alan and Daniel had claimed the front row with Luke and John from Chris R.P's old class. They sat talking loudly, swiping their floppy curtained hair from their eyes, and awaiting Mr M's entrance eagerly. Here, in the top GCSE English set, there was no danger of a slap from the back row, gob in your hood, a kidney stolen from Science secreted into your schoolbag. Having survived the lower years, they were finally free to fully be their loud, posh, front-row-hogging selves.

Even Coconut Joe and Peanut Andrew had been relegated to the second row.

Arianna sat in the back with Tess and seethed. Alan. Daniel. Luke. John. Tess called them Mr M's disciples. Then Arianna came up with The Oxbridge Four.

'They sound like a terrorist group,' Tess had said.

'They are,' Arianna had replied.

She understood now the urge to gob in their smug, floppy hair, to trip them up and watch them smash their faces on the floor, mash lumpy custard into their arrogant orifices.

Mr M entered the class and The Oxbridge Four sat up, attentive, eager. He was tall and wiry, with a slight paunch visible under his jumper. His dark hair was perpetually messy, cut in a style that made Arianna think of all the members of Blur.

'Dickens, Dickens, what the Dickens!' he exclaimed. Mr M waved a battered paperback in the air and then opened it, leafing through the pages. 'So. We arrive at Miss Havisham's along with Pip. A spinster. Jilted at the altar. Mad, bitter. In perpetual stasis.' Mr M paused, raised his eyebrows. 'Stasis?'

Luke's hand shot up.

'Still. Inactive,' Arianna murmured.

'A state of inactivity, sir,' Luke announced.

Mr M pointed at him with his book.

'Correct.'

Tess turned to Arianna.

'It's a Greek word,' she explained quietly.

1999

DANA

Dana strode into Maths and sat down, still shaken by her argument with Candace. She took off her coat. There was a whistle from the boys. She didn't look up, but it was clear that the new bra her mum had got her off the market and the V-neck jumper she'd borrowed from her was having an effect. She was already plumper than her skinny mum, which meant the top clung tightly around her newly acquired curves. She sat a little straighter and experimented with a pout.

The sums were taking longer today. Dana tried to focus, but the boys' stares bore into her. Then suddenly class was over and, for the first time, she hadn't completed the work.

'Dana. A word,' Mr Austen called out. She turned back into the classroom as the last of her classmates left. His fingers made a steeple as he glared at her from his desk.

'Sub-par,' he said. 'Do you know what that means?'

Dana shook her head.

'Lower than average. Your work and your output has been sub-par for a few lessons now.'

Dana felt herself turn a deep crimson.

'Is there a reason for this? Something I should know?'

Dana shook her head, forced out a quiet 'No, sir.'

He looked at her searchingly, trying to understand. Then he seemed to come to a conclusion. 'I would advise you to think carefully about how you use your time,' he continued, 'and, in particular, who you share it with.' He paused and looked hard at Dana.

'Permit me to be blunt. There are many Candace Crawfords, and they will come and go.' Dana looked up at him with surprise at the mention of her friend's name. 'You have potential, certainly as a mathematician, and I trust that you will continue to do well at this school, but you must also be discerning, especially with the company you keep and whether it aids in you achieving that potential, or serves as a distraction.'

Dana's mouth fell open. She turned to look at the door that the boys who had spent the lesson whispering about her had just walked out of.

'Is that clear?' he asked eventually.

Dana turned back. 'B ... but she ... she didn't ... there's nothing bad about ... she's my friend.' Dana managed.

'That's enough now,' he said firmly, and busied himself with the pile of worksheets on his desk.

1999

CANDACE

'Who's got bigger tits, you or Dana?' one of the boys behind her leaned over and whispered. The others snickered.

'Have you ever measured them to see? Like, with a tape measure? Maybe you measure hers and she measures yours.'

Candace continued sketching in her notepad as the teacher, oblivious, droned on about how you can gain a C at best if you take the lower paper in Maths.

C. for Candace. She couldn't wait to be done with this shithole. To burn her maths books and English books and never have to wrestle with another worksheet, another essay, never have to read another fucking book. Her days were measured in fifty-minute prison sentences she had to endure. And now Dana was in the top class in Maths. Riri and Tess in the top class in English. And she was stuck with these gobby wank stains with permanent hard-ons who read their lads mags in the back, chuckling raucously, discussing her tits. Every. Fucking. Lesson.

But not for long. She'd got the letter. Handed to her directly by Miss Thomkins, the Special Needs teacher. She hadn't even looked at the results of her test. If Miss Thomkins approached you, it was for one reason only: it was official, you were 'special needs'. 'Twenty-five percent extra', as they called it, because of the added time you got in exams. She'd chucked the crumpled envelope on the kitchen table when she got home and kept it moving. But soon she'd be summoned. Out of the normal classes, into the special one in the special room with all the other thick kids, while her mates smashed it in the top tier.

'Do you want to go for a jog after lunch time? I could do with a bit of exercise.'

She sat alone, tuning the boys out as best she could until she could get to the next lesson, Science, where they'd all be together again for a precious hour.

'Candace. Oi, I'm talking to you.' One of the boys had rolled his magazine into a baton that he whacked his other hand with. They'd been poring over it in the back row. She'd caught a glimpse as she sat down of a pubescent pop star in a sexy take on a school uniform that showed her smooth, flat midriff and the top of her newly developing breasts, her skirt hiked up to reveal her virgin thighs fastened into suspenders, staring sexily from the front cover. Written horizontally across her left side were the words 'Ten Girls We're All Waiting to Turn Sixteen'. Along the right edge of the cover, a selection of celebrity cleavages were positioned in order of most arousing to least arousing, their heads cut off.

Chris R.P stepped into the room, late. He nodded an apology to the teacher and walked round the back of the classroom, grabbing the magazine out of the boy's hand and whacking him around the head with it.

The teacher spun around. 'Out.'

Chris stopped, turned and walked back out.

Candace sighed, continued moving the pencil across the page, the image appearing gradually under her hand.

The teacher had turned back to the board. And now one of them was rubbing his own nipples and talking in a high-pitched tone that was meant to be her and her best friend discussing their tits with each other.

I'll rise, she thought. *I'll rise, I'll rise, I'll rise.*

Candace shaded in the final touches to her elaborate picture: a beautiful bloom of smoke forming a giant mushroom-shaped cloud as flame and debris rained down on the terrified, violently dismembered male faces below.

'Jay got his ear pierced.'

'Ohmydays. When?'

'I saw it this morning when he was walking up the hill.'

'That is so hot.'

'I know. He looks like Lenny Kravitz but goth.'

'Did he speak to you?'

'No, but he looked at me when I passed him.'

'Like actually look at you.'

'Yep.'

'Ohmydays.'

Candace sat quietly, pretending not to listen, as Dana, Arianna and Tess discussed their latest crush: Jay, from the Year Above. He played guitar and was shagging one of the Florian girls. They were all wearing plastic goggles and leaned over the Bunsen burner like gossiping witches, merging into one boy-obsessed entity, eager to make the most of their precious hour together.

Candace was still smarting from Dana's comeback. And now Dana had taken off her jacket to reveal some skin-tight top she'd blatantly begged off her mum that made her tits stick out. So Candace kept her head down while they freaked out over some brer who'd never give them the time of day.

'Tess, you should have talked to him. He's in a band,' Dana insisted.

'Are you joking? I only just managed to remember how to keep walking,' Tess said.

'Didn't you do Music GCSE at the same time?'

'Last year, yeah,' Tess said. 'But no one spoke to each other. We just sat in a room and did the theory with Mr Tamworth watching us.'

'Mr Tamworth and Jay? Bloody hell. I'm surprised you didn't orgasm then and there!' Dana exclaimed.

The three of them shrieked with laughter.

'Shut up you lot, we'll get kicked out,' Candace snapped.

Dana shrugged. 'So what? Tess has already got her music GCSE. Arianna got her Greek one two years ago. You're going to be a famous artist and live on a massive boat on the Thames and I am going to work for CERN and create my own black hole, so . . .'

It was a peace offering. That compliment about her art. And Candace *had* been a dick to her first.

'Does my boat have a jacuzzi?' Candace asked.

Dana grinned. 'And a hot, naked butler called Pedro.'

1999

DANA

They parted with Tess and Arianna at the school gates. Dana felt Mr Austen's disapproving glare from the depths of the Maths department as she and Candace walked home together. She felt guilty, like she was doing something wrong, and at the same time even worse for being part of such a horrible conversation about her best friend. It wasn't Candace's fault she couldn't concentrate in Maths. But she hadn't been able to explain.

They walked in silence for a while until they reached the corner.

'Dana, yeah?'

Dana looked up.

'Safe.' Jay nodded as he walked past, one side of his perfect mouth curling into a lopsided smile.

Dana's stomach lurched. She tried to hide her surprise as they watched him bounce down the street.

Candace glared at Dana. 'What the fuck?' 'How does he know your name?'

'I don't know.'

'He legit skinned his teeth at you and everything.'

Dana felt her face grow hot.

'We need an emergency meeting.' Candace said. 'I'm calling Tess. What change you got?'

They squeezed into the bright red phone booth by the bus stop, ignoring the smell of stale piss, the tiny business-card-sized pictures of half-naked women with huge breasts and bums that were wedged in the frame between the glass. Candace fed the coins into the slot, dialled the number.

'Hello, is Tess there please?'

They waited, Candace holding the receiver at an angle so Dana could listen in too.

'OhmydayswejustpassedJayandhelegitcalledDana'sname outandskinnedteethatherandeverything.'

'Shutupnohedidn'twherewhenwhereareyounow.'

'Greenmanonthecornercomewego Dana's.'

'AhshitIcan'tI'vegotpracticebutI'mwithRi.'

'Okay. Tell Riri.'

Candace replaced the receiver just as they heard Tess call Arianna's name loudly.

Jay. Gorgeous, perfect Jay from the Year Above. His manly seventeen-year-old body. She was pretty sure he even had chest hair. She considered his grin and the way he bounced when he walked. It did funny things to her insides. And her private parts. As the high rise she called home loomed into view, she sped up, as if the words would tumble out too early if she didn't get to the flat in time, if she didn't find her mum on the sofa, doing her nails, Enders on in the background, so she could tell her about Jay.

'Hi love,' her mum called from the living room over the sound of the TV.

His jacket was slung over the other jackets, his boots taking up space on the mat. They were sitting side by side on the sofa, Mum with her fluffy slippers on, her legs neatly closed, he with his legs wide apart, his arms folded, taking up most of the seat, the room, the air.

'Good day?' her mum asked.

'Yeah,' Dana replied.

'I'll make dinner in a bit. Have a biscuit and come and sit down.'

Dana noticed something move in Uncle Don's arms. A flash of white against his paint-flecked jumper. A tiny ball of fluff with big green eyes looked up at her from inside his giant hands.

'What's that?' she asked.

'Got you a little pal,' Don explained. 'Restless little fella.' The kitten leaped from his arms and trotted towards Dana.

It had a white face and chest with thin brown stripes across its top. Its legs were skinny and its little body was full of curious energy. It stuck its perfect little nose out, sniffing at her before batting her cautiously with a tiny little paw. Dana gasped and put her hand out. It bit her playfully.

'Can we keep her?' Dana looked at her mum.

'You better ask Don.'

Dana turned to Don.

'Course,' he said, then he exchanged a look with her mum. 'But you'll have your work cut out with that one. Might need an extra pair of hands around the place.'

1999

TESS

'Got your spare strings?' Linton asked.

'Yep.'

'I'll leave some food in the oven. We're having dinner with the Windy Revolutionaries,' Linton quipped.

Tess sighed. 'They've all got dandruff and holes in their jumpers. And they smell of mothballs.'

'Which is why Elke and I will go instead.'

'Fine.'

'Go well, my Samwise.'

He kissed her on the forehead. Tess pulled away and looked with alarm at Arianna who tried to hide a smirk.

The two girls stepped out into the cold Saturday morning.

Arianna was still grumpy and sleepy. She hadn't had any breakfast, saying she'd grab some when she got home, *after* she'd gone back to bed. They walked in silence to the bus stop.

'You legit do this every weekend?' Arianna asked.

'Yep.'

'I don't get up before midday. Ever,' Arianna exclaimed.

Tess shrugged. 'I'm kind of used to it.'

'Don't you ever just want to sleep?'

'It's just … you have to … practise,' Tess tried.

Arianna glared at her grumpily. Tess tried to think how to explain. She felt guilty, that her stupid, dweeby orchestra practice had forced Arianna to wake up so early on a Saturday. She had been so excited to have her stay over that it hadn't occurred to Tess to worry about the next morning. She had done this routine for so long now that it seemed normal. In this moment she was realizing just how abnormal it was, *she* was.

Tess thought of the talks Linton had given her on the days she needed some coaxing. About discipline, commitment, examples of famous musicians, artists, sportspeople, revolutionaries who had dedicated hours, years, decades of their lives to excel, to make change. She wondered how many mates all these exceptional people had had. How many sleepovers they'd missed, how many people they'd pissed off, annoyed, let down. How many parties they'd had to skip. How long they'd all stayed virgins.

They boarded the bus in silence.

ARIANNA

Arianna stepped out into the late afternoon. The sun warmed her face, but there was a chill to the breeze. She slowed her steps, tried to be mindful of her tendency to rush when she didn't need to. She was done for the day. Finally. Kind of. She had rushed from a multi-agency meeting to a pre-trial visit and on to three calls with three separate detectives – none of whom had made any progress on her clients' cases, one of whom refused to speak to her because who was she anyway? She'd had a precious hour at lunch to catch up on the paperwork that never lessened before speed-walking to the station to make a court hearing. So, she'd got some exercise in, at least, and was therefore allowed a more leisurely pace from the bus stop through her old neighbourhood, on her way home.

She passed a row of boutique shops that used to be a launderette, a betting shop and a Woolworths. Across the road, what used to be a greasy spoon caff was a place that now charged eleven pounds for a boiled egg and toasted soldiers. She watched a mum push her designer, three-wheeled buggy into the egg-and-soldiers café. Arianna could have been one of them. Someone who could have afforded an eleven quid egg if she'd kept going, passed the bar, accepted the scholarship, gone for pupillage. Instead, she'd walked away from it all and now just about managed rent on her tiny place in a corner of an area she had really been priced out of long ago. Her old borough, where she'd grown up just a few bus stops away.

She faced forward again, tried to keep from catching anyone's eye, hoping, as always, not to bump into anyone from old times. It was weird living here now. Embarrassing. Shameful, if she was really honest. Like she had failed to launch herself into the world and had had to return to the old neighbourhood and admit defeat. She kept her un-ringed finger stuffed into her jacket pocket and her chin held high. Every corner around here held a memory. Every stop on the bus familiar for a hundred different reasons. The high street, especially, full of spots she fantasized about burning to the ground. But there was a reason for everything. Her Higher Power had deemed it right for her to be here. Maybe to make peace with it all. Maybe to reclaim it. Or maybe to pour petrol over the whole neighbourhood and light the bastard up. Who knew?

Sitting on the bus she felt agitated. It was the tinny sound of the repetitive riff coming from the headphones of the teenager sitting next to her. She turned to glare at him, only to realize what he was listening to: E.G.G.'s 'Yamaha'. Her jaw tightened.

Back at her flat, the thumbnail at the bottom left-hand corner of the screen that was her outstanding paperwork lay waiting to be expanded, worked on, completed, delivered.

Thirty-three women.

But she'd made a promise to Candace. So she started once again. She had already searched for her name, scoured images, institutions she knew Dana had attended, worked at, for any clue. The university she'd blagged her way into. The job she'd managed to keep for almost a whole year. She tried to remember her last boyfriend's name. Failed.

2022

CANDACE

Candace walked around the room, looking at the bodies lying on the ground. Corpses. She adjusted one, smoothed the forehead of another, stood relishing this moment of stillness. She padded silently to the front of the room and pressed play. The corpses stirred.

'When you're ready, turn onto your right side.'

They did, one by one, like dominoes being flipped over, and settled again. She turned the volume on the gentle music higher.

'And slowly come to a sitting position, keeping your eyes closed.'

The dominoes flipped back up.

She sat then, cross-legged like them, brought her hands into prayer position.

'Now open your eyes. Namaste.'

The class gathered their belongings. Candace kept her eyes slightly lowered, discouraging all but the most necessary of conversation, keen to keep the atmosphere of serenity intact. This space, made sacred by her. This practice, that had saved her life. When talking therapies had made no sense when she was numb. Completely numb. From head to toe. Heart to womb. Only on the mat did it come. The gradual re-incarnation of something long dead. A re-awakening. Painful at first, like any birth, almost unbearable. She had cried. Hot angry tears of rage and pain. They had come when she had realized that here, no one could touch her. No one was allowed to unless she said they could. To adjust, to correct, to teach her, yes, but only if she said so.

She had gone to a free class once with another girl from the refuge. They'd giggled all the way through. Thought it was a bit weird. Done impressions of the teacher. Then, months later, Candace had gone back, out of boredom mostly, because it was free. And then because she realized somehow that she had found it, or it had found her: the thing she needed. So she came back again. And with every hour, something began to wake, hurt, come alive, until finally, the fragmented bits of her had been gathered, broken and splintered and shocked, but present and correct, until there was a whole once more.

A ringtone started up. Candace frowned as the owner floundered, trying to silence it. She opened her mouth to admonish her. No phones in the studio space. But then she recognized the tune. 'Yamaha': E.G.G. An image of the four lads bouncing about behind their synths sprung into her head.

For a blissful three hours Candace hadn't thought of her at all, had been fully present in her classes, holding space for her students, checking in with her own body, moving it, stretching it. But now her stomach sank as the weight of the problem returned once more. She'd made a list of all the names she could think of, but she'd have to be careful. She'd been caught, twice: once by Saff, who had called her a hypocrite for telling *her* off for scrolling, who had mercifully thought she was looking at random stuff on her phone. And once by Asha, whose face had tightened and then had looked tired for the rest of the evening. Tired of her, of them, of this relationship.

She switched on her phone. Several buzzes. She noticed a message from Tess.

Quick call??

Candace looked around, typed a quick reply:

I've got fifteen minutes from the station to home.
Talk then?

Arianna sent a brown thumbs up.

2022

TESS

Tess knocked on the door. No answer. She turned the handle and went in. Callum took off his headphones and looked up, flustered, angry.

'Hey,' she tried. 'How's it going?'

'Awfully. What's up?' he demanded.

'I need to make a call. Ten minutes tops. Could you ... ?'

He rolled his eyes. 'Now?'

'Actually, you've got half an hour before—'

'So why did you come in now?' he exclaimed.

'I thought, if I gave you a bit of a heads up you could ... get ready for a break?'

He glared at her. She tried to stand her ground, remember what she had practised.

'Okay. Fine.'

She stopped herself from thanking him.

Tess closed the door and headed to the room on the far side of the landing. Her daughter was trying to attach a fox's tail to her trousers, the matching ears already placed on her head.

'Sinead, Daddy's going to come and play with you in a bit so I can make a call. Okay?'

Sinead did a little awkward jump of joy, only just leaving the ground.

Tess helped attach the tail as Sinead wriggled excitedly. Eventually she heard him shut something loudly, scrape his chair back, take those deep, loud breaths that made her grit her teeth, letting everyone know how under pressure he always was, how important his work was, how busy, how burdened. Sinead looked at her. Tess rearranged her face into a smile, heard the door push open behind her.

'Well hello you foxy little fox. What have you done with Sinead?' Callum sang to his daughter.

Tess edged out of the room.

Downstairs, she flipped open the laptop. Linton's old picture of Angela Davis, now framed on her wall, was just in view, along with her bookshelf, heaving with his collection of books. She angled the camera so it was more visible.

Arianna and Candace joined the call. She waved, regretted it. Arianna was in the same position she had been in the first call. Candace kept freezing as she held her phone up to her face, navigating the walk home, mostly chin and nostrils.

'I found Jay,' Tess blurted out. 'He's in Peckham now. I thought someone could . . . I could get in touch.'

They nodded.

'I know it's not a lot,' she admitted.

'It's a start,' Candace managed. And then froze again.

'Is her mum still in the same flat?' Tess asked.

'She won't know anything,' Candace's voice said over the frozen image.

'But shouldn't we at least try to—'

'No point.' Candace suddenly came to life again as she closed her front door and placed her phone onto something solid, looking up to check for something beyond it, then focusing back on them.

'What about other exes?' Tess persisted.

'There's quite a few. No offence,' Arianna said.

'Let's start with the ones we know.' Candace decided.

Arianna stiffened, but then nodded. 'Okay.'

A click, the groan of a door. Candace looked up with alarm at someone beyond the screen.

'Who's that?' Tess asked.

'Just a ... just my ...'

'Mum?'

Candace's screen froze again, then cut off as she disappeared from the call.

Tess and Arianna stared wide-eyed at each other on the screen.

Mum?

1999

ARIANNA

'But I don't want to share with her anymore,' Lelia whined.

'One more night,' Mum insisted.

'I don't want to.'

Mum and Sandrine exchanged a look.

'Lelia darling, *vien ici*. Can you help me with the food? I have a secret ingredient and only you will know ...'

Lelia dragged her feet to the kitchen counter. In less than a minute, she was fully engrossed in Sandrine's tagine, as Mum watched over Theo's Greek work. There were new lines on her forehead, her silky dark brown hair had strands of grey in it now. She slumped slightly in her chair as if the effort it took to keep upright was a bit too much today. Arianna wasn't sure how much Lelia and Theo had actually understood about their extended stay at Auntie Sandrine's. It was common for them to stay over when Mum was late back from work, or for Maya to be at theirs when Sandrine needed help, but it was the first time they'd all de-camped to Sandrine's flat en masse. It was warm here, especially in the small kitchen that they all crammed into after school. Sandrine had welcomed them with her singsong voice and a smile. It allowed Arianna's mum space to let the brave front drop a bit.

Arianna had woken that Sunday morning to find her mum stuffing things in bags and telling them to pack their things too. All three of them had protested, but Mum lashed out suddenly, screaming at them.

That evening, the kids settled in their new beds, Arianna listened at the doorway as her mum and Sandrine spoke in whispers. About the window sliding open, the creaking of the floorboards outside her mum's room, the shadow of a figure making his way through the house. About how she'd started talking loudly to an imaginary husband, telling him to get up, get the knife and check who was outside. How the shadow had hesitated outside her door. How she'd made more noise, urging the non-existent man beside her to hurry up, rustling and thumping, until finally, mercifully, she'd heard the man retreat back through the bathroom window and out of her home.

She hadn't cried. Arianna had never seen her mum cry. But when she helped serve dinner that evening, there was a tremble in her hands she couldn't control.

But Dad was coming back tomorrow. He had called Sandrine's when no one answered at home. Mum told him what had happened. She didn't ask him to come back early, and he didn't offer. So they had stayed at Sandrine's, until it was safe to go home again.

Arianna could relax. There was another adult here, some-one with enough capacity for care and love to cover them all for now, so she could focus on things like her homework and her crushes, both of which she worked on with meticulous care.

After dinner, Arianna sat in the living room as the two mums put the younger ones to bed. Then they both came downstairs, talking quietly to each other. It was Sandrine who came to sit next to Arianna first. She glanced back at Mum, who came and sat on Arianna's other side, both of them peering over at her homework.

'It's a diary entry,' Arianna explained. 'We've got to rewrite the scene from a different character's point of view, looking at all the rotting stuff, looking at the old woman and her old clothes, her mean words.'

'Old woman? Miss Havisham? *Mon dieu*. If she is old, then we are ancient,' Sandrine exclaimed over Arianna's head to her mum.

'What about Miss Havisham? What would she say about it all? If she could speak, finally in her own words?' Sandrine pushed.

Arianna blinked, tried to imagine this. Soon she was picking out the details she had read in her head, forming a picture of this character, then embodying her somehow, feeling and thinking as she would. The words came to her then. Miss Havisham's words. Raw and fresh and misunderstood. Arianna began to scribble it all down as the two women sat either side of her.

Sandrine got up and headed to the shelf that ran along the top of the living room wall. She'd built it herself using old scaffolding wood, maximizing the use of this small space.

'*Tiens,*' Sandrine pulled a book out and handed it to Arianna. Mum frowned.

'She's too young, *kori.*'

'*Non,* it is the perfect time. Just read the first page.'

Arianna looked at the cover – pink and purple with a lone figure at the centre, a girl in a blue dress with hair as frizzy and curly and long and dark as her own. *The House of the Spirits.* Arianna read the first chapter. It was like nothing she had read before. Magic mixed with history and family. Characters flying away and appearing out of nowhere, intoxicating others with their ethereal beauty and trying to liberate a country falling into dictatorship all at once. It was not Dickens. Neither was it Shakespeare or Wordsworth or Chaucer. It had colour in it. And flavour. And magic. And womanhood. When she looked up, Sandrine had selected four more books and piled them by Arianna. *The Color Purple. The Bluest Eye. Ruby. Like Water for Chocolate.*

'Thanks, but I can't take so many,' Arianna protested.

'I am just returning them,' Sandrine shrugged. 'They are not mine.' She looked past Arianna to her mum.

1999

CANDACE

'I swear I saw her down Balham,' Candace exclaimed from Dana's bedroom floor. The kitten, who Dana had named Jazz, was sitting on her chest.

'Shanice? You sure?'

'She was pushing a buggy and she looked *tired*.'

'Oh shit. She had a baby?'

'Why else didn't she come back to school this year?'

Candace tried to imagine the reality of having a baby. She suddenly felt her throat constrict as a wave of panic rushed through her. The overwhelm, the responsibility. The labour. The sex. The kitten looked at her in alarm. She stroked its back gently.

'I wanna stay here for ever,' Candace said. 'Do we have to go out?' Dana's kitten was the sweetest little thing she'd ever seen. She was already plotting how she could come back tomorrow to play with Jazz and then watch her fall asleep in her lap, that deep kitten sleep, her little belly rising and falling, exhausted and spent from the excitement of the day.

Dana sat in front of the new floor-length mirror Don had brought over, her make-up scattered around her, carefully applying black mascara to her blonde lashes. Puff Daddy was cranked up loud on MTV in the living room, because he'd got them Sky now too.

'It's Tess's concert,' she reasoned. 'She's in a proper orchestra and everything.' Do you reckon there'll be any fit guys in it?'

Candace rolled her eyes. 'You're obsessed.'

Dana turned and batted her heavily made-up lashes. 'Yes, I am,' she giggled.

Linton and Arianna were waiting outside the theatre. Arianna ran over and hugged her two friends excitedly.

'The whole gang, present and correct,' Linton said warmly and led them into the building.

'Can we get some wine?' Dana asked, smiling sweetly.

'You most certainly may not,' Linton said, smiling back as sweetly. He passed each girl a thick, glossy piece of card. 'Here are your tickets ladies, don't lose them.'

Linton led them into the auditorium. Candace had never been in a place like this before. She was suddenly very aware of the velour tracksuit she had chosen to wear, her Timbs with the label still hanging off them, all chosen specially for this occasion. But looking around, she realized she would have been better off borrowing something off Dana's mum like Dana had done. She turned to find Linton watching her.

'Would you do me the honour?' He gestured to the row of seats beside them. Candace shuffled her way along and sat down, looking around at the vast stage in front of her, the ornate domed ceiling above her and all the white people surrounding her. Dana and Arianna filed in after her, with Linton at the end. He folded his coat tidily in his lap. He had his best jumper on, his grey hair neatly combed out and his chin held high. He let the girls take in their surroundings, then he leaned in.

'Tess is in first violins, so she'll be near the front and you'll be able to see her,' he explained. 'We'll be hearing some Rachmaninoff, some Vivaldi, and from what she's been practising recently, I think we'll get some Schubert.'

Ri nodded solemnly like she knew what he was talking about.

'There might be some pauses between movements. Watch me for when we clap,' he said and looked at each of them in turn.

The lights dimmed, the orchestra filed onto the stage and there was Tess, wearing a smart black dress Candace had never seen before, her hair pulled into a bun, holding her violin and bow as she made her way to her seat. The audience applauded. So did Linton. The girls followed. Candace watched Tess share a word with the boy seated next to her, straighten the paper on the stand in front of her. And then the audience applauded again and a man walked onto the stage in a black suit with long bits on the back of the jacket. Dana flattened her hands out and swayed from side to side like a penguin. The girls burst into quiet laughter and then turned to Linton in alarm. But he was chuckling too.

A silence fell as the man faced the musicians and held a little stick high in the air. Tess brought her instrument to her chin and adjusted it, then raised her bow, her gaze focused on the conductor. He took a breath, swept his hand to the side, and the entire stage burst into melody. Candace was stunned at the power of the sound, watching the people just metres away creating it with so many instruments all gathered in one place. She watched Tess, their Tess, that awkward, stiff girl who had been among them all this time, alert and adept and moving that bow so gracefully. This was where Tess went every weekend. This was what she did after school and at lunchtimes and why she missed so many of their hangouts. Cos she was doing this.

Candace caught Arianna's eye, and they shared a moment of quiet awe at their friend, who was doing this next level shit up on that legit stage with a whole fucking orchestra. She looked over at Linton, a look of serene bliss on his face, his chin still held high.

And then the melody slowed, the players looked again at the conductor who signalled the final note. Then silence. Dana, who had been adjusting her tight top and looking at her own cleavage, looked up and brought her hands together. Candace caught one hand and pulled it down just in time. She looked at Linton who folded his hands into his lap meaningfully. They waited for a minute in silence, and then the second movement began. This time Candace relaxed, let the wave of sound wash over her. She was surprised to feel tears prickle her eyes, but they didn't fall.

'Can-I-have-the-chicken-chow-mein-please,' Arianna accentuated every word with a wave of her chopstick as if she was the conductor.

'I'll have the same.'

'Me too.'

Linton frowned from behind his menu. 'Girls, I encourage you to try something different.'

'But chicken's chicken, innit,' Candace reasoned. 'You can't go wrong.'

Linton raised his eyebrows. 'Has this not been an evening of firsts?' he enquired. 'First time in a theatre, first time seeing Tess play, first time hearing an orchestra? Not so bad trying something new.'

Candace sighed. 'Okay fine, you order. But Dana don't eat anything but chicken.'

He ordered, and soon the table was covered in strange looking, delicious smelling dishes. Duck-something, and noodle-this, stir-fry-that, something called Dim-Sum that came in a stack of wooden pots … and chicken Chow Mein. Candace let Linton serve her and the girls a bit of everything and she poked at it suspiciously. Tess was munching happily, and Arianna took a bite out of one of the dumplings, widened her eyes, then she ditched the sticks, grabbed a fork and tucked in hungrily. Candace followed suit and sure enough, it was delicious, all of it. Dana picked out the pieces of chicken and left the rest.

Linton raised a cup of jasmine tea. 'To Tess. Congratulations on an exquisite performance.'

The girls raised their cups too. Tess squirmed, giggled and blushed. Arianna stuck a chopstick in her ear.

1999

TESS

'I can't eat very much because I'm going to be on TV.'

'That's great, Mum.'

Tess lifted her mug of tea and held it out, waiting to cheers. Dagmar looked at her in confusion, then at her plate, the ketchup bottle, the napkin dispenser. Eventually, she noticed her own mug of tea in the corner. She picked it up and looked in it with a huff of disappointment, then she grudgingly clinked mugs with her daughter. Tess sipped hers and watched her mum carefully. Dagmar brought her mug to her lips and took a gulp, grimaced and put it down.

Tess tucked into her fry up. 'The sausage is good. You like the food here.'

Dagmar busied herself moving her fork around the plate in an unconvincing performance. Tess paused again while Dagmar put a forkful of food into her mouth, chewed and swallowed. She took another gulp of tea and grimaced again, looked at the counter to complain or order something stronger, then gave up.

She smelled quite bad. Tess had tried to get to her as early as possible, but it had taken twenty minutes just to get her to answer the door and another twenty to coax her out. It was only when Tess threatened to come into the flat that Dagmar had panicked and rushed to put her coat on, slamming the door behind her. By the time they'd got to the café it was midday. She already smelled of alcohol.

Tess looked at her closely; her mum's restless eyes were still a dazzling blue under the puffiness. The angry red scar that ran down the left side of her face was more visible under her thinning silver-blonde hair. Tess longed to run her a bath, brush her hair and dress her in some of her old stylish clothes, a beret perhaps, like she used to wear. Maybe then she'd remember how beautiful she was. Maybe she'd pick up a pen again, or get out that heavy, dusty typewriter she insisted on keeping. Maybe paint something. Dagmar continued to move her food around and mumble quietly to herself.

'I did a concert. With the orchestra. I'm in first violins now,' Tess offered.

Dagmar looked up at her. Tess smiled hopefully.

'I played violin,' Dagmar said. 'I once played for Nureyev. Just me. Alone. With my violin. And he danced very beautifully. We were at Buckingham Palace I think.'

'No. I don't think that happened.'

'It did!'

Tess looked back down at her food. She'd suddenly lost her appetite. But Dagmar now took a large, defiant bite of her buttered toast.

Tess summoned the energy, tried once again. 'Mum ... I wanted to talk to you about something. I started my period.' Her mum was at least still looking at her. 'I'm quite late. I seem to be a late developer in general ... a lot of my friends ... they already look like full grown women. But me, I'm not ... I haven't even ... Anyway, I just thought maybe you could tell me what to do ... ? Or how – when it happened for you—'

'Professional dancers don't have periods, you know. Like gymnasts.'

Tess let herself into the flat and headed straight upstairs. She stood in front of the mirror and looked at herself. She'd put on make-up today, taken time over her hair and outfit. She'd thought that maybe if she looked really pretty it might make a difference. She remembered what Dagmar used to be like. Moments, days, whole weeks sometimes where her mum was bright eyed, where she gave Tess all her attention. Her outfits were always colourful, accessorized with a bright scarf and hat. Feminine, European, arty.

Tess's jumper fell flat across her chest apart from two little bumps not much bigger than bee stings. Hardly worth wearing a bra for, but Arianna had given her two of her old ones, which she alternated. Tess's torso ran straight into her hips with hardly any cinch at the waist, devoid of any curves. She stood and stared at her disappointing silhouette and longed to finally blossom into the woman she was meant to be.

A knock at the door. He always waited now to be invited in.

'Yep,' she managed.

Linton stepped in and looked from his daughter to the mirror and back again.

'You didn't say hello when you came in. Not like you.' His eyebrows raised an inch.

A sob suddenly escaped her. Linton rushed to her and placed an arm around her.

'Oh, oh Samwise! Oh dear, oh dear ...'

Tess tried to gather herself. Linton waited. Finally, she let out a sigh and calmed.

'How is Dagmar?' he asked gently.

'She says she's going to be on TV.'

'Ah. How nice.'

Tess sniffed. 'I started my period.'

She felt him stiffen. He continued to hug her but now there was a fraction of space between his arm and her body.

'Right,' he managed. 'I suppose we'll need to get some supplies in.' He nodded, and kept nodding, as a dozen Bonos smouldered at them both from the bedroom walls.

CANDACE

Mum . . . ?

Candace played it over and over in her head, trying to figure out exactly how much they'd heard. She thought she had cut off the call just before, but she wasn't completely sure, and she knew she would have to explain eventually. She just had no idea how to.

She had a daughter. She'd had one for eleven whole years and had managed to hide it from almost everyone. Only those who needed to know knew. And that's how it had always been. Except now it had gotten complicated – more complicated. Extra, impossibly complicated. Because as their search for Dana continued, she would have to tell them. Show them.

And then there was Asha. Pulling away day by day. Hurt. Hurting. Weary of this whole situation. Candace felt the heat rise in her. Because what a privilege it was to be tired of this all. To walk away whenever she wanted to. If it was that easy, she should. She really should. In fact, Candace would tell her, invite her to walk her tired ass out of it. Because *she* could.

But then there would be someone else out there. In the world. Knowing about her and her daughter. And that was . . . dangerous.

ARIANNA

Arianna's flat was at the other end of the high street, far enough from the house she had grown up in to avoid it and the adjoining streets. But today she'd have to walk right past it. She had planned it for after work.

Thirty-three cases. Thirty-three women. Thirty-three journeys from the first meeting in their offices, listening to their accounts, holding space for them, focusing on them, honouring their horror and courage, informing them of their choices, the process if they chose to move forward, the timeline, the statistics, the hope and the reality. Holding back her own disillusionment with the very system she had chosen to work in, looking for details, evidence, nuggets of gold that might, just might make a case, that might just lead to justice this time. Seeing the myriad ways it, she, could be pulled apart, dismissed. The holes they could find, the blame they could imply, the ease with which this could all come to nothing.

Sweet F-A.

N.F.A.

No Further Action.

She held rage for them, pain for them, hope for them, going the extra mile, working more hours than she should because it was never enough to make up for what they'd been through. For the broken system that she knew would not give them the justice they deserved.

But therein lay burnout, insanity, loneliness and break-down. So now she tried to stick to the boundaries she had learned to impose on herself: dinner at seven-thirty. Rest. A bit of TV. Phone off at ten. Meditation. Lights out at ten-thirty. It kept her honest. Sane. Anchored.

Today she took the first left after the station, walked the familiar street, turned right towards Chris's nan's place. She slowed as she passed the old family house. Someone had hacked at her mum's old plants, grown from cuttings she'd smuggled in her suitcase from Cyprus. Jasmine and nispero and hibiscus and fig. Bright, fragrant flora that shouldn't have survived these chilly climes. But her mum could make a stone erupt with flowers. She'd planted them in the soil at the front of the house and left them to grow and grow. Wildly. Untamed. Blocking the light through the window so the front room was always dark. Entwining with each other to form a matted single entity too enmeshed to separate. The new owners had taken a chainsaw to it all and levelled her mum's Mediterranean garden. Arianna peered into the newly exposed window, a pang of longing for a family she hadn't seen in years. But it was neat in there. Tidy. Ordered. Calm. Cold. Familiar but not.

When she arrived at Chris's nan's, the front garden was covered over with tasteful black slate, the netted curtains replaced with wooden shutters. Not a doily in sight. An automatic porch light switched on as she neared, so she kept moving past it.

2022

TESS

'Are you joking? Today? Of all days. Think about it, Tess. Why didn't you think about it.'

She knew he would lose his shit. Part of her wondered why she'd bothered to ask. Part of her suspected she had arranged to be busy today, of all days, on purpose.

'What is it exactly you want from me?' Callum continued.

'To look after your daughter,' she replied, trying to keep her voice from wobbling.

'You're better than that,' he scoffed. 'Where are you even going? Is it really essential?'

She paused. Chose her words carefully. 'I'll be back for bath time,' she said, forcing herself to look him in the eye, then walked past him.

As she pulled on her coat, there was a bang. Something had been thrown. Or hit. She forced herself to walk out of the door without looking back.

It was a long journey to Knightsbridge. She felt the pull back to her daughter as the miles increased between them. She'd be fine. Sinead was fine. She was with her dad.

She got off at the same stop as when they'd been rehearsing

and then performing at the Royal Albert Hall. A whole five years ago now, she realized with a jolt. He'd been brilliant. Even had his picture in a broadsheet paper, in full conductor action – baton and opposite arm raised, hair mid flick, a gleam of sweat shining in the pink and blue lighting. The tip of a bow just visible at the edge of the frame. She liked to think it was her bow. She'd got Callum that gig. The Festival Hall one too.

Sometime into Sinead's third year, Tess realized that the only projects she'd done recently were with him. She wondered when that had happened. After Sinead had been born, something had flipped, swapped around. And then, when she had a bit more freedom to pick up her bow again, it was Callum that had got her the few gigs she could fit around childcare.

She focused on her mission. It was a proper lead. The best one they had. Tess had found him online and sent a message explaining it all: she was missing. They were worried. And they were trying to find her, get in touch with anyone who might have seen her recently.

And he'd answered. Sent a message asking her to meet him in Central where he was working.

She passed the construction site, a huge, towering mass of reflective surfaces soaring up into the city sky, and she tried to imagine him doing this. Fixing in a plug socket, running some cables through a wall. Standing back at the end of the day and seeing the fruits of his labours before him. Tangible, visible, significant. And then she saw him standing by the makeshift entrance, a grim smile on his face.

'It's you,' she said.

Chris R.P chuckled, the same boyish chuckle from a time long ago. 'Yep, iss me.'

'You look the same but different.'

He nodded. 'You good?'

'I'm okay. Bit worried about Dana.'

'Yeah. Same.'

'We're just trying to make sure she's okay. She's probably fine. We've been trying to find anyone who might have seen her. And I just thought ... maybe like before, you might have ... might know something that might help? Have you seen her, or ... ?'

Chris R.P shook his head. 'Nah. I haven't seen her.'

Tess's heart sank.

'But I have spoken to her.'

1999

DANA

'I can't go.'

Among the screams of excitement, Dana almost didn't hear her. It took a moment to register what Tess had said. 'What?'

'I've got another concert that night.' Tess's voice trembled.

'No! You have to come,' Dana pleaded.

'Tess, man. Just bunk it this once,' Candace reasoned.

'Could you call in sick or something? I'll do you a note,' Riri suggested.

Tess shook her head. 'It doesn't work like that.'

How could she miss this? Dana was sure that nothing this exciting would ever happen to them again. She had described to the girls, blow by exquisite blow, how she'd found out what tutor group he was in and walked past on Monday morning five times before she finally saw him. He was talking to his mate and would have missed her completely if she hadn't said, 'Jay, right?' a bit too loudly and not quite as casually as she'd planned. But it had done the job. He'd turned and then his exquisite face had blossomed into that lopsided smile, and he'd said, 'Yeah.' They'd screamed when she'd described it.

Then at lunchtime she'd made Riri walk past him in the lunch queue with her and he'd called them over.

And invited them to his party.

They'd waited until they were all together to tell Tess and Candace. They'd already planned their cover story which involved staying over at Candace's, which they would do, eventually, but only after going to the party. Dana had even planned each girl's outfit, hair and make-up, and today was meant to be the trial run. She was finally going to get Tess out of those clunky workmen's boots and take those depressing plaits out of her hair, get some mousse in it. She looked at her friend's sad face and her heart constricted.

The elation they had felt just moments ago was gone. Little Jazz rubbed her head affectionately on Tess. Dana searched for something to say.

'Well, we're not the only ones who are gonna be devastated you won't be there,' she said suggestively. Tess looked up. 'Didn't Dan declare his love to you in History?'

Tess blushed. 'Not exactly,' she replied. 'He just said he liked my face and that I was different to the other girls. Classier.'

'He said she looked clean,' Arianna added.

'The fuck does that mean?' Candace said frowning.

'You are classy,' Dana gushed. 'And clean. You play the violin and you've got all those books in your house and you speak proper. And you have baths and everything.'

'Anyway, she's not interested in Dan,' Arianna added. 'She's got her sights on someone else.'

Tess glared at Arianna.

Arianna shrugged. 'Do I lie though?'

'Ohmygodwho?' Candace leaned forward.

'Is he coming to Jay's party? You've got to come now!' Dana squealed.

'No, he's not coming to the party,' Tess replied. 'Because he's not a student.'

They gasped, but Ri nodded knowingly.

'Whothefuckisit?' Candace demanded.

Tess took a breath. 'It's Mr T.'

Candace frowned. 'As in, the hench dude from the A-Team?'

'No!' Tess giggled.

'Mr Tamworth,' Arianna clarified.

'The music teacher? Oh shit. Big man moves,' Candace exclaimed.

'So that's where you've been going after school!' Dana exclaimed. 'You dirty little minx. Has he popped your cherry yet?'

'No!' Tess exclaimed. 'He hasn't even ... He doesn't even ... see me like that.'

'Are you sure?'

'Yes.'

The front door clicked shut and the girls hushed each other as Eileen and Don walked in.

'Evening ladies.' He nodded.

Eileen put her shopping bags on the kitchen counter and started filling up the kettle. 'Right, who wants tea and biscuits?'

The girls stood up and Dana gathered Jazz gently into her arms. 'We'll have it in my room, Mum,' she said.

Candace stretched as they gathered their things.

'Blimey, I bet you eat big bowls of cereal for breakfast. Bigger than even Dana does.' He nodded to Candace's protruding chest.

'Don! Stop it,' chided Eileen. She gave him a whack on the arm. Dana turned a deep purple and hurried through the door, pulling Candace with her.

1999

ARIANNA

'He got Elke to talk to me.'

'Oh shit.'

'She came into my room while I was getting changed and sort of leaned on the windowsill like it was normal to see me half naked.'

'What did she say?'

'She just went straight into it, no foreplay, just, "*I know that you have started your period, Tess, and there will be some more changes to your body that we will discuss. Your vagina and your armpits will grow hair. Your breasts will eventually develop too. And you will begin to feel strong sexual urges. This is all normal.*"'

'Shut. Up.' Arianna turned to her in horror. 'She said that?'

'*Ja.*'

'Where was your dad?'

'Hovering somewhere downstairs,' Tess replied. 'He did, however, leave a mountain of tampons and pads outside my room. Enough to last me the rest of the year.'

Arianna sighed. 'I started mine when I was in Cyprus,' she began. 'I woke up with all this brown stuff in my knickers. I thought I'd shat myself. But then I realized it was coming out of the wrong hole so I told my Yiayia and she jumps up all excited, gets me to take my knickers off and get in the bath, and then she calls her sister and my auntie, and by the time I'm out, they're both over, along with a neighbour who hands me a bag with the biggest pads I've ever seen. Like, ones old people wear when they can't get to the toilet in time. I was legit waddling about like a penguin.'

Tess laughed.

'Hi Tess.' They turned to find Dan standing next to them. He tossed his curtained hair to one side. 'Nice jumper,' he said, formally.

'Thanks ...'

Arianna glared at him. He hovered, then he looked down at a small notebook he was holding in his hand as if he'd just noticed it. 'Ah yes. Been doing a bit of writing.'

'Okay.'

'It's for a thing Mr M's got us doing. Poetry group. We discuss poems and then we get to read some of our own out. Spoken word, that sort of thing.'

Tess nodded. Arianna rolled her eyes.

'You should come,' he said, as if he'd just thought of it.

'Um, thanks?'

Dan nodded a few times and then turned clumsily, then headed to the front of the class where he sat with John, Luke and Alan. Alan slapped him on the back as he sat down.

'That was the baitest thing I ever did see,' Arianna declared. 'He legit thinks he's Lord Byron or some shit.'

'What's this poetry group thing?'

'Apparently Mr M's started up this thing after school where they sit around and read poetry out loud while they wank each other off in a big wanky wank circle,' Arianna said.

Tess giggled as Arianna did an impression of the poetry wank circle. She stopped abruptly as Mr M walked in. He was wearing double denim today – a light blue shirt with darker blue jeans.

'Poetry,' Mr M began, ruffling his hair. 'The most enigmatic of literary forms. And it is my job to demystify it for you.' He looked at his watch. 'And I've got about three months to do it.'

The Oxbridge Four guffawed. Arianna contemplated setting them on fire.

'So, let's start by naming some poets and maybe we can home in on a few to read. Anyone?'

Four pale hands shot up in the front row. He pointed at each in turn.

'William Blake', 'Wordsworth, sir', 'Percy Bysshe Shelley', 'Sir, wasn't Shakespeare also a poet?'

'He was indeed.'

Dan grinned at the other three. He glanced briefly behind him. Arianna rubbed her eye with her middle finger.

'Yes, yes and yes. All strong contenders and all, I am pleased to say, on the syllabus. So . . .'

Arianna raised her hand. This time she didn't wait to be noticed.

'What about Benjamin Zephaniah? And Maya Angelou? Are they on the syllabus, sir?'

Mr M raised his eyebrows. The Oxbridge Four turned in their seats.

'I believe Dr Angelou is, Arianna,' he nodded.

'What about Sappho and Grace Nichols?' she demanded.

'Indeed.' Mr M paused as he regarded her for a moment. He tapped the desk in front of him, then he began. 'Inside the Wolf's fang, the mountain of heather. Inside the mountain of heather, the Wolf's fur. Inside the Wolf's fur, the ragged forest ...' His voice took on a deeper more resonant tone. Arianna froze as he seemed to direct the words at her. Then, halfway, he turned from Arianna and faced the class, addressing the rest of the poem to them all. She realized she'd been holding her breath.

'... Inside the Wolf's tongue, the Doe's tears ...'

She could feel Tess's eyes on her. Arianna smirked dismissively but continued watching him as he delivered the final lines.

'Ted Hughes. Poet Laureate,' he said in a throwaway tone. He turned, plonked a pile of photocopies in front of Alan and waved his hand. Alan jumped up and started distributing the sheets to the class.

They analysed the poem. The structure, the imagery, the rhythm and poetic devices. He asked them about its meaning and Mr M and the Oxbridge Four bounced thoughts and answers between them at the front as the rest of the class looked on. Arianna seethed. She sat taller, her breaths faster, a strong desire to be seen suddenly forming inside her.

'Are you okay?' Tess asked.

'Didn't his wife commit suicide?' Arianna blurted out.

'Who? Mr M's?'

'No, Ted Hughes.'

'I . . . I think I remember Linton saying something . . .' Tess replied bewildered at her friend's intense emotions.

The pips sounded the end of the lesson. 'Homework is to choose a poem, any poem and learn it by heart,' Mr M announced over the bustle. 'Stretch yourselves. Find someone obscure, different. Take a leaf out of Arianna's book, if you will.'

Arianna paused in surprise. The boys at the front looked up as if seeing her for the first time.

As they filed out into the corridor, Tess rushed off to practise. Arianna felt a tap on her shoulder and turned to find Mr M standing beside her.

'Thursday evening. Poetry club. Come.'

She wasn't going to go. The thought of Luke, Dan and Alan performing their shit poems made her want to stab herself in the eye with a Bic.

She contemplated 'Still I Rise,' as she walked home, decided the line about being the hope and the dream of the slave would make everyone laugh at her. Maybe some Sappho? But then she'd be branded a lesbian for the rest of her school life.

She found Theo and Lelia alone in the living room, eating snacks.

'Where's Mum?' she asked.

Lelia shrugged.

Arianna looked in the kitchen. It was empty. She bounded

up the stairs and knocked on her mum's bedroom door. No answer. She opened it and looked in. Her mum was in bed, clutching a water bottle with her eyes closed, leaning to one side.

'Mum?'

She opened them slowly and looked at Arianna.

'It's 4 p.m.'

Her mum looked down, her face deflated, her shoulders hunched.

'Did ... has ... Dad gone?'

She nodded briefly.

'Are we going to Auntie Sandrine's?'

She didn't answer.

It had been a while since she'd last found her like this. It was when he left that things were the worst. It always took some time to adjust. Arianna hovered at the door.

'I've got to do a poem. I need to choose one and learn it,' she offered.

Her mum sighed, looked annoyed.

'Anyway, I'll ...' Arianna gave it a moment more, then headed downstairs. In the kitchen, she took some crisps and chocolate from the cupboard.

'Can I have some?' Theo asked.

'What's that in your hand?' Arianna accused.

He looked down sheepishly at his hand which was already lost in a crisp packet.

She sat with them in front of the TV and watched a man in a broom-cupboard talk to a puppet gopher.

*

An hour later they heard a creak. Soon after, the smell of food wafted through to them. Their mum peered in from the doorway. *'Ade,'* she ordered.

They got up and headed into the kitchen.

She sat watching the three of them eat, then she placed something in front of Arianna. A book of poems.

TESS

Tess had made it back to the station without crying, but now she couldn't control the sobs convulsing out of her. Everything Chris R.P had told her had made her want to ask a hundred more questions, until she couldn't take in any more information. She thought she'd managed to thank him before she'd walked away, stunned.

Tess let herself in, realizing she had no idea what time it was, only that she needed a hug, a drink, to talk it through, make sense of what he'd told her. Urgent footsteps descended. Callum looked at her, wide-eyed. She softened, opened her mouth to begin to tell him—

'Sorted?' he asked.

'Well . . .'

'Good.' He swept past her, grabbed his jacket and shut the door behind him.

Tess stood, too shocked to cry, then rushed upstairs to find Sinead.

She was in the bathtub, playing with some colourful

floating balls, seemingly unaware of the ugliness of the
adult world around her. Tess knelt down, pushed it all aside
with great effort to give this moment to her daughter. Sinead
looked so much like Dagmar. She seemed, as she grew, to
resemble her more and more. Certain movements, expres-
sions, seemed uncannily Dagmar's. Someone Sinead hardly
knew. She'd met her once, the Christmas after Sinead was
born, when Dagmar had managed to make it over for a couple of hours, but both grandmother and granddaughter had
been wary of each other and kept their distance. Sometimes
Tess worried, when Sinead had a tantrum or made things
up or did anything eccentric, what else had been passed on
from grandmother to granddaughter. But, no, Sinead was a
normal, healthy, happy four-year-old, doing the things that
four-year-olds do. Nothing more.

Tess put Sinead to bed, read her a book, kissed both eyes
and switched off the light. She walked past the two other
bedrooms – one their bedroom and one his studio. The
plan had been to fill them with kids. Their kids. She had
been adamant that she would have a proper home – not a
council flat – with a garden. And a family, a big one, not
just two of them rattling around trying to fill up the quiet,
the empty spaces. But as her fortieth year neared, she knew
now, with certainty, this was it. Nothing to do with biology,
everything to do with them.

He had left the radio on in the kitchen. She went to
switch it off, have a moment of peace to get her thoughts in
order. A new song started. 'Yamaha'. By E.G.G.

Tess hurled her phone at the speaker. It hit the side with

a thud and fell to the floor. She grabbed it and hit the radio over and over. It stopped. She stood, panting. A crack had formed across the screen of her phone.

2022

ARIANNA

Arianna sat in the room of a police station in Croydon and tried to focus on her laptop screen as she waited for her client to finish their interview. There was a lot of waiting around, hours often, time she used to catch up with paperwork. But today she felt pulled to her phone.

She should have replied to him by now. Any longer and she would officially be ghosting him. And that made her a dickhead. Like all the other dickheads on these apps. Wasting peoples' time, lacking in basic respect, basic communication skills. Fucking around and messing with peoples' hopes, peoples' feelings. But she carried on scrolling through the profiles of people hugging dolphins and drugged tigers instead.

She didn't have time anyway. She never had time. Arianna was time poor, and everything-else-poor. And the first thing they asked her on these dates was what she did, and when she explained what she did, she saw them stiffen, their features freeze in a supportive, understanding, liberal smile that they tried hard to really mean, as they put two and two together, wrestled with the person they thought they were and their visceral desire to run.

She'd liked his beard. That's how it had started. And something about the way he had presented himself. Like an open book – one of her favourite things. They had started messaging because of his beautiful beard. And then the world stopped.

Arianna had been relieved. Quietly, guiltily, knowing how many thousands of people were stuck in a living nightmare. How many women. But for her, being allowed to stop for one blessed moment, then a day, then whole weeks, with no judgement, had been heaven. Beholden to no one. Answerable only to herself. No need for the guilt that nipped at her heels every day because she could never do enough, the FOMO that haunted her lonely weekends, the thought of the world moving forward, people writing actual books and having actual careers, relationships, babies even, spending time with their loved ones, belonging with someone, because no one could meet anyone and there was literally nothing happening. Anywhere.

And so she had allowed herself that time to do the minimum. Cook, eat, read, keep in touch with a handful of people. There had been pressure, as a single, childless woman, to help others. She had dodged it all. She had lived through her own nightmare long before, survived, come out the other side, faced things, named them, felt them, claimed them, let them go, walked away, rebuilt her life many times, gathered the splintered parts of her and patched them back together. So, while the world burned with fever, she had allowed herself reprieve.

They had planned to have their first date that weekend,

but then the world locked down. And then he'd messaged, asked if he could give her a call to check she was okay, if her family had everything they needed. And they hadn't even met.

They started messaging, slowly sharing details, careful to finish with a question that would lead to more conversation. There were boundaries too. They fell into chatting every other day, giving each other space, respect, breath. She'd tried not to look forward to it, tried to maintain the fierce independence she had painstakingly cultivated over so many years, reliant on no one but herself. But it was often the only interaction she had with someone other than a client or co-worker.

And then the rules relaxed.

He asked her if she'd like to meet.

She hadn't replied.

She told herself it was really about the fact that he had typed,

Garage > Jungle.

That it was doomed from then anyway.

A buzz. Her phone lit up. She lit up with hope. Then she frowned. It was Tess.

Arianna couldn't get her to slow down. Tess strode away from the station, Arianna just managing to keep up. She'd never seen her like this. Tess could be snide, bitter, passive-aggressive, but never all-out angry.

'I still don't understand what's happening,' Arianna said,

her breath already laboured from the pace Tess had set. 'I thought we had all agreed to a call.'

'We did. But that was just to make sure Candace would be home,' Tess explained, checking the map on her phone briefly. Tess's phone was jacked. Arianna noticed a big crack across the screen, splintering the streets on the map so they didn't quite meet each other.

'So, we're ... ambushing her?' Arianna asked.

'We're getting the truth out of her so we can stop running around like idiots,' she spat back.

She had heard the same thing at the end of the call. A girl's voice, saying 'Mum'. Arianna wanted answers too, but this seemed intense, out of proportion. Tess's rage didn't make sense.

They turned into a maze of giant warehouses that eventually led to a dockside, Tess strode to the edge, overlooking the water. Then she turned again towards a cluster of boats in the distance, checking her broken phone once more. Arianna followed. They reached the boats, long and slim, curtained windows and plant pots on the roofs. Tess paused, chewed the inside of her mouth. She peered into one window after another, then stopped. They stood in front of a squat, medium-sized houseboat sitting humbly among the others docked along the pier that extended into the river. In the small window, the picture of the sunflower they had both seen on their video calls.

Tess hesitated. What did one do? She couldn't reach the door to knock without stepping aboard, but that didn't seem right. There were voices, two of them, coming from inside. One was Candace, her familiar cadence and tone, but deeper, wearier. The other voice, a girl's? She stepped onto the boat, it swayed slightly. The voices quietened. She knocked. 'Hello?'

The sounds of footsteps rushing. Candace's face peered out from inside. She opened the door.

Candace, the woman, stood before them, older, wizened, but the expression was familiar, quintessentially hers. And angry. 'What are you doing here?'

'We need to speak to you properly,' Tess said.

'We were going to video call,' Candace clarified.

'No, actually, we're going to speak in person, in there, and you're going to explain what the fuck is going on and why you're making us run around like idiots on your stupid mission while you lie to us.' Tess's eyes sparkled with rage.

'What are you talking about?' Candace asked.

'Don't even try that shit,' Tess said, and barged into Candace's home.

'Oi! You can't come in here!' Candace yelled.

Arianna followed behind them both. The tiny home was pristine. The furniture and décor was worn but warm, chosen and positioned thoughtfully to maximize space. It was delightful in here. Cosy, bright. Arianna tried to imagine living somewhere like this, felt that she understood something new about her old friend, standing in her tiny, lovely place. There was an actual teapot on the small coffee table. Two cups half-full. A yoga mat rolled neatly and leaning by the door. A golden buddha on a shelf. And all around the walls was art. Candace's art. Beautiful sweeping images of brown bodies in motion, rich with colour, landscapes suggested in sweeps of brushstrokes, faraway lands, Africa, India, the places that made up Candace.

And a timetable on the fridge. A school timetable.

'Get out. Now.' Candace's face was a hot red.

'You need to explain what's going on, Candace,' Tess insisted. The three of them, standing in the boat, almost filled the entire space. 'Where is she?'

'Who? Dana? I don't know. That's the whole—'

'No, not Dana. The girl.'

Candace froze. 'How do you—'

'Doesn't matter. What's going on? Why do you have her here?'

Arianna looked from one to the other, frustration rising in her now. 'Will someone tell me what the fuck is going on?'

A creak. Then, from the doorway at the far end of the boat, she stepped into the room. Tess and Arianna gasped. The hair, the eyes, the expression, fearful, questioning. The limbs, the lips. All of her.

'Come in darlin,' Candace said gently.

The girl stepped forward and rushed to the safety of Candace's side.

'This is Saffy. My daughter,' Candace said pointedly.

Arianna's jaw dropped. 'Your daughter? I don't understand.'

'That doesn't make ... When did ... How long have you ... ?'

'Eleven years,' she replied. 'Saffron is thirteen years old. She has been my daughter for eleven years.'

It was uncanny. The skinny, lanky limbs. The translucent

eyelashes, the frizzy blonde hair. It was like a mirage. Like their missing friend had returned as the girl they first knew, all those years ago.

Dana.

1999

CANDACE

Candace looked at the two different shades of gunk in her hands. One was an orangey tan colour which Dana had found in the bargain bin at Woolworths. The other was a dollop of her dad's brown shoe polish. She brought her palms together and mixed them. Eventually it formed a paste that was still nothing close to her skin tone. She looked into the mirror, gritted her teeth and smeared it onto her face.

'This is mingin',' she exclaimed, as the chemical smell of polish attacked her nostrils. Her face was already beginning to itch.

'It looks great!' Dana encouraged. 'Put loads on.'

Dana reached for the orangey-tan bargain-bin foundation and slathered a load over Arianna's face and neck. Candace tried to emulate Dana's method. She couldn't wait to get home and wash it all off.

'Hold still.' Dana attacked them with a blusher brush, then mascara and lip-gloss that smelled of fake sugary strawberry. Dana's face looked quite a lot like it had that time she'd dressed as Scary Spice, but this time she had added heaps of mascara, eyeliner, lipstick. She gave an odd, high-pitched giggle and shrugged her shoulders at her reflection.

A wave of annoyance rose in Candace. 'What the fuck was that noise?'

'What noise?'

'That weird squeak you just did.'

'It's just my laugh.' She did it again and Candace grimaced.

They had sold their free dinner passes for two pounds a day and saved to get matching halter-neck tops from the Arndale shopping centre which they wore with knock-off Wonderbras that made their tits look massive. Dana kissed Jazz goodbye and smuggled them out of the house before Don could see them. Candace and Riri wore their Reebok Classics with their boot-cut jeans, Dana's heeled boots clopped noisily along the street all the way to the bus stop.

As they sat waiting, Candace pulled a bottle out of her pocket and her two friends gasped.

'Is that Vodka?' Arianna asked.

'Yep.'

'Have you got anything to mix with it? Like cranberry juice?' Dana asked.

'Do I look like Wetherspoons to you?'

Candace kissed her teeth and handed Arianna the bottle. 'Hold it while I spark this.' She took out a wonky joint from her pocket and a lighter.

They were nicely tipsy by the time they jumped off the bus, especially Dana, who'd hogged the bottle. She was singing loudly and making sex noises, but she quietened down as they approached the house.

The muted thump of the music was audible from the street. Dana strode up to the door and gave the buzzer a long press, then thumped on the door for good measure.

A blast of sound hit them as a teenager with ginger curls and a smattering of facial hair opened the door.

'Hi, Jay invited us,' Dana said.

The teenager swayed slightly as he looked at Dana, then at Arianna and Candace. 'Hey, I know you.'

'You play drums in Jay's band, don't you?' Dana asked.

'Yeah . . .' They stood in silence until he realized it was his move. He stepped aside and beckoned them in.

Drummer boy grinned at Candace as she passed him, so she attempted a friendly nod. Her face was beginning to burn.

In the living room, people stood around holding plastic cups in a haze of smoke, nodding to the music. She recognized almost everyone there as being from The Year Above and even from The Year Above That. Some turned as the newcomers walked in and Candace noticed that some girls gave them dirty looks as they passed through. Not Karla though, who smiled as they passed her. Karla Malik. Candace had clocked her on her first day of school. Then again when she watched the first netball match. Now she saw Arianna do the same.

'Does she go to our school?' Arianna asked over the music, trying not to stare.

Candace nodded. 'Yeah, two years above. Apparently, she's banging one of the teachers.' Arianna's eyes widened.

She watched Arianna look back at her. Karla was swaying

to the music, paper cup in her long slender fingers at the end of her perfectly toned brown arms, her jet-black hair with that gentle curl to it. She was wearing red lipstick that accentuated her mouth, which turned up gently at the sides. Candace poked Arianna, who closed her mouth and stopped gawping.

Candace's fake Wonderbra made her tits burst out of the halter-neck top, almost touching her chin. She vowed to keep her jacket on and gave silent thanks for her Reeboks. Dana was making a beeline for the decks set up at the far end. By the time Candace and Arianna had caught up, she was already behind the decks talking loudly in Jay's ear.

Candace and Arianna stood to the side nodding to the happy hardcore cover of 'Sweet Love'. As the soulful vocals ascended, Candace wished she'd brought another zoot with her. As if by magic, she opened her eyes to see Jay leaning over the decks, holding a slimmer, more streamlined one out to her: a superior roll. She took it, dragging deeply twice, thrice, before passing it over to Ri. It hit her hard and quick. This was skunk. The kind of stuff her brother and his friends messed with. She took a few deep breaths to steady her mind and took the blunt off Arianna after just one puff.

General Levy's 'Incredible' filled their ears and the room erupted in loud approval. But suddenly a jarring, scratching sound reverberated around the room and they turned to see Dana leaning on the turntable, trying to steady herself. Candace put out a hand, but Jay was already pulling her up, resetting the record, and they resumed their bouncing.

Jay held Dana firmly around the waist, and with his free

hand, lined up record after record, looking over to Candace
and Riri for their musical approval. Arianna raised a gun
finger at 'Original Nuttah'. Candace closed her eyes, swayed,
opened them, and looked over to the decks once more. Dana
was gone. So was Jay. The scraggly drummer guy who'd
opened the door had taken over behind the decks and
Candace couldn't see Dana anywhere.

Then a tall one in a holey jumper with dirty blond hair
moved in closer to Riri. Candace thought his name was
Damion, the bassist in Jay's band. She watched Arianna
attempt to dance with him, matching her moves with his
gangly flow.

Candace sighed. She'd expected Dana to pull, hoped that
maybe she and Riri could stay together, but now he was
saying something in her ear and she was nodding. Then
Bass Face was pulling Arianna into the crowd, and they
disappeared too.

Candace retreated into the corner nearest the decks and
kept to an understated two-step. The night suddenly seemed
a long, lonely prospect. Drummer Boy didn't have Jay's ear
for a banger, but he was looking at her intensely, smiling
over the turntables. She smiled back briefly, looked down.
And now he was beside her, moving closer, holding onto
her hips, staking his claim. Candace went with it, trying to
catch his rhythm. Now he leaned in and they were kissing.
His tongue worked its way around her mouth in a rhythmic
circle. He tasted of rolies and Polos. His hands squeezed her
back but didn't venture any further. It seemed to go on for a
long time, the smoke and the music and the thick atmosphere

giving it a dreamlike quality. She thought of what a milestone this was, how she knew she would replay this night over and over. She thought of what it would mean at school next week. But mostly she thought, as she kept her eyes squeezed shut, of Arianna and Dana.

He murmured something she didn't quite catch and then pulled her gently out of the corner, through the room, into the hallway, and up the stairs.

She started to panic. They were heading to a bedroom and she was not at all sure she was ready for whatever was going to happen next. At the top of the stairs, Drummer Boy opened a door and then quickly closed it again.

'Occupied,' he said.

But Candace heard the new high-pitched laugh Dana had adopted come from behind that door, and she pushed the door open once more. The room had a slanting roof and two electric guitars mounted on the wall. There was a lava lamp and a double mattress on the floor and Dana was sitting in Jay's lap holding a third guitar, strumming it clumsily and looking up at Jay with an expression Candace knew she had copied off Phoebe from *Friends*. Jay sat behind her as he patiently tried to show her some chords.

'There you are,' Candace exclaimed, the two bandmates shared a nod. She plonked herself on a beanbag in the corner and Drummer Boy arranged himself around her.

'Cee! Listen. I can do Chili Peppers.' Dana was slurring her words. She leaned down over the guitar and almost fell forward, frowning with concentration and placing her fingers on the fret. Then she strummed, sang some words about being taken to the place she loves, rearranged her fingers once more, strummed again, sang about being taken all the way. It sounded awful. Jay chuckled, gently pulling the guitar out of Dana's hands.

Drummer Boy lay sprawled on the floor around Candace. He rubbed her leg.

Dana leaned over and retrieved a bottle that was propped by the bed. She took a swig and offered it to Candace. As Candace took the bottle, Dana pulled her closer. Candace thought she wanted to whisper something, maybe give her a sign that they should get out of here. But instead, she felt her friend's plump, wet lips on her own and realized they were kissing. There was a quiet exclamation from one of the boys. Then Dana let her go and giggled mischievously before focusing back onto Jay.

'That was hot,' Jay exclaimed.

Dana pulled him into a snog. He let the guitar fall softly to the bed. Candace felt her fella's hand rub her back more urgently and she glanced over at Dana who was now pulling herself on top of Jay with drunken determination.

Candace gamely turned back to her guy and initiated the snogging. Her heart was racing, still reeling from the sensation of her best friend's lips on hers, now replaced with thinner, drier lips and soft facial hair. Soon she heard her friend's enthusiastic panting a few feet away and felt the hands on her back move lower, take a handful of her ample bum and squeeze.

Dana was now letting out little gasps of delight. Candace began to panic. Was Dana having sex? Candace opened her eyes, trying to control her panic, as he shifted even closer to her and she felt his erection against her hip.

Candace began to plan her escape. Could she maybe slow things down, make it seem as if it had reached a natural end and then disentangle herself from him, take her friend with her out of the room? Did she have to push him off and run? Could she ask for a bit more drink? If she didn't do something, would it just keep going?

She wasn't ready. She knew that now clearer than ever. She wasn't ready.

Candace took several deep breaths, preparing herself to interrupt the heavy petting. Just as she was about to say something, another voice cut through.

'Ah shit.'

They all turned to find Jay sitting up, holding his hands out and looking down at his lap. Whitish-green liquid seeped slowly down his front. Dana burped, releasing more vomit onto him and the bed. Jay jumped up and swore. Candace pushed herself free and ran over to Dana, helping her up and holding her unfastened top over her breasts.

'Where's the toilet?' she demanded.

Candace led Dana out of the room, pushing a couple of doors open until they found the bathroom. Dana fell out of Candace's arms and into the toilet bowl. Candace rubbed her back as she barfed over and over, the smell of her friend's sick wafting into her nostrils and making her heave too. Soon they both had their heads over the toilet, heaving in tandem. Then the door burst open and Candace looked up to see Arianna over the sink, burping violently into it too.

1999

TESS

Tess called Candace's number three times.

'Still haven't surfaced, I'm afraid,' answered her dad, again.

At 10 a.m. she decided to head over. That had been the plan, that she would at least join them the next day to catch up with the goss, relive the experience vicariously through her friends.

As the bus wound its way around the houses, she wondered what she would find when she got to Candace's. Had Dana had sex with Jay? Was she a woman now? Had the others had sex with someone too? Even Arianna? Would Tess be the last one left, probably in the whole year? She thought of Mr Tamworth and cringed.

She'd lingered on Friday afternoon after her violin lesson, waiting for him to do the rounds of the music rooms. Since he'd taken over as Head of Music, he had introduced a policy of keeping the music rooms open at lunchtimes and after school. He'd made it known that anyone was welcome to come in and use the instruments, no questions asked. Mr Tamworth would do a turn through the department every hour to check in, offer creative input, hover long enough to listen. Tess lived for these moments, lingered for these moments. On Friday, she'd been alone, lost in a piece she was trying to write herself. Something different, funky, experimenting with plucking the strings and beating out a rhythm on the body of the instrument.

'Great stuff.' Mr Tamworth's deep voice startled Tess and she dropped her bow.

She retrieved it, then froze, desperate to find something to say. Her mind went blank.

'Very jazzy. It puts me in mind of early Jamiroquai.'

Tess's eyes lit up. 'I love Jamiroquai!' she gushed, and then clammed up again.

Mr Tamworth nodded and began to turn away.

'Herbie Hancock!' Tess blurted. He turned back.

'I've been listening to Herbie Hancock,' she explained.

Mr Tamworth nodded appreciatively. 'Herbie on the strings,' he said. 'Very original. You should listen to some Jaco Pastorius. He's a bass player, but a jazzy one. Might be a good bridge.' He made a bridge with his hands and Tess contemplated his long, lanky piano-playing fingers.

'Thanks,' she managed.

Mr T continued his rounds and Tess tried to continue making musical noises as she replayed what had been the longest most intimate conversation they'd shared.

It was dark by the time she left. Tomorrow, she had a whole day of rehearsals and then a concert while her friends went to the most important party of their lives. They would come back changed, having hung out with, danced with, snogged, or even shagged people while she was surrounded by awkward music geeks who were nowhere close to having sex. Even Dan's attentions seemed to have waned. Maybe she should respond more enthusiastically next time she saw him. The thought of snogging him made her stomach clench, let alone letting him see her naked. But if he was the best chance of her becoming a woman, she would have to crack on.

A car beeped and slowed on the road. She clenched and gripped onto the strap of her violin case. Then the car slowed and stopped ahead of her. The window wound down. Tess froze.

'Tess?' Mr Tamworth's deep voice called from inside the car. She rushed over to the passenger window and peered in. He was rummaging around in the glove compartment. For a moment she thought he was clearing the seat for her to get in.

'Aha!' he exclaimed and held out a CD to her. 'Jaco. There you go. Have a listen.'

'Thanks.'

'Safe home.' Then he drove off.

She had guarded this moment carefully all weekend, waiting to share it with Riri, Candace and Dana. An offering of something in exchange for the wild anecdotes they would all have about the best night of their lives. But if they'd all shagged Year Aboves, then her stupid story about Mr Tamworth handing her a CD through a car window was a joke.

Candace's mum let Tess in, and Tess made her way upstairs. She listened outside the bedroom door and heard nothing, so she knocked and pushed the door open. 'Hello?'

The room was dark, but she could make out Arianna

topping and tailing with Candace and Dana on a mattress on the floor. Arianna stirred first, stretching grumpily and then perking up as she caught the smell of the Maccy Ds Tess had bought on the way.

'What time is it?' Candace asked.

'Almost eleven.'

'Oh shit.' Arianna hauled herself up to a sitting position, Candace squinted, reached over to the curtain and pulled it open. Dana was still asleep, her mouth wide open, one leg poking out of her sleeping bag. Tess hovered, not knowing where to put herself. She held out the brown paper bag. 'I brought this.'

Tess passed the breakfast over. Candace looked inside, placed it between her and Arianna on the bed.

'Mum! Tea!' she suddenly bellowed. Arianna flinched and then scowled at her. Dana let out a snore and settled again.

Tess perched awkwardly against some drawers and looked at her bedraggled friends. Candace's thick curls hadn't been wrapped in a headscarf like usual. Instead, they were a dishevelled, frizzy mess that stuck out dramatically to one side in a hairsprayed lump. The morning light caught her skin too, which was usually dark and smooth, but Tess saw that the side of her face had erupted in angry red lumps. Arianna's eye make-up had run and her looser curls were stuck to the side of her face. A faint smell of sick hung in the stale air.

'So . . . ? How was it?' Tess asked.

Candace and Arianna looked at each other. Tess's heart sank. The moment seemed to expand cruelly, where the three of them shared the secrets of the night before and Tess was left on the outside, waiting for them to gather themselves, order all the life-changing events into something coherent they could share with her.

Then Dana let out a long, loud burp. They looked down at her in alarm. Tess started to giggle, then Arianna, but she stopped herself when she saw Candace seething silently at the other end of the bed.

Dana opened her eyes slowly and looked around in confusion. She wiped drool from the side of her mouth and tried to focus on who was in the room. 'What's so funny?'

Tess skipped off the bus three hours later still giggling to herself as she pictured all three of her friends vomiting in unison in Jay Thomas's bathroom. No one had shagged anyone. No one had left her behind. And now she was going to spend the afternoon listening to Mr Tamworth's CD.

As she approached her block, she saw a figure hovering at the bottom of the outdoor stairwell, hunched in layers of clothes with a purple velvet hat pulled low over her face. Tess hesitated and then quickened her steps towards her.

'Mum, how long have you been waiting?'

'I couldn't remember the door.'

'It's the red one. On the third floor. Come on, we'll go in together.'

But Dagmar didn't move. 'I can't stay long. I'm going to Russia. They'll call me any time.'

'Well, you can wait inside until they do.'

'I brought you something.' She began rummaging in her handbag, muttering to herself. She pulled out a crumpled brown paper bag with something hard and probably stale in it. Then a handful of partially used tissues. A packet of liquorice.

'Ah. This one.' Dagmar pulled something out and handed it to Tess. It was a mobile phone.

'What is this?'

'It's very important I can reach you. I don't know where in the world I will be.'

'I can't afford it. I—'

'They could send me anywhere. You can't call but I can. You can keep it switched on and you have to charge the battery. But I can call you, so wait for my call.'

'But you can just call the landline—'

'*That is where they listen!*' she hissed. She glared at Tess and tapped the side of her head. Then she turned and hobbled off. Tess watched her go, then stared down at the heavy, plastic brick in her hand.

1999

DANA

Dana flinched against the daylight. She carried last night's outfit in a plastic bag and tried to practise looking spritely and fresh for when she was under Don and Mum's scrutiny. She hoped they'd be engrossed in the Enders Sunday Omnibus so she could slink into her room with a cuppa and spend the rest of the day in bed hugging Jazz and trying not to think of how she would have to avoid the whole of The Year Above for the next two years until they left school for good.

Candace wasn't talking to her. She had drunk her tea, munched her Mcbreakfast and turned her back on them all, feigning sleep till they gathered their things and left. Dana sighed, wondering how many days it would take for her to be forgiven this time.

She let herself in and paused, listening, but the flat was quiet. They were out. She headed to the bathroom, stuffing her puke-covered outfit under layers of other washing in the plastic basket, and then went to the kitchen. She filled the kettle and switched it on. Then she turned around and screamed. 'Mum! You scared me.'

Eileen sat quietly on the sofa blowing smoke out into the room.

'What are you doing just sitting there? Is the telly broken?'

Her mum brought the cigarette to her lips once more and Dana noticed the tremble in her hand.

'Mum, are you okay?'

Eileen nodded. 'D'you have fun at Candace's?'

'Yeah.'

'Good.' Eileen looked away again into the middle distance and took two more puffs of the cigarette. Don's absence hung heavy in the small flat.

'Tea?'

Eileen looked at her and blinked. 'Yeah.'

Dana brought it over, milkier and sweeter than usual. She switched on the TV but changed the channel away from the soap dramas and onto a rerun of *Birds of a Feather*. They sat like that for a while, the canned laughter punctuating the silence, Dana watching her mum from the corner of her eye as she lit another fag and bit the skin at the edges of her fingers in between each drag.

After a couple of hours, Dana headed to her room. It was only then she realized someone else was missing.

She called Jazz's name quietly, but heard no jingle of her collar. She called again out towards the hallway, then checked in her mum's room. No Jazz. Dana didn't want to ask her mum, to break the spell she'd been lulled into by the TV, so she quietly searched every corner of the rest of the flat. It was only when she returned to her own room and looked under her bed that she saw a flash of terrified little eyes glaring back at her, cowering in the far corner.

'What you doing, Jazz?'

Dana spoke quietly and soothingly until finally Jazz crept out. She held her and stroked her until she fell asleep and then Dana lay her gently on the bed. Soon after, the sounds from the living room quietened and Dana heard her mum head to bed too.

Dana let out a silent roar of triumph. He was gone.

She lay on the soft, clean carpet and let her mind drift back over the night before. She buried her face in her hands as she remembered how hard she had tried to stop the room from spinning, to keep her stomach from convulsing. Then her mind wandered back to Jay. She had been so close to Losing It with him. He'd even sucked on her boobs and put his hands between her legs. A rush of heat washed up her body at the thought of Jay's lips and hands on her. She focused her mind intently on nothing but those sweet moments they'd shared – first in the living room behind the decks, the bass booming through her as he held her around the waist, and then up in his room as he leaned his perfect, warm, solid body against hers. She replayed it over and over, her breath catching. Then she crawled to the mirror that was leaning against the wall. Dana took off her clothes and sat staring at the reflection of her naked body. These breasts that had suddenly developed, that had made the boys notice her, that had put her on the map, their pale areola with nipples standing pertly in the middle. Her thin waist and thick thighs. Dana opened her legs wide and stared at her vulva, the mousey hair beginning to form around it, the layers and folds of dark, wet skin. She watched herself as she touched the spot she knew was the most sensitive part. She kept her eyes wide open as she tapped and rubbed, tapped and rubbed, held her breath and then, almost silently, let out a final gasp.

CANDACE

'Fun night was it?' Candace's dad dunked a forked piece of sausage into some gravy and chomped at it.

'Yep,' Candace managed. The smell of the meat was turning her stomach. Her mum sat next to him nibbling quietly, a vague smile on her face.

'So, tell us the goss. Who kissed who. Who fancies who?' he urged.

'No one. Nothing. It was just . . . some friends hanging out.'

Her dad exchanged a look with her mum.

'Fair dos,' he shrugged and shovelled some mash in with the banger.

Candace didn't even pretend to eat. She sat there until she couldn't handle his amused scrutiny any longer, until she almost longed for her brother to turn up, smash some shit up. He'd been missing for over three weeks this time. They'd stopped bothering to check with each other, to ask his friends.

Candace dreaded his return and missed him deeply. That messed-up hench brother of hers who tormented her, who brought chaos into their weird little home, who had the same dark-dark skin, the same thick curls, the brown eyes flecked with gold. Who seemed to know her every thought and feeling however hard she tried to avoid his eyes. She held onto the waning memories of them when they had first arrived here as foster kids. He'd already started turning wild, stealing things for them both to eat in the placements and homes before this, even though they were generally well-fed, knocking things over just to relish the crash and mess. But at least he let her in on it then, shared his loot or shot her a look as he calmly shoved a vase onto the floor. It had been them against the world.

He'd reined it in long enough for John and Brenda to take pity on them. He'd channelled all that raucous energy into goofy jokes and enthusiasm for John's vintage car chat, good-natured rugby tackles that were almost hugs. A month into the ink on their adoption papers drying, John had woken to find his car keyed, and someone had done a steaming piss on Brenda's new carpet.

Candace scraped her chair back noisily and got up.

'Er, manners!' exclaimed John, a bit of sausage juice escaping from his mouth.

'PleasemayIbeexcused,' Candace mumbled.

He paused for a moment and then sighed. 'Well, since we're not going to get any gossip out of you: you may leave the table.'

Candace headed upstairs, brushed her teeth and washed her face, wrapping her hair carefully like she'd seen them do on the Cosby Show. Her white parents had looked a bit bemused the first time they'd seen her with her hair covered up. She hadn't bothered explaining, ignoring the dad-joke about joining the Gurkhas.

It was still early, but she was exhausted and deflated. She was angry with Dana for leaving her on her own, for taking it too far. For making them the laughing stock of the party. And as usual, Dana had slept soundly, not a care in the world, while Candace took off her boots, tucked her in, put her on her side so she didn't choke to death on her own vomit.

Candace touched the side of her face and winced. Her skin felt raw, the angry red lumps that covered her face burned. She vowed never to wear make up again – even if it wasn't mixed with shoe polish – and cursed Dana for getting her to slather it on. She thought of Dana's face, pasted with thick layers of the orange stuff, the dark mascara she worked over and over into her lashes, the eyebrows she painted on and the smell of burnt hair. The dumb giggle and coy shrug she did a hundred times a day now. It made her look so fucking dumb. But then an image came to her of the old Dana, the original Dana, before the boys and the tits and the tight tops. Her blonde, almost translucent eyebrows and lashes that made her look permanently surprised, her frizzy blonde hair scraped off her freckly face into a pony tail, the way her lips moved when she was doing sums in her head, the fierce de-termination on her face when Candace passed her the ball in netball, the strong, graceful pivot to the hoop, the elation on her face when she scored, her kindness, the way she always knew when Candace was upset before she had to say any-thing, how easy she was to laughter, how ready she was with a hug, her warm body, the feel of falling asleep holding her hand. She'd been too pissed to share a bed with her last night. Candace had been disappointed, tucked her in nonetheless.

Candace moved her hand past the soft swell of her belly, down under the elastic of her pyjamas and pressed two fingers firmly on her G-spot. She pressed and released. Pressed and released, thinking, but not thinking; imagining, but not clearly enough for it to mean anything. As her body tensed and then exploded with pleasure, she let out a guttural moan, a tear falling into her pillow at the same time.

She woke suddenly and gasped in shock, trying to understand what was happening. She looked up to find her brother standing over the bed, holding her by the forearm so tightly she winced.

'Nathan!'

He gripped harder.

'What you been doing you dirty bitch?' He smelled awful. Of piss and bins and stale sweat. She tried desperately to pull her arm away, but his grip remained firm and she whimpered as he yanked it and pain shot through her shoulder.

'Get off me!'

His eyes were bloodshot and wild looking. His wispy facial hair grew in unshaven tufts across his face. 'You been touching yourself? You putting your fingers in your own pussy?'

'No!'

He suddenly pulled her fingers to his face and inhaled deeply. Her arm felt like it was being wrenched out of its socket. She tried not to scream.

'Fuck me, you stink. Who were you thinking of eh? Was it one of your girlfriends? You fucking dyke.'

'Stop it!'

'You were, weren't you? I bet it was Dana Evans. Was it Dana? Was it?'

'No!'

'It was, wasn't it?'

He swung his other arm around from behind him and he was holding the airgun. Before she could register what was happening, he aimed it at her palm and shot her point blank.

2022

CANDACE

'I don't know who the dad is. She never told me.'

Candace had sent Saffy down the pier to a neighbour's and watched her out the window as she went, scanning the riverbank for any lingerers. Then she made a fresh pot of tea.

'I thought it was just the usual shit. She'd either call or turn up. If she called, I'd travel to wherever she was. Bournemouth first. Then Basingstoke. Then the outskirts of Fuck Knows Where. He'd dumped her again. Taken all her money. Again. The house was always in a state. Cigarette butts and dirty dishes and unmade bed. I'd clean up, cook, open some windows, give her all the cash I had, then head back. If she turned up at mine, it meant she'd been kicked out, lost her job, usually both. I'd sort her out, and then she'd disappear again.'

'New number. New job. New address. New fella,' Arianna chanted. They'd been through it too, several times. But they hadn't realized they'd all been doing it. 'Then it would start all over again.'

'She turned up one day with this tiny girl.' Candace's voice caught, remembering the moment she had first set eyes on Saffy, her heart contracting all over again.

'I was living in a bedsit. One room. I was raging at her for not telling me she had a child. But I said they could stay, for as long as she needed, as long as she promised to sort herself out properly this time, for the sake of the little girl.' Candace sipped her tea, smiled ironically. 'It was so lovely. For a good two and a half days, just the three of us.'

Candace's smile faded as she remembered Nicole, her girl-friend at the time, who'd turned up to find Candace suddenly living with another woman and her child. One of many casualties of this predicament she had found herself in.

'Then I woke up to Saff shaking me, telling me she was hungry. I got up, started making breakfast. Dana was no-where. It was only when Saff was sitting down and eating, I saw the note. Just one word: "Sorry".' Candace shrugged. 'That was it.'

She watched their minds racing to process this, include it in the timeline of the last few years.

'But how have you managed to ... What about social services ... school ... the law?' Arianna asked.

Candace nodded grimly. 'Yep. All of the above. I've had to manage it all somehow,' she began again. 'That's why we moved here. It's an alternative community. Lovely people. Hardly got a pot to piss in, but generous to a fault. Also, everyone's got their history. We don't pry, just take each other as we find them. We kept to ourselves for a long time. It took ages for me to trust anyone. But as she got older, I had to figure some things out. I did some research, asked around quietly. Then I made the call to Social Services before they made the call to me. There was a home visit, lots of questions asked, of me and of her. Questions about Dana and her whereabouts, how long Saff had been left with me. And then the wait. I didn't eat or sleep for a week, until finally I got the call. No Further Action.'

Arianna bristled at those three words. But Candace was smiling with relief. For her, this was a good outcome.

'We were on their records now, but Saffy was clearly fed, nourished and well-clothed so no further action would be taken,' Candace continued. 'She could stay with me, as long as she kept going to school. School's a big deal as far as Social Services are concerned, so I walked my little blonde-haired, blue-eyed daughter to her first day at school.'

She watched them take this detail in. The hundred ways in which she, a brown woman, raising a blonde child, would be viewed. The hundred ways she was forced to navigate the world differently.

It had been so lonely. And horrifying. The gradual realization that she had been left with this child for good. The silent rage and desperation that she'd tried hard to hide from that tiny little girl as she adjusted her entire life to accommodate her. And then the love that gradually grew between the two of them, abandoned by the same woman. The thousand tiny milestones as they moved from shock to survival and then to a love so fierce Candace had never known anything like it.

'What about ... Have you seen her at all since ... ?' Arianna asked.

'Dana?' Candace sighed. 'That's what I was trying to tell you. She calls. Every year. On Saffy's birthday. She calls and listens down the phone until she hears Saffy's voice, knows she's okay, and then hangs up. A different number every time. I was confused the first couple of years, then raging. I screamed at her a lot. She never spoke, just waited until she was sure, then she was gone again for another year. I started talking to her, in the silences, asking her if she got the documents I emailed her, to all the many email addresses I've got for her. All she has to do is sign them so that I can be Saffy's official guardian, so that she really belongs with me, so no one can take her away from me, so *she* can't turn up and take her from me.'

Her voice broke as the dread rose in her. The thing she expected to happen every day of her life. The thing she dreamed of almost every night. The reason why she hadn't been able to hold down a relationship, because either she or they got spooked. Until she met Asha. Brilliant, gorgeous, savvy Asha, who also came from a complicated family situation, raised by her mum's friend even though her grandma was her official guardian. She didn't seem fazed by Candace's white child.

But it was Candace's obsessiveness, her paranoia, checking the curtains ten times a night, staring at the bankside waiting for that figure to appear again, or for Dana to turn up and decide she wanted her back. And the fact she'd called Dana's name out in her sleep, more than once, that was destroying the longest relationship she'd had so far, the best relationship. Especially since the missed call this year on Saff's birthday, when she'd searched for Dana and found nothing. It consumed Candace. And Asha was getting tired of it.

2022

TESS

'Sorry,' Tess said, finally speaking. 'I shouldn't have barged in like this. I don't know what I was thinking, ambushing you in your own home. I'm sorry. Really.'

Tess had only been a mother for the last four years and it had been so tough, lonelier than any other time in her life, and god knows she had been lonely in the past. And, of course, it was also wonderful and joyful and exhausting all at once. But she had had almost nine full months to prepare for it. She couldn't begin to fathom what Candace had been through. The shock of being left with someone else's child. The waiting, the unexpected rearranging of her life, the slow realization Dana wasn't coming back, the decisions she'd had to make, the sacrifice, unable to even ask for support because it had to be kept secret – so she could keep this tiny person alive, because that was all that mattered now.

Candace shrugged. 'I knew it would have to come out eventually.'

Tess wished she'd asked Chris R.P more. She had a hundred more questions about every detail of his account. But she'd fixated on the one: the fact that Dana had a child. That

Chris had got a call late in the night and rushed out of his home, left his own wife and kid behind, disappeared for almost twelve hours because Dana had tried to have an abortion. But she was too late, past the legal limit, so she'd tried to do it herself. He'd found her in a terrible state, got her to hospital, and the baby had survived, miraculously. He'd pressed for her to tell him who the dad was. She remained silent. It was the first time she'd contacted him, but not the last.

Tess cleared her throat, spoke quietly. 'So, the good news is, Dana's alive.'

1999

ARIANNA

Arianna cringed as Tess walked in and sat beside her. Every year on this day Tess would wear black in mourning for Kurt Cobain. She heard titters from the side of the classroom and sighed. Worse, she felt Tess's eyes boring into her, waiting for a comment about her outfit, approval of her dedication to their musical heroes, an excuse as to why she too hadn't turned up in black. It was exhausting.

'Are you pissed off with me?' Tess said, when Arianna didn't react.

'No.'

'What is it then?'

'Nothing,' Arianna insisted.

'Have I done something wrong?'

'Tess, man. Allow me. I'm still waking up.'

The pips went and Arianna sighed. 'Come on then, lets twos the headphones.'

They walked awkwardly out of the classroom, sharing an earphone each. Tess had recorded Mr Tamworth's jazz CD onto a tape and Arianna tried to look enthusiastic as a snare drum, trumpet and bass guitar ran up and down the notes. It was definitely clever, whatever these musicians were doing, it just didn't move her.

'SLAG.'

They both pulled out their earphone at the same time and spun around. A group of girls had their backs to them, but their shoulders shook as they tittered. Arianna frowned and then turned back, placing the jazz back into her ear, Tess following suit.

They reached Science and saw Dana arriving from the other direction, smiling at them.

'SLAPPER.' This time Arianna saw the girl shout it as she passed Dana. Dana's face dropped.

'Oi! Come back here and say it to her face!' Arianna shouted. But the girl had disappeared back into her group, which hurried down the corridor.

'What was that about?' Tess asked.

Dana shrugged. Her face had turned a bright red.

'Where's Candace?' Arianna asked.

'I dunno. She wasn't in registration,' Dana replied.

'Maybe she's sick.'

As they took their seats in the science lab, the sound of retching came from one of the tables at the front. It was followed up with, 'Careful with that Bunsen burner. You wouldn't want to choke on it.'

'Okay, thank you everyone,' Mr Okika said as he strode into the classroom, putting an end to the guffaws from the boys at the front. 'I'm sure there is nothing more exciting than the periodic elements we will be studying today.'

He started writing letters and symbols on the board and asked the class to identify them.

Dana knew the answers. Arianna knew she knew them. But today Dana kept her hand and head down as her cheeks blazed red and the boys at the front shouted out the correct formulae instead.

At lunchtime, the three of them stood holding out their free school meal passes, waiting for someone to buy them. But today it meant they were sitting ducks as the rest of their year filed past.

'Lost your appetites have you?'

'Still got a mouthful?'

'Is it true you gagged so hard on his dick you threw up?'

'Did you all get popped by the big boys?'

'Oi, where's Candace? Is she too sore to walk today?'

'Fuck off, Ryan. I'm gonna tell her you said that and watch her kick three shades of shit out of you,' Arianna yelled back as someone slapped two pound coins in her hand and took the pass.

Daniel walked over and stood in front of Tess; the rest of the Oxbridge Four stood a polite distance away.

'I just want you to know that I know you had nothing to do with what happened at the party,' he said solemnly to Tess. He counted out three pounds and placed them softly in her palm, holding up her lunch pass as he sauntered away.

'Let's get the fuck away from here,' Arianna said.

Tess nodded. 'I know where we can go.'

She led them to the music department. Arianna noticed

the immediate change in atmosphere. It was calmer, more contained. A variety of experimental sounds drifted from behind the doors on either side. Tess found an empty room and ushered them in.

Arianna, Dana and Tess settled themselves on the carpeted floor surrounded by music stands, instruments and a wall display on the Fibonacci sequence. They pulled out the sandwiches they'd prepared at home and chucked packets of crisps, sweets and other sharables into the middle.

Now they knew what the story was: that they had all been giving the older boys blow jobs and thrown up in the process. Arianna felt numb. She glanced at Dana, who'd hardly said a word all day. Arianna wished Candace was there to give as good as she got, to scare the shit out of anyone talking about them, to fully challenge each accusation until she'd exposed it for the utter shite it was and made the utterer of said accusation look like a dickhead. Arianna's retaliations didn't come close.

Tess picked up a bass guitar lying on the floor. She found the end of a lead nearby and attached it, followed the length of the lead to the amp and pressed a big red button. It came to life with a buzz. Tess played a note. It rang out deep and loud. She played another, her strong, dextrous fingers making light work of the thick strings, and quickly worked out a riff. Then Arianna played a simple beat on some tabla drums. Dana started humming and turned it into some lyrics. Something about where her Candace was, ending in 'My Candace, my Candy Rain . . .' By the third time around, Tess was harmonizing and then they all had a go at improvising a verse.

'I was walking along, just singing my song when they started shouting at me,'

'You're a slut and a slag and you blew all the lads and threw up at Jay's party,'

'Is it true? Did you do it? How far did you go?'

'But there's only one question we want to know,'

'Where's our girl, where's our girl, where's our ... Our Candy Rain?'

They shrieked with joy as they ended on a harmony, Arianna trying her best to do a drum roll.

As the pips sounded, they headed out. But Dana froze the moment she stepped into the corridor. Jay and his friends, including Damion, the guy Arianna had spent that evening snogging, stood talking with Mr Tamworth. He was wearing a different cardigan today with holes in different places and he flipped his dirty blond hair from one side of his head to the other. She remembered his wiry but firm body against hers and felt a rush of heat at the effect she'd had on this older boy. She'd remembered the toilet paper in her bra after they'd started and was relieved they'd stopped before he'd discovered it.

Arianna set her jaw and stepped forward. Tess and Dana followed reluctantly as Arianna strode right past the lads.

'Hey, Dana, wait up.' They all froze as Jay called out.

He walked over. Dana turned slowly around.

'Are you okay?' he asked, looking genuinely concerned.

'Yep.'

'Just so you know, I didn't say anything. To anyone. It wasn't me,' he said solemnly.

Dana could barely look him in the eye. 'Yep.'

'Honestly.'

'Okay.'

Jay nodded and turned away.

Damion smiled at Arianna. She smiled briefly back and then led her friends out through the double doors.

The halls filled with kids rushing out of the building at the end of school. Dana gave them both a quick hug and then headed off. Tess lingered, looking hopefully at Arianna.

'I've got another thing,' Arianna explained. Tess waited for more, but Arianna held a hand up. 'Laters,' she said quickly and walked away, pushing against the tide of schoolkids keen to get out.

She made her way to the door at the end of the corridor. This one had no rectangle of reinforced glass that you could peer into like the classroom doors did. On a silver sign at its centre, it said 'Head of English'. She had never been into Mr M's office before. She knocked loudly, pushed the door open to find Mr M perched on the edge of his desk facing a circle of chairs. Daniel, Luke, Alan and John all sat holding books. She considered turning around and leaving. Then she saw Karla, beautiful perfect Karla Malik from the year above, looking as radiant and serene as she had at the party, sitting with two others from her year.

Arianna felt a flutter of something confusing.

'Arianna,' Mr M exclaimed. 'Pull up a chair.'

She forced herself forward and sat in a seat one away from Karla.

'Coffee?' Mr M held up a large glass container of dark liquid. Arianna noticed that the others were holding polystyrene cups.

'Yes please,' she said. Mr M poured her a cup. She took a big gulp and tried not to grimace at its bitter taste.

'We do the dance. She twirls away. My arms are momentarily empty . . .'

Arianna looked up with a start as Mr M began his incantation by heart, projecting his voice loudly in this small room, enunciating each word, gesturing with one hand. '. . . This back and forth, across the stage of time. I do my dance with you.' He finished and held the silence before taking a contemplative sip of coffee. The students nodded their appreciation, many of them with looks of rapture.

'Something I've been working on this week.' He smacked his lips, breaking the spell. 'Any volunteers brave enough to follow?'

Daniel raised his hand.

Mr M bowed. 'I pass the quill to you.'

Daniel opened his notebook and cleared his throat. 'You, a muse, whose music woos my blues away each day. Even as your heavy boots stomp a beat on my heart you leave a sweet tune in the air as you depart . . .'

Arianna stifled a smirk and tried to remember the words to recount to Tess later.

When Daniel was done, Mr M let the silence linger before he spoke again. 'Great stuff,' he said. 'Strong use of syntax and rhythm, internal rhyme and drawing on a rich variety of inspiration too.'

Daniel beamed.

Alan was next. He'd written a haiku about stepping on a snail. He looked at Mr M with such hope and reverence, that a simple nod from him seemed to rock his world. Arianna wished he'd just suck his cock and get it over with.

Each member of the group took their turn. Karla had chosen E.E. Cummings. In her milky voice the simple love poem sounded perfect to Arianna. She wondered who would have stolen Karla's heart, who would be worthy of this perfect being just a year older than, but a universe away from, the likes of Arianna.

Mr M nodded, looking at the floor contemplatively, then he raised his eyebrows and looked at Arianna expectantly.

She wasn't sure if it was the caffeine or something else, but she felt twitchy and light-headed, almost nauseous.

'So, I've got a poem … It's something I read and … liked … So.' She cleared her throat.

'It took a hurricane to bring her closer to the landscape …' she began. As she spoke the words from the book her mum had given her, she thought of that complicated woman who'd known her all her life but who she somehow didn't know at all. 'Tell me why you visit an English coast? What is the meaning of old tongues reaping havoc in new places?'

She thought of her dad telling her mum to stop shouting, how her mum had tried to explain that this was just her normal speaking voice. She thought of her wildly gathering people to her, desperate to create her own community out of strangers in the café, unassuming posties, homeless people in the park. How she planted cuttings smuggled over in her suitcase in the sunniest spot and tended to them, insisting they flourish in a climate they were not made for. How she insisted on Greek in the house, pretended not to understand if they fell into English. How she had annotated this very poem in that book with her own insightful analysis in perfect written English.

'Talk to me Huracan, Talk to me Oye . . .' These were not Arianna's gods, or her mother's. But she replaced them in her mind with the names her mum had written in the margin.

Athena, Circe, Medusa, Sappho.

'Come to let me know that the earth is the earth is the earth.'

Something about that final line overwhelmed her. She became lost in a recurring dream she had that Cyprus was just across the road from England. That she could cross over whenever she liked into the warm, bright sunshine and sit with her Yiayia for a spell before crossing back and hanging out with Tess. Introducing her best mates to her cousins, going back to her old school where she was king and kids were kids, popping back over to shop for CDs and DMs.

She blinked, spent, and looked up. Mr M held the moment. 'A solid first offering,' he said and turned to the group. 'Same time next week.'

Embarrassment coursed through Arianna at his tepid response. She kept her eyes down as she made her way out of Mr M's office. The Oxbridge Four jostled each other ahead of her and Arianna was suddenly angry. What a load of pretentious bollocks. What even was that? She started practising impressions of them all in her head, vowing to call Tess when she got home and share the utter hilariousness of the whole thing. They could make it into a skit, the four of them, beatnik poets saying obscure things that rhyme, sitting in a circle brown-nosing Mr M. How fucking ironic they were the ones who'd been accused of blowing the boys when there was a whole circle of people desperate to suck Mr M's dick just for saying 'onomatopoeia'.

She was so caught up in her monologue they almost collided, and it was only because Candace flinched and swerved that they didn't.

'Candace! Where have you been? Are you okay?'

Candace held her massive art folder in front of her like a shield. She stared down at the floor and nodded.

'Have you been in art?' Arianna asked.

She nodded again.

'All day?'

Arianna looked at Candace's face closely. She looked tired, raw. 'Do you want to talk? You can come over mine . . .'

For a moment it looked like Candace was considering it, then she looked even sadder and shook her head. Arianna didn't know what to say. Candace turned and walked away. As she adjusted her folder, Arianna saw with a jolt that her left hand was wrapped in a bandage. Arianna almost called after her, but then she felt a tap on her shoulder. She turned to find Mr M standing behind her.

'Have a go at writing something of your own. For next week.'

Arianna found a notebook from last year's History class that was only half full. For two hours she scribbled phrases and groups of rhyming words, themes and reams of freewriting that all sounded awful and utterly shite and cringeworthy. Except for maybe this bit. And these three words. And that line too.

It was late when she finally switched off the light. She tried to stop her mind from reciting her own words over and over. She imagined reading it to the group, except there was no one else in the circle, just her and Karla. What would it take to impress her, to shock her, to get her to really see her?

Arianna turned over onto her stomach. She lifted her top and stroked her breasts, just beginning to fill out. She pulled the pillow down between her legs and thrust her pelvis onto it. As she thrust and thrust, she pictured herself looking up from below. But then the image changed and she was looking down on herself. And as she came, so intensely she surprised herself, she gasped in shock at what had popped into her mind. What she had imagined was what *he* would have seen, Mr M, if he was on top of her.

1999

TESS

Tess squatted over the toilet and held her breath. Her whole body braced itself as she pushed her fingers between her legs, trying this third time to do it with more force. The dry, woolly end of the tampon met the lips of her vulva and inched into her, only to stop at the same point as before. That wasn't right. It was still hanging out of her. There was something wrong. She gritted her teeth and tried to force the tampon further, but it met with a resistance as solid as a wall. She pulled it out with an angry sigh and sat on the loo with her head in her hands.

She was meant to be practising three pieces for LSSO rehearsals this weekend. Three complex, seminal orchestrations that required more quickness of thought, more dexterity than ever before. But she knew that no matter how long she spent practising she would receive the same feedback she had been receiving for weeks now. She was incredibly accurate and her timing was impeccable, but her playing lacked passion, lacked expression. Depth.

She lacked depth.

Tess pulled open a sanitary pad and placed it in her pants.

She returned to her room. Sitting on her bed, she glared at the violin nestled in the open case on the floor, the sheet music waiting on the stand. She looked up to the section of wall where a collection of half a dozen pictures of scribbled notes were tacked, lyrics jotted down on foraged notepaper – now hallowed paper, now venerated words, songs that were the most precious jewels in the musical canon, written by hands attached to the gods of music: Lennon, Dylan, Morrison, Jagger.

Tess reached for her maths book and tore out several blank pages. She grabbed a pen and began to write. It flowed like a wave, coursing through her and out of her hand in furious scribbles. Misunderstood, underestimated, passed over, looked through, words of love and frustration, of loneliness and a deep longing to be known, to be truly seen. Sometimes the pen deviated from the letters, sketched and shaded instead, illustrations that expanded until they reached and merged with the words, all that had been simmering inside her. And musical notes, snatches of melody, jotted on hastily drawn lines, joining the sketches, the letters.

She kept writing, kept sketching, love letters and hate letters and poems that rhymed and didn't, lyrics that segued from verse to chorus to bridge, pictures that undulated and travelled, elucidated and stirred, gave form to thoughts that could not be expressed in words. Whole sections crossed out, scribbled out, stabbed at and banished, only to be revived just below. She wrote and sketched and composed until the muscles in her hand began to ache, and still she pushed on, until she gasped with pain as her fingers seized into a wonky claw. She shook it out and sat back panting and dazed.

A tinny electronic refrain broke the silence. It repeated again. Tess blinked. She looked around, trying to find the source. She lifted the sheets of paper scattered across the floor as the refrain repeated once more, clicking out a rhythm, vibrating. She flung open the door, scanning the landing, and then she heard it repeat right beside her. Her blue parka was hanging on her bedroom door. She rummaged in the pockets and pulled out a solid plastic weight. The melody increased in volume. She pressed the green button on the phone uncertainly, brought it to her ear.

A groan. Some words slurred so badly Tess couldn't make them out.

'Mum?'

Dagmar took a breath, Tess could hear her gathering herself, making an effort to speak clearly.

'Where are you, Mum? ... No, I don't think you're in a desert. I can hear traffic in the background .... I don't think you've been kidnapped by Arabs, Mum ... They're not the reason the flat is a mess ... No one's listening in on the call ... No, they're not. Mum ... No ...'

1999

DANA

The morning felt harsher than usual, like one of those spotlights beamed from the helicopters that sometimes circled, searching for someone, locking onto them, making it impossible to escape, hide. Her limbs went weak, her chest constricted. She pushed on, but the feeling of being out there, exposed to those names, those gestures everyone had suddenly unleashed on her, the filthy looks and words, made her chest tighten. She paused, trying to calm herself down.

Slag.

Slapper.

A bus pulled up and she realized she was leaning on a bus stop. She got on. Dana hesitated as she considered climbing to the top deck, decided to play it safe and sit downstairs among the mums, babies and grannies.

'Dana!' She saw a familiar face grinning at her from the back seats. It took her a moment to place him. He had filled out. There was a shadow of a 'tache under his freckly nose, but his curly lashes and warm easy smile were just the same.

'Chris! Ohmygod.' Dana sat next to her old schoolmate,

giving him a warm hug. She saw him take in her face, glance briefly down at the rest of her.

'Rah, girl done turned into a grown woman,' he exclaimed with surprise.

She giggled and touched his upper lip. 'What's this then?'

Chris R.P chuckled and blushed. 'It's my bum fluff innit. Growin' it out so I look like a big man.' His voice went deep on the last two words and Dana laughed with him. It was a relief, to be in the company of someone who didn't know about the rumours.

'Where you off to?' she asked.

'Work innit. Told you, I'm a big man now.'

'What are you doing?'

'Sparky. I'm doin' an apprenticeship with my cousin.'

'Like proper, full time?'

'Yeah.'

'Do you like it?'

'Yeah,' Chris nodded. 'It's helping people. Fixing things. Turns out I'm good with my hands.' He grinned.

'Are you now?' Dana asked. Something new passed between them. Dana looked closer at this man-boy who she knew so well and yet didn't know at all. He looked back at her with the same searching familiarity.

'You goin' school still?'

'Yeah,' she shrugged.

'Arianna still good?'

'Yeah, she's like my best friend now.'

'Is it? She still good at English and that? She was always getting top marks. Dealing in high-brow books while we was still reading some basic Ladybird shit.' He shook his head fondly.

'Yep, she's well clever.'

Chris side-eyed her. 'You can talk,' he nudged her. 'I remember, Maths and Science and that. You was cleverer than the bods in the front.' She looked up, expecting derision, and saw only pride. It disarmed her.

'This your stop ain't it?' he said without breaking eye contact.

Dana hesitated. Maybe if they just stayed on this bus, going round and round the city, everything would stay okay.

'I might stay on a bit longer,' she suggested.

Chris raised his eyebrows and then nudged her. 'Who are those bods gonna copy off if you don't go in?' he reasoned with a gentle authority she'd never seen in him before.

'Fine,' she said, shrugging. 'Laterz.'

He put a hand on her arm. 'I'll be passing back this way. Meet you after school?'

She shrugged again. 'Maybe.' She turned and stepped off the bus, allowing herself a glance through the window as it drove away. Chris R.P glided by, shaking his head and grinning at her.

'I swear down,' Arianna insisted. 'I saw her after school holding her art folder.'

'Yesterday?'

'Yeah.'

'She must have been up there all day.' Dana frowned. 'Come, we go check at lunch.'

'I thought we were going to do more music,' Tess complained.

'I've got to finish this writing thing for tonight,' Arianna said.

'How about after school?' Tess suggested.

'That's the writing thing.'

'I've got to go straight back,' Dana said, thinking of Chris.

She looked at Arianna, wondering if she should tell her she'd seen him. But some part of her wanted to keep this new Chris, Chris 2.0, to herself for a bit longer.

The pips went and the three friends scattered in different directions.

Dana stepped into Maths and braced herself. But the boys were huddled together and engrossed in something that emitted a beeping sound, followed by what sounded like a siren, then a car alarm and then another electronic jingle. The boys gasped and cackled as one of them showed off all five sounds and three functions of his new pager. Without the scrutiny of the lads on her, Dana felt her brain clear again until there was nothing but the figures and the lines and dots that connected them somehow. She worked steadily. But she didn't raise her hand. Or her head.

Dana found Tess and Arianna holding out their lunch passes in the usual spot. A boy mimed a blowjob using his hand and his tongue in his cheek, staring at her as she passed. She grabbed her friends and marched them up to the Art department. Ms Gail looked up from her desk at the back of the room, placed in front of the stock cupboard which was open to reveal shelves of coloured paper, boxes of oil pastels, charcoal and paint, brushes and easels.

'Hi, Miss. Is Candace here?' Dana asked.

Ms Gail nodded meaningfully to her left and returned to sorting through paint brushes.

Large canvases covered with in-progress artwork leaned against drawers, desks and sculptures. In the far corner of the room, huddled at her own desk, with a mug and large pieces of thick art paper laid out before her, was Candace.

'Where have you been all this time?' Dana was suddenly full of rage at all the times she'd needed Candace over these last few days. At the dickheads who'd called her those names, at this shitty school, at that shitty man who had upset her mum, at the horrible things Mr Austen had said about her best friend, at everything.

Dana took a step forward and then stopped. Candace's left hand was bandaged around the palm and knuckles. She held her pen with her right hand, which she never did.

'What happened?' Dana asked. She saw the clench in Candace's jaw, knew how hard she was working not to cry over that dickhead brother of hers.

Dana looked down at Candace's artwork. It was so different. The life-like imitations of real images that Candace usually produced with her left hand had been replaced with a series of abstract sketches, epic and broad and full of life and motion.

A series of light thunks made them turn. Ms Gail plonked

paper and a selection of pens and pastels onto the table. She looked at the three friends.

'Sit down then.'

In the toilets after the final pips had gone, Dana teased her hair and pressed her face with the new blotting paper she'd bought from The Body Shop. She chose some tinted lip gloss instead of lipstick and contemplated what kissing Chris R.P might be like.

The girls had gone. She waited a moment longer, hoping to avoid as many students as possible, and then slunk out.

He was waiting at a distance from the bus stop, watching that buzzing murmuration of kids which he had been a part of not so long ago, keeping a low profile. He clocked her and smiled shyly. 'Wah gwan, you good?'

'Yeah. Good day at work?'

'Yeah.'

'So, where you taking me?' Dana asked, tilting her head to the side.

'Where d'you wanna go?'

'How about we get Burger King and take it to the park?'

They started walking down the hill, through the back streets, keeping space between them.

They laid out their takeaway between them on the bench facing the pitch, the concrete shelter offering a privacy of sorts. They shared fries and sauce and even bites of burger. Chris put an easy arm around her and they sat watching the three different games of football before them. As the daylight faded she turned to him. He held her chin gently. They kissed and kissed and kissed.

He walked her to the doorstep of her tower block. They were both flushed and dopey with happiness. She leaped up the stairs to the fifth floor, practising what she would tell Eileen first – the kiss? Chris's 'tache? Candace's hand? She almost tripped over the big work boots parked on the mat and grabbed at something hanging on the door to steady herself. Don's bulky jacket draped over the others once more.

1999

CANDACE

For a blissful two days, they'd gotten into a routine so sweet Candace prayed it could stay like this for the rest of her school years. She left home early, arrived early, helped Ms Gail set up the paints and paper, the charcoal and crayons. She tidied piles of things, washed jars of coloured water, rinsed each brush thoroughly, stapled the edges of displays back into place and opened artbooks onto inspiring pages. They shared a quiet company she had never known before, an easy peace punctured by the roar of classes, which subsided every hour to reveal the serene haven she had created once again.

At lunchtime she'd switch on the radio. Candace had shyly suggested some classical music, remembering that evening she'd listened to Tess play at the concert. Ms Gail had nodded and found Radio 3. Candace sometimes liked to imagine she was a posh white man in his forties, planting bold swipes of colour on his canvas, one of many in a series that were sure to be displayed in a gallery as soon as he was finished, listening to other posh white men conduct music written by dead posh white men that inspired every assured, posh,

white brushstroke. Now that she was forced to use her right
hand, this was the persona she channelled. She'd decided that
morning his name was Kenneth.

The throbbing had dulled to something manageable that
didn't keep her awake. The ruptured skin was still purple at
the edges, the dark hole had begun to fill in, pink flesh and
white sinew and brown skin reforming. It turned her stomach
to look at it.

But now the time had come to head back to class. She
hovered over a jar of paintbrushes, adjusting them slightly.

'Thanks, Miss,' she said quietly.

Miss nodded.

As she neared her home, she felt the weight of her art folder.
It was satisfyingly heavy now, with the fruits of her labour,
a body of work slowly grown through the hours she'd spent
with Ms Gail.

She noticed a figure leaning against the railings of the
front garden. Her stomach clenched. He sat straighter and
watched her approach. Candace decided she would scream
this time, the minute he made any kind of move. But as
she neared, she noticed that the frame was smaller, the
shoulders narrower, the movement and posture familiar
but different to her brother's. It was Warren, Nathan's mate.
He stood.

'You alright?' he tried. Candace glared back at him.

He looked down at her hand. She thought she saw him
smile, or wince.

'Nathan's not here,' she said.

Warren shook his head. 'Nah, I'm not ...' He swallowed, started again. 'He got it off me. The airgun. It's mine.'

Candace frowned.

'I let him have it cos ... well, he's quite persuasive.' He looked up at her then.

'Once he had it, he wouldn't give it back. I had a go in the end, tried to force him to go back home and bring it, but he kicked me in the head. I had concussion for days. He started bragging about shooting you and your mates up. I felt sick. I couldn't sleep. And then he comes round the squat up in Roehampton a couple of days ago pissing himself laughing cos he shot you point blank.' His voice wavered. He looked down again at her hand. 'Is it ... How ... are you ... ?'

Candace didn't answer.

'I got a few of the lads together and we got it off him. He didn't like that. He's fucked off now. Maybe for good.'

Warren turned to gaze down the road. Then back at Candace again. 'I just wanted you to know—'

'What you got a gun for in the first place?' Candace exploded. 'What did you think was gonna happen?' She was seething with white hot rage and Warren took it.

'Look, if there's anything—'

'Fuck off,' she spat.

Warren nodded, walked away.

Candace breathed deeply, forcing the sobs down into her belly, blinking back the tears until she was sure they wouldn't spill. Then she let herself in.

They were sitting on the sofa, a wheedling New York voice

coming from the TV. Dad burst out laughing and slapped his leg. Mum smiled vaguely.

'There she is,' he exclaimed. 'Come and watch this.' He pointed at the screen and turned the volume up. Candace saw a small Jewish man with glasses and a New York accent pushing away the advances of an impossibly stunning white woman at least half his age. Eventually, he succumbed.

'This guy,' Dad continued. 'Genius.'

'Hungry?' her mum asked.

'Nah.' She carried her folder upstairs.

1999

ARIANNA

'Can someone help please.'

Arianna turned up the volume on the TV, drowning out her dad's huffing and puffing. She had been home fifteen minutes. The more he banged and huffed, the more she seethed. Eventually there was a clatter so loud, the two younger ones turned to her with alarm. She hauled herself up.

In the kitchen, a pan and a pot sizzled with another two dirty pots stacked beside. He was making pasta. With tinned tomatoes. He looked at her expectantly and gestured in the general direction of the food, huffing so loud and long she thought he might give himself an asthma attack.

'I'm only one person,' he exclaimed. 'There's only so much I can do.'

Arianna didn't move from where she leaned on the door frame, glaring at him. He continued to look at her expectantly. His neediness knew no limits, especially when he was actually doing some dad-ing.

He gestured again at the pots and pans, the sink, the cupboards that held plates and the drawers that held cutlery. 'The kids need to eat,' he said to his eldest.

Mum was out somewhere. Arianna pushed herself off the doorframe and stepped into the kitchen, finishing what he'd started, cleaning up, calling Theo and Lelia to the table. They ate quietly while her dad slumped in his chair, making a show of how exhausted he was.

He collapsed onto the sofa the minute dinner was done. Arianna washed up, then took her schoolbag up to her room and started studying.

She was alone, walking against the wind tunnel between stairwells when he called out to her. They sheltered inside at the bottom of the steps. Damion's dirty blond crop looked even more rock 'n' roll in the wind and his pale features were bright with the sting of the cold and the joy at bumping into her.

'Been trying to catch you,' he said. 'I had fun. At the party.'

Arianna blushed.

'Are you okay?' he said uncertainly. He looked at her with genuine concern. Dana had gotten the brunt of it, she was an easy target. Everyone was jealous of her, waiting to get some dirt on her, bring her down a peg or two. But Arianna was less of a threat. More of a six out of ten, as Alan had once informed her. An acquired taste, he had added, looking at her dark curls and tanned skin, so there was less need to call Arianna a slag.

She nodded.

'Do you wanna hang sometime? Maybe Friday? We could go park.'

Her stomach flipped. She shrugged. 'Okay.'

'Sweet.' His face broke into a smile. For a moment he hovered, unsure what to do next. Then he leaned in, kissed her on the cheek and bounded off.

Tess didn't come to English. She had music practice. So, Arianna would have to wait until tomorrow when they were together again to tell her. She rehearsed how she'd describe Damion's invitation in her head as she packed up her things at the end of the lesson.

'I've got something for you.'

She wasn't sure she'd heard right. She turned to find him looking down and thought she'd been mistaken. The others continued to file out. Arianna started to follow when he spoke again.

'Here it is.' Mr M held out a book to her.

She took it from him and looked over the turquoise cover decorated in ornate Arabic patterns with a purple star at its centre, the name Rumi in gold lettering.

'Thank you,' she said.

'Have you heard of Rumi?' he asked.

'Yes, of course,' she lied.

'I thought so,' Mr M said, pleased. 'Bit of inspiration for your own writing.'

She waited until she was in bed before opening the book. She drank in the translated words eagerly, studiously, and then lustily. They spoke of spirituality and magic, of exotic faraway wisdom she tried hard to comprehend. Also of love, of passion, of adult concepts and feelings. Of adult acts.

It was just a book, they had studied all sorts of plays and

novels that dealt with adultery and murder and madness, even accidental incest. She felt it all so hard, had been told by her family how sensitive she was, what a drama queen she could be, how wild her imagination was. This was just another book. So why, deep down, somewhere she didn't have words for, did she feel a line had been crossed? She didn't know to trust this instinct. And yet she felt it. Knew it.

2022

ARIANNA

Dana is alive.

The three friends sat in Candace's small living room area, the light from outside beginning to wane, the cosy interior darkening, the tea in the pot stewing, turning cold. But they didn't move.

'I met with someone who spoke to her,' Tess said.

'Who?' Arianna asked.

'A friend. Someone she called for help.'

'Jay? Did you meet up with him?' Candace asked. 'Does he know where she is?'

'No. I mean, yes, I got in touch with Jay. I'm meeting him too. But there's someone else . . .' Tess looked at Arianna. 'Chris.'

'Chris R.P? What did he say? Where is she?' Candace jumped in before Arianna could.

'Things got strange a couple of years ago,' Tess continued. 'When the world locked down. She called Chris out of the blue, after years, and then started calling him almost every day, checking in on him, asking about his family. Chris was surprised to hear from her, but relieved she was okay. But then it started to get intense. He tried to keep it friendly, respond whenever he could, tried to ask her if she was living with anyone, if she needed anything. She'd just fob him off. And then she disappeared again.

'He tried calling her number. It would ring, so it hadn't been disconnected like the other three numbers he had for her, but she wouldn't pick up. But then the whole world had gone weird, no one knew what was normal anymore, and who was still alive.

'And then a month later she called again. In the middle of the night, around 3 a.m. She sounded different. Chris said he thought she was on something. She was talking a mile a minute, about the news and politicians and the fake stories they were making up, to keep us all imprisoned while they made millions out of us. She said she'd been looking into it, reading stuff, watching stuff, really seeing for the first time ever, the Truth. At first Chris just listened, then he tried to calm her down. Then he started to challenge some of the things she was saying. She got aggravated, started shouting, telling him he was a blind follower, a lemming. He looked exhausted just telling me about it.'

'She started calling every night. Sometimes she'd already be in the middle of a sentence, overwhelming him with the so-called truths she'd unearthed and a strange mix of all sorts of stuff. Quantum physics mixed with religion mixed with conspiracy theories mixed with astrology, poetry, politics, fake news, philosophy. Chris had reminded her he had two little ones now, that she couldn't just call in the middle of the night. Then she stopped calling again. Just like that. And he was back to worrying where she'd gone.'

'Weeks went by. Months. Then a letter came, sent to his nan's address and forwarded on. Pages and pages. From her. First about him and all he'd been through, what she saw in him, how she forgave him for everything. Then pages on all her transgressions. A list of every time she'd asked something of him, the times she hadn't been there for him, the numbers, emails, addresses she'd used and then cancelled, the calls she'd never answered, even the calls she'd made to him recently, the inappropriate times ... Each individual incident that had ever occurred between them. It was insanely detailed, like she'd spent weeks recalling it all and writing it down, confessing it.'

Arianna nodded. A moral inventory. Step four. She had spent six months doing her own.

Tess continued. 'Chris said that at the end of the letter, she had asked for his forgiveness. She called a week later. She was calmer, asked him if he'd read the letter, and if he forgave her. He said of course he did. He said he wished he could have done more to help her. That's when she started talking differently, asking him if he'd like to meet up, come with her somewhere. Meet some people. By then the rules had relaxed a bit. Chris asked her a bit more about this group and she told him all sorts of things.'

'Like what?' Candace asked.

'Well, he didn't say much more, he just kind of laughed and said it sounded like she'd joined some kind of ... cult.'

2000

DANA

She woke up early, thinking of him. His lips, his smell, his warm open face. The soft hairs on his upper lip that brushed her when they kissed. Their private world, the way she felt so excited and at ease all at the same time. A heat and a throbbing started low in her. She gasped with surprise and opened her eyes. They were all lying on the mattress on Tess's bedroom floor. Riri was sprawled out next to her, Candace at the other end, Tess neatly tucked into a foetal position and sleeping quietly as a mouse near Dana's feet.

Dana got dressed quietly and made her way downstairs.

Linton looked out from the kitchen as she put her bag down in the hallway and reached for her coat. 'Up with the rising sun? Can I make you some tea?'

She paused. It was too early to meet Chris anyway. 'Yes please.'

Linton smiled. 'Would you like a fried egg on toast? I always add five drops of Tabasco, and it is perfection. But that is optional.'

'I'll take the fried egg but hold the Tabasco, please.'

'My Baby Just Cares for Me' played jauntily from the living

room. Dana sat at the kitchen table. There was a new piece of art on the wall above the picture of the woman with the afro. One of Linton's girlfriend's art pieces. Tess had told them she was practically taking over the whole flat with her stuff. Dana watched Linton hum and cook and wondered if he had got his leg over last night. Did people that old still do it? He had grey hair and everything. She decided he must have. No one was this perky this early in the a.m. without having got some the night before. Or even this morning ...

'Tess tells me you are a great mathematician,' Linton said.

'Er, yeah. I'm good with numbers,' she replied.

'It sounds to me like it's more than that. You have a brilliant mind.'

'Tess is the one with the brilliant mind,' she insisted.

Linton smiled.

'Did you know that the part of the brain you use to read and play music is the same part of the brain you use for Maths? If Tess is gifted, then you must be equally so.' He punctuated his final point with a flick of the spatula.

He served her two eggs on brown toast, then sat opposite her and carefully tapped exactly five drops of Tabasco onto his eggs. 'Brain food. For a marvellous brain.'

He saw her out. The girls were still fast asleep, and she decided to walk to Chris's nan's house. She counted her steps as she went.

The net curtains in the window twitched. Then a stern looking elderly lady opened the door wide and looked down at her.

'Good morning. Is Chris in please?'

His nan called upstairs to him, delivering the information that a girl was waiting on the doorstep. Moments later, he was there, looking elated and surprised and scared all at once.

'I'm going out for a bit, Grandma,' he called over his shoulder as he shrugged on his jacket and closed the door.

They rushed down the road and turned the corner before stopping. He always took a moment before he dived in to kiss her, taking her in first, checking she was with him. She loved that. And then his soft lips were on hers, the hairs tickling her gently, the heat in her stomach travelling down to between her legs.

For a moment they lost themselves in each other, desperate to push this feeling as far as they could. Then he checked himself and looked around to see who else was about.

'Can we go back to yours?' she asked.

'My nan's?'

She nodded.

He looked at her, lust still in his eyes, and contemplated the idea of being somewhere indoors together, somewhere private. His smile faded. 'I can't.'

'Are you embarrassed of me?'

He frowned at her. 'What you talking about?'

She shrugged.

'First of all, she wouldn't let you up the stairs,' he explained. 'We'd have to sit at the kitchen table where she could keep an eye on us while she's listening to her Jesus music.' He shook his head. 'She *loves* Jesus.'

Dana laughed, then got serious again.

'It's just, I'm ready,' she said.

He took in her words, his eyes lit up, a chuffed, surprised half-laugh escaping out of him. Then he took a deep breath in and let it out slowly.

'How about yours?' he suggested.

Dana hesitated a moment.

'Not right now,' she said. They both sighed with frustration.

But she'd figured it out. On the way home, she'd made a plan. Mum had Auntie Naila's keys for when she went to her time share in Spain and Eileen took care of the plants. And Auntie Naila was going away soon. She would find out exactly when, get the keys and take Chris there when it was empty.

'The fuck is your problem. Eh? EH?!' The minute she opened the door she realized it wasn't the TV. It was him. She froze on the doorstep.

'Look at me when I'm talking to you.'

She heard her mum whimper, say something she couldn't quite make out. Then there was a thump.

A jolt ran through Dana. Her breath caught.

Dana forced herself to walk into the living room. Her mum was face down in the cushions on the sofa, Don standing above her panting, his fist still curled.

Don looked up at her. 'What you looking at?'

Dana's voice caught in her throat. Her mum raised her head slowly, mascara and tears running down her face.

'Dana,' she gasped.

'I said what you looking at,' he demanded.

'Mum,' Dana whimpered.

'Oh, that's it. Now you're gonna start. Fuckin' hell. You're both doing my head in.'

A new ripple of fear passed over Eileen's face. 'Out you go love, back to your room.'

'That's right, fuck off out of here and get out of our business.'

Dana couldn't move.

'Is there something wrong with your hearing?' Don took a step towards her.

'Get out!' Eileen suddenly shouted. Dana felt the blow of her mum's words like a punch. She ran to her room and shut the door. It wasn't long before the shouting started up again, his deep rage-filled voice; her whimpering, reasoning, begging. Then another thump, and another one. A crash and a tinkle. The stomps of heavy footsteps passing right by her door. And finally the slam of the front door.

Dana crept back into the living room, terrified of what she might find.

Eileen sat on the sofa, sniffing and gingerly wiping the make-up and tears from her face, a cigarette lit and held in a trembling hand. The coffee table was overturned and Nana's vase lay in pieces on the floor.

Dana began to cry. She rushed over to her mum and put a hand on her.

'Mum,' Dana pleaded.

But Eileen remained rigid.

'You're bleeding,' Dana said as a trickle of crimson bloomed from the top of her right cheek. Eileen wiped at it.

'Stop fussing,' she hissed.

That night, Dana lay in bed heartbroken and terrified, exhausted but unable to sleep. She felt the nervous footsteps of her cat on the bed. Jazz lay herself down in the crook of her leg trembling, her little ribcage expanding and contracting with fearful breaths as Dana stared wide-eyed at the ceiling too terrified to close her eyes.

2000

CANDACE

The smell of trampled grass, the streaks of it across her muddy knees, the heat and sweat on her face despite the cold incessant drizzle, as she pushed herself to her limit, focused everything on the ball, on the goal, on the sprint, up and then back down the pitch. Homing in on the calls of her teammates, the instructions coming from the side of the pitch, allowing herself exactly two seconds of frustration every time a decision didn't go her way, then wiping the slate clean, pushing forward. The strength of her body, the skill and lightness of touch, the shoulder drop, the pivot, the pass, the clean receive, the fake, the nutmeg, the double fake, the lob, the heel, the volley, the one-two, the set pieces, the purity of seeing a play that you practised for weeks put into action in real-time. The game. The beautiful game.

She was Gary. She was always Gary. Even if Gary had retired as England skipper, she'd always be Gary.

Candace stole the ball off the girl she was marking, clean, without even touching her, nudged it with the outside edge of her left foot and sent it the other way up the pitch. Little Bernie S sprinted up the middle calling for it. Candace passed it a couple of metres ahead and it landed in front of Bernie's feet perfectly. Bernie glanced up at the goal and then decided to pass it back. Candace's first touch sent it right back to her and Bernie sent it flying past the goalie, smashing into the back of the net.

Candace ran to Bernie, Bernie ran to Candace, elated laughter escaping from them both as they bumped chests and embraced. Miss White wasn't even trying to hide her pride.

6-0. And it was only half-time.

'Right, gather round,' Miss White began. 'Well done, all of you. And I mean all of you. It takes the whole team. Let's not get cocky – Bernie, I'm looking at you – it's not over yet and that midfield is no joke. Keep focused. Keep passing and communicating. Keep the pressure and the pace up right until that final whistle. I want another six. Got it?' She looked straight at Candace. Captain Candace.

'Yes Miss,' she replied loudly, and the other girls echoed her.

'Right. Keep warm.'

The team jogged back onto the pitch.

'Six nil. Are you joking? The boys' team could never,' Bernie exclaimed.

'Not even Jordan P and Romesh ever got a hat trick each in a game,' Candace replied.

When the final whistle blew, Candace fell to her knees and covered her face, deep sobs of joy escaping with the last bit of breath she had left. She felt Bernie jump on top of her, and then one by one the rest of the team, until she thought she might be crushed. But what a way to go.

'It's coming home, it's coming home, it's coming . . .' Bernie led them in the chant, standing on the dressing room bench. The girls joined in, fists raised, voices deep.

Candace sat on the bench and looked at little Bernie, the shortest in their year by a few inches, and Candace the hench-est. They were an unlikely pair, but it worked. The problem was, Bernie was an annoying little shit off the pitch. Candace had punched her in the face no less than three times over the years, but there was no denying the girl could play football. She had a perfect centre of gravity that allowed her to turn on a sixpence, fake and dazzle and laugh in your face and be halfway up the pitch before you realized what had happened. And she'd assisted on as many goals as she'd scored, which led to more generosity on Candace's part. She knew Bernie had grown up in care. Imagined a stint surrounded by older boys which had allowed her to hone her skills, gain some re-spect, give her something to pull out and play when needed. Or maybe even just hours of boredom where she kicked a ball around until she got good.

It was the best day of Candace's life, but she suddenly felt a pang. Why wasn't Dana here? Why weren't they celebrating together, heading home together, exhausted and spent having left everything on the pitch, re-playing the glory moments over and over? She was probably out somewhere covered in make-up, wearing her mum's garms and getting felt up by some loser.

Their goalie, Sara, grabbed Bernie's face and placed a wet kiss on her cheek.

'Ugh, get off me you lesbian,' she exclaimed.

'Fuck off Bernie. You're the lesbian,' Sara countered.

'Say that again to my face.' Bernie stepped up to Sara, who looked down at her and smirked.

'Come on, say it again,' Bernie insisted.

'Leave it, Bernie, man. Why you gotta start something every time?' one of the other girls reasoned.

'She called me a fucking lesbo.'

'You are a fucking lesbo.'

'I mean it, I'll fuck you both up.'

'Relax, Bernie. We know you're not the real carpet muncher in this team,' Sara said.

Bernie turned, her eyes sparkling again. 'Carpet muncher! That's rank! Who's the real carpet muncher? Tell me!'

Candace kept her head down as she continued getting changed.

'Everyone knows,' Sara shrugged. 'It's obvious.'

'Is it someone in this room?' Bernie pressed, looking around at each girl.

'Eugh, fuck off,' someone exclaimed.

Bernie's eyes stopped briefly on Candace.

'You best not even look at me,' she growled.

'Relax man,' said Sara. She turned to face the centre of the room. 'It's Miss White, innit.'

The girls burst into laughter.

'Miss White drinks from the furry cup, you know!'

'I bet she's begging to come in here and take a goooood look!'

'Miss White the carpet muncher.'

They laughed. And shouted it over and over.

White hot rage blinded Candace for a moment. 'Shut the fuck up. All of you,' she growled. 'How you gonna talk about her like that? She's done nothing but look out for us, drive us here, there, make sure we get home safe, train us up to be the best fucking team this school has seen, give us all the glory and you gonna start dragging her name?'

Bernie smirked. 'Calm down love, we was just having a laugh—'

'*Take* her name out of your mouth,' Candace seethed.

They dressed in silence.

Candace left her boots on the doormat and ran a bath. Lying in the hot water she finally felt the weariness in her limbs. She looked down at her body and marvelled at the muscles on her legs, flexing the ones above her knee and seeing the ripple, before going floppy again as the lactic acid coursed through her once more. She turned over, holding her breath, immersing her face in the water, staying there for as long as she could. Images of soft lips, bright eyes, firm breasts, gentle hands, began to creep into the edges of her mind. But then Bernie's face, scouring the changing room, interrupted her thoughts.

She turned back around and hauled herself out.

ARIANNA

Arianna stabbed a full stop onto the page, slammed the textbook shut and pictured a time in her life where she would never have to do Maths again. Or Science. Or Geography. It felt like those days would never arrive. Just like her boobs.

The doorbell rang and she rushed down, taking the stairs two at a time. She heard Dad welcoming the girls in. She ushered them back upstairs. Her mum appeared in the hallway in her coat and snuck out behind them, glancing at Arianna sheepishly.

The funky riffs of 'Blood Sugar Sex Magik' accentuated their chatter as they got ready for the gig.

Candace lit the tip of the solid with a lighter and pinched some off, crumbling it on top of the line of tobacco in the King-size Rizla Arianna balanced between her fingers. She tore a section of the cardboard off and rolled it into a roach. Then she placed it carefully at the end and Arianna moistened her fingertips on her lips and began to roll, finally sealing the paper with her tongue and twisting the end. She held out the final result.

'Riri, man. That's baggier than my jeans,' Candace exclaimed.

Arianna glared at her then handed it over. She pushed the bedroom door closed and stuffed a towel against the gap at the bottom, then opened a window.

She was nervous. They all were – especially Tess who was the shortest with the flattest chest and generally looked five years younger than she actually was. All this time and effort might be for nothing if they didn't make it past the bouncers on the door. She tried to think positively, visualize the perfect outcome, call on her powers to manifest a night of dancing and cheering and watching Jay and Bass Face and Drums Dude do their thing on the stage at the Half Moon pub.

They were soon stomping down the road to the venue, chattering excitedly and getting more nervous the closer they got. They joined the queue, Dana and Candace in front, heavily made up, cleavage high and proud. Arianna had ponced a cigarette off someone and lit it up in the hope it might make her look older.

'ID,' the bouncer said, hand held out, not even looking at them. Candace handed over her fake ID. He looked at it for a long time, held on to it and extended his other hand towards Dana. He scrutinized that one too.

Voices were raised inside the doorway and the bouncer next to him tutted and headed in.

'Terry,' he called moments later from inside. The bouncer returned their IDs.

'Wait there,' he instructed the girls.

The doormen surrounded someone at the paying booth just inside the door and were arguing with him. Dana grabbed the girls and walked behind them, straight into the venue, the fivers they had brought to pay for entry still in their pockets. When they were safely ensconced in the crowd they turned to each other and laughed incredulously.

'That was some jammy shit.' Arianna exclaimed.

'We've got money for drinks now.' Tess said.

'Okay, but Dana and me will get them,' Candace insisted.

There were lots of familiar faces from The Year Above and older. Arianna saw Karla's friend Sara who had been at the poetry meeting with Karla, near the stage, but after craning her neck to survey the crowd, Arianna saw no Karla.

Suddenly Tess turned to Arianna, her eyes wide. 'Ohmygod.'

'What?'

'Mr Tamworth's here.'

What? Where?'

'*Don't look!*'

'*I don't know where I'm not looking.*'

'Two o'clock.'

Arianna slowly turned her head. There, indeed, was Mr Tamworth, elbow perched on a ledge, beer in hand. And right next to him, leaning against the back wall and looking straight at her, was Mr M. Her heart started beating rapidly. She forced herself to turn away, as Candace and Dana returned, holding two glasses each.

'JD and coke,' Dana said.

Arianna was suddenly painfully self-conscious. Tess was also concentrating hard on not spilling it and generally trying not to make a fool of herself in front of her Teacher Crush.

And then two large figures appeared in front of them.

'I told you to wait outside. I haven't checked your IDs yet.'

The distress and humiliation Arianna was feeling was mirrored in her three friends' faces as people turned to look at them. 'Alright, hold on,' she said, and fumbled in her pocket for her fake ID, as Tess did the same.

'And what's that you're drinking?' the bouncer demanded loudly. Even more heads turned their way.

'Coke. It's just coke,' Arianna said. She felt the laminated plastic in her back pocket and began to pull it out.

'It's okay, they're with me.'

They looked up to see Mr Tamworth standing beside the bouncer. 'They're just here to listen to the music.'

'Well, that's very nice but they can only do that if they have ID.'

'Sure, but they are actually gifted musicians who are also in a band and we're scouting the venue out for a possible gig.'

The bouncer didn't look convinced.

'Tess here is a bit of a prodigy,' he continued.

'Eh? Prodigy? You know Prodigy?' The bouncer suddenly perked up.

Mr Tamworth hesitated only half a second. 'Yes. Prodigy.'

'You're scouting for them?'

'Sure.'

A newfound respect replaced the boredom on the

bouncer's face. He dropped his hand and disappeared back behind layers of bodies.

Mr Tamworth looked at the four girls. He glanced at their drinks and turned away, returning to where Mr M was standing. The two men spoke, glancing at the girls.

The boys took to the stage and there was a ripple of excitement as the crowd edged closer. Arianna squeezed Tess's hand, while she was still recovering from Mr Tamworth's intervention.

Beautiful Jay placed a beautiful hand around the mic at the front of the stage. 'Yo,' he said. Everyone cheered. Dana whooped extra loud. 'This is called Sleep Walker.'

Drums Dude counted off four with his sticks and launched into a funky beat. Damion came in with a baseline and Jay strummed a riff on the guitar, then turned into the mic and began to sing. Candace glanced over at Arianna with a look of dirty funky appreciation on her face. By the third song, people had let loose and some at the front were dancing. Dana headed into the mosh pit and befriended an old rocker with a long grey beard, taking a swig of his pint.

It was a great night, one of the best. Damion made a point of searching for Arianna in the crowd. When he found her, he grinned, and she grinned back. She contemplated him up on the stage. She wasn't really into skinny guys, but he really could play the bass – that was hot.

When the music was done the lights brightened in the venue.

The boys emerged from backstage and received a hero's welcome from the remaining crowd. Dana rushed over to

Jay, enveloping him in a drunken embrace. He laughed it off as Candace rushed over and pulled her back.

Damion made his way over to where Arianna and Tess stood. He hugged Tess first and thanked her for coming. Then he turned to Arianna and smiled.

'Did you have fun?' he asked.

'Yeah, it was wicked,' she replied.

Jay came over to join them.

'That loop pedal thing you did was pretty cool,' Tess said.

Jay's eyes lit up.

'Thanks, man. Come check it out.'

Jay beckoned Tess over to the stage to talk loop pedals. Mr Tamworth joined them, and Arianna could tell Tess was trying not to look back at her with alarm as these two gods surrounded her and included her in their music talk.

Arianna turned back to Damion, and suddenly, he kissed her, in front of everyone. Butterflies and heat coursed through her. He pulled away and looked at her, beaming.

'Damion. A word, please.'

Mr M was standing behind them, his expression hard to read. Damion followed Mr M to the back of the room. She watched as Mr M spoke, and Damion slumped slightly. Then he nodded and said something briefly back. Mr M patted him on the shoulder and headed out.

Damion returned looking flushed.

'You okay?' Arianna asked.

'All good,' he said. But it clearly wasn't.

'What was all that about?' she asked.

'Ah, just a bit of ... real talk.'

Arianna frowned. 'What does that mean?'

'Nothing. Look, I'm gonna pack up yeah?' He smiled briefly and then turned away.

The four girls gathered once more.

'Let's go back to Jay's,' Dana suggested.

'We haven't been invited.'

'Well, where's the fucking party then?'

'At Arianna's house.'

'Is Mr Tamworth coming? Tess, have you shagged him yet? Oi! Mr T! Come to our party! Tess wants to—'

'Shut up!' Candace hissed and shoved Dana.

Tess blanched. Mr Tamworth looked over, his jaw set solid, and he strode over. Candace glared at Dana so hard she didn't dare open her mouth again.

'Detention. Every day. For two weeks,' he said then added, 'Safe home.'

The vibe was sombre the next morning back at Arianna's. No one was in the mood for Dana's hangover – especially not Tess. Her cheeks remained flushed with anger as she silently got dressed.

'Are you going already?' Dana asked her when she finally stirred, oblivious to Tess's pain. Tess continued gathering her things in silence.

'You got rehearsal?' Dana tried again.

Arianna saw her out. She couldn't remember seeing Tess this upset or angry. When she returned, Candace was sitting with Dana, whose face was blotchy. She looked up at Arianna.

'I'm so sorry,' she cried. Arianna exchanged a look with Candace.

'S'okay.'

'It's not,' Dana wailed. 'I fucked it. Tess hates me cos I'm a dickhead.'

Candace didn't say a word. She let Dana cry it out, then she took her home.

Mum was cooking a roast, Dad huffing and puffing as he peeled potatoes, Mum seething with every exhale as she did everything else. Arianna grabbed a banana and retreated back upstairs.

'Arianna!' her dad blustered in. 'I've got enough to do without having to climb all the way up here to call you for dinner.'

'Relax. You peeled a potato,' she spat back.

Mum hovered as they ate. Then she put on her jacket and scarf.

Dad looked up. 'Where are you going this time?'

'Out.'

'Again?'

Mum suddenly turned, a dangerous glint in her eye. 'Do you want to have this conversation? Are you sure?'

Mum glared at him, then she turned and slammed the door.

Arianna hovered near his tutor room and waited until she saw him. Then she strode towards and past him, close enough for there to be no mistake. Damion turned in surprise. He almost smiled, then he caught himself, gave her an apologetic look instead and turned to his friends. Her heart sank. Tears welled up, but she gritted her teeth and only let them fall when he was well behind her.

By the time she made it to her tutor room she had composed herself again.

'We've got detention, remember?' Tess said as the final pips went.

'I know. I just have to do something first,' Arianna replied.

She stomped to the English department and waited. Mr M followed the last student out.

'What did you say to him?'

'Hello Arianna,' he said levelly. 'Is there a problem?'

'What did you say to Damion about me?'

'I'm going to need you to calm down and stop shouting.'

'You chatted shit about me to him and now he won't even look at me,' she seethed, her voice trembling with the terror of talking to a teacher like this.

'If you swear at me again, I'll put you on report.'

Arianna shook her head in disbelief.

He sighed. 'Arianna, I have a duty of care, to you and all students. You are fifteen years old. You were in an establishment that sells alcohol talking and doing other things with a boy who is older than you. I voiced my concerns and they were taken on board. That is all.'

'But it's not your business—'

'I'm afraid it is.'

'But you ... you ...' she didn't know where to start. The poetry, the books, the secretive looks, the singling out, the hanging around in pubs with his students. At gigs. Why was he suddenly playing the Teacher Card?

'Look,' he said. 'I can see how frustrated you are. I under-stand.' He took a step closer, his eyes boring intensely into hers now. 'Write it, Arianna. Use it. Channel it. Turn it into work.'

He held her gaze a moment longer and then turned and walked back into his classroom.

2000

TESS

Tess made her way on her own to the music department for the second time that day. She had seen him at lunch, but only in passing. Now she would have to face him properly. And the girls had left her on her own. Again. She turned into one of the music rooms, knowing it would only be a matter of time before he checked in there. An electric guitar lay plugged into an amp. The drumkit had been set up. A bass guitar, a sax and two mics on stands in a circle. Maybe Jay's band had jumped straight back into rehearsals again. She stood in the doorway, unsure whether she should go in.

'Where are the others?' Mr Tamworth was suddenly standing by her.

'They're on their way,' Tess said as levelly as she could.

He looked at his watch. 'Let me know when everyone's here. In the meantime, if you could tune the instruments please.' He nodded at the room and disappeared back into his office.

Tess sighed. She lay her bag on a table, took off her coat, picked up a guitar. She tried to shove a metal box on the floor out of her way and then did a double take. It was a loop pedal.

'Where's Ri?' Tess looked up. Candace and a penitent look-ing Dana stood at the door.

Tess shrugged and looked back down. They shuffled in. Tess could feel Dana's gaze on her and she ignored it, strum-ming a chord instead.

'That sounds wicked,' Dana said.

'It's a C major. It's basic,' Tess replied.

Arianna stormed in looking like she was going to cry.

'What's wrong?' Tess asked. But Riri was so angry she couldn't speak. She shook her head and chewed on the inside of her mouth. For a moment the other three forgot any other tensions and exchanged looks.

'Ah, you're all here,' Mr Tamworth reappeared in the door-way. 'Right. Consider this your first band practice.'

'Our first what?' Candace asked.

'I told the gentleman at the venue that you were in a band. You wouldn't want to make me a liar now would you? So, you have mics, leads, instruments and amplification.'

'This is all for us?' Dana said incredulously.

'Correct. Dana, I suggest you try the drums. Candace, I hear you have a wonderful singing voice. Lead vocals please. Arianna on bass. Tess, grab the sax.'

He stayed with them for two hours. He taught Dana how to use the bass drum, the snare and the high hat. Arianna was shown finger-work and scales, root notes, thirds and fifths, and soon she was rocking a bassline. Candace tried out some lyrics and they all pitched in. They had a chorus. And maybe a verse and a half. Then Tess did her thing, her fingers flying across the notes as she breathed into the sax, playing with Candace's melody, echoing it, deviating from it only to return and harmonize with her voice. It was actually decent.

'Same time tomorrow ladies. Make sure you're on time please. And put the tables back,' he said and left.

The phone. The fucking phone. She'd left it in her coat and hadn't checked it for weeks. It was dead. She charged it. The pixilated screen said she had messages, all from the same number. The first few were long, slurred stories about adventures and conspiracies, abruptly cut off when she ran out of time. Then a swear word and nothing more. Then just the sound of the line going dead.

'You ready already?' Linton said with surprise the next morning as Tess appeared dressed, and coated, her violin already slung over her shoulder. 'You're two hours early.'

'I'm meeting Arianna first. We're doing some stuff for our band.'

She could tell he wasn't convinced.

'Take some breakfast,' he said, watching her carefully.

She took two buses and walked another fifteen minutes to Dagmar's flat. It was too early for her to be out, but late enough that she should be getting up. Unless she'd been on a massive, three-day bender. Tess rang the bell and waited. She rang again, more incessantly, and peered through the letterbox. A stale whiff greeted her.

'Mum?' she called through the gap. 'It's me, can you open up?' Tess waited a while longer, then, on a desperate whim, she rang next door's bell. A figure appeared through the frosted glass and opened the door. A middle-aged woman in a saree looked at her inquisitively.

'Hi, my name's Tess. I'm Dagmar's daughter from next door.'

The woman's face lit up in recognition. 'Come in, come in.'

'Actually, I'm just trying to get hold of her. She's not answering the phone and she won't come to the door.' Her voice trembled on the last word.

The woman nodded. 'I think I have a key,' she said and rummaged through a drawer in the hallway. 'This one. I'm sure.'

They went outside together and the woman tried the lock. As Dagmar's door opened, the woman hesitated on her threshold.

'Maybe I should go in first,' Tess said quickly.

The woman nodded. 'I'll wait here, okay?'

Tess stepped inside.

The smell of stale sweat, wine, beer, vomit and piss assailed her. It was much stronger inside than the whiff she had gotten through the letterbox. The hallway was fairly tidy, but Tess knew most of her mum's tricks. Dagmar kept the area people could see presentable, even as the rest of the house, and her person, fell apart. Tess forced herself forward. She found Dagmar slumped on the floor in the living room, leaning against the sofa, snoring lightly. Empty cans, upset wine bottles, takeaway cartons with cigarette butts floating in them, dirty plates surrounded the floor and the surfaces. Tess burst into tears. Then she swallowed hard and wiped angrily at her eyes. She turned quickly and headed back to the front door.

'Found her!' she said as chirpily as she could.

The neighbour who had been discreetly looking down the road, turned back around. 'Is she okay?'

'Yep, just sleeping it off.' Tess rolled her eyes.

The woman held her gaze. 'Would you like some help straightening things up?'

'No, no. Nothing much to do really. Apart from make her a strong coffee.'

The neighbour's eyes softened. 'It's nothing I haven't seen before. We've both been living here a long time. I've known Dagmar—'

'Have you got your key? Don't want to forget that. Thanks so much.' Tess was already retreating behind the front door.

The neighbour sighed. 'I'm Shammi. I'm home all morning. Knock if you need anything. Okay Tess?'

'Yep.'

Tess placed her violin case down in the hallway, stepped over her mum and into the kitchen. She found some bin bags and started to fill them.

2022

CANDACE

Candace watched Arianna and Tess step off the boat and scanned the area before closing the door. Saffy had eventually returned from the neighbour's when she hadn't been summoned, putting a stop to what could have been an endless conversation of shocking revelations. Candace's ears were ringing, she was exhausted, and relieved to have her daughter back. She tried to hide the worst of it. 'Are you hungry? There's food—'

'Why were you sitting in the dark?' Saffy demanded.

'I didn't notice,' Candace said.

Saffy frowned. 'Who are they anyway?'

They're old friends. From school. From when I was your age.'

'Did you always have such a laugh together?' she said sarcastically.

Candace sighed. 'Actually, we had loads of laughs. We were laughing all the time. Until ...'

Saffy waited. Candace shook her head.

'When are you going to tell me what's going on?' she

demanded again, but this time there was concern in her voice, thirteen-year-old worry.

Candace's throat tensed. Saff watched her so intently, there wasn't much she couldn't hide from her daughter anymore. She'd been through so much already. Candace knew it wasn't realistic to assume she'd be able to keep her away from life's pain for ever, but every day that she did felt like a huge win. And she'd prepared her as best she could, because although Saffy looked ethereal and angelic, Candace's daughter was also savvy, street-smart and no one's fool. Not even hers.

'Saff, I owe you a proper chat, about all this, but I'm knackered and it's late and you've got school tomorrow.'

Now Saffy tensed, ready to start the same argument they'd had several times now. But then she stopped herself. Candace sighed with relief. School was a point of contention; a card Saffy had recently realized she could play – a power move. She'd been so diligent and willing for so long, Candace even suspected she enjoyed school, but the day she got caught bunking and saw how desperate Candace had been, was the day she realized she could use it whenever they argued, whenever Candace set a limit, a boundary, for her teenage daughter. Now every dispute ended in a threat to skip school and Candace walked the impossible line of trying to hold her ground and at the same time not let on about the terror at Saffy being taken away by Social Services if she dropped below ninety-percent attendance.

It had worried her, how compliant Saff had been when she was little. She hardly questioned things growing up, hardly ever challenged her. From that first day when Dana left, she had just looked at the door expectantly, until she didn't. Candace had always tried to be honest with her about their situation. Explaining that she hadn't given birth to her, but that the person who had wasn't able to take care of her and so she came to live with Candace. That she would always be there for her. That *she* would always walk back through that door.

So maybe she should be grateful that Saff was turning into such a strong-willed young person. More like Candace than . . . anyone else.

Saffy turned away and headed to her bedroom. Candace went to pull the curtains closed and peered out once more. Where was she? What was this cult thing? And how would they find her? The last words Chris had told Tess rang in her head. *You don't need to find her. Because she'll find you. All of you. Don't you see? She has to.*

Candace froze. She was sure, through the dark and the drizzle, that a figure had retreated behind the warehouse opposite. She waited, straining to see. Eventually she drew the curtains closed, folding them tightly over one another, and backed away.

2022

ARIANNA

'You're angry with me,' Tess said, as they rushed through the drizzle towards the station.

Arianna rolled her eyes. Tess did this a lot. Did and said controversial things and then put all the focus on how pissed off *you* were instead of how shitty *her* behaviour had been. Arianna held her tongue.

'Yep. You're angry with me,' she said again.

Of course Arianna was angry with her. She was raging. She'd done it again. After all these years, when they'd fallen out so badly the first time around, here she was playing the same game again, and Arianna was over it.

'I just did what everyone asked me to do. I found out where Dana was—'

'Yeah, you did. Well done.' Arianna spun around. '*You* did it. Before anyone else. You got there first. Again.'

'Again? What do you—'

'Just, if it's okay, next time, could you keep me out of the dramas, please? I don't need to be dragged across London without knowing what the hell is going on because you won't tell me a thing just so you can have your big moment.'

'My moment?'

'Who did you imagine you were? Was it Jessica Fletcher? Or more of a Hercule Poirot vibe?'

'What do you mean, "Again?"'

Arianna looked at her with disgust. Then she shook her head and carried on walking.

'No, really, what do you mean?' Tess insisted.

'This isn't the first time you've used Chris, is it?' Arianna accused, picking up her pace so Tess had to almost jog to keep up. 'This isn't the first time you tracked Dana down, met up with her in secret and only thought to tell me months later.'

'That's not fair. I tried—'

'Did you? Really?'

'Yes! I tried so many times to tell you, but you were so far up your own arse you wouldn't even speak to me—'

Arianna stopped. 'You know what I was going through,' she said, hurt.

'But that wasn't my fault, you'd just disappear all the time and every time I tried to talk to you, you would—'

'Fucking hell, Tess—'

'And then I finally got to tell you and then you were so angry you didn't speak to me for a year—'

'How the fuck have you managed to make this about you? Again?' Arianna spat.

Tess stood, speechless.

Arianna turned and rushed down the station steps.

DANA

He was lying across the sofa, one dusty workboot-shod foot up on the armrest, the other on Eileen's freshly vacuumed carpet. He was playing with Jazz, who held out a tiny paw and batted at his enormous hand before retreating again. Dana's stomach clenched.

'Alright love? Good day at school?' Eileen turned and plonked a dish on the kitchen table.

'Yes, thanks.' Dana kept her eye on the cat. Don had Jazz on his stomach so that even when she retreated from him, she was still on him, surrounded by him, the very ground she stood on.

'You still doing good in Maths?' he said.

'Yes.'

'Good girl.'

He chuckled as he waggled a finger at Jazz who, in a moment of boldness, attacked it with paws and teeth. He gasped and retrieved his finger, looking at it for damage. Dana readied herself to grab the kitten. And then he chuckled again.

'Vicious little blighter, in't ya?'

Dana realized she'd been holding her breath.

'Right. Dinner's ready.' Eileen announced.

'I'll just ... wash my hands,' Dana replied.

As she walked out, Dana picked Jazz up from Don's stomach, careful to keep her eyes on the kitten, and took her to her room.

'Oi, Dana. This one's for you. Oi. I'm talking to you.'

Dana looked up.

'Why was six afraid of seven?'

'Why was what?'

'You heard. Why was six afraid of seven?'

Dana looked at her mum, who nodded encouragingly.

'I don't know.'

'Because seven ate nine.'

Eileen shoved Don and pretended she was struggling to keep her food in her mouth while laughing. But Don kept glaring at Dana.

'What's up with you?' he demanded.

'Nothing.'

'Why you being a moody cow? We're trying to have a laugh.'

Dana looked down at her plate. 'Please may I leave the table?' she asked her mum.

'No, you may not. I've got Vienetta in.'

Dana waited and watched for a week. Then she grabbed Auntie Naila's keys off the hook when her mum was in the kitchen and put them in her bag. Dana counted the condoms again. She left half an hour early the next morning and let herself into the flat across the landing. Auntie Naila's home, which was almost as familiar as her own. When her mum had the cleaning job, Dana spent a year being picked up from school by Auntie Naila and brought back here till her mum was done. A ripple of guilt rose in Dana as she thought of the kind lady whose flat she was about to use to lose her virginity in. But then determination set in. Dana decided against the bedroom, it was too disrespectful. Plus, it smelled of her, which would put Dana off. Instead, she eyed the carpet in the small living room and pulled the coffee table to the side. She opened her school bag and pulled out a smaller bag crammed with a sheet and towels. Dana stuffed them behind the sofa and ducked out of the front door, closing and locking it behind her.

The day dragged. She tried hard to act normal but could tell from Candace's reactions that she was being weird. Finally, after band practice, she hugged them all a bit too tightly and escaped.

They were both nervous, shy, like they'd been when they first started going out. She led him to the living room.

'We've got to set up the sheets and stuff,' she said, and pulled the plastic bag from behind the sofa. He looked bewildered but helped her lay it all out on the floor. She pulled two cushions off the sofa and lay them down too. Then she looked up at him.

'Can we just chill for a minute? Like, chat for a bit,' he asked.

'Yeah, sure,' she said.

They sat on the sofa. The chat was stilted, nervous at first.

But soon they were cracking their silly jokes and she was teasing him. Then they kissed. They paused at the same time, smiled, then they made their way down to the floor.

They giggled over trying to put the condom on. It took two tries.

It hurt more than she let on. Once he was out of her, her tummy ached and if she moved too quickly a sharp stab of pain shot through her. But she hid it well. They stayed another half an hour. Then they gathered the towels – one with a small trickle of blood slowly spreading across it. She let him out first, then she waited a minute and snuck out too.

Eileen and Don were arguing. Dana crept to the bathroom and stuffed the sheets in the wash basket. Her stomach was throbbing now and she was desperate for a cup of tea and a hot water bottle. But as she hovered in the hallway, contemplating going into the kitchen, Don thumped something and raised his voice.

She turned back to her room, gingerly crouched down to check Jazz was under the bed, then she curled up into the foetal position and tried to breathe through the pain.

CANDACE

Dana had developed another fake laugh. A different one. Not the ditsy blonde one she used to do around boys which she'd copied off that woman from *Friends*. This was loud, shrill, an explosion that came from nowhere because it wasn't preceded with a joke. Candace found herself jumping in fright as Dana looked at her intensely, desperately, willing her to join in. She'd also started doing big nervous blinks.

Detention was over now, but they still rehearsed most evenings. It was wicked being the lead singer of a band. The name kept changing every week, but Tess said they'd only need to make a final decision once they had a gig booked. Gigs. Proper actual gigs. She thought she might shave one side of her hair and dye the other pink. She'd always wanted an undercut, but Bernie's smarmy face filled her thoughts every time she considered it, shouting dyke at her over and over. But if she was a legit rock chick, then no one could say anything. This week they were Sub Deep. Last week it was Jazz Kitten. Also, Rising Purple, The Rare Ones and Viscose.

They were in Spanish when it happened. A knock at the

door and Miss Thomkins, the Special Needs teacher who helped the thick kids trying to scrape a GCSE, peered around the door. 'I wonder if I could borrow Candace.'

Candace's heart started pounding. All eyes turned to her. She had known this day would come, but she'd assumed she'd get a heads up at least, not be dragged out halfway through a lesson in front of everyone. Candace forced herself up, gathered her things and did the walk of shame across the classroom. Miss Thomkins smiled kindly as Candace heard the class start up again, as normal, with all the normal kids carrying on with their normal class.

Her mum had tried to talk to her last week about the letter they'd received. Candace had accused her of calling her a retard and stomped up the steps. She'd forgotten about it, until now.

'I bet you're glad to be missing class,' Miss Thomkins quipped. Candace glared at her. They walked in silence to her Special Room where she did Special Work with the Special Kids.

'Twenny-five percent extra. That's what I get in the exams,' Candace explained to the girls later that day.

'That's what you *are*.' Arianna quipped. 'A whole twenny-five percent extra.'

Candace felt her insides unclench. They weren't looking at her funny, or worse, with pity. They were just taking the piss as normal.

Normal.

They'd gotten through another band practice and smashed their new song. Dana had had a go at a drum solo which ended with them all falling about laughing. It was good to hear Dana laugh again, properly.

'Are you alright?' Candace asked quietly as the two of them walked home.

'Yeah. Course,' Dana replied.

'Sure?'

There was a long pause.

'Can I stay over?'

'Yeah, sure,' Candace replied. 'Do you wanna go get your stuff?'

'Nah. Can I borrow yours?'

At home, Candace yelled down the hallway that Dana was staying over and they rushed upstairs. They slept, side by side, like old times. Holding hands.

The next morning, they left early and went back to Dana's. Her flat was empty, apart from little Jazz who cocked her head to one side as they entered. They gathered Dana's stuff, enough for a week, and packed a bag of Jazz's food. Dana picked Jazz up, but the minute she tried to carry her out of the front door, Jazz started meowing with fear and clawing her way out of Dana's arms. The kitten rushed back inside the flat. They tried once more but Jazz refused to leave the flat.

'Help me make a thing for her.' Dana said eventually.

They emptied a shoe box and cut a hole in the side. She got a towel and her favourite scarf, and placed it all under the bed. Dana made a safe space for Jazz there. Then they left.

2000

ARIANNA

They were definitely bigger. Anyone could see that. Fuller. Arianna stood sideways looking at her boobs in the mirror. She imagined them growing before her very eyes. Bigger and bigger until they were as plump and round as her mum's were in those pictures of her in the sixties – all silky brown flowing hair and oval eyes and curves packed tight into big-collared shirts and flares. And smiling in that hopeful, carefree way she'd never actually seen in real life. That's all she asked for – that she take from her mum's side and get some tits.

Her fake Wonderbra was in the wash so Arianna stuffed some tissue paper into her normal bra. She put on her favourite purple jumper over black jeans and all her rings and necklaces. She drew the eyeliner on thick and headed downstairs.

Mum stormed out of the kids' room holding Theo's bedsheet at arms-length, a dark wet patch expanding in the middle. She rushed right past Arianna on the landing, a whiff of fresh piss accompanying her.

'Theo! Bathroom. Now,' her mum yelled. Arianna stood in

front of her mum, waiting. But she pushed past Arianna and stomped back up the stairs swearing in Cypriot.

Arianna walked downstairs and scanned the kitchen. The table was bare, apart from the fruit bowl stuffed with receipts, batteries, elastic bands and also some fruit. Arianna sat and closed her eyes. She imagined the sound of the kettle was actually the hum of aeroplane engines, that she was on a flight back to Cyprus. Her Yiayia's face filled her mind. She swallowed down a sob and made herself breakfast, then she slung her bag over her shoulder and walked to the hallway. Lelia was sitting on the bottom step, a card in her hand.

'Happy Birthday,' she said shyly, gazing at Arianna with a reverence that pissed her off immediately.

'Thanks,' Arianna said. She opened it. A big number sixteen with googly eyes stared back at her. Inside was a poem about how she was her best friend and how she wished one day she would be just like her. Arianna closed it and stuffed it into her bag. Lelia's face crumpled.

Tess nudged the other two as Arianna turned the corner and all three of them burst into 'Happy Birthday' Tess doing harmonies. They forced her to wear a giant badge.

'I got you this.' Tess said, putting an envelope on the table as they sat in registration. Inside was a card with a picture of two blonde girls hugging.

'Dear Arianna / aka Ri-ri / aka Cypriot Goddess / aka Funky Bass Player / aka English student extraordinaire,
   HAPPY SIXTEENTH BIRTHDAY! You are awesome

and also my best friend and I love you but not in a lesbian way but if you decided you were a lesbian that would be okay too oh no I'm rambling all over your birthday card over and out Tess.'

Arianna giggled.

It felt like it was all of their birthdays. Tess had also made a cake with Linton's help and they scoffed the whole thing in the music room at lunch time while Arianna opened her present. It was a big box. And heavy. Inside were brand new purple Doctor Marten boots and a yin yang necklace.

'We all chipped in,' Candace grinned.

They were the most beautiful things Arianna had ever seen.

As she walked to her next lesson, she heard her name called. Damion-Formerly-Known-As-Bass-Face was rushing up the corridor towards her. He handed her an envelope. 'I just wanted to say Happy Birthday,' he said, smiling sadly, and walked off.

Arianna opened the envelope. A hand-drawn purple heart with the words 'Birthday Girl' in cool gothic writing filled the front. Inside it said:

> 'For what was
> And what could have been.
> No regrets
> My beautiful Bass Queen.
> D x'

*

'Shall we go Wimpey's?' Tess asked.

'Ooh! Yes please!' Dana exclaimed.

'I'll meet you there. I've got someone to thank first,' Arianna replied.

'What? Who?' Tess's face dropped.

'Chill. Please,' Arianna said, a spark of annoyance in her voice. Tess looked like she was going to cry.

'Okay, no sweat. We'll meet you there. Get the grub in,' Candace reassured.

She'd hoped she might catch Damion outside the music department. To say thank you, maybe ask him for some music advice, since they were both legit bass players now. She'd been picturing them both hanging out in a music room together, flirting over a guitar, maybe kissing again.

'Arianna.' She turned and saw him leaning around the entrance to the first floor.

'Could you come to my office for a sec.'

Arianna stared at Mr M. 'Now?'

'Yes,' he said sternly, and disappeared.

Arianna looked around one more time and then made her way reluctantly to the English department. She knocked on Mr M's door, and he called for her to come in. She stepped inside and then stopped in her tracks. Mr M was leaning against his desk. Behind him six large candles burned, and music was playing softly from somewhere. He had a notebook in his hands and he studied it for a while. Arianna stood uncertainly until he finally looked up, taking off his glasses. He launched into a poem.

'How to find the words
For something that cannot be.
How to make you see
What you do to me.
How to know what to do
When every move is wrong
How to let you hear
My forbidden song
How to find the words
To say it has to be
Because even forbidden,
You mean so much to me.'

He spoke it directly to her, not reading from the page, but off by heart. Arianna felt like she was in a dream, not quite in her body. He put the book down and stepped towards her, then past her. He turned the key that was in the lock she hadn't noticed was there, and then before she understood what was happening, he had grabbed her face and was kissing her.

His adult lips felt harder and thinner than any others she'd kissed before, his stubble coarser, rubbing against her face. Then he pulled back and looked at her. He smiled and kissed her again, harder this time. This time his tongue pushed into her surprised mouth and she tasted his taste, more mature, sourer, more adult. A noise escaped from her. He paused. She turned and unlocked the door. Then she fled.

She ran and ran. Through the corridor and out of the building, out gate and down the street, ignoring her aching muscles, her rasping breath. She ran and ran until she found herself at her front door. Then she doubled over, gasping for breath and trying to make sense of what had just happened. Her heart beat wildly, her hands shook and her stomach was flipping over and over.

She calmed enough to get her key from her bag and opened the door. As she stepped into the living room, she saw balloons and a banner.

'Happy Birthday!' Theo, Lelia, Dad, Sandrine and Maya shouted in unison, and her mum walked in with a cake and candles.

'Wouldn't miss my girl's sixteenth,' her dad beamed proudly.

'Dad. I . . . I—'

He put on his old rock 'n' roll vinyl and the kids did the twist.

In bed, finally, her mind reeled. Had it really happened? What had happened? What did it mean? What would she say when she saw him on Monday IN HIS ENGLISH CLASS?

Should she have seen it coming? Did she do this? Was she really more powerful than she thought? Able to manifest even the most unthinkable things into reality? How did she even feel?

What would she tell the girls?

It was only then she remembered: she'd left them waiting for her in Wimpey's.

2022

ARIANNA

'I'm so sorry,' Arianna exclaimed.

She waited, quietly present, as the woman next to her processed the news.

'How could it not be enough?' the woman asked. 'They had the kit, with the evidence. They had my phone, with his messages. What more could I have ...'

'You did way more than could ever be expected of you. You were amazing, every step of the way, Sian.' Arianna didn't waver for a second as she kept every thought and feeling of her own about this archaic, broken system they called Justice out of her voice.

No Further Action.

Again.

Even she had allowed herself some hope this time. Silly.

'What if he does it again?' Sian asked. 'To someone else?'

'Sian, listen to me. This isn't on you. Nothing he ever did or might do is your fault. What you did by reporting him was to send all the responsibility and the burden of this right back to him, where it belongs.'

'But he won. He's proven he's innocent.'

'No Sian, they believed you, the police officers told you as much. They just decided there wasn't enough evidence to proceed to court.'

'What more could they possibly need?'

'You're right. And if you'd like to request a review of the decision, we can do that. But right now, please understand how much you've already done. Because of you, and because of the courage and strength you've shown over this last impossible, horrific year, it means he's on their radar now. He's officially on record and he'll know every action of his will be scrutinized. Because of you, there is a much lower chance that anyone else will go through even a fraction of what you've been through.'

'I don't feel like much of a hero right now.'

'You never asked to be a hero. You're a human being who deserves to live her life without the shadow of this hanging over her anymore.'

Even during the worst years, the Rock Bottom ones, she hadn't missed a day of work. She turned up and delivered, over and over. So, Arianna had been promoted quickly, from regular ISVA to Senior ISVA to ISVA manager. Just like all those years before, when she had achieved straight As despite everything: four A-stars and six As for GCSEs. Three As for A-level. He'd taken pride in that, as if it was his own achievement, as if he had been such a good influence on her, as if he'd made her into the straight-A student she was. She understood now that it would never dawn on him that she had achieved all that *despite* him, not *because* of him. That she was in fact a miracle-worker to have just survived him.

She'd worked a full-time job and studied Law in the evenings for four years, adding all the extracurricular mooting and mock trials to her already impossible schedule, to boost her chance of a pupillage, to make this young brown woman doing a night course stand out among the thousands of Oxbridge graduates who had direct connections to the barristers and chambers she had been so desperate to be invited into.

And then she'd walked away, just before her final exams, to become an Independent Sexual Violence Advocate. Because she knew personally how desperate the need was, how unfathomable the epidemic of violence was, how huge the gap between the emotional and legal support for these victims was. So, she worked tirelessly to bridge that gap. To bring not only her presence and empathy, her humanity and counselling skills to these women in their darkest moment, but also her advocacy, her four years of legal knowledge, and her fierce determination to mould this unfit, archaic, white man's Injustice System into something that might serve a handful of women. And because of this she was an alchemist, turning shit into gold: a magic worker, a trailblazer.

But now she was learning to be careful. Because the real reason she had gotten those grades as a girl was that it hadn't occurred to her to be anything less than perfect. To be everything to everyone. No limits. No boundaries. You could do anything to her, put her through anything, demand absolutely anything of her time, her mind, her body, her spirit, and she would give it, perfectly, completely, betraying and abandoning herself over and over again. Because that's what she had been trained to do, by everyone in her life.

So now she said No. Now she let herself lie in on weekends. Sometimes she didn't exercise, left a list half-ticked, an email unanswered – sometimes for a whole twenty-four hours. It felt scandalous. She felt so deeply responsible for everyone all the time that at first, she couldn't sleep with the discomfort of it, broke out in night sweats as if she were an addict. And that was why she had sought The Rooms.

The first relationship you worked on was with yourself. She knew she was in the right place when she saw the chairs placed in a perfect circle, the literature presented as if in a bookshop window. Five different types of tea, three different types of milk. And everyone punctual, on time, filling their service-roles diligently, perfectly even. A room of perfectionists, trying to get clean one day at a time.

It was a Monday evening. She always front-loaded the week so she could take it easier the closer she got to the weekend – a kindness to herself that Future Arianna would thank her for. She had brought the meeting with Sian to a close by 7 p.m., had sat with her as she processed the decision, the devastation, found the beginnings of acceptance. By 8 p.m. she was in a fellowship meeting. They finished with the Serenity Prayer. She often felt lighter, grateful, serene even, by the end. And understood.

Arianna stepped out into the night and headed to the bus stop. She switched on her phone and waited for it to warm up. She looked at the dating app and thought of him, his beard and smile, his kind, patient messages, and seriously considered replying this time. Maybe she was ready now. Her phone vibrated. She had messages, emails and a missed call. A Facebook, Insta and Twitter notification. Voice mail. She opened them one by one.

They were all from Dana.

2000

TESS

'How hard can it be?' Dana said as the clippers started to buzz. Candace glared at Dana, then squeezed her eyes shut. 'I swear if you fuck it up, I'll end you,' she said as Dana brought the clippers to her head.

Tess watched her friend's thick brown curls fall to the floor and tried not to gasp.

Dana left a mass of curls on the right side of Candace's head. Candace took the scissors and chopped them short. Then Dana applied the bleach. While they waited for Candace's dark hair to turn, she did highlights in Arianna's hair too, copying from a picture of Scary Spice she'd brought with her.

It took ages for their dark locks to lighten, twice as long as the instructions said. But then it was done and Dana applied the final pink tint to Candace's hair. By the time she was finished with her, Arianna's head was starting to burn. They rushed to the bathroom and washed it out. The highlights were so light against her dark curls she looked like a badger, but a cool one. Dana applied some of the pink dye to the ends of her own hair too.

It was Candace's barnet that stole the show, though. Dana had done a decent job of the undercut and the shock of pink hair down the side of her face was sick. She looked pure rock 'n' roll . . . And strangely, more herself than she'd ever been.

'What can we do to my hair?' Tess asked after she'd waited patiently.

Dana held one of her tight, golden curls appreciatively. 'Nothing,' she replied.

'What do you mean?'

'We can't touch your hair. It's perfect,' Dana explained. 'Plus, there's always one girl in the band who's the *au naturelle* one. Like Chilli in TLC. That's you.' Dana grinned.

Three of Candace's mum's towels were ruined, covered in bleached patches with pink around the edge. And there was a dollop of dye that had dripped onto the bathmat too. Candace stuffed it all into the washing machine.

'Come,' she beckoned.

High Street Kensington was a strange and brilliant place, because right in the middle of the line of designer boutiques, full of posh Sloanies wearing pearls and riding boots, was a small entrance that led to an underground market. Literally under the ground. As they descended, the girls were assailed by rock music on one side and techno on the other, second-hand denim and things made of leather and piercing booths and a whole stall that only sold silver skull jewellery and another one where everything was rainbow coloured and then a cave that was full of neon glow-in-the-dark raving gear.

Candace made the first purchase – stripy black and purple

tights. Tess bought a little goth-green skirt with pixie bells hanging from it. Dana bought a bright pink boiler suit. Arianna bought a belly top with the acid smiley face printed on it.

Then to the piercing booth. Arianna went first, because she was the oldest.

She squeezed Candace's hand as the gun pierced a bright silver stud into her left nostril.

'Sick,' she managed through watering eyes.

They all had it done, then Candace got one at the top of her earlobe and bought a septum ring too. When she put it in, with her new hair, even she couldn't hide her elation. She walked different. Felt different. From the inside out. Or the outside in. She was still her, but magnified. Defined. Reduced to her essence. Tess couldn't fully explain it, none of them could, but finally she was Candace, and her outside matched her inside.

Tess looked at them all. The transformation was complete. They were gig-ready.

2000

DANA

'Mum?' Dana called quietly from the door. She hadn't been home for four days. Her stuff was still at Candace's, but the ache to be with Eileen was now a physical pain, and she was desperate to show off her new look.

A scream made her blood freeze. She rushed into the living room. He was dragging her around by her hair. Eileen flailed about trying to grab his arm. Then he shoved her hard into the coffee table. Dana cried out and ran over to her. Eileen's pupils rolled back into her head.

'Stop it! Stop!' Dana screamed.

'*Stop it! Stop it!*' he mimicked in a pitiful girly voice. 'Oh, you're back now, are ya? You give a shit now do ya?'

'Leave her alone.'

'Don't you tell me what to do.' He gritted his teeth and brought his face close to hers. A speckle of his spit landed on her. Then he stood up straight and kicked Eileen in the back with his booted foot. She opened her eyes in shock. Dana screamed again. Then he stomped out of the flat, slamming the door.

'Mum?'

Eileen heaved herself onto the sofa and lay panting and disorientated.

'Mum.' Dana tried to get her mum to look at her. 'Don't let him in again. Let's change the locks. Chuck his stuff out. I'll help you. Mum, please,' she begged.

Eileen wouldn't speak. She wouldn't blink. Dana didn't know what to do. She thought of knocking on Auntie Naila's door but knew Eileen would never forgive Dana if she did. So, she made her tea, covered her with a blanket.

'Would you run away with me?' Dana asked Chris. They were at his cousin's house. He'd given Chris the keys and told him they had two hours while he took his missus to the cinema.

Chris looked at her to check she was serious.

'No.'

'Why not?'

'Because . . . we haven't got any money, we haven't got anywhere to go . . . and my nan. I couldn't leave her. You know that.'

Dana looked at him for a long time. Then she shrugged.

'I was just taking the piss,' she said. 'Just testing you to see how much you fancy me.'

'I don't fancy you,' he said. 'I love you.'

He wanted to walk her all the way to Candace's, but Dana gave him a brusque hug and set off on her own. But then, as Candace let her in, she turned to look outside once more, and thought she saw him nod at her from across the road.

2022

ARIANNA

Arianna sat in yet another police station, a wad of casework wedged into her handbag, a hopeful book in her lap: *The Artists Way*. She'd bought it as a gift for herself the first time they'd got a guilty verdict – one of only a handful over the years she'd been doing her job. She'd promised herself that these hours of waiting for her clients would be when she studied the book, practised her writing exercises, in the hope she'd have enough material she could piece together into something bigger. A book? She'd written mostly about Cyprus, about her beloved Yiayia, long dead now, the jasmine scent and rosewater, the lemon tree and the fig and pistachio infused treats, the gossiping aunties and the relentless cicadas. But also the scar that ran through the centre of the divided island, the violent history that overshadowed life there. Yiayia's filthy swearing and the deft way she broke a chicken's neck for Sunday lunch. Raving with cousins in Ayia Napa and creeping home as the hot dawn dried their sweaty clothes stiff. She knew it was good; had no idea what to do with it other than to keep writing.

But today there was no chance of concentrating on

anything. Because Dana had called, and emailed, and messaged, and that was all Arianna could think about.

The door to the waiting area opened and a woman holding a file entered the room and sat nearby. As Arianna made eye contact, her heart skipped. The deep brown eyes, the slender figure, the silky black hair cut now into a professional bob.

'Karla?' Arianna exclaimed quietly before she knew what she was doing.

Karla Malik turned to her and smiled inquisitively.

'I think we went to school together ...' Arianna began.

A shadow passed over Karla's face. Arianna noticed now the faint lines at the side of her eyes, a weariness in her gaze despite her retaining that radiance Arianna had been captivated by as a girl.

'I'm sorry, I don't ...'

'I was a couple of years below you, so you wouldn't remember me. I'm Arianna.'

'Oh yes, I think I remember ...'

'Don't worry, you don't have to pretend.'

Karla laughed then, and it was beautiful. She realized she'd never seen her laugh before. Not at school, not at Jay's party and not at ...

Arianna's heart sank. She suddenly felt like the room itself was pitching, the ground tossing her off balance. Her vision blurred apart from the very centre of it where Karla sat, looking at her questioningly.

The poetry group. In the office. That had been the last time she'd seen her. Then she'd disappeared. And the rumours had started, about her shagging a teacher. The realization struck Arianna with a jolt.

'Are you here to ... Do you mind me asking what ... ?'

'Oh, I work in Fraud,' she replied.

'Oh!' Arianna exclaimed with surprise. 'What kind of—?'

'All sorts,' Karla said. 'We've got quite a few live cases, all different, and at different stages, so I'm kept busy.'

'That's great.'

'What are you in for?'

'I work as an ISVA. An Independent Sexual Violence Advocate,' Arianna explained.

'Oh right,' Karla said, Arianna thought with genuine interest.

'I support people, women mostly, who are going through the process of reporting,' and then because she couldn't help herself, because she didn't know if she'd ever get another chance, 'Quite a variety too. Some are recent incidents, others are nonrecent cases, from years ago, decades sometimes. Almost all are by perpetrators known to the victim, often in a position of trust or power. Family members, partners, teachers even.'

Karla nodded.

She was studying Arianna's face, putting two and two together, like most people did when she explained what her job was, asking the question in her mind that hardly anyone dared ask outright. Coming to her own conclusion.

The door swung open once more. A plain-clothed policeman nodded at Karla. She stood.

'Good to see you again,' she said, and walked out.

2000

ARIANNA

Arianna strode into school staring ahead of her. She had him for second lesson today and she had no idea what to do. She was the one who had run away. Maybe he felt rejected. Did she owe him an apology?

'Hey, did you hear about Dana's mum?' Tess asked when they met outside tutor group.

'Yeah, Candace told me.'

'It's so messed up. Like, what's she gonna do? Just stay at Candace's for ever? What about her mum? What about her cat?'

The situation with Dana played on Tess's mind enough for her not to notice every damn thing that was going on for Arianna for once.

As they got closer to second period, Arianna began to feel sick. Then the pips went and they were walking to his classroom. And then she was walking through the door and there he was as they filed in. He didn't look at her at all. He launched into a discussion on the two writing voices in *Of Mice and Men*. He chose the boys in the front to read a page each. Arianna's face flushed a hot red and her heart beat wildly as she tried to make sense of why he was ignoring her. As the class left at the end of the lesson, she passed him. He looked up and smiled coldly, formally, then looked away.

'Maybe we could write her a song. Or we could do a sleepover at mine, but she could stay the whole week if she wanted. Maybe we could—'

'Tess, man. I beg you. Give it a rest,' Arianna snapped.

Tess looked at her, hurt. 'Why are you angry with me?'

'I'm not, I just … It's a lot right now.'

'Did I do something wrong?'

'No, no. I just … I'm gonna … go for a walk, okay?'

Once Arianna was alone, her feelings began to overwhelm her. Her chest tightened, she couldn't breathe properly. She started to hyperventilate there in the middle of the play-ground. Tears threatened to burst and she rushed to the nearest toilet and slammed the cubicle door before letting it all out. Eventually, she wiped her face and sorted herself out in the mirror.

As she stepped out, Damion walked by.

'Are you okay?' he asked.

'Yeah, yes. I'm just … Our mate Dana, she's going through some stuff and we're all a bit …'

'If you ever want to talk … I mean … Like, we could just talk …'

Arianna looked up at him. She saw longing in his eyes, a tension, wrestling with whether he should be talking to her or not. She softened.

'Yeah, I'd like that.'

'Yeah? Okay, well, just let me know ...' He smiled and walked away. She took a deep breath and headed to History.

Tess was waiting for her, watching her carefully. Arianna tried to reassure her with a smile. They made it through another hour then filed out into the hallway once more.

'Ah, there you are.'

Mr M was suddenly right in front of her. 'I've taken a quick look and made some notes, so see me later to talk through them.'

He handed her a notebook that wasn't hers and walked away. She had no idea what he was talking about. She hadn't given him anything to read. She put the notebook in her bag, her mind whirling once again. Tess didn't notice. A part of her wished that she had.

'So, I say we go to the chicken shop and take it to Candace's,' Tess continued, oblivious.

'Okay.'

'Yeah? Great! Shall we go straight after school?'

'Sure.'

'I'll tell Mr Tamworth I can't make practice today. It's an emergency.' Tess skipped down the corridor to the Music department. Arianna waited a beat and then pulled out the notebook. It was empty. She flicked through it and found a bright yellow card wedged among the blank pages.

'29A EVERLY CLOSE, SW11. OPPOSITE THE BANK. 7PM. X'

Her heart began to race. Her face burst into a smile she tried to suppress.

'Sorted!' Tess jumped in front of her. 'Let's go.'

Arianna slammed the notebook shut. 'Ah, shit. I've got to talk through those notes with Mr M.'

'What?'

'Yeah, he just said.'

'Should I wait for you?'

'Nah, no idea how long I'll be. Just go and I'll find you there.'

Tess looked at her searchingly. 'Are you having sex with Bass Face?' she suddenly blurted out.

'What?'

'Because I'd be fine with it, it's just ... you've been acting weird for ages and I don't know why and ...' Tess's voice caught in her throat. 'I'm sorry, I just feel like there's so much horrible stuff happening and it's like I don't even know you anymore.'

Arianna felt a pang of anger. 'I'm not shagging Bass Face, okay? And you'd be the first to know if I was.'

'Promise?'

'Course.'

Arianna watched Tess head off, counted to a hundred and then followed her out.

She had a whole hour and a half to kill. She thought of going home first, but the thought of more demands, more people wanting something from her, scrutinizing her, pulling at her, made her chest tighten. So she walked slowly until she got to the bank, and then sat at a bus stop for another hour until it was time.

She rang the bell. It felt like ages before he answered. His glasses weren't on and he was wearing baggy trousers and a tight T-shirt, the curve of his middle-aged paunch just visible beneath it. His feet were bare.

'Hi,' he said softly and turned inside, leaving the door open for her.

She hesitated, then stepped in. He'd disappeared down the hallway and she heard the strum of a guitar coming from the far end. He was perched on the sofa in the living room, guitar in his lap, picking broodily at the notes. Arianna stood uncertainly in the doorway. He continued to play and then launched into a song. She recognized some of the words – they were the same ones he had read out to her the day they'd kissed. He played the whole song while she stood there in her coat. Then he strummed the final chord and looked up at her.

'That was lovely,' she said. He continued to strum the guitar and look at her.

Then he suddenly stopped playing and put a hand over his face. It took a moment for her to realize he was crying.

'Are you okay?' she asked.

'I'm sorry,' he managed, wiping his eyes. 'I'm just so confused. I don't know what I thought I was doing when I invited you here. It's mad, really. I could lose my job and you could get kicked out ...' Arianna blinked with surprise. Could she? Get kicked out of school? Just before her exams? '... I've just been so deeply unhappy for so long and I've been with someone who doesn't understand me. Sure, she's hot and beautiful and everyone was amazed when we got together because on the surface we look like the perfect couple but ... until I met you I had no idea what I was capable of feeling.' He looked at her then, piercingly, intensely.

Arianna nodded, trying to keep up. She looked around and saw pictures of him and a grown woman, on holiday, in formal wear, a silly one with her tongue out, matching rings on their fingers, and remembered a woman's shoes by the front door, a woman's coat. Arianna started to back away. What was she doing here? Whose house was she in? Why?

He stood up and put the guitar down. He took her hand in his. The feeling was so strange, holding Mr M's hand.

'Arianna, I'm scared too. I'm terrified of what you do to me. But I am a very creative soul, and so are you. I think we really get each other, and I think ... I think I love you.'

Arianna felt like she was in a dream, outside of herself again, like that time he had kissed her.

And now he was kissing her again, caressing her face. And she was kissing him back, so he kissed her some more, and then his tongue snaked into her mouth once more, and she stood there kissing her teacher.

He guided her to the sofa. Then he leaned over her and began to kiss her hungrily, roughly, like he had before, except this time she was under him and she couldn't really move and, even though she was beginning to panic, she tried to go with it.

And then Mr M was touching her boob, caressing it and squeezing it and then reaching under her top. She remembered too late about the tissue which fell out of her bra as he undid it. Arianna was mortified and quickly swiped it to the side. He looked at her topless body.

'God, you're beautiful,' he said. And then he buried his face in her small boobs. She looked down at the top of his head, the grey strands of hair between his brown ones up close now. He stopped and straightened up on his knees and his erection – Mr M's erection – protruded from inside his trousers. He reached for her trousers and began to unzip them. She panicked, not knowing how to slow this down. Then he pulled them off, and her knickers and she was naked, in front of him.

'God, what do you do to me?' he said as he took his clothes off. And then Mr M was naked, towering over her. Mr M's erect penis was inches away from her. She tried not to stare at it. He began to part her legs.

'Wait, please,' she managed to say. He paused and looked at her questioningly.

'What?' he demanded.

'It's just . . . I'm not . . . ready to . . . I think this has gone quite far and . . . er . . .'

He slumped slightly, his penis beginning to lower with disappointment. Then he put his hand to his forehead and swiped at his hair like he did in class when he was about to tell someone off. Then he looked at her coldly.

'Can I at least cum?'

She froze.

And then she nodded.

He sighed in frustration and leaned over her. She lay there quietly as he pumped away, sometimes using his other hand to squeeze at her boob. It took a long time.

'I've thought about you, you know,' he said as he pumped, his voice catching with the exertion. 'I think of you all the time when I touch myself.'

'Really?' she asked.

'Yeah, all the time. You're in all my fantasies Arianna. And do you know my favourite one? The one I think about the most when I touch myself?'

She shook her head.

'I imagine you're a refugee. And you've got to come and see me and let me do this to you, so you can stay in the country.'

He gasped and shuddered. She closed her eyes.

He got up and walked to the bathroom. He returned and handed her some toilet paper to clean herself up. He pulled on his trousers and sat on the edge of the sofa with his head in his hands. She wiped his semen from her body and looked around for somewhere to put the slimy paper. He wouldn't look at her. It was clear she'd fucked up, but she didn't know how. So she got dressed.

'Are you okay?' She asked uncertainly. 'Shall I just—'

'It's not your fault,' he said finally. 'I don't want you to feel bad. It's my fault if anything for expecting you to know these things.'

'What things?' Arianna asked, embarrassment already forming in her stomach.

'Look, I know you've probably just fooled around with a couple of boys, but I'm an adult and I have needs. And it's not really the done thing to turn up here and get me all excited and then . . . I have to . . . do that.'

Her face burned with shame.

'I just . . . I guess, with the song and everything. I wanted our first time to be really special. Not like that.' He turned away.

'I'm sorry,' she said quietly, and let herself out.

2000

TESS

'There you are. It's been so long I hardly recognize you,' Mr Tamworth quipped.

'Sorry sir' Tess replied.

'Well, I've got some news which you can pass on to the rest of the band: you have a gig.'

'What?'

'So, you'd better figure out what you're actually called by Friday 3rd. Two weeks from now. Well, a bit earlier actually because Ms Gail's going to make up some posters for you.'

'Are you serious?'

'Very. So, a few practical things. I'll need permission from your parents, and of course they're welcome to come. I'll be driving you there, but if they could take you home that would be best.'

'You'll drive us? In your car?'

'I think the minibus will be better, what with all the instruments.'

'Yes, of course.' Tess blushed.

He looked at her closely. 'I know it's not been easy. I think it would be a good thing if you could rally everyone for this.'

She nodded. 'Oh and also, I've still got your CD. I'll bring it in, I just forgot. It was really good,' she gushed.

'Oh shit. That is big time,' Candace exclaimed.

'We'll finally get to wear our outfits,' Tess said excitedly. 'Dana you can wear the boiler suit. It matches your hair and everything.'

Dana managed a smile. Tess could tell she was already starting to plan the way she would style them all, the little Dana touches that would make them look like a proper band. Tess wanted so much for them to get lost in the excitement, for Dana to start talking a mile a minute, for Arianna to start coming up with the blurb for the poster, for Candace to don her septum ring and become her alter ego – Rock Candy.

'We can get ready at mine. We can stay at mine. Linton can bring us back. That way it's easy,' Tess enthused.

For a blissful two hours that afternoon in rehearsals, they forgot everything else and got through a whole five songs. There was a moment where Arianna seemed to disappear somewhere in her mind and Tess felt panic rise in her, the sense that she was losing Arianna to something she didn't understand. So Tess played louder, asked Arianna questions about the lyrics she'd written, the bass line she was playing, until Tess brought her friend back.

ARIANNA

In her dreams, she is the magic. So powerful she can make anything happen. A sorceress presiding over her spells. Her visions. Her potions. Her cauldron. And now the cauldron is a pot, on a hob. On a cooker that is covered in pots that are boiling, cooking, brewing. And there is an oven, roasting. The grill too, toasts and blackens, as she tends to first one, then the other, back and forth as they bubble and bake. Then one begins to bubble over, spilling onto the flame that rages higher. The grill catches fire and the thing in the oven is burning. She tends to one only for the other to rage. She can't keep up. She rushes to the tap and throws water on it all, but it only burns higher, angrier, fed not quenched or sated, but demanding more of her, the flames beginning to engulf her too.

Arianna woke up gasping for air.

At school she walked towards his office and found him in the corridor outside. She passed him back his notebook. On the back of the yellow card tucked in it she'd written, *I'm ready.*

2022

CANDACE

'I've been distracted,' Candace began. 'I've been scared – more than usual.' She looked up then, tried to laugh, because it was an in-joke between them how terrified Candace was, all the time. Asha softened a little but remained quiet.

'But the main news is that I'm letting go of that. I've decided not to waste my life, and yours, worrying.' Candace steadied herself. 'It's been crowded, in this relationship, and that boat of mine is small enough as it is.' Asha still didn't laugh. 'I'd like it to be just us. The three of us. That's what it should have been all along.'

They were sitting on the grass in the park. It was where they did all their serious talking. Partly because they didn't get much time in the boat alone. Partly because when they were at Asha's they always ended up in bed. Even now three years in, they were hot for each other.

But with Asha, it was so much more. A whole other level that Candace had never experienced. A history they both understood, a desire to be better, a kindness within them both that had survived the darkest of times, and a deep attraction that didn't seem to be going anywhere. It blew her mind on a daily basis that love like this was possible. That she'd found it at this point in her life. And she knew that somewhere deep inside, she still didn't fully trust it.

It scared her how easily she was ready to give up on it sometimes. How the defensiveness would kick in and she was ready to end it all, send Asha packing before Asha walked out of her own accord. And if she was really honest, how she sometimes used Saffy as an excuse, a shield to stop people getting too close. And worse than anything was the fact that Candace had had to face that sometimes she had been so defensive, so hostile, cruel even, that *she* had become the aggressor, the very type of person that she had been exposed to over and over in her life. And now she was trying to make it right.

So they sat, again, in the park, to work through it together.

'Saff loves you – I love you. And Saff ... Saff is ... savvier than I give her credit for. And our world is much better for having you in it. Fact.' Candace said. 'Could we maybe ... start thinking about moving in together?' She saw Asha's eyebrows rise a touch. 'Maybe, over the next year, we could work towards that?'

2022

ARIANNA

The cappuccino sat cooling in front of Arianna. The last thing she needed right now was caffeine. She had wrestled with herself about whether to call Candace at least, but it was happening so quickly she convinced herself she hadn't really had time. And then Tess had staged that dramatic confrontation without letting Arianna in on it until it was happening, without even telling her she was meeting with Chris. She owed Tess, at least, nothing. With Candace it was sensitive, Saffy being left in her care for so long. And then there was the asking of Forgiveness. Dana must be working some kind of self-help programme and Arianna was the only one who understood that. Even Tess, with her alcoholic mum, had scoffed at Arianna for going to those 'pseudo-religious American meetings'.

So, Arianna had decided to meet Dana alone. It seemed that this was what Dana wanted too.

At first she wasn't sure if it was Dana at all. She'd set up a variety of identities with obscure names that sounded like quotes from poets, Romantics, if she remembered correctly. Mostly dead white men's work. Skylark and Daffodil and Ode with a long thread of posts sharing philosophical, existential quotes that Arianna couldn't quite identify. They seemed to be connected to some of the literature of the twelve-step groups she was now familiar with, but also different. Some of it quasi-religious, a Churchill quote thrown in, more poetry. But her message to Arianna was consistent across all mediums.

> Hi Arianna
> Do you remember me?
> I'm sorry for everything.
> I hope you can forgive me.
> Because I forgive you.

Arianna had responded. And then they were chatting. And then Dana had asked if they could meet. Arianna was about to suggest that very weekend, but Dana beat her to it. Tomorrow perhaps? She was nearby. She could meet anywhere Arianna wanted.

She had no idea why Dana had chosen her out of the three of them this time, but now the door to the café opened and her lost friend was walking towards her – older, hardened, the sparkle dulled – but it was Dana.

2000

TESS

'Right settle down quickly.'

Tess looked around at the girls in her year, crammed into one classroom for a whole day of PSHE. They'd had the most cringey hour on pubic hair and breast development from Miss McGee, followed by a workshop on relationships. Now Miss White, flustered and grumpy, stood at the front of the class looking like she might cry. 'I mean it!' she exploded suddenly. 'I would much rather not be here either, believe me. So don't give me an excuse to send you all back to Geography because I will.'

They quietened, shocked at how distressed Miss White looked.

She sighed. 'Now. Today I have the pleasure of discussing contraception with you.'

There was a ripple of amusement. Miss White glared at them until they were silent once more.

'As you may know, there are several options when it comes to choosing a contraceptive when you are considering sexual intercourse. Some are more effective than others. Contraception is used to prevent an unwanted pregnancy, but it is also a way of preventing sexually transmitted diseases from being passed from one person to another.' They could tell she was struggling through this speech that she'd had to memorize and deliver. She stopped, taking a deep breath before continuing. She talked through the pill and the diaphragm and the rhythm method, asking them for the pros and cons of each. Her distress only increased as the class went on.

'So the next method we will look at is the condom. This is one here,' she held up a square packet and the class stifled another smirk. 'And this is a model of an erect penis.'

Miss White reached under the desk and pulled out a white bust of a torso with an erection. The class burst into scandalised laughter.

'So the first thing ... is to ... try and open it ... without ...' she fumbled awkwardly, her face reddening. It was awful. She finally managed to open the packet and, with her thumb and forefinger, pulled the moist condom out with disgust. She swallowed and turned to the model of the erection.

'So what you do is ... you just ... you've got to ... find the right way to ...' she tried to unravel it and it almost escaped her fingers.

'I'll do it.' Dana jumped up, but then Arianna stood, walked to the front of the class and took the condom from Miss White. She placed it on the tip of the erection and pulled it down until it was covered. Miss White sighed with relief.

'Thank you Arianna. I won't ask how you—'

'Fuck this shit.' Candace's chair scraped back noisily, and she stormed out of the classroom, slamming the door behind her.

Tess looked from Dana to Arianna to the door in bewilderment. Once again, she had no idea what was going on. Once again, she had been left behind. Once again, she was the last to know.

2000

CANDACE

Candace kicked a bin; the bang reverberated loudly. She stormed through the foyer, down the stairwell and out into the cold air. She kept walking, knowing that five storeys of classrooms looked down at her solitary figure, outside in the middle of a lesson.

She walked until she got to the far end of the grounds, turned to the section of grass where she'd played endless football matches, done countless drills, runs, kicks and headers, where she'd lost herself for hours on end in blissful physical activity. She kicked at the fence, twice, tried to push over a netball hoop. It teetered and then righted itself, so she kicked that too. She found the cluster of bushes in the blind spot around the corner where students went for smokes and, crouched on her haunches, head in her hands, she tried to breathe.

She felt crazy. The whole world didn't make sense. None of it. It kept tipping her and everyone she knew upside down, swiping the ground from under their feet, giving and snatching, punching and stroking, saying one thing, meaning the opposite. And she wanted out. Of this shithole of a school.

Of this piss stain of a city. Of her skin. Of her feelings. Of her head. Just for one goddamn moment, she wanted a bit of peace. For the world to make sense. For her to make sense.

The pips sounded, followed by the noise of hundreds of children pouring out into the lunchtime air. She looked down at the carpet of butts she was squatting on and heaved herself up. She ducked into the sports hall, headed to the equipment cupboard at the far end and grabbed a ball. The door nearest her groaned open. Miss White stepped inside.

'You alright?'

'Yep,' Candace replied.

Miss White looked at Candace steadily. 'It won't always be like this,' she said. 'It won't always be this hard. This ... lonely.'

Candace stared at her, refusing to give her any sign she understood, desperate for her to keep talking.

'You will find your team. They'll get you. They'll welcome you in. Cos they'll need you as much as you need them. Like family. They'll look like you and talk like you and feel like you. You've just got to be patient. Keep on keeping on until it gets good. Cos it will. I promise.'

A sob threatened to escape from Candace, but she gritted her teeth until it passed.

Miss White nodded, closed the door behind her. Candace stood alone, holding the ball. But she felt like a weight she hadn't known she'd been carrying this whole time had just been laid down. She felt her limbs buzzing, fizzing with this new lightness, and she stood, exhausted and relieved and surprised, staring at the door.

There was a chuckle from the back of the cupboard. Candace froze. She waited to hear it again, but there was only silence. She stepped into the small room packed with sports equipment and could just make out a mousey fringe and a ponytail. Candace lunged forward and pulled Bernie out by her hair.

'Ow! Get off me you dyke.'

'What are you doing spying on people like a fucking pervert?'

'You're the fucking pervert. I heard you. Both of you. I knew it! I said, didn't I? You're both lesbians! Aaaaah ha ha ha!' She laughed with delight. Candace yanked her hair hard.

Bernie screamed and looked at her with genuine fear before bursting into nervous laughter again like a hyena.

Candace glared at her. 'If you open your pissy little mouth and start spreading rumours, I swear I'll fuck you up. Do you understand?'

2000

ARIANNA

It had hurt so much the first time that she had passed out on the bus home. She had woken up just in time to press the stop button and gingerly lower herself onto the pavement.

It had been four times now. She'd sneak to his when he told her to, and they'd make love and then he'd tell her about his life, the small town he'd grown up in where he was a big fish in a small pond, misunderstood, bursting with potential, and his plans for when he became a successful writer and they could both leave that cesspit of a school. He probably had enough songs for a whole album too, plus he was quite advanced in Krav Maga. She'd listen attentively as he lost himself in his own stories.

Then her favourite bit, when he'd turn to her once more, give her all his focus. This grown man. He'd say amazing things to her that made her stomach fill with butterflies. Then he'd say things that made her blush. And then they would Do It all over again. It often lasted quite a long time. He said that made him an exceptional lover. She had nothing to compare it to, so she assumed the failing was on her part. To fully appreciate his efforts, not to hurt so badly afterwards that she could barely walk, not to orgasm herself. So, she started to make the appropriate noises and noticed how this excited him further. In an attempt to speed things along in the hope it would all finish a bit sooner, she often reached two, three, even four fake orgasms each time. Finally, she would get dressed and leave.

But it was time. Even though he had sworn her to secrecy, she had to tell someone, not just confide it all in her top-secret diary that she kept at the back of her wardrobe. She was a woman now. And she needed another woman to talk to. To try to make sense of this dream-like life she was living, this double-life, and all the confusing feelings and thoughts that came with it. Maybe someone could help her figure out what was normal, what was wrong with her and how she could fix it so she could be the lover he desired her to be. Maybe Dana would know.

She hopped off the bus and waited on the kerb. As her eyes swept both ways across the busy main road, Arianna caught a glimpse of familiar blonde frizz: Dana was standing at the bus stop across the road. Arianna made to call her name, but then she saw Dana lean into another figure. And then she watched her friend tilt her head up and kiss Chris R.P.

By the time Arianna had crossed the road, Chris had gone. She put her hand on Dana's shoulder. Dana turned, confused, then elated, then terrified.

'Ri!' she exclaimed.

'What the fuck?' Arianna demanded.

Dana started to turn red.

'Was that Chris? My Chris? What the fuck Dana?'

Dana seemed to be lost for words.

'How long ... Were you even going to tell me?' Arianna demanded.

Dana nodded weakly.

'Fucking say something!' Arianna yelled. 'Who's next? Eh? Candace's brother? Tess's dad?'

Dana's expression turned to shock. Tears welled up in her eyes.

Arianna shook her head. 'They were right. You are a slag.'

Arianna stormed up to her room. Everyone was a scheming liar. Herself included. All she did these days was lie. To her mum, her dad, to her friends, to him, to herself. Lie, lie, lie. She suddenly felt exhausted, had no idea when it had gotten so complicated.

She heard the front door shut downstairs. Arianna looked out of the window and saw her mum heading at a pace down the road. Arianna jumped up and grabbed her coat.

She rushed out and jogged along the street until she saw her mum in the distance. She suddenly needed to know where her mum kept disappearing to in the evenings. Enough lying. Enough shit going on behind her back. Arianna tried to think back to how often she disappeared. Mostly when Dad was around so that someone was with the kids, but sometimes, if Theo was at a friend's and it was just Arianna and Lelia, she would sneak out too. And then she was back and snapping at them as usual.

She was in a rush. It was hard to keep up with her. Arianna began to falter. Was she ready to see where her mum was sneaking off to? Who her mum was sneaking off to? It began to dawn on Arianna that maybe she was more like her mum than she realized. She had always been told she took after her dad – his hair, his mannerisms, his features – but if she was sneaking out to her lover almost at the same time as her mum was, did that mean she had picked up her behaviour without realizing? She couldn't imagine her mum snogging anyone – not even her dad – especially not her dad. She couldn't imagine her in the throes of passion, or the intimacies of companionship. But then she was pretty sure her mum had no idea what her daughter was capable of either. As Arianna rushed down the street after her mum, she realized with a pang that they hardly knew each other at all. When had that happened?

Her mum turned the corner and headed across the main road. On the other side was the park that ran along the edge of the River Thames. The gate was locked, but there was a gap in the iron fence behind the bushes to the side that her mum went straight through. Dusk was beginning to set in and Arianna followed her mum's small figure hurrying across the grass to the far end of the park where it met the water. Her mum stopped and put two hands on the ledge overlooking the river. Arianna hid behind a tree, waiting to see who else would join her. She waited. They both did.

And then.

There was a burst of orange light as the sun passed between the arches of the bridge as it set over the water. It lit up her mum's face and she turned to meet it, a look of such relief and gratitude and sorrow on her face. A release from the daily slog, of her roles and labels, an escape to a place full of sunlight and water.

Arianna thought of the young, curvaceous woman in the photos she'd seen. The island girl who had travelled so far to start anew. The one who had escaped the traditions and limitations of small island life for the freedom of this city, only to find herself stuck at home, alone, keeping three kids alive. Facing burglars alone. And the cold. So much cold.

Her mum kept her face raised towards the sunset the whole time. Then, as the last rays left her face, she turned and made her way back home.

2022

ARIANNA

They hugged. Dana had always been warm, effusive – the warmest and most effusive of all of them. But then she seemed to check herself, her embrace loosened and she stepped back.

'I can't believe it's you,' Arianna said as they sat. 'How are you?'

'Good.' Arianna could tell Dana was holding back, trying to suss how safe Arianna was, if she would judge her, scrutinize her, report back to the old lot. Arianna felt the urge to reassure her.

'Mad how old we all are now,' Arianna tried. 'I need an extra half an hour in the morning just to make myself look human,' she quipped.

'You still look the same,' Dana said kindly.

'So do you, exactly the same. I recognized you straight away,' Arianna replied.

Dana grimaced. 'You must be married now with five kids.'

'Ha! Quite the opposite,' Arianna retorted. 'I think I've unticked more boxes than I've ticked to be honest.'

Dana softened slightly.

'How about you? Married?' Arianna stopped herself from asking if she had any kids.

Dana raised her chin, looked at Arianna steadily.

'I'm really good, actually. The best I've been in a long time, thanks. Do you see much of the old lot?'

'Not really,' Arianna replied. 'Just one or two now and then. I try to stay away from the reunions and all that.' She paused. 'I did see Tess recently. And Candace.'

Dana's expression changed. She seemed interested and fearful at the same time. 'Oh yeah?'

'Yeah,' Arianna said. 'It was weird without you.'

Dana kept her gaze steady. Arianna imagined it was hard to hear about them meeting without her. And then there was Saffy.

'Where did you meet?' Dana asked.

'Online, actually,' Arianna explained. 'Everyone's so busy we couldn't find time to meet in person.'

'So you haven't seen them in real life?'

'Well, actually, we did kind of spontaneously meet up at Candace's. She's got a little boat she lives on. It's lovely. Small but . . .' Arianna felt like she'd said too much.

Dana suddenly looked like she might cry. Arianna realized she must be picturing where Saffy was living, where she was growing up. It dawned on her how loaded this whole interaction was. So full of things unsaid, people un-mentioned.

'Are they okay?' Dana managed.

'Yeah, yeah, they're okay,' Arianna said gently. 'They're

worried about you. They'll be happy to know you're okay.'

Dana blinked back tears. 'I'd love to see them,' she said. 'Could we meet up? All of us?'

2000

DANA

Candace cackled dirtily at her own filthy joke and looked at Dana who tried to smile. She hadn't told anyone about her argument with Arianna. Because she'd have to tell them about Chris first, and then they would all say what Arianna had said. She *was* a slag. And none of them would trust her anymore. Candace nudged her hard, looked at her with concern, also annoyance. Dana's weird mood was ruining her punchline.

There was a knock at the classroom door and Dana saw Candace's cheeks flush. She sighed and began to gather her things. But when the door opened, it wasn't Miss Thomkins come to take her to her twenty-five-percent-extra-special class, it was Miss White.

'Sorry Miss McGee,' she said. Then looked around the classroom. 'Dana, could you come with me please?' Dana shared a look with Candace.

'Dana, we're going to go to my office,' Miss White said gently as they walked down the corridor.

Dana stopped. 'Why?'

'We'll have a chat in there.' Dana forced herself to follow.

Miss White closed the door gently behind her.

'We got a call from your neighbour, Miss Naila Levent. She says your mum's been hurt.'

'No,' Dana pleaded. 'What did he do? Where is she?'

'She's being taken to hospital. I can take you there and you can ask a friend to come with you—'

'I want to see my mum,' Dana wailed.

'It's okay. We're going to arrange that. Now who would you like to go with you?'

'I . . .'

'Would you like me to ask Candace?'

Minutes later, Candace burst in. She hugged her as Dana cried so hard she couldn't breathe.

Auntie Naila was sitting on a plastic seat in the Intensive Care waiting area. She stood when she saw the girls. Dana ran to her.

'Where is she?'

'It's okay, Dana. Look at me. She's stable, okay? The doctor said she's going to—'

'WHERE'S MY MUM?'

'In here.'

Dana opened the door to a small room with a bed in the middle. Eileen lay, her head turned away, looking small and thin, brittle, under the covers. There were monitors and tubes and one eye was purple and swollen shut. Stitches ran across the side of her face and there was what looked like a cigarette burn on her arm.

Dana wanted desperately to hold her, but was terrified she'd hurt her. She sat on the seat facing her mum and took in each injury, each individual bruise with renewed horror. She didn't even notice Candace and Auntie Naila come in.

'We've got to go now, Dana,' Auntie Naila said. 'I'm going to take you back to mine and I'll bring you back here first thing, okay?'

Dana held her mum's inert hand. Then she let herself be led away.

Candace and Dana went into the flat. In the living room, the kitchen table was upturned, a streak of blood on its edge. She called out for Jazz, but Jazz wouldn't come. Candace helped her move the bed away from the wall. Jazz wasn't under it. They went from room to room, calling her name. Dana shivered, then she realized that the balcony door was open. They never left it open. She rushed outside, but the cat wasn't there. With growing horror, she leaned slowly over the fifth-floor balcony and looked down. But there was no sign of her cat.

She sat on the floor, numb. Candace held her hand, watching her.

Dana turned to her. 'Will you run away with me?'

'What?'

'Will you run away with me?' she said again, flatly, clearly.

'Where would we go?'

'Away.'

'But you can just stay with me.'

'Not for ever.'

'Why not?'

Dana stared at Candace.

'I dunno, D,' Candace tried. 'We got our exams. You got

to do your maths. What about all that? You're gonna get As.'
She took a breath. 'I won't leave you, though, okay? Whatever
happens, I won't leave you.'

Dana looked away.

'And you can't leave me, okay? Dana? Look at me. You can't
leave me.'

2000

CANDACE

Candace woke to a face full of frizzy blonde hair. Dana was curled up in a foetal position, clinging onto Candace's arm like it was a float keeping her above water. They had whispered late into the night trying to find a way. She offered to steal some money from her parents to help Eileen get away or change the locks or hire a hit man to kill Don. She'd even considered finding her brother, getting him to go over and fuck him up, injure him in exactly the same ways he'd injured Eileen.

Eventually Dana began to stir and Candace saw the moment she passed from blissful ignorance to remembering the horrors of the day before.

Her dad was whistling 'Delilah' downstairs. The song was cut short as he closed the front door behind him. Candace walked downstairs and into the kitchen. Her mum sat frozen at the table, her strange half-smile pasted on her glazed face. Candace stepped past her and grabbed some breakfast.

They walked to school in silence, joining the growing tide of kids heading towards the imposing glass and metal building that loomed over the surrounding area.

More kids poured out of the bus stopped across the road and one looked over at them, clocked Candace, and turned to whisper to her friend. They cackled with laughter and called to someone just stepping off. It was Bernie. Her high-pitched hyena laugh joined theirs and they rushed up the road, turning around every now and then to steal glances at her.

'Let's do it,' Candace said.

'What?' Dana turned to her.

'The thing you said we should do. Let's do it.'

'Run away?'

Candace nodded.

'When?'

'Soon as we can. There's just one thing I've got to do.'

Candace left Dana waiting at the bus stop and strode towards the school. She caught up with Bernie a few metres from the gate and pulled her aside.

With one hand, Candace pushed Bernie further into the estate that surrounded the school until they were round the back of the buildings where no windows overlooked.

'Get off me,' Bernie protested. 'Stop feeling me up like one of your girlfriends—'

Before she could finish, Candace punched her square in the face. Bernie squealed with shock. Candace dragged her further into the bushes and punched her again. Bernie let out a nervous laugh and tried to dodge her. But Candace pulled her to the floor by her ponytail. She kicked her in the stomach, and once in the face. Then she left her, a crying mess on the floor.

Candace walked away, panting, and into the tide of kids making their way to school. She strode through them one last time, heading in the opposite direction. She thought of Ms Gail. And Miss White. Of her artwork. And the coming fixtures. The gig. Fuck. The gig. A sob escaped from her as the flow of kids rushed past her towards the building.

Then Candace straightened up and kept walking.

2022

ARIANNA

Arianna's stomach was churning with nerves. The potential for this to go tits up in a myriad of awful ways was overriding any sense of excitement or promise of a tearful, joyous reunion.

She hadn't called Tess. It was petty, she knew, and not what Dana had wanted exactly, but Arianna reasoned that reuniting with Candace and her daughter was huge enough.

Also, Dana seemed determined to make this a surprise. So Arianna hadn't even told Candace what was happening. She had, of course, thought about the fact that springing Dana on Candace and Saffy was completely out of order, so Arianna had at least made sure Candace would be alone.

But Dana had insisted they go to the boat. Arianna assumed Dana wanted to see where Saffy had been living all this time, so she had agreed. Remembering Candace's reaction when she and Tess had turned up uninvited was making Arianna less and less sure of this plan. But she hoped that above all else, the fact that she was delivering Dana, alive and in the flesh, would trump everything. Dana might even finally sign the guardianship documents Candace was so desperate for, and Arianna would have been the one to make that happen. Not Tess.

Dana had been keen to get the address and details of their schedules so they could arrange it. Arianna hadn't seen her this organized and proactive in years. She suspected Dana also wanted to prove that she was more responsible now, more capable.

And now Arianna was at the boat. She had come early, fifteen minutes before Dana would arrive.

She heard voices and stopped dead. They were coming from Candace's boat. Loud ones. She stood outside on the pier, trying to listen to what was being said but she couldn't quite make it out. Her heart was thumping wildly. Saffy shouldn't be there.

She knocked, the door swung open and Candace ushered her inside. 'Are you listening to this?'

'To what?' Arianna asked, looking around the room. It was empty.

Candace went to the radio and turned it up. 'It's that teacher. Mr Whatsisname. The one you all fancied.'

Arianna's stomach sank, her vision went weird and she couldn't breathe properly. 'Who? Which one?'

'Mr Tamworth. The music guy. He's on the radio. Talking about our school.'

Arianna almost collapsed with relief. It wasn't him. They listened to the special programme on Radio 4 about the amount of famous musicians who had come out of their school. Jay Thomas and his band. The Garage Crew. The E.G.G. boys. And the interviewer wanted to know why the music teacher thought this was? What was so special about their regular comprehensive school that had produced such musical geniuses?

Mr Tamworth cleared his throat. 'Well, actually, the question we should be asking is why so many *more* haven't got the recognition they deserve. Tess Morgan's band for example. They were creating innovations in music, pushing the boundaries of genre when they were teenagers. Where are they now? What about her?'

It was the first thing he had said, in the whole interview. He'd put respect on her name first, above all others. Arianna shakily grabbed her phone out of her bag and called Tess's number.

She didn't answer, and Arianna didn't leave a message. Regret coursed through her. If only Tess had been here for this moment, if only they'd all been together, Dana included, for the moment Tess had finally got a fraction of the recognition she deserved. It was a small win, but it meant something to them all. They'd all watched the E.G.G. boys' astounding trajectory. They'd been elated that some of their own had Made It, from their little corner of the world. But it had also left a bitter taste, because why them? And why did they not only get the music deals, but why had John had an exhibition of his mediocre artwork in New York of all places? And who had given Luke a publishing deal for his children's books about the adventures of a patois-speaking gerbil? What about *her* writing dreams? What about Candace's artwork? What about Dana?

Dana.

Arianna looked at her watch. The fifteen minutes had passed. Any minute now Dana would appear.

'Tea?' Candace asked. 'Or shall we wait for Tess?'

'Tess isn't coming.'

'Who are we waiting for then?'

2022

TESS

She had over twenty missed calls. Mostly from Callum. Voice messages too. She didn't know where to start, so decided not to. She was suddenly and completely over it all. She had done enough, run around like a madwoman trying to bring everyone together, just like she had all those years ago, and it hadn't worked then either. She hadn't managed to keep one friend. And she'd failed again now. And she'd failed at a family and a home and a loving relationship. But there was one person she refused to fail: her daughter.

It was dark in the house. Tess closed the door quietly, climbed the stairs and looked in on Sinead. She was sleeping with her head to the side, her arms tucked under her and her bum in the air. She was awesome: the awesomest.

In the other bedroom a dark lump of a figure lay on his side of the bed. She could just make out his features in repose. There was a softness to him, no sign of the anger that tensed up his face in the daytime. She wished they could be like this; knew that what was required of her now was the opposite. She undressed and lay down beside him. It was over.

Tess turned to switch off her phone. A message. From Jay.

2022

ARIANNA

They waited. And waited. With every minute past the time Dana was meant to arrive, Arianna felt sicker. Candace refrained from asking questions. She didn't like surprises but had tolerated Arianna's mysterious hints about a meeting with a twist. But an hour in, Candace started to see the worry on Arianna's face turn into something darker.

'Er . . . it's just . . . Saff's coming back in a bit. So . . . ?'

'What time?' Arianna asked quietly.

Candace checked her phone. 'Well. Any moment. Three minutes ago, to be exact.'

Arianna tried to keep her voice steady.

'Does she have a phone?'

'Who? Saff?'

Arianna nodded.

'Why?'

'Can you call her?' she asked, even more quietly.

'What the fuck Arianna?' Candace's voice rose with growing alarm.

'Just call her. Please.'

Arianna could see Candace trying to breathe, keep calm. She called her daughter's number. It rang and rang.

And rang.

PART TWO

2001

TESS

'What about the girl in your French class?'

'Which one?'

'You said you did some coursework together.'

'Tara? She's into Take That.'

'Oh. Wasn't there someone who played the clarinet?'

'Lucy's friends with Arianna's new crowd. She was just polite. Once.'

'Who gave you the candle? For your birthday?'

'Dawn Jones? That was two years ago.'

'Still—'

'No. Just, no.'

He'd started a list, when he saw her crying first thing in the morning, again, of all the girls he could remember her mentioning in her year, who might want to be her friend. It was so pathetic. She couldn't bear it.

She showered, dressed, looking at her good bits (legs), despairing at her bad bits (still no boobs), ate a morose breakfast and then headed out.

She dreaded seeing her. It was the same every day, like bumping into your ex a hundred times a day, except there was no sympathy or friend to make you feel better and tell you what a wanker he was and that you were better off, because *she* was that friend and *she* was the one who'd broken up with you. There was no rebound sex either. There was no sex, full stop. Because she still looked like a fucking child.

'Tess! Wait up.' Daniel rushed away from his Oxbridge Terrorist gang and over to her with that hopeful/delighted expression on his face that made her insides feel weird. 'Hey.'

'Hey.'

'I was gonna ask you actually, if you've listened to the new Jamiroquai album?' he asked, self-consciously tossing his curtained hair.

'Er, yeah. I have.'

'I thought so,' he grinned. 'Yeah, cos I was just listening to it last night and I thought of you cos ... cos I knew you probably listened to it and I thought ... Was it ... What did you think?'

'Yeah, it's funky.'

'Funky, yeah. Yeah, I thought it was funky.'

'I like some of the jazz riffs and the bass lines.'

'... Bass lines, totally.' He nodded and gazed at her. 'Wicked. Yeah. Well, thanks for ... if you hear of any other good albums then ...'

'Yeah, sure,' Tess replied.

'Okay.'

'Okay.'

He walked back towards the terrorists. She walked on into the sixth form common room, alone.

There she was, wearing a Gap hoodie and blue boot-cut

jeans, laughing loudly at something one of the mousy-blonde girls had said. Kate? Katie? Or was that one Phoebe? From this distance she couldn't tell. She only allowed herself one glance, took her in in one go, was careful not to look up again. She found a seat separate from, but adjacent to, another group and plonked herself there, listening to their loud, confident voices travel across the room, to her old friend's new, unnatural cadence, discussing something vacuous at a decibel that everyone had to endure. Tess pulled an NME from the front pocket of her sax case and buried her face in it.

2001

ARIANNA

'I've already saved a grand and then I've got another two hundred coming in from Nana. So in six months I'll have close to two thou. And I'll get time and a half at Gap over Christmas,' Kate explained. Her mousy-blonde hair was styled in a Rachel cut, the oversized Gap sweatshirt falling perfectly over her petite frame.

'Is two thousand enough to buy a car?' Katie asked, her back turned to Arianna, her front leaning eagerly towards Kate.

'I only want something simple,' Kate admonished lightly, her green eyes twinkling. 'But Luke did say that he'll match whatever I save.'

'Ohmygod. He totally loves you,' Phoebe gushed.

'Shotgun on our first ride!' Katie shouted.

'Shotgun on the second ride!' Arianna added.

'Oi, oi.' They turned as Luke approached and placed his hands on Kate's slender shoulders. She lifted her chin up and they kissed as the others watched.

'I was just talking about you,' Kate twinkled.

'Were you now.'

'Yep. Apparently you're going halves on a broom-broom with me.'

The pips went. Luke put his arm around Kate and she let herself be led away. There was a silence as the three remaining girls watched her go. Phoebe started studying her timetable intently, avoiding eye contact with the others, while Katie stretched. 'Right,' she said to no one in particular, gathered her things and walked away.

Arianna hastily did the same.

'*Vite! Asseyez-vous.*' Arianna slunk into Ms McGee's A-Level French class. She clocked Tess without looking at her directly and sat far enough away, but not so far that it looked like she was making a point of it.

'Arianna – I mean, Tess, sorry. The pluperfect *s'il vous plait.*'

This happened at least once a week. They didn't even look that similar. Especially now that Arianna was wearing more understated, womanly clothes and Tess still insisted on looking like some sort of indie elf. It was awkward. They both managed a grim smile as they reddened. Then Tess began to conjugate.

2001

TESS

'At the end of the day, I don't think some random Belgian pol-
itician should be making key decisions about British policy.'

'Fair observation, James,' Mr Sebastian said. 'So, who
should be making decisions about British policy?'

'People we've elected to represent us.'

Mr Sebastian looked across the room. 'Lucy.'

'But we elected politicians who then voted for us to join
the EU, so we're part of a bigger elected body who also make
decisions in the interest of the EU as a whole—'

'But is it good for British business?' he pressed.

'To be able to do deals with the whole of Europe? Yes. To
be able to travel and work across Europe, to study and even
live in some of the most developed, progressive countries in
the world? Yep.'

Tess sat with the rest of her year who were seated in the
back half of the common room. The Year Aboves populated
the front half and dominated the debate, Mr Sebastian, the
head of sixth form, conducting it all. It was compulsory to
attend, every Wednesday after school, and even *she* didn't get
a pass for her music practice.

There was nothing she hated more than these useless fucking debates. They were as vacuous as the real things in those elite colleges of dusty learning that Mr Sebastian aspired for them all to attend after Sixth Form. Exercises in egotistical wit and intellectual parrying with absolutely no heart or passion, no care for the real human cost of the issues they so facilely debated.

'Harry.' He motioned to a student sat near the front.

'The Referendum Party's concern is that trade could be adversely affected. But it's also concerned with our identity being diluted and control over our own country being weakened. And the party's rapidly increasing popularity is testament to the fact that a lot of Brits feel the same.'

Tess could tell exactly who was desperate to be invited on The Trip. It happened every year. Mr Sebastian would choose an elite few who he deemed to show enough promise to have the chance at a place at Oxford or Cambridge and take them on a trip to those hallowed institutions before personally mentoring them through the application process. But she also knew who would be chosen. And it wasn't her. Or Arianna, despite being predicted to get straight As. It wasn't Joe or Andrew either.

'Fuck's sake,' Tess mumbled.

'Tess, do you have something to say?' Mr Sebastian glared at her. Heads turned. She froze, but then sat up straighter.

'It's not even that popular,' she said. 'It's just making a lot of noise and is funded by a billionaire who is chucking up adverts all over the place and stuffing propaganda down our throats. It's just money,' she exclaimed.

'I'm sorry, but there are legitimate concerns—'

'Yes, there are legitimate concerns,' Tess continued. 'Lots of them. Especially for small businesses and rural communities and workers' rights. But that billionaire isn't interested in any of that. He's just worried that he and his mates will have to finally answer for some of their dodgy business practices. And the truth is that even though the EU is far from perfect, the alternative is even more terrifying. Because at the moment it's the only thing that's protecting us from the far right in this country decimating our rights.'

Tess's face was hot. Her heart was beating fast. A snigger came from the side of the room and Tess turned to see the Kates laughing quietly. Arianna sat beside them, her eyes to the ground. Mr Sebastian was still looking at her. She waited for him to say something, but he turned to one of the white boys at the front.

'James.'

And just like that, Tess's impassioned contribution was dismissed. Tears of frustration prickled her eyes, but she clenched her jaw, fought them down and sat through the rest of the debate in silence.

2001

ARIANNA

'Concern for the workers ... rural communities ... Trotsky ... Lenin ... oppressed pixie-tie-dye-jazz ...' Phoebe exclaimed in a high-pitched voice.

It didn't sound anything like her, but Katie laughed anyway.

'She's so intense. Like all the time,' Phoebe said.

'Isn't her dad some kind of revolutionary?' Katie asked Arianna.

Arianna shrugged. 'Not really. He's just ... political.'

'I bet they just sit around at home discussing the downfall of capitalism,' Katie riffed. 'Like, what's for dinner? Thatcher's head. Can you read me a bedtime story? Sure, 1984. Chapter one ...'

'Why are you even in that band with her?' Phoebe turned back to Arianna.

Arianna shrugged again. 'Something to do. Looks good on the CV. I'll probably quit soon.'

Kate turned back to Phoebe. 'You're just jealous cos Daniel fancies her.'

'Ohmygod you two would be so perfect together,' Katie

gushed. 'Why is he wasting his time with that weird ...
pixie.'

'I don't even care,' Phoebe said.

'But it would be so perfect. Kate and Luke. You and Daniel.
Ohmygooood.'

'Shut UP, Katie. I don't even fancy him.'

'Yes you do,' Kate pushed. 'And you'd actually shag him.
I don't think Revolutionary Pixie Dust knows how to shag
people.'

'Pixies don't have the right holes.'

They cackled. Arianna tried to mirror their amusement.

TESS

Tess took the doobie from Bubs and inhaled. She passed it to Wesley as the three of them nodded thoughtfully to Bubs' latest vinyl acquisition: Goldie's *Timeless*. Tess absorbed every detail of the production, which seemed to intertwine with her gentle high, spiralling ever upwards and sending her mind in several directions at once as she began to form her own iterations, remixes, then fresh compositions, inhaling the specifics of this new broken beat, the layers of samples and the contrasting vocals; exhaling a fresh new take of her own. And yet, there was something familiar within it, bringing to mind Linton's deeper, darker dub records, the Sound System era he described so passionately, sped up, taken apart, and re-formed into this new musical evolution. To the others, she seemed to be nodding along, like them. But inside she was fizzing, analysing, improvising, composing.

The doorbell rang. Tess tried to hold on to the music in her head.

Arianna walked into the bedroom carrying her bass guitar case. She nodded appreciatively to the music and to them, but boredom was already visible in the corners of her features.

Wesley held out the zoot for her. She shook her head.

'I'm good thanks,' she replied.

Bubs was already at his keyboard switching through some sounds and trying to match it to Goldie's production. At the drumkit, Wesley was starting to emulate the complex beat of the record with impressive speed.

Arianna tuned her bass slightly inaccurately, which made Tess wince. Even worse, Arianna insisted on keep her nails ridiculously long now, and they tapped annoyingly on the frets as she played, making the notes fuzzy. She was a decent musician, Tess thought, could pick up a riff easily, but she never practised, and those fucking nails ... Tess hadn't realized how hard she'd been silently willing Arianna to tweak the A-string just that little bit more until Arianna frowned at her.

'Right,' Tess said and picked up her saxophone. 'Let's warm up with a couple of familiar ones, and then I reckon we get into something new.'

Tess led on the songs, bringing each instrument in at the right time. Both numbers sounded strong. They were a good band. Solid. But she felt a sadness and frustration bubbling beneath. She pushed forward into the new song, inspired by Goldie's sound.

They picked a few of Bub's synth sounds. She played the sax into the mic and added plenty of reverb, looped it. She sang some vocals in her high, haunting, young-sounding voice, trying not to cringe at the sound of it, and looped that too. Then she turned to Arianna. She played a simple bass line on her sax and Arianna translated it onto the strings. Then Wesley jumped in with a drum roll that segued into that complex, impossibly quick drum beat. Tess brought the reed to her mouth once again, adding a jazzy improvised melody.

They revelled in their new creation, Bubs adding new sounds to the bridge, the chorus, Wesley breaking it down in the middle eight, Arianna holding it all together with a simple riff. Tess conducted them to a slightly messy ending, and Wesley chucked his sticks in the air in celebration as Bubs played a Pull-Up horn on his synth. Even Arianna forgot herself for a moment, holding up two gun fingers in delight and glaring at Tess hard, a fierce old sparkle in her eye that Tess hardly ever saw anymore.

Tess beamed. 'Let's go again straight away, get this cemented.'

'So what's that, five tracks now?' Bubs did some maths on his fingers. 'That's pretty much a set. I reckon it's time.'

'You reckon?' Tess asked.

'Let's do it,' Wesley said.

Tess looked at Arianna.

'Yep, sure.' It was the best Tess was going to get from her, but they both knew that Arianna had been as lit up by their new song as any of them. So why did she seem so eternally bored?

'Okay,' Tess said. 'Let's book our first gig.'

They crowded onto the tiny balcony once more and Wesley lit up the doobie Arianna was already packing up.

'There's a night up in Central,' Bubs explained. 'Called MetalHeadz. All new sounds like this. We should go.'

'Goldie plays there?' Wesley asked.

'It's his night. He curates it. Him and all his crew.'

'I'd love to go.' Tess exclaimed.

Wesley and Bubs nodded. Tess looked over at Arianna. She kept her head down, busy zipping up her guitar case, then she straightened up, said 'See ya,' and left.

Tess's stomach sank, with sadness and also relief. She felt so silly and immature in Arianna's presence, like everything they talked about was dumb kid's stuff. At least now she could just be her immature kid self with these two pot-heads without being eternally judged. But part of her had left with her friend, was always with Arianna. Except now there was a mysterious part of her life that Tess could not follow her to. Not the vacuous half-friendships she had with those bimbos at school, but her weekend missions, the reason why Arianna was already halfway out the door before rehearsal had even started.

Tess sighed. 'Oi, play that jungle LP again.'

Bubs grinned, complied.

2001

ARIANNA

Arianna hurried along the street as quickly as she could, the bass weighing her down. She was sweating by the time she got home. She sprayed herself with the Dewberry perfume Kate, Katie and Phoebe had got her for Christmas, all four of them now smelling of the same sweet, fruity fragrance. She grabbed her overnight bag.

Her mum stood in bedroom doorway. 'There's food.'

'I'm eating out.'

'Where?'

'Candace's.'

'Don't be back late.'

'I told you, I'm staying the night.'

'Again?'

'Yes.' Arianna brushed past her, down the stairs and back out.

Waiting at the bus stop, she felt the weariness of the week descend. She was always tired. Always rushing.

She got off at the same stop as Dana's. The first time she'd taken this route again, she had sobbed when the familiar high-rise came into view. She even knew the window to look up at as she passed.

Where was she?

She'd never got to tell Dana about Mr M. They'd just disappeared, her and Candace hadn't shown up for school the next day, or the next. She never got to say sorry for the things she'd said that night, when she'd seen her kissing Chris. And now she didn't know where they were. Then all the drama happened with her being caught with Mr M, the headteacher getting involved and Mr M leaving the school and she'd had enough of her own worries.

Weeks had gone by, then months, and still they hadn't shown up. She and Tess had called their homes, but no one answered. Linton had come in to have a meeting with Miss White, to see if he could help, put pressure on the school to do more, but it hadn't led to anything, and by then, she and Tess weren't really talking any more.

Arianna headed up the hill. He hated her being late. Just like he hated her smelling of cigarettes or weed, wearing colourful nail polish or her hair up.

He buzzed her in. And there he was, leaning in the doorway of his new flat, a kitchen towel draped over one shoulder.

'Hey, sorry I'm late—' she began, but he pulled her to him, his tongue in her mouth before she'd crossed the threshold. He groped her body hungrily under her coat. His familiar adult smell and taste, the prize she had travelled here for, his desire for her elating, affirming, defining.

'I'll show you how you can make it up to me,' he murmured.

He led her through the hallway and she managed to drop her overnight bag in a corner without breaking stride. To her confusion, he walked them into the bathroom. 'Now you can show me how sorry you really are.'

Behind him, arranged around the sink, window ledge and the edge of the bath, were open magazines, showing pictures of naked women in a range of sexual positions being fucked by anonymous men. Arianna's frazzled mind rushed to catch up as Mr M stared at her expectantly. She blinked and fashioned her shocked expression into a cheeky grin. Then she began to peel off her clothes.

Each room had a different theme, something new they were to enact, prompted by the images in the many, many magazines displayed around his flat. The climax was in the living room, where a video played on the TV of something even more extreme than what had come before. By the end, Arianna felt nothing but the hot, stinging rawness in between her legs as she lay on the living room floor. She adjusted herself slightly and winced, her back also on fire from the open wound caused by the friction against the carpet.

'You're amazing,' he said huskily. 'You get me in a way no one else ever has. That was incredible. You're incredible.'

She found a position on her side which seemed the least painful and rested there, propped up sexily on one arm.

'I'm just so ... passionate,' he continued. 'I've got so much passion to share. And for the first time in my life, I've met my match.'

He took her free hand and kissed it.

'Next time it's your turn,' he said mysteriously.

She stiffened, tried to look intrigued rather than alarmed. She wasn't sure how she would manage any more.

'Next time?' she asked.

'I'm all yours. Whatever you desire.' He shifted closer until his face was inches from hers. 'Tell me your fantasy Arianna, and I'll make it come true.'

Arianna's exhausted mind went blank. She pushed herself to think of something as he waited expectantly. 'I've had such an amazing night, I don't think I could possibly want anything else.'

'Sure, but next time?' he pushed.

'Well . . .' she began, hoping something would come to her as she spoke. 'I guess I've always kind of liked the idea of . . . making love under the stars.'

Mr M's eyebrows rose.

'Like the two of us somewhere secluded, with a blanket, on some grass . . . just . . . fooling around . . .'

He smiled with amusement, then shook his head. 'So innocent. Bless you.'

Arianna frowned. 'What?'

'Nothing.'

'What's wrong with my fantasy?'

'It's just . . . a bit . . . basic.' Then he hauled himself up. 'Hungry?'

Was she hungry? She couldn't tell. She'd been starving on her way there, envious and desperate for some of the takeaway Wesley was ordering when she left. That must have been hours ago. Now, the burning sensation on her back and between her legs seemed to obliterate all other feeling.

She gritted her teeth as she got up and headed to the bathroom. She cleaned herself up as best she could and inspected the wound on her back. Then she grinned. It was kinda hot, she decided. Evidence of just how mad and hardcore her life was now. Better than any shitty night playing some bootleg computer game and eating egg fried rice with a bunch of teenage skunk heads.

'Let there be light,' his voice boomed from the booth looking down over the auditorium. Arianna shielded her eyes as the stage was illuminated from above. She was almost used to this routine now. He would nudge her awake on Saturday morning, painfully early, so they could have sex again before they got ready for his workshop. She often hadn't recovered from the night before, but her body had started to learn to bear it. Perhaps this was what true womanhood was.

He'd brought her a glass of water and reminded her to take her pill. She dutifully popped it into her mouth and washed it down in front of him. It was the least she could do. He'd been through so much for her, proven his love to her in a million ways. It was her gift to him, so that he didn't have to worry about condoms and they could be spontaneous, express their passion whenever and wherever they wanted.

Alan was the first to arrive. His loud, boisterous voice ricocheted off the dark walls as he strode into the theatre.

'Greetings, and salutations.' Alan saw Arianna on the stage and bowed deeply. Something passed between them. Now that people knew about her and Mr M, she'd noticed that she was looked at by men in a new way, the kind of way boys and teachers alike had looked at Dana. She was sure that she wasn't most people's type. Phoebe had explained how she and Kate were the kind of girls everyone fancied, but that Arianna was more of an Acquired Taste. Something she'd been told before. But she was having sex now, she was on the map, and their radar.

'Al, you foolish boy, come here.' Mr M appeared from the shadows and pulled his ex-student into an aggressive bear hug. The others arrived. Jim, Kevin, a tomboy called Sal – all older than Arianna by two or three years, all previous students of Mr M's who turned up every Saturday for his creative workshop. Alan and John, two of the Oxbridge Four, were the only ones from her year. Arianna had fallen into a strange, unspoken agreement with them both where they shared this extra-curricular experience, led by their former teacher, who kissed and touched Arianna possessively and openly in front of the group, but they practically ignored each other at school.

'Spread out. Move around. Limber up both body and voice,' Mr M projected. The chatter quietened and they fell to it, as if in a trance.

It was a mix of improvisation exercises, creative writing, performance and Krav Maga which always ended in a thoughtful reflection by Mr M illustrated by an anecdote about his life. Now that he had been liberated from his academic role, Mr M combined his many passions into this weekly offering and charged them a fiver each. Arianna insisted on paying too because she was a feminist. They adored him, these misfits, most of whom had been spat out into the real world too soon. He became someone they could attach themselves to as they attempted to navigate the wider world. He became their anchor.

TESS

Tess waited in the café a few streets from Sinead's school. She had put on make-up. So stupid of her. She looked old, out of shape, a flustered, middle-aged mum. She grimaced at the funky outfit she'd chosen, the way a couple of the mums had glanced at her battered old Dr. Martens at the school gate. What did she expect would happen? She'd launch herself into her new life, start an affair with Jay Fucking Thomas and become the rock star she was always meant to be but also an attentive full-time mum? Sure. Why not.

She had lain awake most of the night figuring out the rest of her life, so she looked extra old and tired today. But she'd made a plan: she would gather some money, get in touch with old connections, line up half a year's work – gigs, recordings, sessions, depping, anything – call in favours from neighbours and other mums and push for a fairer balance of childcare. She suspected Callum would be forced to do more looking after his own daughter if they were separated.

The house was in her name. When Linton died, she found out he'd bought their council flat. Despite his values and politics, he'd bought the flat when the offer was made in the

'80s and ensured his daughter was set for life. A year after he died, Tess had forced herself to sort through his things. She'd kept most of it. A year after that, she sold the flat and bought a house in the only area she could afford – the opposite corner of the city. She was already with Callum. It turned out he had savings, fifty grands worth, but he only mentioned that after the sale. So, he'd kept his savings intact, and she'd invested all of hers in the house they lived in.

And now, they hated each other. The last couple of years had cemented that. She'd thought, in that bizarre year where the whole world had stopped, when all the concerts and jobs had been cancelled, when they were forced to apply for financial help and stay at home, that they would at least be gifted some time to establish themselves as a family. Sinead had been so tiny then. Instead, it had been the loneliest time of her life.

Well, now it was her turn.

Linton had never met Callum, but she could imagine what the expression on his face would have been if he had: similar to when he'd met Daniel.

Daniel.

Tess tensed.

She'd already had to walk out of a newsagent's this morning when the song came on. She hoped she'd be able to get through a coffee here without upending the table. They were playing it everywhere.

She snapped out of her musing, realized she'd been mumbling to herself, looked up, and there was Jay.

2022

ARIANNA

Arianna let herself into her flat and rushed to her laptop, her ears still ringing with Candace's screams, her chest throbbing where Candace had hit her over and over, demanding to know where Saffy was, who had taken her, what she'd done. Arianna had explained that she'd met Dana, agreed for them all to meet, given her Candace's address. She'd called Dana's number over and over while Candace did the same with Saffy's. Dana's was already disconnected. And Saffy's continued to ring and ring.

Arianna wanted to call the police, but Candace laughed bitterly in her face. 'And say what? That her mum kidnapped her own child? I've got no rights, Arianna. None. I'm not her mum. I'm nothing to them – to anyone. There's no one to call.'

Her journey home had started with her begging a Higher Power she'd only just started to believe in to make this better. Bargaining, making promises, if only Saffy would come home. Then the horror at the part she had played in this, in Dana taking Saffy from Candace. She felt herself start to go numb, to check out. But then, as she walked, the Recovery kicked in, the years of New Behaviour she'd practised to re-learn how to be in the world, to break old patterns in-grained from a lifetime in her own family, from years of being used, by him.

She'd wanted an acknowledgement so badly. For so long she'd wanted someone to say Sorry, to name the things they had done to her, and to Make Amends. She had also come to accept that that wasn't likely to ever happen.

But now *she* had fucked up. *She* had hurt someone.

And now *she* would make amends.

2022

CANDACE

Candace called Saffy's number for the hundredth time. As it rang and rang, she pulled open the front door and stood searching the embankment for her daughter. Her neighbours stood in the doorways of their boats. She realized they must have heard the shouts and screams, must have watched as she threw Arianna out and slammed the door. She turned to them. 'She's gone. Saffy's gone.'

Within minutes, Stu was patrolling the north side with his dog; Leah and her partner heading south. Candace rushed between the giant, dark warehouses, calling Saffy's number over and over.

As another call went unanswered, she spun around in frustration.

That's when she saw someone duck behind the far building.

Candace pelted towards them. She heard their footsteps echo around the empty buildings, but Candace was strong and fast, after all the years of sports she had done as a girl. And soon she was gaining on him and, with every last bit of strength she had, she jumped on him and dragged him to the ground.

'What the fuck have you done with her?' she screamed. 'Where is she?'

He was lying with his face to the ground. Candace hauled him over. He held his hands up over his face, but he didn't fight back. She stopped hitting him long enough to move his arms and found herself staring into a face so familiar it took her breath away.

'It's okay,' she heard him say, as Nathan sat up and put his arms around his little sister.

2001

TESS

'So, we'll confirm the date, get some rehearsal spots booked in. I'll reserve the minibus, then we can get Ms Gail to mock up some flyers,' Mr Tamworth said.

'Would you be able to ... could you ... do all that?'

'It would be an honour,' he beamed. 'They'll be lucky to host your debut gig, Tess. I have an inkling they and you might look back on this as a bit of a moment.'

Tess burst out of the music department, buzzing. As she entered the sixth form common room, Kate, Katie and Phoebe looked up from their huddle. Tess locked eyes with them, then changed course, veering towards a table and picking up a newspaper instead. She counted to ten, then put it down. Tess stopped herself from searching for Arianna. She would have to wait until French and tell her then.

'There you are!'

Tess spun around.

Daniel strode over, grinning awkwardly.

'I was meaning to ... Basically I was messing about this weekend and I made a thing ...' He rummaged around in his schoolbag and pulled out a cassette tape. He handed it to her, nervously.

'What's this?' On the front of the plastic case he had written 'For Tess' in graffiti style writing and neon pens. On the back was a list of tracks.

'A mix tape?' she asked.

'You've probably heard most of them already . . .' he trailed off uncertainly.

'Thanks. This is . . . really nice.' She smiled despite herself. His shoulders lowered with relief.

'Good. Great. Well . . . enjoy.'

Daniel swept his sandy-coloured curtains out of his face and did his backwards walking, only turning away from her at the very last moment. Tess turned to find Phoebe glaring at her from across the room.

Tess strode home, realizing that the first person she'd get to tell was Linton, laughing because she knew exactly the proud expression that would break across his face. The lights turned red. She crossed. Mid-way she let out a squeak as she looked at the man passing her.

He looked up, an easy smile spreading as he recognized her. 'Tess, right?'

'Chris? Oh my god.'

He looked exactly the same, but different. Still that easy way about him, warm, kind, boyish. His voice was deeper and he had tufts of curly hair growing under his lip and on his chin. He asked about Arianna of course. She told him she'd got As in her GCSEs. Even some A stars. He chuckled

with pride, nodded, like he hadn't expected any less. Then
Tess asked him if he still saw anyone from school.

Chris asked her if she remembered Dana.

And Candace.

Because he'd seen them in Balham last week.

Tears sprung to her eyes. She demanded he tell her where
exactly he'd seen them, what they'd said, how they looked.

Chris told her everything he knew. And he told her about
the pager. His cousin's old work pager that he'd given to Dana
before they'd run. He'd made her promise to keep it with her.
Then he wrote down the number on Tess's arm.

Now she sat in the living room dialling the number on the
landline, Linton watching quietly beside her.

'Hello, Anthony Parris's pager. Your message please.'

'Hello, um, please could you say, Dana this is Tess, call me.'
She recited her phone number. 'End of message.'

ARIANNA

Arianna stared at her protruding belly in the mirror. It looked bloated, bizarre, a roundness to the underside of her chin that had never been there before. She looked closely at the angry red spots pushing out from under her skin around the edges of her face and she applied more concealer until they were pasty beige lumps. Then she headed downstairs.

'Come and eat breakfast *kori*,' her mum called from the kitchen.

'Not hungry,' she called back.

'Wait!' Lelia pleaded as Arianna slammed the front door.

Arianna strode down the street and soon heard Lelia's footsteps behind her.

'Why didn't you wait for me?' she asked breathlessly.

'You know the way,' Arianna shot back. Lelia fell into silent step. They stayed that way until they arrived at the bus stop, then Lelia rushed ahead to her group of friends and soon the giggles started.

Arianna watched her younger sister's easy fun with envy. Lelia was different with them, the centre of the banter. She hadn't realized she was so funny and fun. Arianna couldn't remember the last time she'd shared a laugh with a friend. She suddenly longed for it so urgently, it was a physical pain. She had to look away.

Phoebe took a large, hungry bite of her sandwich. Katie placed a Granny Smith on the table. Kate took out a series of pills and swallowed them, one by one, allowing herself a sip of water. Phoebe's chewing slowed, then stopped. She put down the rest of her sandwich guiltily. Arianna's lunch space remained empty. She, too, looked demurely down.

'Arianna!' She looked up to find Lelia's friend Maya rushing towards her, her face full of fear.

'What's wrong? Where's Lelia?' Arianna demanded immediately.

'Tanya Price pushed her into the wall for no reason. She didn't even—'

'Where is she?'

Maya led her to the lower foyer toilets where Lelia was with two friends, sniffing and wiping away tears.

Without saying a word, Arianna spun around and walked back through the crowded foyer until she spotted Tanya. Arianna shoved her into the wall and held her there.

'Touch my sister again and I'll fuck you up. You understand?'

'Get off me!' Tanya protested.

'Do you understand?'

Tanya nodded. Arianna held on a moment longer, then let go and walked away, heart pounding.

By the end of the day, Lelia was laughing again. Arianna

followed her and her friends as they walked down the hill after school. Arianna had started walking too, instead of taking the bus, for the exercise mostly, hoping she could shed some of the weight she had gained. She'd never been this big, this spotty, this emotional.

At the bottom of the hill, Mr M was standing on the corner of the high street, twiddling a rose between his fingers, watching her. Arianna looked fearfully at her sister, but Lelia was too engrossed in her friends to notice. Arianna waited until they turned the corner before she approached Mr M.

'What are you doing here?' she asked.

He pulled her to him and kissed her hungrily. She looked around with alarm at the passers-by when he finally released her. Mercifully, none of them were her mum. He still had an arm firmly around her waist and was pressing the rose into her hand. She stepped back, feigning surprise and delight, and managed to free herself.

'I knew you'd be missing me, so I thought I'd surprise you,' he grinned. He held out a hand.

She hesitated. 'I don't think ... I mean ... someone might see ...' she tried.

Mr M hardened. 'What are they going to do? Fire me? Oops, that already happened. I am free of those archaic rules and regulations. We are free to express our love openly now.'

'But the school might ...'

'Might what?'

'Or my mum ...' she begged.

'Are you ashamed of me, Arianna?'

'No! Of course not. It's just ... I'm on my period and I'm

feeling really . . . shit at the moment and I've got band practice in a bit—'

'Hey, hey. Come here.' He stepped closer. 'You're beautiful. You make me hard just standing there.' He took her hand and pressed it against his erection. She looked around again desperately. 'And you keep forgetting, I'm a man. I don't care if you're on your period. I can handle it.'

Arianna took a few steps down the side street, desperate to get off the main road, pretending she was trying not to cry. 'I'm just a walking hormone at the moment. I mean, why so much blood for one miniscule egg you can't even see with the human eye?' she quipped.

He looked at her then with pity.

She frowned. 'What?'

He sighed. 'It's not just the egg, Arianna. It's the whole lining of your womb that is shed during ovulation. That's the reason for "all the blood".'

'It was a joke.'

She hated it when he did that. Reminded her of how young she was. Anger coursed through her suddenly. What the fuck was he doing anyway? Why did he suddenly show up and start snogging her on the street? Exactly like he'd done the week before the headteacher had quietly asked him to leave? He'd seen Mr Austen across the road, she was sure. And he'd turned and grabbed her face, kissed her, on purpose. When she'd pulled away, Mr Austen had been staring at them. Then Mr M had grabbed her and they'd run. He had been elated, buzzing from the controversy. And hard.

And then she'd been invited into Miss White's office to

talk. Just to check in and see how she was. If there was anything she wanted to talk about. Anything at all. Arianna's
heart had been beating wildly; she knew exactly why she was
there. The shame. And the elation.

And then Mr M had cornered her on the stairwell to tell
her he'd been asked to leave. He had lost his job. Because of
her. He told her he was going to leave his wife and they could
be together, properly. It was such a huge sacrifice. All for
her. She had gone home that night and lain in bed, her mind
whirling, and wondered how she'd ever make it up to him.

'I love it when you get angry,' he said now.

She let him lead her down the street, to the side door of
the youth theatre where he ran his Saturday workshops. He
unlocked it and led her up into the sound booth. She was
so relieved that they were off the street that she let him pull
down her jeans and bend her over the sound desk, a blob of
blood falling onto the carpet below.

2001

TESS

Arianna was late. Again. Tess's face prickled with angry tears. Why was she like this? It was so fucking rude. So unprofessional.

Wesley and Bubs looked on nervously.

'Right, let's just ... start,' she decided.

The doorbell rang.

Arianna burst in and looked straight at Tess. 'Sorry,' she said. 'Sorry,' and looked down, hurrying to get her bass out. She looked flustered at least: actually sorry.

'Now that we're all here I can finally tell you,' Tess began. 'It's been confirmed. We're playing The Half Moon. Two weeks from today.'

'Oh, shit,' Wesley gasped.

'For real?' Bubs asked.

Arianna looked up from her tuning. 'Wicked,' she said huskily.

Tess softened.

They were all stoked. Elated. Bricking it. But only Arianna really understood what this meant. She'd been at the gig when Jay's band had played, almost two years ago. She'd been there at the original band rehearsals with Candace and Dana, at Kensington Market when they'd had their makeovers, the build up to their first gig which had never happened because their two best friends had disappeared a few days before. And now they had a band again, and a gig. And Dana and Candace's absence was felt harder than ever.

It was the best rehearsal so far, the promise of something concrete to work towards made all the difference. They worked through their repertoire and then on a funked-up re-mix of Herbie Hancock's Cantaloupe Island. Arianna stayed a whole twenty minutes extra, experimented with some slap bass, which they decided to keep. It was the first time in a long time Tess had seen that mischievous, creative spark in her ex-friend's eyes. But then her face darkened and she started packing up. She was going to rush off. Again. And again, Tess wouldn't get to tell her about Chris and Dana and Candace and the pager. Because Arianna always had one foot out the door.

'We're gonna have to put some extra rehearsal hours in,' Tess said loudly.

Tess saw Arianna roll her eyes.

'You could actually be a decent bassist if you practised a bit,' Tess blurted out. 'And cut your nails for god's sake.'

Arianna paused, then finished packing up and left quietly.

Tess stumbled into the flat at eleven, buzzing, high, after another sesh with the boys. She closed the door quietly, shushing herself as she pulled off her DMs. Linton's shoes were missing.

'Magwitch? Are you there?' she called.

Silence. He was out. Probably with The German.

Tess clomped into the living room and switched on the light. She checked the notepad by the phone. No messages. No return call from Dana. The answering machine remained dark. Tess sighed. It cost almost five quid to leave a message on that pager. She picked up the receiver and dialled the number once more.

'Call Tess,' she said, reciting her phone number again.

Tess switched off the light and stumbled up the stairs, but she was too awake. She wasn't ready to call it. She grabbed her Walkman, put the headphones on and pressed Play. 'My Favourite Game' by the Cardigans played followed by the Cranberries and then 'I Am the Walrus' kookoo-kachooed in her ears. She giggled and opened the folded sleeve of the cassette cover where Daniel had written out the nonsensical lyrics in tiny letters. At the bottom was his number.

Tess leaped up from her bed and headed back downstairs. In the dark, she dialled.

'Hello, sorry, is Daniel there please?'

2022

ARIANNA

Arianna went back through the messages Dana had sent her, analysing every word of her emails, then her socials. Dana had left her the same message on Facebook, Instagram and Twitter, and though she'd signed off with her name, her handle read *The Doe's Ear* and her icon was of something obscure. An illustration of a rose, with some writing at the centre. It didn't take long for Arianna to find the reference. 'The Sick Rose' by William Blake. Arianna felt a pang of sympathy. But no, there was no excuse for what Dana had done, however sick or desperate she was.

She scrolled down, reading recent posts about *Making Amends*. Step Nine. Arianna felt sick. Dana had contacted her to ask for forgiveness. She'd sent Chris the letter detailing all her mistakes, her shortcomings. Did she really believe that taking Saffy from Candace was some sort of amends? For what? Not being there for Saffy all those years? It was so twisted and selfish. This was not what amends was meant to be.

She scrolled further, more poetry. This time Rumi followed by a bible quote:

'Very truly I tell you, no one can see the kingdom of God unless they are born again.' – John 3:3

And then a series of articles on Covid, on Government Lies and Vaccines, on how to live Outside the System, on Censorship and MeToo Madness and Men's Rights and Climate Fraud ...

'For we do not wrestle against flesh and blood, but against the rulers, against the authorities, against the powers over this present darkness.' – Ephesians 6:12

Then a picture of a cross: a tattoo – huge and thick and dark, along a forearm. Bumpy, uneven, hairy skin. Not Dana's.

And then more poetry. Poetry Arianna knew off by heart. Her vision blurred. She was exhausted. The images and words swam around her frazzled mind and she pulled the screen shut.

2022

CANDACE

Candace sat looking into her brother's face. His hairline had receded, his eyes were edged with fine lines, but they were alert and they watched her closely. When he'd held her, she felt a bulk to him that was new. Not the wiry, restless frame of his youth, but something softer. He leaned forward in his chair, in her home – her brother, in her home – concern etched on his face.

'We're gonna get her back,' he said. 'End of.'

Conflicting emotions coursed through Candace. How dare he rock up suddenly out of nowhere after all these years and talk about 'we', talk about 'getting her back' like he knew who she was, what they'd been through. How could she trust him in any way? But also, who else did she have? Who else understood that they couldn't involve the police? How desperately helpless was she right now? And how much did she long to believe him, to let him in, to have him back, to not do this alone?

'How long have you been watching us?' she demanded.

'A while,' he replied. 'On and off. Just checking in on you.'

'That's weird,' she said.

'It's all I knew to do,' he explained. 'I wanted to make sure you were okay, but I didn't think I'd get much of a reception so, I just rocked up when I could. Kept an eye on things, but kept my distance, let you be.'

Candace stared hard at him. 'Were you scouting the joint? Waiting to break in, jack some valuables?'

He winced. 'Nah, it's not like that. I'm not like that anymore.'

'Did you have something to do with her being taken?' Candace asked. 'Do you know where she is?'

'I wish I did. I wish I'd been there when … But I got here too late.'

He looked at her. And she knew he was telling the truth. She saw the change in him. The fight was gone, the speed with which he used to turn to destruction. Something had calmed in him. He'd paid a price; she had no idea how many years he'd been in and out of prison, she didn't want to know, or how he'd broken that cycle. Only that he was looking at her now like he really saw her, like he wanted to be there for her, like he meant it.

'I didn't give birth to her,' Candace explained. 'But she's my daughter. When she was little, she—'

Nathan held a hand up. 'I know. You don't have to …'

Candace stopped, relieved. He'd seen Saffy, knew exactly who she looked like. And he knew *her* better than anyone in the world.

'How did you find me?' she asked.

'I have my ways,' he said mysteriously. But seeing the panic on her face, he added: 'Warren. It was Warren.'

'I've got to get her back,' Candace sobbed. 'I need her home.'

2001

TESS

Tess walked past the neat, terraced houses overlooking the common, her strides lighter without her sax or violin case slung over her shoulder. She looked down at the black and white mosaics patterning the walks through the front gardens from the gates to the doors. The bay windows beside them and the two levels above, the loft extensions, all looking out to the greenery across the road. Tess vowed to one day have a house of her own, just like these ones. Fill it with a family of her own. Listen to her children clomp up and down the stairs. Her very own tribe. Wake up to greenery filling her eyes, rather than the smell of piss and bleach. To have walls thick enough not to hear the neighbours. A garden.

She turned into Number 34. It had a nice gate. A swirly one. The front garden had a rose bush in it and the door was cherry red. She rang the bell and suddenly blushed with nerves. The door swung open and Dan's equally flushed face greeted Tess.

'Hello,' he said self-consciously.

'Hi.'

'Would you like to come in?'

She stepped into a nice hallway with floorboards. A woman appeared from a room beyond the stairs, smiling. She wore sensible jeans and a green jumper that matched her eyes. Her straight, sandy-coloured hair was cut neatly in a bob and she had tiny turquoise stone studs in her ears. Tess's stomach fluttered with longing.

'Mum, this is Tess. Tess this is my mum, Sue,' Dan gestured from one woman to the other.

'Hi Tess. I've heard lots about you. It's nice to finally meet you,' she said warmly.

Tess's face flushed again. 'Thank you. Nice to meet you.'

'Daniel tells me you play violin?'

'Yes.'

'And you're in an orchestra?'

'It's like, one for students, so it's not a proper one or anything. But we do concerts.'

'That's fantastic.' Sue smiled at Tess. 'I'll leave you to it,' she said, and turned back into the recesses of the house.

'Okay, well, shall we ... would you like to ... come up?' Dan gestured awkwardly.

'Sure,' Tess replied, although she felt a strong urge to head the same way Sue had just disappeared, to stay in her presence a little longer.

At the top of the house, Dan pushed open the door to his room. Two big windows let in plenty of daylight, despite the grey sky. It was painted a greyish blue with a neat display of football posters on one wall and a Sade poster above his bed. In the corner was a table with black turntables on it, two speakers either side and a plastic box underneath it, holding a few vinyl records.

Dan stood in the middle of the room watching Tess. She walked to a window. It overlooked a garden, covered in grass and edged with plants. She could see Sue sitting there with a book, her bare feet crossed at the ankles, sipping from a mug.

Tess turned back in.

'That's Sade,' she said, pointing to the poster.

Dan nodded. 'Yep.'

'Are those yours?' Tess pointed to the turntables in the corner.

'Yeah. I got them for my birthday.'

They were expensive, almost professional standard. She squatted down by the modest record collection, sifted through it and picked one. He gently took the record and placed it on the turntable. He lined up the needle and pressed a button that brought it down gradually onto the record. Linton's old sound system had no such button. There was a loud scratch whenever he manually placed the needle down, before it settled into the grooves and the sounds of Burning Spear, Nina Simone or Little Richard played through the quiet crackling of the vintage vinyl.

Through Daniel's state-of-the-art speakers came the sound of Ms Dynamite's 'Booo!' Tess raised her eyebrows. The garage beat kicked in over the vocals and Dan bounced up and down, not quite on the beat.

'I just bought it yesterday,' he said.

He placed one side of his headphones over his ear, the other just off it. With a flourish he pulled out another record and placed it on the neighbouring turntable. Then he clenched his jaw and began to fade in the new track. There was a jarring few seconds where two beats and voices played simultaneously through the speakers, and then the track segued into a much slower beat, Cypress Hill's high-pitched bars replacing Ms Dynamite's London flow. Tess re-arranged her face from a grimace into a smile and tried to nod along.

Tess was relieved to see him put down the headphones.

'I'll just let the album play,' he said with a shrug.

They sat on his bed and nodded to the music. He lifted one hand up to Tess's hair, stroking it. As 'Insane in The Brain' segued into 'Hits from The Bong', Daniel leaned over and kissed her.

ARIANNA

Arianna's stomach growled loudly as she walked through the school gates with Katie, Kate and Phoebe. She had been experimenting with how long she could get through the day before having her Slimfast. She'd managed two o'clock yesterday. And on Sunday she'd managed to get to 4 p.m. But still her stomach protruded unnaturally, the acne inching from the edges of her face to her cheeks, and the last two mornings she'd woken up and immediately burst into tears.

Katie suddenly put both arms out, stopping the group in their tracks. She was staring, wide-eyed, ahead of her. Tess walked into the Sixth Form building with Dan, his arm draped over her shoulder.

'You're fucking kidding me,' Phoebe exclaimed.

They turned to Arianna as if she would have some kind of explanation. Arianna fought through her astonishment and managed a shrug.

She followed the girls in as they chatted animatedly about this new development, Phoebe suggesting bitterly that Kate might have a new bestie now that Luke's mate was going out with Tess. Arianna's mind whirred. She'd had no idea.

She was almost angry at Tess for not telling her. But then she thought about everything she hadn't told Tess, thought back to the last time they'd seen each other, Arianna rushing in late to rehearsal, leaving quickly, Tess's harsh words. She looked down at her fingernails, freshly filed now, the callouses on the tips of her fingers smarting at the extra practise she'd put in over the weekend after time with Mr M.

They sat apart, as usual. But Arianna watched Tess surreptitiously, looking for a change in her. Was her head held a little higher? Did she move and sit and walk with more assurance? Had she actually had sex? She desperately wanted Dana and Candace to be there. For the four of them to congregate to welcome Tess into Womanhood and also get every last gory detail out of her. Dana would do that bit. Candace would question Daniel's prospects, character and general worthiness, and they'd all revel in it, dissect it, and shriek with joyful laughter at this new milestone as if it were their own.

'What is it you actually do in the band?' Kate asked, placing her books and pencil case on the desk next to Arianna in the next lesson.

'Mostly bass. Bit of vocals,' Arianna replied.

Kate looked perplexed. 'And you meet every week to practise?'

'Yeah. Fridays.'

'With Tess?'

'And the rest of the band. I head off as quick as I can,' Arianna explained.

'So, you don't really hang out with her then?'

'No,' Arianna grimaced.

'Did you know about her and Dan?'

Arianna shook her head.

'I guess he'll be going to watch her play,' she mused, joining the dots, knowing that Luke and the rest of the lads would go too. It baffled Arianna that anyone was into those floppy haired, posh Oxbridge wannabes, but now apparently both her new and old friends thought they were boyfriend material.

'A gig,' Kate mused. 'Should be fun.'

Arianna felt a wave of gratitude. If Kate was coming, Katie and Phoebe would come too. She reached out and hugged Kate spontaneously. She felt so much bonier than Arianna expected. It was the first time they'd touched each other, exchanged any kind of gesture of friendship. It was awkward.

'I just don't get it,' Phoebe exclaimed, again, as they sat together at lunchtime. 'Like, what does he see in her?'

'And what does he think's gonna happen? They're not actually going to have sex ever, so what's the point?' Katie added.

Arianna was already getting tired of the relentless dissection of her old friend, but she held her tongue. Kate also held her tongue, but she allowed herself a smirk, making it clear she approved, despite being above it all at the same time.

'It'd be like fucking a frigid, half-caste troll,' Phoebe suddenly announced. All three of them shrieked with laughter. It was loud enough to make several people, including Tess, turn around from the other end of the common room.

Arianna stood, suddenly appalled, and headed to the toilets, slamming the cubicle door. She sat with her head in her hands and tried to breathe. Silent sobs burst out of her for the third time that day. Then, even though it was only one-thirty, she glugged down the entire can of strawberry flavoured diet shake.

She remembered with a jolt that she hadn't taken her pill that morning. Waves of panic coursed through her. Her head was all over the place, her body, skin erupting uncontrollably.

It had been just over five months since she'd gone to the doctors, alone, making sure to book with someone at the practice whose name she didn't recognize. A man, so that he might be a bit awkward about it and just get on with prescribing it for her. He'd asked if she was in a committed relationship. She had answered Yes. He'd asked if she had an adult that she could talk to. She'd said there was a teacher she was close to. He looked at her a moment longer, and then typed up the prescription.

Mr M had been through so much for her. All he asked was that they be able to be spontaneous with their passion. It was the least she could do.

Arianna rushed home and up to her room after school. She opened the drawer and rummaged through her socks until she found the bundle that hid her contraceptive pill. She popped one out and swallowed it.

One knock and her mum pushed open the door. Arianna shoved the pills back in the drawer.

'Fuck's sake. Wait till I tell you to come in. I could be naked.'

Her mum glared back. 'You haven't eaten.'

'Yes, I have.'

'Are you hungry?'

'No. I just ate.'

She remained standing in the doorway. 'Lelia and Maya will look after Theo. I will come with Sandrine.'

Arianna looked up. 'To the gig?'

Her mum nodded.

Arianna softened. 'What about Dad?'

Her mum shrugged.

'I guess I'll be cancelling my Krav Maga session then,' Mr M announced.

'You don't have to do that.'

'I should be averaging four to five a week, really.' He sighed. 'But for you, anything.'

'Really, it's just a stupid gig. To be honest, I'm kind of dreading it.'

They were both surprised when her voice broke on the final word.

She'd never looked so bad. Her skin had been fully taken over by angry red pustules that multiplied every time she inspected her face. She'd developed a double chin and now her bum was expanding at the same rate as her gut. The thought of being on stage in front of everyone she knew made her feel sick. And she couldn't stop crying all the time.

'Hey, hey. Look at me.' Mr M put a finger on her chin and raised her blotchy face to his. 'I don't care how mediocre it is, okay? You think I got this good at all that I do without lots of trial and error? Of course not.'

'It's just—'

'Don't worry. I'll do a double sesh at the weekend.'

'No, but my mum—'

'Shh. I want to do this. For you.'

Arianna nodded.

'There she is. Our very own pop star.' Dad rose from the sofa.

Arianna looked over his shoulder as he hugged her, as her mum, who remained sitting quietly, watched them. He held her at arms-length.

'Wouldn't miss it for the world,' he said. 'How about lunch, just you and me?'

'Ah, I just got back. I've got a few things—'

'Ah, come on. Come and have a fry up with your old dad.'

They headed out together, down the street to her dad's favourite café. Ordered two of the same set meal.

'Three hours I was delayed.' He shook his head, staring into the middle distance. 'Then it was gridlocked all down the M11. I couldn't even get a sarnie or have a piss. I reckon I'll do the M1 next time, see if I can at least get somewhere dry before dark.'

He took a sip of his tea.

'I'm gonna sing a song. At the gig,' Arianna tried.

'Oh yeah?' he looked at her, his eyes settling on her for a precious moment.

'It's only a cover, but if it goes well, we might include a few more next time.'

'You still doing good in English?'

'Yep.'

'Good girl.' His eyes drifted to the middle distance again. 'Cos I wouldn't recommend this life on the road. Not everyone can hack it.'

Arianna sighed quietly. 'I better get going,' she said.

'Yep, okay.' He screwed up his face, patted his jacket pocket. 'You haven't got any cash on you, do you? It's just . . .'

Arianna paid the bill.

That night she dreamed it again. Of cooking on a cooker just like Yiayia's. A pot or pan on each hob. The grill above alight too. The oven below roasting. She tried to alternate between each, stirring and turning and flipping. But she couldn't keep up and she heard the crackle of something burning. Now acrid smoke escaped from one of the pans. Another caught fire. She rushed to put it out, just as the grill also burst into flames. Arianna threw water on it all only to have the fire roar angrily as if she'd thrown petrol on it. The flames engulfed her. She jolted awake.

TESS

Tess felt a wave of excitement before she'd even opened her eyes. She beamed at her ceiling of music heroes in ripped jeans and black leather, smouldering down at her.

She stepped into the mouth-watering smell of ackee and saltfish and some morning Miles Davis. Linton had his cooking apron on. In another pan, two fried eggs crackled.

'What's all this?' Tess exclaimed.

'Special breakfast for a special day,' he declared.

Dan was waiting for her at the corner as he had done every morning since they'd become official. Tess found it a bit cringey. The way he kissed her on the lips right there on the street, putting an arm around her and then walking like that all the way to school even though their strides were completely different, making an irregular rhythm that seemed to start Tess's day off on the wrong foot, literally. But today she skipped up to him and experimented with a peck on the lips. He was surprised, delighted.

Today she was untouchable. The glare of the Mousy Blondes washed off her. She bounced to the centre of the common room, right up to the invisible line between her year's territory and the Year Above's. Damion and Jay turned to her and smiled.

'Looking forward to tonight?' Jay asked.

'Yep,' Tess replied.

'Let us know if you need a hand loading the van or setting up,' Damion added. 'We can head over a bit earlier if you like.'

Tess felt an arm snake around her waist and turned to see Daniel standing beside her.

'Safe.' He nodded to Damion and Jay.

'Safe.'

Dan looked at Tess. 'Shall we . . .'

'Sure.'

Dan led Tess out of the common room. Tess saw Arianna ducking into the toilets. She disentangled herself from Dan and followed her in, just as the door to a cubicle closed and locked.

'Arianna?' Tess called.

There was a pause, then Arianna opened the door.

'Hey,' Tess said.

'Hey.'

'You okay?'

'Yep.'

'Cool. Um, I was just wondering what you're going to wear tonight?' Tess asked. Arianna's face dropped. Then she rallied in that sharp way she did, focusing intently on the task at hand. 'I was thinking baggy, flared jeans with a rip and then my purple vest? I've got those platform boots from Camden market too . . .'

'That sounds wicked.' Tess said.

'You?'

'DMs, that skirt from Ken Market, and I thought my Nirvana T-shirt might be cool ...'

'You could tie up the bottom. Make it ... sexy.'

Tess giggled. 'Yep. Sexy.'

Arianna giggled too. It came out in a rush of relief. It was only then Tess realized how close Arianna had been to crying.

Tess frowned with concern. 'You sure you're okay?'

'Yep. Yes.' Arianna's focus hardened. 'So. Dan,' she said.

Tess blushed. 'Oh yeah. It's not ... I mean ... we've only just ... It's quite new so ...'

'That's wicked.' Arianna said, kindly.

'Yeah?' A wave of gratitude coursed through Tess. She longed to tell Arianna everything, the way she would have if Candace and Dana were here too. But there seemed to be a huge chasm between them even now. Arianna seemed so far away, despite Tess being able to reach out and touch her. Before she knew it, Tess's eyes had welled up.

'Sorry,' Tess said, backing out of the toilets. 'Thank you. See you after school, yeah?'

Tess wiped angrily at her eyes and took several deep breaths as the toilet door shut behind her. When she looked up, Phoebe stood glaring at her a few metres away. Tess turned in the other direction. It was all so fucking stupid and exhausting.

The day passed in a blur of nerves and excitement. Tess's mind was full of the set list and the musical arrangements, the riffs and melodies. And then they were loading up the minibus with Mr Tamworth, Jay and Damion, even Arianna mucked in. She looked lighter, happier.

They picked up Bubs and Wesley along the way. And then they were unloading and setting up and Mr Tamworth was orchestrating the sound check and Tess was asking for more sax in the monitor and they were running through the opening number.

Tess and Arianna headed to the toilets to change and do their hair and make-up. Arianna tugged at her top with frustration.

'You look great,' Tess tried.

Arianna grimaced. 'Thanks, but I don't,' she said bluntly. '*You* look great.'

Tess shook her head, looked at her tiny, bee-sting boobs in the mirror. They fell into silence. There was so much to say, and this wasn't the time.

Eventually Arianna sighed, not so much ready as giving up. 'Shall we?'

Tess nodded.

The band looked out from backstage onto a sea of familiar faces. Dan, Luke, Alan and John. Kate, Katie, Phoebe. Mr Tamworth and so many other teachers. Linton and The German. Arianna's mum and French auntie. Even her dad. Dan's mum. Pretty much the whole sixth form. And in the corner, standing in the semi-darkness, away from everyone else, Tess thought she saw Mr M. She turned to Arianna, but Mr Tamworth had arrived backstage, blocking their view.

'Everyone ready?' he asked, looking at Tess.

Tess looked at Arianna, Bubs and Wesley. 'Let's do it.'

Tess was suddenly and completely shitting herself. Her terror was mirrored in each band member's eyes.

'Okay, so apparently we're doing this,' she rallied. 'But we're good. Because we've practised the shit out of this set and because ... well, we're actually good.'

Feedback whined in their ears. The crowd quietened.

'Thank you all for coming this evening for what promises to be a very special offering from a brilliant new band.' Mr Tamworth's assured voice boomed through the PA. 'You know them as your peers, friends, sons, daughters and students. Tonight, they are Sub Deep!'

A loud cheer and Tess led her band onto the stage. In the glare of the warm coloured lights, she lifted her sax. Arianna looped the bass strap over her shoulder. Bubs and Wesley nodded at her. She turned, mercifully half-blinded by the lights, and stepped up to the mic. 'Er, hi. We're Sub Deep and we're gonna play some songs. Thanks.'

Bubs' synth sounds filled the venue, then Wesley's drumbeat kicked in, followed by Arianna's bass riff. Tess let it run a few bars and then came in with the melody. It was shaky at first, but they got through their first song. They were doing it. On to the next one and then, for the third, Arianna stepped up to the mic and sang. It was simple and beautiful and raw. Soon they were near the end of the set and Tess's special arrangement, the one she was most nervous and most proud of, started up.

She'd created a melody in her head and then divided it

up between the bass, the synth and the sax. It was an idea that had appeared fully formed one morning in her head. Played individually, each part was a strange series of notes in irregular random rhythms. But put together, they formed a whole, a tune that danced across scales and phrases and instruments, building to a crescendo, only to be disassembled once more as, one by one, each instrument stopped playing, until only Tess's sax was left. The applause was louder than ever.

They finished with the live drum 'n' bass piece, the front of the crowd bouncing about in appreciation, the double-time beat ending the gig on a high. And then it was done. They left the stage to demands for more. But they didn't have any more. They hadn't planned an encore.

'Shit man. That was next level,' Wesley said as they huddled, bewildered and elated in the tiny dressing room.

'Sick. Utterly sick,' Bubs added.

'I think that might have actually been good,' Tess exclaimed.

There was a knock at the door and Linton's face appeared, his eyes moist with emotion and pride.

'That's what I'm talking about,' he exclaimed hoarsely and pulled both Tess and Arianna into an embrace. He turned to the boys, shook their hands. 'Well done, well done.'

Dan appeared and pulled Tess into his arms. 'That was amazing.' He kissed her on the lips. Tess beamed back at him and then remembered Linton, who stood watching, his eyebrows raised. 'Um, Dad, this is Daniel. Dan this is my dad, Linton.'

Dan stepped clumsily towards Linton. 'Pleased to meet you, Sir,' he said formally, holding out his hand.

Linton's eyebrows remained raised, a dangerous smile spreading slowly across his face. 'Hello, Daniel,' he said. 'Daniel ... ?' he enquired.

'Daniel Wilson. Please. Call me Dan.'

'It's a pleasure to meet you, Daniel.'

Tess looked instinctively towards Arianna, who was glaring at her, wide eyed. Mercifully, Mr Tamworth's arrival interrupted the moment.

'Congratulations to you all. A fantastic night.' He beamed at them, his eyes settling on Tess, who found herself in the centre of the three most important men in her life. A crowd was growing outside the dressing room and so the four members of Sub Deep stepped out to receive their flowers from friends and family.

Arianna was pulled into a hug by her dad as her mum watched from further away, a silent, fierce look of pride in her eyes. At the far end of the room, Tess saw Mr M once more. She looked back at Arianna, now being embraced by her auntie Sandrine, and wondered if the rumours could possibly be true.

It had been a cruel quip that had travelled through their year to Dan and then to Tess. Something about how Mr M had been fired for shagging a student. And that student was supposedly Arianna. Alan had joked that that was the only reason why she had won English student of the year over the rest of them. Dan had thought Tess would laugh along with him when he'd told her, assuming that after she'd been dumped so brutally by Arianna, any dirt on her ex-bestie would be gleefully received. Instead, Tess had shouted at him for the first time, demanding he tell her where he had heard this and what exactly he knew.

Tess scrutinized Mr M. Tried to imagine him touching her friend, kissing her, putting his grown man's dick in her. When she turned back, Arianna was staring straight at him, frozen.

2001

ARIANNA

He smouldered at her from across the venue, took a sip of his pint, smacking his lips loudly, savouring the drama of it all. Arianna felt sick. Auntie Sandrine was still congratulating her, telling her how proud she was watching her grow into this gifted young woman. Arianna tried to take in her loving words, but her mind was racing, trying to figure out what to do. She hadn't realized until that moment just how completely she had been living two lives. It was exciting, a dream, her own little X-rated movie, and it seemed impossible that it would intersect here, in this room, in this moment. She felt herself split in two, tried to fathom how she would be both dutiful daughter, regular teenage band member, and at the same time lover to her teacher. And he stood, waiting. He'd missed his Krav Maga to be here tonight. To support her. She nodded gratefully to Sandrine, let herself be embraced once more, then made her excuses, began to cross the room.

'Arianna!' She turned to find Kate, sipping a drink, Luke's arm around her shoulders, Katie and Phoebe flanking them.

'Well done,' Kate offered.

'Thanks. Thanks for coming,' Arianna said.

'It was fun,' she said simply.

She felt a hand on her shoulder and turned. Damion.

He grinned. 'You were great.'

'Thank you,' Arianna managed.

Damion looked to the corner of the room and backed away.

She walked towards Mr M, feeling the eyes of her family, the eyes of her peers and teachers on her. He watched her every step.

'There she is,' he said loudly. 'Our very own rock star.'

Oxbridge-Four-Terrorist Alan stood beside Mr M. They had been chatting. And now Alan glared at her, seemingly resentful at this interruption. She stopped a few feet out of Mr M's reach.

'You're here,' she said.

'Wouldn't have missed it for the world.' She felt like she was in some sort of strange game. He watched her closely, titillated by the controversy he was creating.

'Did you ... enjoy it?' she tried.

'Very much,' he answered, wry amusement on his face.

'We were pretty nervous at the start,' she filled the silence, 'but we got into it eventually.'

'That you did.'

She was desperate to get back to her friends, her family, to this special moment, felt that she couldn't possibly leave him.

'So, I should probably help pack up,' she said eventually.

'Heading off already?' he said, a tad too loudly.

'I just ... I have to ... pack up and ...'

He downed the rest of his pint and stepped forward. She tried to smile, tried to make out to the people behind her that this was just another fan, congratulating her on a great show. Mr M loomed closer as if he were going to kiss her, right there and then.

At the last moment he moved his face to her ear. 'I'll wait for you outside. Take you home and congratulate you properly.'

She reared back, laughing loudly. 'I can't do that. My family are here . . .'

'You can slip away,' he insisted. 'I'll be waiting.' He turned and, nodding to Alan, exited the venue.

Arianna glanced at the other teachers standing near the bar. They were looking at her with concern. Not everyone in the room was staring at her, but enough of them were. Damion's face was hard to read. Tess was openly shocked. Her dad was mercifully lost in conversation with Linton, and Sandrine was facing the other way. But her mum glared at her from across the room.

Arianna headed swiftly to the stage and joined the band packing up the equipment, busying herself with looping leads around her arm. She felt Tess's gaze on her but didn't look up.

'Afterparty at MetalHeadz then, yeah?' Bubs suggested.

'Definitely,' Wesley confirmed. 'Everyone's coming right?'

They looked at Arianna. She felt pulled in a hundred directions. 'I can't,' she said.

'It's the afterparty. Our afterparty.' Bubs insisted. He'd never asked anything of her before. She hadn't thought he really cared about her either way, but as he looked at her now, it seemed to mean something to him that she join them.

'Why can't you come?' Tess demanded.

'I have to go to this other ... thing.'

'What other thing?' Tess pushed.

'I just can't come, okay?' Arianna's voice suddenly broke. She gritted her teeth, trying to stop the anxious tears that were threatening to burst from the stress of this impossible situation. Tess quietened.

They carried the equipment out to the minibus, the cool of the night air calming Arianna's nerves. Free from the lights, the smoke and the heat, she could breathe again. She lingered a moment after the others had gone back inside, leaned an arm on the cool brick wall of the venue.

A hand turned her roughly around. Before she could get her bearings, he was kissing her, hungrily, pushing his groin into her and his tongue into her mouth.

'I thought you'd never get out of there,' Mr M growled. 'Come on.' He took a step in the direction of his home.

'I'm staying,' she said quietly.

'Arianna, I've been out here waiting for you to finish mucking about with your—'

'I told you not to wait for me.'

'Are you serious?' His voice hardened. He reached out and grabbed her hand. 'Stop playing games, Arianna.'

Games. The word seemed to ricochet around her body. She had felt like a mouse being pawed to death in front of everyone she knew. But apparently *she* was the one playing games.

'I said I'm staying.'

He looked at her, surprised. She looked back, equally surprised at herself. Then, before she could change her mind, she turned and walked back into the venue.

Her mum stood quietly near the entrance, her coat in her arms. Arianna tried to calm herself, look normal. 'I'm going out with the band,' she said. 'I'll be back later.'

'Later tonight?' her mum demanded.

'Yes,' Arianna confirmed.

'And you're going out with Tess.'

'Yes.'

Her mum glared at her, searching her face for the truth. Arianna turned away, stepped back into the venue. The other band members looked up.

'I'm coming,' she said.

2022

ARIANNA

They Do the Dance. Around and around. There are candles. On a desk. And grey carpeting and strip lighting. And a door with no window that locks from the inside. And they dance in the space between the desks. They Do the Dance. The two friends. But they are women now. She and Dana. Someone is playing guitar. A man. Naked. Singing a song about How to Find the Words. Reciting a poem now called We Do the Dance. And now Dana takes her hands, shows her his arm, the one holding the guitar. Now it turns to reveal a tattoo. A big dark cross covering his hairy forearm. Arianna doesn't understand, until the ink begins to fade, the cross begins to disintegrate to reveal beneath it a smaller, more intricate design. Some letters. A poem . . . ? No: too short. A name . . . some initials. Her initials. And his. Intertwined. She gasps. And now—

Arianna wakes and sits bolt upright. She rushes to the laptop and clicks on Dana's icon. She scrolls until she finds the words, the quotes of poems she knew she'd heard before. She knows who wrote them. She sees the picture on the screen of the arm she recognizes now. And the skin is bumpy and uneven because the thick, black ink of the crucifix is covering an earlier tattoo, one that she can still see the outline of underneath, protruding through the dark ink.

No, she moans. *No, please no.*

But it is.

And now she knows who Dana has taken Saffy to.

And it's all her fault.

TESS

'Congratulations,' Tess said. 'On everything.'

'Cheers.' Jay smiled. He was smashing it. His band had stayed together through college and kept in touch with Mr Tamworth, who had steered them to a record deal. Then Jay had started producing on other people's albums. And now he'd moved into music for TV and was smashing that too.

There was a moment where he should have congratulated her too, but instead, Tess thought she saw a flash of something resembling pity, before he quickly moved things on. 'Let's be honest, I'm not the real success story,' he said modestly.

Tess tensed. She knew her face looked weird now, her smile tight, but she couldn't help it. She hadn't expected the conversation to arrive here so quickly. Hadn't quite planned how to handle it. And now here they were.

'Yes, of course,' she said, hoping it landed somewhere between impressed and non-committal. 'Have you seen them around? Since you're all gigging and stuff?'

'Actually, we've collaborated on quite a lot of stuff over the years,' Jay replied. 'I've worked on some of their albums, they recorded some stuff for the last TV show ...' he trailed off as if the list was endless.

Tess's stomach sank. She'd had no idea. She wanted to scream. They'd had this secret life, playing music together, supporting each other's creative projects, careers, while she begged and scraped a gig. And Mr Tamworth was involved in it all too? Why had it turned out like that? Why hadn't anyone thought to include her? Why was Daniel such a dick?

She remembered the first time she'd seen him in his new guise. Someone had shared an image from their first single. Alan, Luke, John and Daniel. The Oxbridge Four. They'd gone to Cambridge together in the end. And, for reasons no one could fathom, they'd emerged as an electro-pop band. They played synth. All of them. Daniel was the lead because he also sang. Cool phrases and words like 'Retro' and 'Game-Boy' and 'Pac-Man' that were looped and played through the synth. He could only do one hand at a time so the others did the other hand, and someone else did the drums on another synth. Basic, tinny beats that sounded like someone had pressed the Demo button: Level One. And the riffs. Simple, childlike stuff.

Stuff that Tess had taught him.

The first single had made her jaw drop. It was so basic, but it was her tune, note for note. The second one had yet another tune she'd taught him as the main hook, and the third. The whole first album was in some way based on the simple riffs she had taught Daniel all those years ago. And much of the second album too. But it was 'Yamaha', their breakthrough single, that had launched them to global stardom. She had watched, gobsmacked, as the country, then the world, fell in love with E.G.G. They were everywhere. Now signed to the biggest record label on the planet, touring the world, playing the fucking pyramid stage, being played in every clothes shop, café, on every phone, radio station, by every DJ, on adverts too. 'Yamaha' was fifteen years old now and she still heard it everywhere.

And every note of it was Tess's work. The riff. The bassline. The fucking drumbeat.

And he'd never made contact with her, never mentioned her in any of the hundreds of interviews he'd given about the unique sound of the band that had launched a whole new genre of music. Now labels were falling over themselves to sign another E.G.G. and a hundred different iterations of white boys were creating albums on a four-track in their bedrooms at their mum's house and making a fortune.

She realized now what she had hoped for from this meeting with Jay. Some solidarity. An ally to scoff at how ridiculous E.G.G.'s trajectory had been. A proper musician who had practised and committed to music for years while they were growing up, just like her, talking to her as an equal and bemoaning the state of the industry and the state of them: interlopers, fakers, who'd blagged their way to the top.

Jay had no idea that Tess had taught Daniel those riffs. No one did. That so much of his music was based on her work, stuff she'd made up on the spot, it was so easy, and then watched him labour for days to learn to play it. But now she saw instead that Jay was their ally, creative ally, that this whole time there was a scene – a wank circle, as Arianna would have said – polishing each other off for years behind her back. Tess felt tears begin to prickle her eyes. She was going to cry in front of Jay Thomas.

Jay leaned in, seemingly oblivious to her turmoil. 'It's really nice to see you. Thanks for tracking me down.'

She shrugged. 'S'alright,' she said.

'I was surprised, though. Bit of a blast from the past.' Jay's eyes were questioning.

She owed him an explanation. Where to start? 'Yeah,' she began. 'So, I basically got in touch originally about something really random, but then it got sorted, but then you called, so ... here we are.'

Jay's gorgeous face looked even more confused. 'Something random?'

'It was to do with Dana. I don't know if you remember her—'

'Dana, yeah.' Jay smiled. 'Course I remember her. How is she?'

That was all Tess needed to know. Jay knew nothing about Dana's whereabouts or the current drama surrounding her. There had been no moment of guilt, of covering up, of hesitation, or anything other than innocent, genuine ease as he remembered her. What a luxury that must be.

'She's fine,' Tess replied.

'Good,' Jay nodded.

'But I'm glad we met, anyway. I'm actually starting to work again too,' she heard herself say. 'Yeah, I took a few years off because I wanted to do the whole mum thing, but now I think it's time to jump back in, so ... if you ... I'm just ...

keen, really, to ... get in touch with old connections, line up some gigs, recordings, sessions ... that kind of thing.' Her face was red hot.

Jay nodded eagerly. 'Yeah, sure. I didn't know if you were still ... But yeah, of course. I'll put the word out.'

'That would be amazing,' Tess said.

'Actually,' Jay began carefully. 'I didn't know whether to say anything as it's quite sensitive but it's you so ... They're having a bit of trouble. The E.G.G. lads. One of them's gone AWOL and, you know what their schedule's like, they've got a studio booked in L.A., they've got sold out stadium gigs, live radio stuff, and they're down to three at the mo. I'm trying to help but I'm tied up with TV stuff. Shall I mention you? It's pretty basic stuff. You'd pick it up in a heartbeat.'

TESS

Tess peered down the line of people queuing to get into the club. The band, their mates, half the sixth form were here, coming to their unofficial afterparty. She clutched her fake ID and begged a god she didn't believe in to get her through these pearly gates just this once.

She looked at Arianna. Only now did she begin to get a sense of what her life had been these last few months. And there was so much she still didn't know. Her face had changed. Her body had filled out. She'd lost something and gained something all at once. Just as Tess was beginning to catch up, get a boyfriend, Arianna had moved further into womanhood, further away from her, again. There was so much she wanted to ask her, but she had no idea where to start. Dana would have known what to say. Candace would have come right out with it, demanding through the rights of Friendship that Arianna let them in on every detail. She thought of Arianna rushing from rehearsals, her moodiness, how pathetic their childlike banter must have seemed, the tears she'd swallowed down in the toilets, the terror on her face just an hour ago.

But she was here, with them now, beside her in the queue. And she looked lighter, genuinely happy to be in their company, for once. Tess realized they would spend the night raving together in a club. She felt a surge of joy.

'Your singing was really good,' she gushed. 'It got the loudest cheer.'

Arianna seemed surprised. 'No, it didn't.'

'It did,' Tess pushed. 'We should get a few more songs down. For next time.'

Wesley and Bubs nodded. Jay and Damion turned around too.

Arianna looked suddenly vulnerable. 'I just . . . I'm not the strongest singer. I'm okay, but I'm not . . . Aretha or Mariah or anything.'

'No one's Aretha,' Tess retorted. 'Apart from Aretha, obviously. No one's asking you to be Aretha.'

The bouncer waved another lot of people through. He didn't even glance at Tess and Arianna, or their fake IDs as he ushered them in. And then they were in the dark of the foyer and handing over their tenners and then walking through the double doors into a wave of sound, smoke and lights. Into the Leisure Lounge.

A large space with rows of airport lounge seats stretched out before them. Twenty-somethings in baggy jeans and hoodies, tank tops and chunky trainers, boots and neon raving gear, milled about, drinking, talking and skanking. The jungle beat, the booming bass, the samples and vocals reverberated from the sound system and Tess headed towards the far end of the room where a light-skinned man with long dreds and a goatee nodded as he selected another record and lined it up, leaning into the headphone that rested on one ear. Tess stood in front of him, listening intently, lost in the layers of production, in his deft mixing of one track into another. Arianna stood nearby, transfixed. Eyes closed, she seemed to be leaning into the music, nodding slowly, letting it wash over her, in her own world, one that Tess longed to be allowed back into.

Then a cold plastic glass was proffered as Dan arrived, nodding enthusiastically, slightly off beat. Soon, Jay and Damion came over with the rest of the band, the Kates, the Oxbridge Four.

Then a man squeezed between them. He took the cigarette out of his mouth and grinned back at Tess, revealing a line of gold teeth. He stepped behind the decks clapping in appreciation at his comrade's set. The club joined in, whistling and blapping. And then he took over. The energy was raised further. Across the dancefloor heads bounced, hands were raised. Tess watched the DJ's every move, feeling the bass shake up her chest bone.

The record got pulled up abruptly. The music stopped. Goldie picked up a microphone. 'What you saying, MetalHeadz?'

The club erupted in appreciation. Daniel whistled loudly.

Then Goldie doubled down, raised the volume and the bar, and dropped something new.

Tess looked at Arianna and they both laughed with delight before the bass kicked in and Arianna closed her eyes, lost in the wave of blissful sound. They danced.

A few songs in, a group of men weaved their way through the crowd and joined Goldie behind the decks. They stood out, smarter and whiter than the rest, an older man at their centre, looking out across the club and nodding at them all. He caught Tess's eye and smiled briefly. Goldie turned and shook the man's hand, and as the man leaned forward, the light caught his face. Tess's jaw dropped. She tried not to stare at him – literally two metres away. She looked around, but no one else seemed to have clocked him. Then he receded back into the shadows behind the decks.

Tess raised her arms and bounced with elation. She tried to emulate Arianna who was shedding something, becoming lighter, more fluid, and knew this was a night they would remember for ever.

They made their way out of the club in the early hours. They were all spent, but it was a good spent.

They headed to the kebab shop and ordered steaming portions of food that came wrapped in layers of greasy white paper. They leaned and sat on a wall nearby, shovelling handfuls into their mouths.

'That was David Bowie,' Tess said.

'What was?' Daniel asked.

'That guy. The old white guy. In the club. With his entourage. That was David Fucking Bowie.'

Greasy jaws dropped open, a piece of meat plopped onto some paper.

*

They got the night bus back. Daniel draped a heavy arm around Tess as she sat facing Arianna across the aisle.

'I know where Dana and Candace are,' she suddenly blurted out.

Arianna turned to her, blinking sleepily.

'I saw Chris, a few weeks back. He gave me a number for them and—'

'Chris? My Chris?' Arianna frowned.

'Yes, but I've called and called and—'

'And you're only telling me now?' Arianna's voice had an edge to it.

Tess's stomach sank.

'I tried to tell you, but—'

'When?'

'Loads of times—'

'When?'

Tess's mind suddenly went blank.

'Where are they?'

'I don't know exactly but—'

'Where's Chris? What the fuck Tess?'

Bubs stood and pressed the button. Daniel pulled Tess up and they headed down the stairs and off the bus.

'Have you seen them?' Arianna demanded as they stood on the street.

'No . . .'

'So . . . ?'

Tess looked at Arianna. She wanted to explain but realized she didn't have much else to tell her.

'So, that's it? I can't believe you didn't tell me.' Arianna glared at Tess and then turned, shaking her head as she made her way home.

'Are you okay?' Dan asked.

'Yep. Yes,' Tess rallied. She turned and smiled at him, trying to salvage a trace of the feeling she'd had just moments ago.

Dan hesitated, held on to her hand, longing in his eyes.

'Come back with me, Tess,' he pleaded.

'I kind of need to sleep in my own bed tonight. It's been a huge day.'

'I'll sleep on the floor, I don't care. Just come back.' He stroked her shoulder, pulled her to him, kissed her longingly. Her ears were buzzing, her heart was hurting, her legs ached with exhaustion, and they both smelled really bad.

He looked at her closely, then he sighed, raised her hand to his mouth and kissed it. 'Goodnight, Tess,' he said and started to walk away.

'You can come over for a bit,' she suddenly blurted out.

He turned.

'We'll have to stay downstairs, but ... we could play some music?'

They tiptoed into the living room in the dark. She went to switch on the light, but he put his hand gently over hers and pulled it away from the switch. They stood, snogging in the living room doorway. His kisses were tender, gentle, his lips soft. Tess was surprised to feel her body relax a notch. He felt it too, and began to kiss her harder, his breath quickening, his hands holding her more firmly. Tess's body suddenly stiffened. He pulled back, sighed.

'Why don't you show me how to play something?' Dan suggested.

Tess blinked with relief. 'Like, on an instrument?'

'Yeah.'

'Um. Well, my dad's sleeping so . . .' Tess looked around and clocked the keyboard in the corner. The flat wasn't big enough for a piano, so Linton had procured a decent second-hand Yamaha with weighted keys. And a headphone input. Tess switched it on. She put the headphones over Daniel's ears and pressed a button. His face lit up as the piano turned into a clavichord. Then a xylophone. Then an 80s synth. He found the Demo button and pressed it, bouncing around at the cheesy tune, pretending to play along. Tess giggled.

'Go on then,' he encouraged. 'Teach me.'

She started with a simple riff. His clumsy fingers struggled, his sense of rhythm just off. She got him to try it with his other hand. That was even harder, but Daniel was determined. She watched patiently as he learned to play the three notes in the right order. Then she taught him something new, another simple tune, this time getting him to try and play it with both hands simultaneously. He took to the task solemnly and eventually started to make progress. An hour later, he took the headphones off.

'I'll leave you to get some rest,' he said softly.

'Can we kiss like we did when we came in?' she found herself requesting.

He nodded quickly. 'Sure! Like this?'

He approached her slowly. She guided his hands to her

face and he remembered how he had held her, kissed her gently once more. She felt herself soften once more. This time he kept it gentle and not too long. Then he pulled away. Smiled a little sadly.

'Goodnight Tess. Well done for today. You were amazing.'

Tess sat on the sofa in the dark. It had been the best day of her life. She replayed every moment of it. Flashes of music, her band onstage, the cheers, the smile from Arianna, the club, Mr Tamworth, Daniel, Goldie, David Bowie.

The corner of the room flashed red, then dark, then red again. She sighed, remembering that she hadn't charged her mobile phone, which meant her mum must have called the landline. Tess hauled herself up, padded towards the machine and pressed play.

'Tess? It's Dana. Call me on this number.'

TESS

John, Luke and Daniel sat in the back room of the record store in East London, preparing for the intimate performance they would be playing in a few hours' time to launch the release of their new collaboration with Alex from Blur. There was a queue already forming outside when Tess walked in. She felt slightly sick, nerves mostly, but she held her head high.

Luke saw her first. 'Hey, Tess!' he exclaimed.

Daniel jumped up, walked over enthusiastically, self-consciously. He was wearing an Adidas tracksuit that Tess was pretty sure was a replica of one that the Beastie Boys had worn. Under the outfit, the cap, the chains and the trainers, it surprised her how old he looked. She realized he must be thinking the same about her. She'd seen pictures of his wife, a beautiful mixed-race woman younger than him. And their three kids were stunning, of course. And now Tess and Daniel were hugging, and then she was hugging Luke and John too. So, it was Alan who'd gone AWOL.

She was to be the new Alan.

'Good to see you,' Daniel exclaimed, and it looked like he meant it.

'That's Adidas.' She pointed at his tracksuit.

Daniel blushed, looked down at his outfit.

'It is,' he said. And suddenly he looked like he always had around her. And this outfit seemed a bit silly when someone who had known him when he was just Daniel and not Daniel-From-E.G.G., was looking at him. And the other two looked from him to her, and, in that moment, with a surge of surprise, Tess realized the power she had. Daniel, in his finery and fame, seemed to have reverted to being the eager, awkward kid he'd always been around her. And his whole career, every song, had in some way been a twisted homage to her.

'So ... you're famous pop stars,' she said.

They laughed. Daniel blushed some more.

'Musicians,' Luke corrected.

'How are you?' Daniel asked.

'Yeah, good,' she said.

'That's great, Tess.' He seemed relieved.

'So ... Alan,' Tess said.

The remaining band members exchanged looks.

'Yeah, Alan,' Daniel echoed. 'Look, it's long and complicated and we'll get into it properly later, but, basically, he's ... taking a break for a bit. Figuring some stuff out. These last few years have been a bit ... strange.'

'We love him like a brother, but like a brother, he's a pain in the neck,' John added.

'Anyway, the main thing is, we've got to keep on keeping on. And we're seeing it as a chance to change up, expand, get some fresh input on our – on the sound,' Daniel corrected himself.

'I've been meaning to hit you up for ages,' he said. 'We were so stoked when Jay said you were working again. I've heard you've been smashing it on the old fiddle. So look,' Daniel looked at his watch, then checked in with a woman who was busy typing things into her phone that Tess had only just noticed in the corner of the room. She nodded. 'We've got about an hour,' he continued. 'Shall we ... talk music stuff?'

ARIANNA

Realization is a strange process. The dawning on you of the truth. Sometimes it comes as a lightning bolt, a key detail revealed that brings all other details together into a singular knowing.

Sometimes it's a slow awakening, years long. Of life experiences that teach you something different to what you had been told was normal. A maturing into a woman who knows and sees and relates to people, and the world which relates back until she has new language with which to understand her own story.

Arianna had dated. People her age. And went to their homes, witnessed other families, other dynamics. She was astounded to realize that they wanted to wait before they jumped into bed with her, wanted to take things slow, asked questions about her pleasure, were invested in what *she* wanted. At first, she had no idea. What were her preferences? What did she like/dislike? She'd never been asked before, so her mind had drawn a blank. But she decided to find out. Alone and in company, Arianna had gone on a journey of exploration to find out what she liked and didn't like. Food.

Words. Material. Textures. Smells. Fingers or mouths. And she started to find the answers. And to tell them. And some people received this so calmly it was as if it was not the huge revelation she thought it was, but a common part of human interaction that should have always been a given. Others were filled with rage at the audacity. Her audacity.

She lived with her increasingly angry family and studied as she worked full-time, four years of night school, and learned even more things. She learned about Property Law and Contract Law and Family Law and Criminal Law. And somewhere in her second year she learned about Sexual Violence and Abuse and Coercive Control and this new term that had just become Law called Grooming, and she realized what had been done to her.

But even then, Arianna did what she had always done. She carried on. She kept working from 9 a.m. to 5 p.m. and studying from 6 p.m. to 9 p.m. five days a week, until she reached the weekend and had a breakdown.

Her mum found her in a foetal position on the floor and stood over her, telling her eldest to get up. Eventually Arianna did. She herded them all into the living room, sat them down and told them what *he* had done to her over the course of three years. She was shaking but no one reached out to her, no one touched her. Then Arianna had taken herself off to bed. In the morning, her dad had left, her mum and Lelia were arguing, Theo rushed past her and out of the house, and no one mentioned it again.

The next day, Arianna had gone alone to the Rape Crisis Centre in Croydon. A woman called Jade guided her into a room, and then, in faltering words she had held in for decades, Arianna tried to describe each individual incident she could remember. Jade listened, for over an hour, gave her tissues, mirrored her devastation, sat quietly with her. She said, 'I'm so sorry' and 'What happened to you is awful' and 'You should never have been put through this' and 'What he did was a crime' and 'I believe you' and 'What would you like to do next?'

The following week Jade met Arianna outside the police station and they went in together. For two hours Arianna described once more every incident she could remember to the detective as another watched from behind a mirror. The detective asked her the date, time and location for each one. She couldn't even remember his address. Then she handed the police officers a box full of her teenage diaries. Because since there were no witnesses and no forensic evidence, Arianna's teenage diaries became the main source of evidence.

She'd continued, with work and studying, only taking the afternoon off those two times. She got some free counselling and tried to make sense of the strange, exhausting dream she was living in. She forgot her dad's birthday, Lelia screamed at her for being so selfish and wouldn't let her sign the card. Theo, now in his twenties, told her the vibe in the house was shit now, and it was her fault. Months later, Arianna went back once more to the centre where Jade waited with two detectives who handed back her diaries.

There just wasn't enough evidence. So there would be No Further Action.

But.

They believed her. They said as much. The police officer told her that she worked with a bunch of dinosaurs and they did their best where they could. She said she would make sure this went on his record, that they would express concern at him being left alone with minors, and that this would be seen by prospective employers any time he applied for a job.

Jade sat with her for another hour. She talked of Arianna's courage, how she'd done right by that wonderful younger Arianna who had been through so much. Given her a voice, named, in terms of the law, what had happened to her, and most importantly, let *him* know that she knew. Named him for what he was and sent the weight of this knowing, of his actions back where it belonged: onto *his* shoulders. Because what Arianna deserved was to thrive now – not just survive – and maybe this could be the beginning of that.

A week later, Arianna quit her degree and moved out.

What happens to the men who have been outed?

What happens to the ones whose history has finally caught up with them? Named for the violent transgressors they are, but spared the full wrath of the law because, in the end, it's his word against hers? Word. Words. Not strong enough to convict, but once spoken, forever in existence. Marking him, tainting the upstanding, professional decent persona he'd created, convinced himself of. Sullying his Record. What happens to the ones who live in purgatory, the liminal space between society and prison, vindicated but unemployable?

Had she wondered? She'd tried not to. Tried to put all her efforts into focusing on herself. On tending to the void left by so many losses: family and study and prospects and Cyprus. Leaving her family behind left her Yiayia devastated and confused. They needed her and now she was tending to herself. And something about that was unforgivable. Her mum's rage at her selfishness had isolated Arianna from almost everyone she knew. She punished Arianna ruthlessly for abandoning her. But she'd also given her daughter the tools she needed to rebuild. Because Militsa knew how to build community in the coldest of places. Slowly, tentatively, over years, Arianna took steps to reach out to neighbours, support groups, survivors, filling that deep, lonely void, rebuilding her life and connections just like she'd seen her mum do as an immigrant.

And Arianna, older than she would have liked, single and estranged, had her bedsit now. She was queen of her own tiny castle, beholden to no one, cocooned in the safety of her own four walls and healing, finally.

Arianna never forgot the one person who had stayed by her through the hardest thing she had ever done. Jade had been a living angel, guiding her through the legal process, by her side at every turn.

So, Arianna became an ISVA just like Jade. And in true Arianna style, she became the best. Promoted faster than any other woman in her field, she was soon managing a team of other ISVAs and her own caseload of women.

Arianna also never forgot what the police officer had told her that day.

The system's broken Arianna. It's not fit for purpose, not even close. But we do what we can.

So Arianna chose to work within this broken system

and do what she could. And because of her legal training, Arianna was the thorn in the police department's side. She knew when they were cutting corners, not fulfilling their legal duty to the survivors she supported. And she made calls, sent emails, filed complaints, and got officers moved off the case if they didn't serve her women well. Loyal and dedicated, exhausted and burnt out, Arianna kept on keeping on in the hope that every now and then, she could help bring about Justice for someone, if not for herself.

But now, after all this time, she would have to look up the very person she had hoped she'd never have to discuss or look at or name ever again. Because the words quoted by Dana online were his. The poems were his. And the arm was his. And she'd been there all those years ago to watch as the tattoo under the tattoo had been etched into his skin.

She knew who Dana had run to. And it was all her fault.

ARIANNA

She slept till midday. Then she lay in bed, listening to the noises of the household drift to her from downstairs as she replayed the night before. The bliss of the dancefloor, the greasy kebab, the laughter, the stage, the sound, the lights, the applause. She sobered as she remembered Tess telling her she'd seen Chris, knew where Dana and Candace had been all this time. The hurt on her face as she'd walked away. And then there was him. The glee he took in causing a scene. The shock on his face as she pulled away from him, returned to her friends. It turned him on, seeing her squirm, causing controversy, taking her away from everyone else. Arianna pulled her contraceptive pills from the drawer and chucked them in the bin, kicking it for good measure. Then she took them back out, popped each one individually and flushed them down the toilet along with her diet shake.

On the way to school the next morning Arianna stopped at the corner shop. She bought chocolate. And two packets of crisps. Smelly ones. She queued by the magazines. The one next to her had pictures of celebrities, women, cut through the middle so that their cleavage and pouted lips were in the top half, their legs and barely covered groins making up the lower half. The caption read: 'Which Half Would You Choose?' and a speech bubble underneath said 'Bottom half every time – two holes.' – Clive, Wanstead.'

She found the girls in the common room, Phoebe and Katie perched on the table listening intently to Kate.

'Morning!' Arianna announced.

They looked up briefly, then turned back.

It wasn't until Jay passed by that anyone spoke to her.

'Great night,' he called. 'You smashed it.'

Arianna beamed.

As the pips went, Kate put her hand on Arianna's shoulder. 'I'm dying for a fag. Wanna come?'

Arianna shrugged to hide her surprise. 'Sure.'

They made their way to the far end of the car park, the sixth-formers' smoking corner. Kate pulled out a packet of B&H and offered it to Arianna. Kate took a few indulgent drags and looked out across the car park.

'That's so much better,' she sighed.

Then she turned to Arianna. 'So. Mr M, turning up at the gig. What was that about?' her voice was breezy, her stare piercing. Arianna's heart started to beat wildly. She wasn't sure it was the nicotine she'd just inhaled.

'Yeah ... random ...' she said.

Kate continued to watch her carefully. 'What exactly happened with him leaving last year?'

Arianna searched for something to say that wasn't a lie, but wasn't the truth.

'There's been some wild rumours going around,' Kate

continued when Arianna remained silent. 'Luke's been hearing all sorts, mostly from the lads, about you meeting Mr M outside of school ... going to some sort of workshop he runs ...?'

'Oh that. Yeah. I think I saw Alan there, so I guess he must have mentioned something to Luke ...?'

Kate waited for more. Arianna tried to look bored.

'I know Phoebe and Katie can be a bit ... clingy sometimes,' Kate confided. 'We don't really get to hang out much just the two of us ...'

'No.'

'They're sweet, it's just, they don't really get what it's like being in an actual relationship,' Kate said. 'To talk man problems with, you know?'

'Yeah, totally.'

'Anyway,' Kate sighed. 'I'm not one to judge. I keep an open mind, so ... yeah,' she concluded with a shrug.

They stubbed out their fags and headed into the lunchtime crowd. Phoebe and Katie were sitting on a bench at the far end of the playground, looking lost without their queen bee.

Someone called Arianna's name. She turned to see Damion walking over.

'Recovered from the weekend?' he asked.

'Almost,' Arianna replied.

Damion smiled, then he looked suddenly nervous. He pulled something out of his back pocket.

'Er, this is for you,' he said solemnly. He placed it in Arianna's hand and backed away.

She looked down. It was a cassette. On the front cover he'd written 'Not Aretha ... or Mariah: A Mixtape for Arianna.'

By the end of the week, she already noticed a difference. Her jeans were sitting lower on her flatter stomach, the red lumps on her face were receding and she only had the one chin now. She'd also stopped crying randomly. And had started eating again. Voraciously. Passionately. Enthusiastically. She vowed never to take another pill ever again.

She turned up for rehearsals five minutes early. Tess was setting up a mic for her and took Arianna's bass.

'I've been wanting to tune this properly for ages,' she said.

Then Tess launched into a familiar bass line that slid down in semi-tones and soon Wesley had picked up the riff. A few bars in, Tess nodded to Arianna, Arianna smiled in recognition. She leaned into the mic and began to sing 'Glory Box' by Portishead.

It was a great choice for her voice. Arianna kept it simple, close to the original, and Bubs came in with chords that kept the focus on her vocals. They beamed at each other.

She stayed an hour after practice. Got a portion of special fried rice all for herself. Then, weary and satisfied, Arianna made her way home.

At the corner of the road, he was waiting, leaning against a wall just out of the beam of the streetlight, a small book open in his hand.

'I missed you,' his voice cracked with emotion.

Mr M pulled her into an embrace, sighing.

*

He led her back to his. Arianna tried to recover from the surprise at finding him suddenly there, suddenly walking back with him. She tried to hold on to her anger at him, but he kept looking at her with such pleading that by the time they reached his flat, she had melted. He cupped her face in his hands, actual tears coursing down his face.

'I'm sorry, Arianna,' he said. 'I didn't realize how much you mean to me. The thought of losing you . . . I couldn't . . .'

Arianna was speechless at the effect she was having on this grown man.

'The truth is, I was jealous. All those guys looking at you up there on the stage, undressing you with their eyes. Even the teachers, now that they know you're sexual, that you're with me, they look at you differently.'

'I know what men are like,' Mr M continued. 'I know what goes on in their heads, and I wanted everyone to know . . . you're mine.'

She smiled despite herself, melted a bit more. It was real. What they had. It was true what he said. They had a connection like none other and she couldn't believe she had been ready to walk away from it.

'I'm sorry too,' she found herself saying.

He nodded. 'Don't ever pull away from me again,' he said softly. A steelier look came into his eyes. Then, to her surprise, he pulled her back out of the front door.

'Come,' he said.

'Where are we going?' Arianna asked as he walked with determination down the night road, holding her hand tightly. She realized with growing horror that they were walking in the direction of her home, and she tried to figure out how to stop whatever confrontation he was planning from happening.

'Will you just tell me?' she pleaded.

'It's a surprise,' he replied.

Arianna was so relieved when they turned away from her street that she asked no more questions. They crossed an empty road to the local park. The same park she had followed her mum to a few months back.

'It's locked. It's gone midnight—' she protested.

Mr M crouched down by the tall railings and crisscrossed his fingers, creating a step for Arianna to climb.

'Ladies first,' he said.

Arianna stepped up and over the metal fence. Mr M followed, scrambling awkwardly up, his shirt riding upwards and exposing his belly as he tried and failed the first time to make it over. He landed heavily on the other side, then he grabbed Arianna's hand again.

He led her off the concrete path that surrounded the edge of the park, and onto the wide expanse of grass, divided by white lines into several football fields. Arianna yanked her hand out of his and stopped.

'What are we doing here?' she demanded.

He turned, a spark of excitement in his eyes, and then impulsively kissed her in that hungry, messy way that signalled his arousal.

'Trust me, Arianna,' he said as he groped her bum. Then he pulled her even faster towards the middle of the playing field. They got to a goalpost and he pushed her up against it, already pulling at her clothes.

'Please?' Arianna's voice was shrill as she tried to keep up. She looked around at the darkness, knowing how many people jumped that fence every night, how many people would still be walking around, watching. She couldn't properly see his face in the dark, but she tried to make eye contact as he continued to grope and pull at her.

'This is for you, Arianna,' he growled.

'What?'

'You asked me for this.'

'For what?' she asked.

'You said, Arianna, you said you wanted to fuck outside. So I'm going to fuck you outside.'

Arianna's mind was racing, trying to make sense of what he was saying, even as she tried to slow him down, keep some clothes covering her breasts, her lower half.

'I live to make your dreams come true,' he said.

With a surge of strength, he yanked down her clothes, exposing her breasts, then he had pulled off her pants. He turned her around roughly and she reached out for the goalpost to steady herself. Before she knew it, he had pushed himself inside her and she gasped.

That was when she remembered, muddied and shocked, what she had said about making love under the stars.

2022

ARIANNA

Arianna scrolled through almost two years' worth of posts. Somewhere in 2020, Dana had started re-posting content from an organization called The Xanadu Foundation. There was no website, but an image of a majestic, ethereal city rising to the heavens graced their socials, along with a similarly confusing mix of quotations from the Bible, twelve steps, Hollywood movies, poetry, conspiracy theories and positive affirmations. The latter were typed on backgrounds filled with forests and waterfalls and each quote was attributed to the same name – Marlon Bysshe Blake. In among them were invitations to workshops entitled things like, *Words as Weapons*, *The Great Lie*, *Shedding Shame Seizing Success*, *Media Manipulation and Pharma Falsehoods*, *Tough Love in the Age of Victimhood*, and, sickeningly, *Women's Self-Defence Classes*. Between these were posts with a singular date and a postcode. The newest of those was for tonight.

She promised herself she'd go as far as the entrance, get a sense of the event, see if she could spot Dana or Saffy, and then leave, head to Candace's and make a plan together.

Arianna arrived at the hotel near Canary Wharf. An uber-modern part of the city that was bustling with office workers on weekdays; a ghost town at the weekend. A queue snaked around the side of the building, and Arianna found herself joining it. More people arrived behind her, then the line moved forward, past the security guard, through the entrance, into the lobby where the same image of a mystical city with the letters TXF guided them into a large, carpeted conference room.

She kept her beanie hat on, hiding her curly hair, her clothes were baggy and dark. People clustered around stands that were arranged around the room, signs that read PX1, PX2, PX3 and so on up to the number twelve. At the centre of the room, several rows of chairs faced a stage. She should leave now, she thought as the crowd started to sit, before whatever was going to happen happened on that stage. He wasn't meant to come near her, she knew that much, but she had no idea where she stood legally if she sought him out, voluntarily attended an event she knew he'd be at.

But she hadn't seen any of them yet. Not Dana, not Saffy and not him. This was still a wild theory she'd concocted based on a handful of obscure social media posts. It was also the best and only lead she had.

So, she sat somewhere in the back among the growing crowd. She caught snippets of discussion about the last women's self-defence class, someone else bragged about the one-to-one coaching sessions they'd had with Marlon himself. Another asked what it was like working with him so intimately? Was it worth the extra payment? But there was no time for the answer because the lights were lowering and the crowd hushed respectfully, piously.

A figure stepped onto the stage and Arianna's stomach sank because it was a familiar figure, from her childhood.

But it wasn't who she expected it would be.

It wasn't Mr M.

It was Alan.

TESS

In a TV studio in Stockholm, Tess stood, caked with make-up, wearing sunglasses indoors and a tracksuit that matched Daniel's, Luke's and John's. The lights were bright and there was a camera trained directly on her left hand.

John started up the tinny beat, pressing the keys with one index finger with the intensity and commitment of a drummer at a fully kitted, Pearl drumkit. Luke came in with the bassline. And then, together, Daniel and Tess did the right hand and the left hand respectively. Then Daniel looked into the camera and sang.

'Yamaha.'

PART THREE

2001

DANA

Dana tried not to keep looking out of the window of the second-floor squat on Balham High Street. She checked her make-up one more time in the wardrobe mirror and bounced back onto the bed where Candace was sitting. A harsh buzz cut through the early morning and Dana jumped back up and headed downstairs.

She opened the front door to find Tess standing there, holding a tub of Marmite. Dana pulled her into a tight hug.

'Ohmygodyoulookexactlythesame,' she gushed.

'You look the same but different,' Tess concluded.

Dana giggled. 'That's such a Tess thing to say.' She looked down at the Marmite. 'Is that for me?'

Tess looked apologetic. 'I didn't know what to bring. I remembered you liked this, so . . .'

Dana hugged her again and pulled her inside. She suddenly became aware of the stained, threadbare carpet on the staircase, the musty smell. As she pushed open the door to their small room, she saw it through Tess's eyes: walls covered in grainy wallpaper, damp patches, a bed in the centre, neatly made by her, and a wardrobe in the corner of the room, stuffed full of five people's clothes, her and Candace's brightly-coloured raving outfits peeping out of the gap in the door.

Candace rose from the bed. 'You caught up with us in the end,' she said.

'Yeah,' Tess said, taking Candace in. Her hair had grown so that the faded pink dye only covered the ends, the undercut growing out now too. She was thinner, they both were. But they were well turned out. Dana saw to that – fresh outfits and make-up. Tess looked around the room. 'This is . . . nice.'

Dana jumped in enthusiastically. 'It's wicked, actually. No school, no grownups, we get to hang out all day and rave all night, and five of us share the bed.' She watched Tess closely, gauging just how shocked, impressed she was.

'Five?' Tess asked.

'We do shifts,' Candace explained. 'The other three work in the daytime, so they've got the bed most nights and we swap with them in the day.'

Tess looked confused. 'So, you don't sleep at night?'

'I told you. We're out raving.' Dana indicated the neon pink outfit and platform boots she was wearing. 'We only got in an hour ago. That's why it still smells of lads in here.'

Dana bounced back onto the bed, striking a pose. She reached for the packet of B&H at the end of the bed and lit one up. 'Fag?'

Tess hesitated, then took one and awkwardly lit it up. Candace watched with amusement.

'So . . . you're happy?' Tess asked.

Candace looked at Dana.

'We're freeee!' Dana exclaimed and spread all her limbs wide at once. Tess giggled. It warmed Dana's heart, it was the best sound ever. Just like how it used to be. Candace was so serious these days. She had to get her really drunk before she'd loosen up, crack a smile, have some fucking fun.

'Do you . . . What do you do? I mean, all day?' Tess asked.

Candace opened her mouth to answer, Dana jumped in once more.

'Whatever we want,' she said. 'Mostly hang out with the locals. We're, like, best mates with all the homeless people in Balham. It's wicked,' she added.

Tess nodded. 'Cool.'

'And we're out every night. Parties, illegal raves, drink whatever we want, do whatever we want, smoke, shag whoever we want.' She cackled. 'Do you want some Jack Daniels?'

'Um, could I have a cup of tea?' Tess asked.

'Sure.' Dana headed to the shared kitchen downstairs and stole a teabag from someone else's stash. They had no milk or sugar. She heated the water in a pan on the one working hob and then rushed back upstairs, handing the mug of tea to Tess. Tess held it without sipping.

'Tess did a gig. With her new band,' Candace said.

'Really?' Dana asked, suddenly hungry for news from their past life, but also scared. Scared she might long for more, miss it, remember the good bits too well.

'Yeah, at the Half Moon.'

'Where Jay's band played?' Dana asked, remembering that

night they'd all got ready at Arianna's, dodged the bouncers and made it into the gig.

'Yep,' Tess said. 'Arianna's in it too. She plays bass and sings.' Candace's face tightened.

'Everyone came,' Tess gushed. 'All the Year Aboves, the teachers, our ... everyone.'

Dana fought the sinking feeling in her stomach. There was so much she wanted to know, so much she wanted to ask Tess. But it was very suddenly too much. So she jumped up and headed to the wardrobe, the one other bit of furniture in the room. She flung it open to reveal a collection of brightly coloured clothes, none of which you could wear underwear with.

It had the required effect on Tess.

'Wow. Is that all yours?'

'Yep,' Dana said proudly.

'But how much ... how did you ... ?'

'Dana nicked it,' Candace chimed in. 'It's her new hobby.' Tess looked at Dana, shocked.

'You hungry?' Dana asked, fighting to keep upbeat. 'We're gonna go Maccy D's and get some brekkie. There's this pimply teenager doing the morning shift and he gives us a free meal if we snog in front of him.'

Tess looked at Candace who remained impassive. 'That sounds amazing, but I've got to go to orchestra practice,' Tess said.

'Already?' There was still so much to talk about, to show her. 'Well, now you know where we are,' Dana managed eventually.

They hugged. Dana didn't want to let go. But then Tess was gone and it was just the two of them again. They sat in silence, until someone's tummy grumbled.

2001

CANDACE

As they slept through the daytime bustle of the High Street, their bellies full of fries and milkshake, Dana clung to Candace like they were on a boat instead of a bed.

Tess's visit had shaken them. They had been in some sort of survival mode for ages now. Running away, finding somewhere to stay, setting up their new life, staying alert, thinking about the next meal, where to spend the next night until they could come back to the room. And then Dana had charged the pager at some posh guy's house after he'd paid for their drinks at the bar. She'd convinced him to let them have a shower so he could watch. Made a game out of looking in his fridge and eating his food as if they were just a bit bored, not really hungry. She'd even thrown on one of his designer shirts and a pair of his warmest socks and pranced around in nothing else, while the pager charged. She'd used his landline to call Tess and leave a message with the number of their local phone box.

But then she'd come. Here. And suddenly their new life had collided with the old. Exposed it for what it really was.

They had been aiming for Miami: made it as far as Balham.

They usually hung out with the local street faces for a few hours. Someone would have the lowdown on where to go for a bite to eat, if the teenager at McDonalds wasn't working that day. Then they'd make their way to a pub or a bar. They kept rotating the venues. They were always dressed to the nines in tight, bright clubbing gear, colourful make up, their hair rave-ready. Dana had nicked it all – the clothes, make-up, hairspray, shoes.

Candace had tried twice to steal some food for them. The minute she walked into the local shop, the cashier didn't take his eyes off her. She tried Safeway but the security guard, who was as brown as she was, followed her through every aisle. She gave up before she'd really started.

But today was a good day. They got a free bus ride into the city and joined the queue for a club in Soho. Dana sashayed to the front. Candace watched as Dana homed in on the security who was in charge, beamed, bargained, joked. He rolled his eyes, turned away, then turned back despite himself. Then the nod. Dana beckoned Candace, and they were ushered in.

It was a new place. They could tell from the self-conscious décor, the fresh bar staff, and the stush clientele in their designer wear, sipping chilled drinks and looking around the room at everyone else but the person they were talking to. Dana and Candace found a spot near the DJ and the empty dance floor. When the DJ eventually dropped something more upbeat, Candace let out a loud whistle. Dana pulled her into the centre of the dancefloor, and they danced.

First, they focused on each other, synching their moves, then they turned outwards, smiling at the other clubbers, sharing a nod of appreciation, a dance move across the space. Someone bit. They dance-walked onto the floor, pulling their mates with them. Then more joined, Dana whooping appreciatively, winding with them in welcome. The dance-floor packed out and the DJ looked at them with relief and gratitude. A tap on the shoulder, and a waitress led them to a table on the edge of the dancefloor with bottles of premium vodka and champagne chilling. A petite brown man in a slick blue suit smiled and shook their hands.

'I'm Maurice, the promoter. Thank you for creating a vibe in this place. Honestly, it's like pulling teeth sometimes.' He gave them his card, said it would be his pleasure to host them at any of his nights. They drank. The DJ joined them when his shift was done. And just like that, they were the heart and soul of the party. Again.

More importantly, they were set for the night.

Sometime in the middle of the evening, Dana disappeared for an hour, but Candace didn't mind. Most people gravitated to Dana like flies to shit. She would make them feel special, then choose the leader, the most tactical one to snog or shag, and whoever was left over would end up with Candace. But every now and then, there was a guy who preferred her. Often it was a kink thing, a taste for something more exotic. Once, a man had paused his pawing of her to shout over the music, 'I've never been with an 'alf-caste girl before,' directly into her ear.

DJ's name was Nathan. Nathan was white and cute and smiled a lot. He made it clear that she was no Second Choice to him. He gave her space to bust her moves, nodded appreciatively as she did. She closed her eyes for a moment and felt the beat. She felt hands around her waist and opened her eyes to find Dana had returned. 'Guess where our new bouncer friend is working tomorrow night?'

'Where?'

'Wembley. Red Hot Chili Peppers gig. He's gonna get us in.'

'Shut up.'

They screamed.

They stayed till the end, got a cab back to Maurice's one-bedder in Chelsea. Candace appreciated the neatness, the tasteful nods to his Mauritian background, the fact that he offered them not only more drinks, but also food.

All four of them piled onto his bed, Dana, Candace, Maurice, Nathan, a naked tangle of limbs. Dana led what came next.

They made it back to the squat a perfect hour after the other roommates had left, both still a little buzzed. They giggled as they lay face to face on the bed.

'Did you enjoy that?' Dana asked Candace.

'Yeah,' Candace replied.

'No but did you actually enjoy it? Like, do you feel satisfied?'

Candace frowned, trying to understand.

'Did you?'

'No,' Dana said.

'What was all that moaning and screaming for then?'

Dana shrugged.

'Ambience?'

They laughed until their stomachs hurt.

Dana lay a hand on Candace's face and pulled her closer. They kissed. Candace was shocked to feel Dana's body push against hers. This was different to the making out they did in front of horny men for their dinner. Candace's breath caught as she felt her friend's hand slide down her body and soon a wave of hot red pleasure suddenly, quickly rose and crashed in her. She tried to recover from the surprise, the elation, the emotion, and then turned to focus on Dana.

ARIANNA

The crowd rippled with excitement as the celebrity stepped onto the stage. Alan stood, a seasoned stage-occupier, down-to-earth-Britishly-humble enough, to put them at ease. He was tall and lanky, his haircut and outfit retaining the echoes of his pop stardom. He'd aged, of course, but the warm light he stood in was kind and Arianna thought she could make out some foundation smoothing him out further. He swept his hair from his face in a gesture so familiar, all accolades fell away momentarily, and he was a schoolboy once more.

'Great to see so many of you here,' he began. Arianna bristled at the strangeness of hearing this deeper version of a voice that had punctuated her formative years, from the front row of her English classes to the after-school poetry club, to those clandestine extra-curricular workshops and then into her adulthood, singing catchy refrains from her TV, retail shop speakers and phones. And now here.

Alan looked down, waited a beat. 'It's been quite a journey. I know some of you have been here from the beginning. Many more have joined along the way.' Several of the audience sat straighter then, proud to have been included as the

O.G.s of whatever this was. 'I've seen this movement grow exponentially, which shows how much of a need there is for it. How hungry we have been for something that gives us the tools to understand our past, make peace with it, be born into our new selves, see through the lies and the oppression that keeps us blind and brainwashed and small, and pushes us to do the work to wake up and reach our full potential – all of us, not just me.' He smiled at the subtle nod to his own monumental success.

'It's hard work, waking up,' he continued. 'But the rewards are immeasurable. We've worked hard to create the multi-faceted programme you get to enjoy now. I urge you to deep dive into it all. Yes, it's a big investment, and no doubt there are many close to you who are sceptical, hateful even, of what we do here at The Xanadu Foundation, but there is nothing more important than this. And we are so committed to you, to making sure as many of you as possible can access this, that we have five different payment plans for every possible financial situation.' Alan spoke with assured conviction. 'What makes us different here at TXF is that we walk the walk. When the people around me started to question what we do here, to doubt, and yes, even to hate, I didn't falter. I've left the band, because they just didn't get it.' There was a collective gasp, mutterings of shock and awe from the audience.

'This movement will continue to respond to the extreme times we live in. And it will continue to commit to you in a way no family, friend or partner ever will. Meditate on that.' Another pause. 'We'll be retreating soon, back to Xanadu HQ, to reassess and re-structure so that we can come back with a fresher, even more relevant offering. Prices will increase too, so if you've been hesitant about jumping in, I suggest you do it today. And wherever you are on the journey, keep going, keep investing, because really, it's an investment in you.'

Alan pointed at the audience, now amazed at his commitment to Project Xanadu. A man at the peak of his career, walking away from it all, for this.

'But we're all here because of one person,' he continued. 'One man. And his tireless vision for a better world. Someone I have had the privilege of knowing for a very long time. Who has guided me and inspired me and been my mentor and, yes, my best friend, for decades.' Arianna's breathing quickened. She tried to prepare herself, had no idea how she possibly could. 'I owe him everything and I know you do too.'

At that moment, two figures appeared from a doorway to the left of the stage. A woman and a child. Dana and Saffy. They made their way to two seats in the front row. Arianna strained, tried to see between the heads in front of her, could just make out the two of them facing forward. Was Saffy scared? So far away from everyone and everything she knew. From Candace.

'Fellow X-warriors,' Alan continued. 'It is an honour and a privilege to welcome Professor X himself, Mr Marlon Bysshe Blake.'

The audience roared, as people in front and beside her suddenly stood up, applauding with vigor. And then there he was, striding to the centre of the stage, a fist in the air reminiscent of the Black Panthers or maybe Nelson Mandela. He wore black jeans with big black boots and a loose white shirt with a frilled collar and flounced sleeves, like something out of a Shakespeare play. His frame was bulkier now, broader and heavier, taking up more space, larger than life. But it was him.

Fear gripped her, then, just as suddenly, rage coursed through her. She looked around as this room of hundreds of people gave her perpetrator a standing ovation. Arianna was suddenly desperate to get out, but she was trapped, among the fevered mob of followers.

The audience quietened as the man who now called himself Marlon Bysshe Blake took the microphone.

DANA

'Oh shit. Dana, wake up.'

Dana frowned but kept her eyes closed.

'Dana man. Wake UP!'

Candace was already out of bed and rushing around the room.

'We overslept. We've got ten minutes before the lads come back.'

Candace threw some clothes at her. Dana hauled herself up, put them on while Candace hurriedly packed a bag. She was so thirsty. She'd do anything for a mug of her mum's tea.

Candace pulled them out of the room, and they started down the stairs. The front door slammed shut below them. They froze, trapped at the kitchen, on the middle floor. Heavy footsteps made their way up the stairs. One paused. A wide-set face with weary, bloodshot eyes peered in. The two girls looked at him. He nodded, then turned and made his way up to the room.

Dana adjusted the wing mirror of a car parked on one of the residential roads off the high street and kneeled down to do her make up. She heard Candace's stomach grumble loudly, felt the hunger in her own acutely. When she was done with her own look, she did Candace's while she said things like, 'Not too much of that pasty shit on my face,' and 'Ow, Dana man, leave some hair on my fuckin' head.' Finally, they were rave-ready again. But the vibe was bad. Dana had to think of something really special to make this better. Then she remembered.

'Right, come on.' She grabbed Candace's arm and started marching her back towards the main road.

'Where are we going?' Candace demanded.

Dana turned to her. 'Wembley, innit.'

A giant neon sign that read RED HOT CHILI PEPPERS loomed above them. Dana grabbed Candace's hand and squeezed it. They made their way around the building, looking for some kind of backstage entrance. They saw a small crowd hovering around a doorway and Dana pushed her way to the front. Two thick-set security men stood looking grimly at the crowd. Neither of them were their doorman from the night before.

'Excuse me, do you know where Trevor is?' Dana asked.

'Who?'

'Trevor. He's working security here.'

The man looked wearily at the other.

'No Trevor,' he said and looked over her head once more.

'Oh, that's a shame. Are you sure? I've got his sister here and she needs to talk to him. It's urgent.' Dana indicated Candace who stepped forward. The bouncer took them both in, then looked away again, but then he reached to his hip, pressed a button, and murmured something into his walkie-talkie.

They waited. Eventually, Trevor appeared. He nodded to the men, then he beckoned the girls with his head, leading them around the side of the building. They reached a loading bay and Trevor spudded a skinny man in a high-viz vest who nodded them in. The music echoed from somewhere deep within the building. Dana looked at Candace wide-eyed as the well-known guitar riff and vocals played mere metres away.

Trevor led them through a series of spaces stacked with rigging, planks, wires, lighting and enormous pieces of set. The music got louder as they travelled further into the heart of the Arena.

They turned a corner and suddenly, through a crack in the layers of rigging and lighting, they could see the stage. Bathed in blue and pink light, was the back of Flea. When he moved an inch, they could see the drummer's hands holding the sticks. The bass kicked into the funky line for 'Give It Away' and Candace turned to Dana, open mouthed.

They looked to Trevor.

'Stay here. Don't move. I mean it,' Trevor said sternly.

Trevor disappeared back the way they'd come. Dana grabbed Candace, they pogoed up and down as they shouted the lyrics in each other's faces and watched as the band strutted and played, just metres from them. The song ended and the crowd erupted. Then, as the lights dimmed, a team of men hauled a huge piece of set into place onstage. The lights came on once more and the view of the stage was completely blocked. They could see nothing, no one, except a huge piece of painted MDF. The concert continued, and for the next hour they stared at the wood, their heroes just out of view. They waited till the end, then they retraced their steps, Dana still hoping they might catch a glimpse of the band, maybe get invited to the afterparty, or into their dressing room. Trevor was leaning against a railing waiting for them.

'Good time?' he asked.

'It was amazing! Thank you!' Dana skipped up to him and hugged him. He let out a deep laugh and held on to her hungrily. Candace stared at the exit as Dana and Trevor disappeared into a dark place between piles of painted MDF boards. They returned a few minutes later.

'Come back next week,' Trevor said, adjusting his clothes. 'Prince is playing.'

They walked through Wembley, heading into town. Dana produced a Snickers bar she'd nabbed from Trevor's pocket, and they split it, munching on it desperately. But it only seemed to make her stomach growl louder. An hour later, Candace was beginning to limp. Dana's own feet were throbbing, and she felt weak from the lack of food. She wanted so badly to just sleep, but they were hours away from being able to go back to the squat. The clubs of Soho were closer, but she couldn't bear negotiating with another bouncer.

They passed a side street somewhere near Shepherd's Bush and she saw a neon sign. 'Pool Club'. Dana pulled Candace towards it.

CANDACE

They clunked heavily down the steps as they entered the dimly lit hall. Six pool tables were arranged across a large room. A neon sign hung on the wall above the bar that said *Bevan's*. A short woman with dyed black hair, heavy make-up and a black leather waistcoat was pouring a pint. Candace saw Dana deflate. Their little number wasn't likely to work with this woman, and they were both desperate for a drink and some food. Candace walked towards an empty pool table next to one that was already occupied by four men. They all turned.

Candace nodded at them. 'Alright.'

'Alright,' they murmured back.

One of the men turned back to the game, aimed carefully, took a shot.

'Not bad,' Candace said.

She and Dana stood by their own pool table, Candace pretending to half-heartedly reach for coins as she watched the men's game. The men stiffened, became awkward in their movements, tried to keep up the banter. Candace pretended to be so enthralled by their game she forgot to start her own.

Eventually one of the lads – undercut and ponytail – missed, badly.

'Where was that heading? Timbuktu?' one of them quipped.

'I'll keep my helmet on next time just in case,' another added.

Candace smirked.

The executor of the clumsy shot looked at her. 'You reckon you can do better?'

Candace shrugged. 'Maybe.'

The men jeered. The woman at the bar looked on. Candace was relieved to see amusement on her face.

The man who had challenged her held out his cue to Candace.

'Go on then.'

Candace took the cue. She steadied herself and leaned over the table, fighting the light-headedness and trying to focus. Without much hesitation, she potted one of the stripes. There was a shifting, some eyebrows rose. She lined up the next shot. It sailed confidently into the hole. And now came a tricky one.

'You've snookered yerself,' Undercut smirked. Candace studied the table for just a moment, then aimed again. The white ball bounced off the edge of the table at just the right angle and hit the remaining stripe, which spun gracefully in an arc and slotted into the far hole.

'Bloody hell.'

'Fuck me.'

'She's only gone and done it.'

Candace glanced at Dana. Dana smiled, the sparkle return-ing. She knew all of Candace's skills. Years of playing with her brother's mates, keeping up with older boys, had honed her tricks until it was second nature, something she could turn on in a heartbeat.

'Black then, yeah?' she checked in with the men whose game she had taken over. The older man nodded. She focused back down.

'Hold on,' Dana's voice cut through. 'What's it worth?'

They turned to her.

'If she pots the black, what's it worth?'

The older man chucked a tenner on the table. 'There you go. Next round's on me. This is the best craic we've had since Timmy smashed his head on the counter.'

Candace tapped at a hole with the stick and swiftly pock-eted the black, then handed the cue back to Undercut. They all clapped. Dana picked up the money and skipped to the bar. The older man held out his hand.

'Well played, young lady,' he said, shaking Candace's hand. 'I'm Benjy. This is Timmy and Rob and that's Wayne.'

'Candace.'

'You've earned your pint, Candace.'

Dana came back with two double JD and cokes and two packets of crisps between her teeth. They clinked glasses and glugged down half the drink in one. Then Dana turned back to the bar.

'Where you going?'

'There's more,' she called back.

Candace saw her pick up a tray of shots and more crisps

and nodded to a man who had appeared at the side of the bar. She laid it on the pool table and everyone grabbed a shot.

'Where did these come from?' Candace asked.

'His name's Matt. He's the owner.'

Candace looked over at Matt. He was in his late thirties, better turned out than the others, but it was all relative. He was nothing special, but in this domain, he was the alpha.

Benjy raised his tiny glass. 'Stingy fucker's never put his hand in his pocket before,' he murmured, as he smiled over at Matt. 'And I've been coming here for years.'

They cranked up the music and had themselves a lock in. The woman behind the bar, Sandra, seemed relieved to have some female company. Dana soon had her dancing on the bar to 'Lady Marmalade' while the lads played air guitar with the cues. Everyone was drunk. Dana and Candace ate five packets of crisps each.

Candace woke up with a start in a strange room, the sound of traffic zooming by outside. She was on a sofa. Dana wasn't there. It was the deepest sleep she'd had for weeks. She hauled herself up and straightened her crumpled clothes. In the small kitchenette connected to this small living room, she poured herself some water, then went to find Dana. She tiptoed out into the hallway and peered through the door to the bedroom that was ajar. Dana lay beside Matt, both of them naked, both of them snoring loudly.

Candace headed to the bathroom. She found toothpaste

in the cabinet and rubbed it onto her teeth with her finger, then she jumped into the shower, lathering herself with soap, washing her hair twice, three times, letting the hot water run over her, breathing in the steam, lingering in the luxury, before drying off and putting her stale outfit back on.

She helped herself to a chicken leg from the fridge as she waited for the kettle to boil. She raided the cupboards, found tea and sugar, also a pot noodle. Breakfast fit for a queen.

'Looks like you've made yourself at home.' Candace jumped at Matt's voice. She had the telly on and was drinking her third cup of tea with three sugars. He looked older in the daylight, a thickness around the waist.

'I've gotta do the stock,' he said with a smirk. 'Stay as long as you like. She's still knocked out.'

The front door closed behind him. Candace cranked up the volume on the telly. An hour later Dana emerged, squinting in the daylight.

'Is that tea?' she asked.

'Yep.'

'Did you have a shower?'

'Uh huh.'

They were soon back on the road. Dana was scrubbed and smelling of spearmint, her face shone clean, make-up free. Her hair, still damp, curled naturally in the city air as they treated themselves to a bus ride with the coins they'd found down the side of Matt's sofa. They made it back to the squat and collapsed on the bed. Candace contemplated

the feel of her full stomach. It was uncomfortable in the
sweetest way. They lay, touching each other's bellies, till
they drifted off.

ARIANNA

Mr M turned the chair that had been placed centre stage for him so that it was diagonal to the audience, almost side on, a microphone in one hand; his other arm obscured his face slightly, adding to the mystery. It was a pose Arianna had seen before somewhere but couldn't pinpoint. He waited for the audience to quieten, his face half in shadow, then he spoke.

'It is heartening to see so many individuals who have woken up,' he began. 'It is nothing short of a miracle that so many of you have succeeded in evading the myriad ways that you are being indoctrinated, to see through it, reject it and get yourselves here. The act of being in this room is an act of resistance. I am in awe of you all.'

Arianna frowned. It was him, it was his voice. But it also wasn't.

'Many of you know of my journey. In my multiple lives before arriving here I have been a teacher, a thinker, a feeler, a lover, a mentor, a musician, a fighter, a writer. I have been fired and blacklisted, witch-hunted and purposefully misunderstood, misrepresented and scapegoated. Because I have had the curse and the blessing of being able to see through the lies, the manipulation, the propaganda and exploitation that makes up the system we live in.'

His accent was different to what she remembered. Not the plumb vowels and plosive consonants of his middle-class upbringing, but a studied, self-conscious take on something more working class, down-to-earth. Almost cockney, but overly verbose, using ten words when he could use two. And the gestures, the half hiding of the face with the flourish of hand movements, was a strange mix of familiar performances she was just beginning to recognize. Marlon Brando, in that film about the war. Bysshe and Blake, the romantic poet and the political one, the one Dana had used in her avatar, the white frilly shirt casting him as some sort of literary romantic revolutionary all at once.

'And so we created our foundation. What started off as a modest offering in a community theatre for a handful of lost souls has flourished into the global movement you are a part of today.'

Arianna was surprised to find herself on the verge of laughter. Because she suddenly realized that she wasn't scared of him, that he had no power over her anymore. It was so fake, so staged, such an obvious amateur performance made up of a hodge podge of appropriated personas that the grown-woman-Arianna could see straight through. Surely everyone else could too. But they all sat, transfixed, as this aging man with a dyed goatee did his bit on a stage in the conference room of a four-star hotel. But then she knew how compelling he could be, how convincing, how manipulative and how charismatic he could seem to someone young or vulnerable or lost or lonely.

'You have woken up,' he continued. 'And many of you have taken the next step, to fully awaken from the induced coma you have been in, and immerse yourselves in the training that will set you free, set the world free. Or maybe you have just arrived, just found us, are just starting out on this path, the road less travelled. Either way, be quick. Our team will indeed be retreating to the wilds of Xanadu HQ. We have one more gathering after this. Make haste. Hurry towards your liberation, for all our sakes.'

Alan appeared stage left. He listened with awe to his mentor's final few words, then he was the first to start the applause, fervently banging his hands together over and over as the audience joined him. Arianna looked on, bewildered. How had Oxbridge Four Alan become E.G.G. Alan, and then given all of that up to start some dodgy scheme with his ex-teacher?

Mr M stood. The crowd cheered louder. As he embraced Alan, Mr M's frilly shirtsleeve was pulled up his forearm and there it was, the tattoo she had seen in the picture, a huge, thick, black crucifix covering what she knew was another, smaller tattoo of her initials and his hidden beneath it. Then he turned to the front row. Dana and Saffy stood and were ushered through the door to the far left of the room along with Mr M and his disciple, Alan.

'Saffy!' Arianna called. But she was drowned out by the cheering. She tried to get to them, but couldn't even get past the people in her row. The lights were raised and the crowd began to head to the different stations positioned around the fringes of the room where bright-eyed volunteers waited with clipboards, pens and wireless payment points.

2001

DANA

A pain in her left hand woke her. Candace was squeezing it too tight. She forced her eyes open and saw Candace staring at her, wide-eyed.

From downstairs, there was loud thump. Then another. She saw Candace's eye dart to the bag they always carried with them, filled with whatever they needed for the day and currently slung in the far corner. A final bang and the whole building shook. The sound of splintering wood as the front door began to break.

'Police!' a muffled voice shouted.

Candace leaped up and skidded across the floor, grabbing the bag as Dana swung the bedroom door open and jumped down the steps two at a time. With a final crash, the front door gave way below them. Dana and Candace ducked into the kitchen next to the landing as they heard shouts, sounds of scuffling and grunting as others in the building attempted to escape and collided with police lower down the stairs.

Candace glanced at her, then rushed out of the kitchen, back up the stairs.

'Candace!' Dana yelled. But seconds later, Candace was

back with their second bag, the secret bag they kept stashed behind the wardrobe, the one with their most valuable possessions. As several pairs of booted footsteps rushed up, Candace climbed into the sink and shoved the window behind it wide open. Then she looked down, shook her head, looked back at Dana with despair. They were on the third floor.

A policeman holding a baton stepped into the kitchen.

'In here,' he shouted, and another policeman appeared. The girls clung onto each other.

'What are you doing here?' he asked. But now they were crying so hard neither could answer. More shouts from downstairs. The policeman shook his head.

'Just go home,' he ordered.

Dana and Candace stepped outside into a sea of black and white uniforms. Some stood guard over a small group they had kettled against the wall. Dana and Candace recognized them. They were people from their building. Others were kicking in the door a few shops down. Candace pulled Dana away. They slunk along the street, away from the uniforms, down side roads and into the heart of a residential area. Surrounded by quiet, cosy terraced homes, they stopped.

'That's it then. We can't go back.' Candace said.

They looked at each other with shock as they realized they had nowhere to go. Suddenly, the few hours they had been afforded in that bed, in that grotty room, seemed like a luxury. And now it was gone. Dana looked away, trying to stay strong, to figure out what was next, but she could think of nothing, no one, but her mum. A lump of despair and desperation formed in her throat. The desire to go back, just for one cuddle, one cup of tea, to be ensconced with her in her bed, under the duvet in her pristine flat, was overwhelming. But Candace was watching her carefully. Candace who had left everything behind to run away with her because Dana had asked her to. So, Dana gritted her teeth and tried to think.

'Matt's,' Dana said, looking up. 'Let's go there.'

'Matt? From the pool hall?' Candace frowned. But it was the only option they could think of. So they headed back to West London.

The doors of the pool hall were bolted shut. Dana tried the buzzer on the door round the back that led to the small flat above, but there was no answer. They waited. When Matt eventually walked around the corner, he looked like a king to Dana.

'Oh hello,' he said, surprised.

Dana skipped over, jumping into his arms and giving him a kiss. 'Surprise!'

'You alright?' Matt asked, trying to make sense of what was happening. He looked at Candace, who stood awkwardly nearby.

'Yep,' Dana replied. 'Just missed you.'

'You better come in then.'

Dana led him straight into the bedroom.

Afterwards, she lay there watching how chuffed he was at the pleasant turn his afternoon had taken. She jumped in while the glow lingered.

'So, I've got a suggestion,' she began. 'What your place needs is a couple more girls.'

He raised his eyebrows. 'Oh yeah?'

'Yep,' she said. 'It's a great place. You got a good thing going. But if you think about it, last night was the best night that place has seen. And that was because of us.'

'So, what do you suggest?'

Dana sat up.

'Well, you're lucky because we are available to help you. And all we want in return is a place to kip.'

'Is that right?'

'Yep.'

Matt studied her carefully. Then he pulled on his boxers and beckoned her into the living room.

Candace sat up. Matt sat in a chair facing the two girls.

'Apparently you need somewhere to stay,' he said.

Candace nodded.

'Right. You can stay here for now. But you're gonna have to earn your keep. Got it?'

They nodded.

'You'll work nights in the pool hall. Drum up a bit more custom. Get a vibe going. Like you did the other night.'

'We can do that,' Dana agreed.

It was quite fun pulling pints, measuring shots, learning all the regulars' tipples. Dana even liked collecting the empties, keeping the surfaces wiped clean. Under her stern exterior, Sandra the bartender seemed to defer to Matt quietly but completely, and made space for the two new girls. Candace had great banter with the guys and paused between work to pot a shot or two. She was in charge of the pool tables, the balls, the cues, the chalk and triangles, she kept the score boards pristine and even refereed the games sometimes, to the delighted protestations of the regulars. Then they retired upstairs, where Dana and Matt would shag and then Candace would sneak into the bed beside Dana once Matt was snoring.

He'd head out by midday and the girls would lounge around the tiny flat, making cups of tea with loads of milk and sugar. And they ate. Bread and cheese and pizza and chips and noodles and crisps and ham and chicken. By the end of the first week Dana noticed that Candace had started to lose her gaunt, sickly hue, her curves were rounding again, her skin clearing. In the mirror Dana saw the cheekbones recede once more, the youthful fullness returning, the shadows waning from below her eyes.

If he noticed the amount of food they got through, Matt didn't comment. He had an authority about him that slightly unnerved Dana, but also elevated this plain man above the others. One night after they'd closed the bar, had a night cap and shagged, he started to talk about his time in the police force. And something landed, made sense. The tendency to seriousness when the other lads were clowning about. Matt didn't so much laugh as raise an eyebrow. But he'd been forced to retire early after he injured his knee. And now that focus and discipline went into the pool bar. And shagging her.

He led them down to the pool hall every night, and they were careful to be ready early. Dana cracked silly jokes, played the radio loud, tried to get him to loosen up. He'd roll his eyes and shake his head, but he seemed to enjoy the lightness that she brought to his place, so she maintained it at all times.

'Up for some fun tonight?' he said over his shoulder as they headed down a week later.

'Course we are! Fun is our middle name,' Dana exclaimed and cackled loudly. 'What did you have in mind?'

Matt shrugged, 'Bit of a lock in. A few shots. Music. Bit of banter.'

'Bring it on!' Dana shouted.

He poured the first round of tequila shots himself. Candace, Dana and Sandra clinked glasses and downed them in one. The regular lads arrived – Benjy, Timmy, Rob and Wayne – and a few more faces who frequented the place. Benjy was quieter than usual, his eyes darting to Matt and back, and he would only look at the girls sideways.

'Alright Benjy,' Dana said. 'You up for a mad one?'

'Something like that.'

It was like squeezing water out of a stone. Candace was trying with the others, she'd set up the pool tables for them, handed them their cues. They nodded, began playing more quietly than usual.

'Bloody hell, you lot need a fucking drink,' Dana exclaimed, and started pulling pints with Sandra behind the bar. They chucked a shot of Jägermeister in each one and finally, they began to relax. At eleven o'clock, Dana cranked up the music. Matt looked on from his high seat at the end of the bar, his perennially ironic expression giving little away. Dana dance-walked over to him and wound her body sexily in front of him. He watched her for a while and then beckoned with his head. Then, to her surprise, he looked over at Candace and beckoned her over too. The two girls exchanged a look as they followed him towards the toilets. Dana tried to make sense of what was about to happen. They might try the old lesbian act, then she could finish him off before he tried to shag them both. He stood by the cubicle door and turned to them, raising his hand. Between two fingers was a small, folded envelope.

'Might as well make it a proper party,' he said. Dana took it from him and he patted his nose, before sauntering out.

It was a mad one. The maddest one yet. They'd have stories for days after this. Dancing on the bar, on the pool tables, lying on the pool table, tops off, chests bared, dares and drinks and more drinks, everyone snogging everyone, someone shagging someone else. Dana wasn't sure where Sandra had gone, but as she lay on the pool table, Candace also lying across the other end, just out of her range of sight, Dana hoped she was having a good time.

They stumbled back to the flat in the early hours. Everything was spinning. Matt carried them both up the stairs, got her into bed. Someone vomited. But they still shagged.

2022

ARIANNA

Arianna breathed in the cold night air, reeling from what she had just witnessed. So that's what had happened to the man who had caused her such harm. That was the story he had created about his legacy, a story that so many had bought into, just like that handful of young souls who used to gather for his weekly workshops so long ago, hanging on his every word. Just like Alan.

Alan. What the fuck *was* Alan? Had he gone from Oxbridge terrorist to pop star to disciple in one lifetime? Or had he always been first and foremost Mr M's biggest devotee? She thought back to the English classes, the back of his eager head as he sat in the front row, the after-school workshops when he was the first to arrive, relishing the horse play, the physical wrestling that often left him winded, bruised, hurt, but touched by the very man himself. They'd remained close, all this time, and now were the face of this . . . foundation.

And Dana. Ushered in and out with Saffy. Her old friend in the intimate circle of trusted 'X-warriors'. Had Mr M got his claws into her too? Arianna had never got to tell her. She'd been so close, she remembered now, stepping off that bus having decided to confide in Dana, tell her about the double life she was living, having sex with this grown man, their teacher, and then she'd seen her across the road with Chris and screamed at her instead. And then Dana had disappeared.

This couldn't be happening. She couldn't have got it wrong so many times. And now there was the unthinkable reality of Saffy being in his grasp. Arianna marched around the side of the building, looking for a back entrance, a car park, anything that might get her to where Saffy was now. But there was nothing. Just a series of vents and the next building attached firmly to the back of the hotel.

'Saffy!' she shouted. She banged on the wall with frustration. Then she turned and rushed back to the station.

2001

CANDACE

She heard the heavy pad of Matt's footsteps. He paused at the threshold of the living room. She could feel his gaze on her even as she kept her eyes tightly shut, tried to stop her body shaking. He watched her for a long time. Then finally, mercifully, the floor creaked again as he turned away and left the flat.

Candace opened her eyes and stared at the ceiling. Her body wouldn't stop trembling, her teeth chattering, her hands shaking so badly she couldn't control them. Her mind was blank. She tried to focus, and dimly, a thought broke through.

You have to get out.

Candace hauled herself up to a seated position and cried out with pain. Everything hurt. Some of it sharp, some of it dull, some of it throbbing, all of it so bad she was scared to move. A flash of the night before. Lying across a green table. Faces leering down at her. Hearing but not seeing Dana. She winced, leaned on the arm of the sofa and gingerly pushed herself up. She limped to the bedroom and looked in. Dana was curled up in a ball in the bed, half covered by a sheet. Purple bruises around her wrists. Thumb prints on her neck.

Her lips swollen. Candace turned to the bathroom. She was too scared to look in the mirror, so she washed her hands and saw bruises around her wrists too, less pronounced on her dark skin but so painful. She tried throwing some water on her face, but it burst into a ringing pain. She gasped, and that's when she caught her own reflection. One of her eyes was swollen to a slit, dried blood was encrusted around one nostril and matted in her hair. She leaned on the sink and cried. But that hurt too. She stood there, gasping. It had gone too far.

Candace hobbled back into the living room, to the corner where the telephone was. She dialled Eileen's number. It rang once, then Don's gruff voice demanded a Hello. She hung up. Defeated, she rang the only number left to ring.

'Hello?'

'Mum?'

A pause. It had been weeks, months, since they had run, since she had last seen her. The silence hung between them. Candace didn't know where to start, to begin to explain why she had disappeared. She was a terrified mass of blind pain and panic and she just needed her mum.

And then a clunk as her mum replaced the receiver. The line went dead.

Candace stood in shock. Her brother's face flashed across her mind, a grim, knowing expression. The tears had gone.

Back in the bathroom, she stripped off her soiled clothes. She raised one leg, then another, and got into the shower. Jaw clenched, Candace washed herself.

She could barely handle the towel on her skin, the clothes.

Candace approached the bedroom once more and stood over her sleeping, injured friend.

'Dana. Wake up.'

Dana didn't move.

Candace put a hand on her shoulder. She shook her lightly, then harder, until finally, with an intake of breath, Dana pushed her away and resumed her sleep.

'Please. Wake up.' Candace tried to pull her up.

Dana opened one eye. 'Stop it, Candace.'

'Dana.'

'No.'

'This is serious. Look at you. Look at what they did. You've got to wake up. We've got to get out of here.'

'What are you talking about,' she said, refusing to look at her.

'Dana!'

'Just leave me alone.'

'WE'VE GOT TO LEAVE.'

But Dana refused to budge. Refused to open her eyes. However many times Candace tried, Dana slumped back into bed. Candace's stomach was hurting so badly she had to sit on the edge of the bed, breathing as best she could.

'Last night. What happened. It was ...'

'Mad party,' Dana mumbled.

'What?'

'It was mental. Everyone was fucked. Mad one.'

'No ... No. That's not what happened—'

'Absolute mad one,' Dana said again. 'Sleep it off.'

Candace sat by her friend, mouth open. Then she got up

and found their two bags. Numbly, Candace transferred some things from one bag to the other. She closed one and left it tucked by the sofa. She put the other on her own shoulders and walked to the front door. The door didn't budge. She tried again, yanking at the door, but it was locked. From the outside. Heart racing, Candace looked around wildly, then rushed into the bedroom and looked out of that window. They were two floors up, but the extension that made up part of the pool hall jutted out to the side and offered a shorter fall. Candace pulled open the window. She looked back at Dana and her face crumpled. She kissed her on her bruised cheek, stroked her matted hair. Dana kept her eyes tightly shut.

Candace climbed through the window and lowered herself onto the roof below. Her body screamed in pain as she landed and she paused, winded. She found a drainpipe and half-fell, half-shimmied down onto the pavement. Another shot of pain. Then Candace straightened up and limped on.

She walked and stopped, walked and stopped, leaning on lampposts to wait for the pain to subside enough to keep going. On busy streets she tried to walk as straight as possible, but still, wary eyes lingered, gave her a wide berth.

Her legs eventually took her back to familiar streets. In South London she chose a side street and sat gingerly on the ground, head resting on her arms, exhausted with the pain of every step. She sat for a long time. In shock. In grief. Out of options. There were places she had to avoid, whole postcodes she had to navigate around in case anyone she

knew saw her in this state. She wracked her brain to think of
somewhere she could go, to get off the street, but the sound
of the phone line going dead when she'd called her mum
replayed over and over. And then that absence of sound,
echoing in her mind.

As the daylight dwindled, Candace began to feel light-
headed. She hadn't eaten all day. She had walked miles.
She usually thought ten steps ahead, packing essentials
into their bag to get them through the day and any curve-
ball that might come at them on the streets. But life in the
flat above the pool hall had turned her soft, her regular full
belly lulling her into a false sense of security. They hadn't
had to pack the bag since they'd left the squat, or needed to
be walking the streets because they had the flat to hole up in
until it was work time. Work Time. Matt's face appeared in
her mind and Candace doubled over and retched. The pain
in her stomach and between her legs was excruciating. She
looked towards the main road. Shoppers, retirees, mums,
workers bustled past. Going Somewhere. She started to notice The Others. The pale man with sunken cheeks sitting
by the phone booth with a blanket over his legs. The woman
with a headscarf standing outside the supermarket selling
the Big Issue. She'd have to be careful. Turf was sacred on
the streets when all you had to your name was a square of
concrete to fight for, and an unfamiliar face from a different
postcode was not always welcome.

She'd have to keep it moving. Shakily, Candace got to her
feet and headed slowly up the road. She soon found herself
in front of the imposing building of The Grand. Sometimes

a club, sometimes a music venue, they'd blagged their way in a couple of times in their previous life.

The light was dwindling. Candace wracked her brain one more time for somewhere to go as she walked down the side and round to the back of the building. She clocked two industrial-sized bins by the back door and hovered long enough to check if anyone else was around. She kept it moving, circling back several times, until it was properly dark and she knew she had to get off the streets. Candace could hear the sound of a band playing inside. The thump of the bass drum, the twang of the guitar. Cheers at the end of the song. People began to pour out soon after. She waited by a parked car across the road. A man took a piss against the wall of the venue, just where she had been standing moments ago. Finally, the lights were switched off, bar staff came out of the back door, chattering, lighting fags. The last out locked up and walked off too. She waited a bit longer, but now Candace's legs were trembling with fatigue, her head light and dizzy with hunger. She needed to lie down.

Candace looked up at The Grand. It was the biggest venue for miles and she had thought that, just like her brother and his mates, she, Dana, Tess and Arianna would end up there most Saturday nights, once they were old enough.

Now she was going to sleep in the bins outside.

The darkness was thickening now. She pushed open one of the bins. It was empty, apart from a little pool of sour smelling liquid in one corner. She opened the other. This was full with empty glass bottles. Among the bottles were pieces of folded cardboard. Candace reached in and pulled some out. The bottles clinked together loudly. She squinted as she peered in once more, hoping to spot some kind of food. But it was so dark now she could hardly see anything apart from the glint of the glass. She'd sleep it off, make it to morning and find some breakfast.

Candace threw the pieces of cardboard inside the first bin and tried to pull herself over the edge. Pain ripped through her body and she fell back to the floor. She tried again. On the third go, she fell into the metal container and the lid slammed shut above her with a clang. It was horrible. There was no window, no way to see outside. She somehow felt more vulnerable there, blinded, surrounded. She tried to calm down, to settle. She arranged the cardboard on the floor of the bin, away from the puddle of acrid liquid and tried to get comfortable. But soon her breathing began to quicken. She began to hyperventilate. She became disorientated, convinced the walls were closing in, the oxygen running out. It was so completely dark, she couldn't see her hand in front of her face. Blind panic kicked in and she burst out of the bin. Candace leaned against the wall outside, trying to calm herself down. Then she pulled her jacket around her neck, allowed herself a sob, and lay down on the cold, hard ground. She tried to think of something that would get her through tonight. Until the light came back. From somewhere deep inside her, a rhyme began to echo. Then the words of the only poem she knew came back to her wholly and completely and she repeated them to herself.

'Still . . . I rise.'

Over and over she repeated the words until finally, awfully, she slept.

Candace woke with a gasp. Something was hitting the side of her face. Liquid. Hot, acrid liquid. Brick filled her eyeline. She remembered where she was. She must have turned over in her sleep. And now someone was standing right next to her and urinating. She squeezed her eyes shut as the liquid splashed onto her neck, her clothes. It seemed to go on forever. Then a zip and footsteps walking away. Candace lay frozen, her eyes wide open now, as the urine cooled quickly and she began to shiver.

She lay there until the first grey light cast a weak pallor on the scene. Candace pulled herself to her feet. She walked shakily, the pain in her limbs, her organs, her muscles and bones screaming now, worse in the cold, after a night sleeping on the ground.

When she reached the familiar block of flats, she waited under the stairwell. Time passed, then Candace saw her come out of the door, her familiar strides bouncing away down the road to the bus stop. Candace waited a little longer, then she climbed the stairs to the third floor.

He opened the door with a look of surprised curiosity. Then his mouth dropped open, his face crumpled, tears springing from his eyes as he took her in.

She was clutching the book in both hands, hands that were shaking violently. Maya Angelou's warm smile peeped out from the battered cover.

Through chattering teeth, she spoke.

'I ... I kept it safe. S-so I could bring it back. I only borrowed it. I never nicked it.'

'Good god, child. Come in.'

Linton put an appalled hand on her elbow and pulled her into the flat.

2022

ARIANNA

'So she's with her mum.'

'No. Well, yes. She's with Dana, who gave birth to her but she didn't raise her. Dana hasn't seen her since she was a toddler.'

'So who has legal guardianship?' Jade was trying her best to make sense of what Arianna was telling her. She'd only just remembered who Arianna was.

'Well, Dana does, but she hasn't been in Saffy's life for ... She's taken her ... to *him.* Surely we can get some kind of ... emergency injunction ... or ...'

Arianna hadn't known who to call. So she'd called the one person who had stood by her through her own police case, who understood how dangerous that man was, hoping Jade might know what to do. To make this all okay.

'Are social services aware? Did they decide she wasn't able to look after her?' Jade asked.

'Yes. Well, no, they just checked that my friend, who is the one who raised her, they checked she's keeping Saffy fed, clothed and in school, but—'

'Has your friend called Social Services? Or the police?'

'No, she hasn't because . . . she doesn't think . . . she's got no legal standing. But she doesn't know about *him*, that Dana's taken her to him. That's the point. A young girl – a minor – is in his company, maybe even living with him—'

'But she's in her mum's care.'

'Her mum kidnapped her and took her to him. And he's running some kind of cult—'

'Okay, Arianna, slow down—'

'It's a lot, I know, but please, Jade. We've got two days before they disappear to god knows where with her. We've got to get her back.'

'Arianna, I'm glad you called me. And I am concerned. Because we both know what he is capable of. What he has done. To you. But I'm an ISVA. My job is to help women who are reporting sexual violence. I'm not a lawyer, you know that, because this is what you do too. So the only thing I can do is call Social Services and—'

'No. I promised.'

'What about a friendly detective or police? You must have met lots through your work—'

'They hate me. All of them.'

'Right.'

Jade sighed. 'The thing is, Arianna, safeguarding is everyone's responsibility. You know this. So someone needs to call them.'

Arianna's chest tightened. Whatever she did, she would be letting someone down. Either breaking her promise to Candace, or putting Saffy at further risk.

'Yep, you're right,' she said.

'So shall I ... ?'

'Nope. No. It's okay. I'll do it.'

It was late. Arianna had called Jade's number until she had finally answered, sleepy and bewildered as Arianna tried to remind her who she was, and to explain why she was calling after all this time. But Jade was right.

Arianna looked up the number and called. But as it rang, she pictured the conversation, the complication of an anonymous tip off to Social Services, the time it would take to process a report of a minor in the company of a man accused of abuse. Accused but not convicted. And the time it would take them to get to Saffy. And Candace's devastated face.

She hung up.

Arianna rubbed at her exhausted eyes and turned back to her laptop. She searched for the Xanadu Foundation and dove in deep, opening Reddit threads and going down rabbit holes until she finally started to find things.

There were a handful of people beginning to speak out, who had been a part of the group for a few years, who had joined at their lowest, most lost and vulnerable, been welcomed in and quickly initiated, slowly isolated from friends and family as they invested more and more of their time and money, thousands, sometimes tens of thousands of pounds into the PX12 programme, which promised the kind of success that Alan had enjoyed. Then they slowly began to question when it would start happening, when things would start getting better, why it wasn't working for them. And that's when the bullying had started, the threats and rage and blame that had silenced them back into submission, until they had gotten so desperate and poor that they had to speak out. She tried to contact them, tried to track them down, but she could be waiting days, weeks, for a reply, and these people were nervous, scared, suspicious of being duped again, sued. And mostly anonymous.

Arianna's eyesight began to swim. She turned away from the screen and buried her face in her hands. She couldn't fathom him getting away with this. Not again.

First thing the next morning, Arianna made her way to the police station.

ARIANNA

'I don't want you to worry, okay?'

'Okay.'

'It's a big change for us, but there's no reason why we can't make it. We have a special bond, something no one else understands. And that's okay, the world just hasn't caught up yet, but if anyone has a chance of making it, we do.'

Mr M watched Arianna closely. 'There will be lots of fresh faces at my new school, new intrigue, temptation, but as long as we're honest with each other, we'll be okay.'

Arianna turned to him. 'What do you mean?'

He smiled. 'You're way too intelligent for me to patronize, Arianna. I'm just trying to be transparent with you. I've been informed by my new colleagues that I've already been singled out as a bit of a catch among the older girls. And we're in this exquisite mess because of temptation, because of your crush on me. I was a married man, remember.'

'Hold on, you kissed me.'

'Not that again,' he rolled his eyes. 'If that's the simplified version of events you're sticking to, then fine. But I'm fresh meat. It's only a matter of time, and I just want us to be prepared.'

She was chewing the inside of her mouth again. Something she only realized she'd started doing when she drew blood a few weeks ago. Arianna did the other thing she had started doing to soothe herself, stroking the bit between her eyebrows so that the frown wouldn't become a permanent line, just like her mum's had.

'And then there's Cyprus.' Mr M tilted his head, reasoning. 'You'll be away for weeks. Did you think about us when you booked the holiday?'

'I didn't ... My mum ...'

Mr M sighed. 'It's okay. I understand. It's all part of being with someone from a different culture. You're so exotic.' He smiled hungrily. She squirmed despite herself. 'But an adult relationship means that decisions must be made with the other in mind. That's what I did when I accepted the new job. I thought of you. I'm discussing it with you. This party you're going to when you get back, did you ask me before you agreed to go? Did you even think of talking it through with me?'

'I ... No.'

'No.' He sighed. 'So you'll be away from me for three weeks and then you'll come back and go to some party—'

'I'll see you beforehand—'

Mr M put his hand on his chest. 'I'm honoured.'

Waves of frustration and guilt flowed through her. He seemed to have an answer for everything, until she was so confused, her own words seemed to tie her in knots, prove his point further.

He put his hand under her chin, tilted her head up to look at him. 'Hey, hey. Come here. It's okay. We're both learning. And anyway, by the time you're back I'll have a whole album's worth of new songs to play you.'

Arianna knew something was up when she got home last Sunday. Her mum wasn't exactly smiling, but there was a sparkle in her eyes that hadn't been there for a long time. She'd cooked *yemista*, one of Yiayia's signature dishes. It took hours to prepare, not something her mum usually had the time or inclination for, but there she was, that morning, defrosting the vine leaves, hollowing out the tomatoes, preparing the stuffing, all the while London Greek Radio playing songs she only sang out loud when she thought no one was listening.

She'd heard her on the phone to Yiayia. After four years she'd saved enough to get them all there again. Arianna knew how elated they both were at the thought of seeing each other, but not one word of that was uttered. By her mum's expression, Arianna knew that Yiayia had launched into a tirade of practical concerns: Where would they all sleep? She'd have to clear out the back room. It gets hot here now, not like before. They only have water every other day. Don't ask your brother to pick you up in the early hours if it's a weekday, he's got work. Get your father a new jumper from *MarsASpeser*. Get me chocolate. And eye drops. And your sister wants the *Cheesonyo* crisps.

They were screaming at each other within minutes. But arrangements were made and they were all going to Cyprus.

Arianna looked at herself in the mirror. Would Yiayia see how much of a woman she was now? Would her cousins know it too? She'd have to tell them the gory details, explain to them how to give a proper blowjob so they'd know what to do when their time came. She'd have to choose her garms carefully for maximum effect. Time to show them what a London woman looked like. And she would tan. And swim. And come back so buff he wouldn't dream of looking at any other pasty girl in his poxy new school.

'Arianna! Homework!' her mum shouted up the stairs.

'I am!' she shouted back.

Arianna sat on the floor of her room and opened her English folder. Inside, her notes were organized by coloured dividers. Outside, it was covered in white Tippex hearts and initials and the secret sign she and Mr M had that she had designed, with both their initials in Greek letters, swirling and connecting. She abandoned her homework before she'd really started. She took a pen and began to copy the design, their secret sign, carefully onto the inside of her palm.

2001

TESS

She'd heard them shagging last night. They were usually very discreet. But she'd heard some kind of whimper from the German through the walls that made her shudder with disgust. She had pressed her pillow into her ear and lay, eyes open, traumatized. But then she realized she also felt relief. Because something had been up the last few weeks and she was sure it was girlfriend problems. Linton looked weary and troubled these days. He still got up early and made her breakfast and saw her out, but behind the practical chatter about plans for dinner and rehearsals, there was something weighing on him. She'd asked him if he was okay and he had smiled weakly, hugged her close and shoved an extra dumpling in her bag. Then there was that time she'd forgotten her French book and she'd doubled back. She was in a rush, flustered, and couldn't find her key. She had rung the bell and he'd opened it and almost looked disappointed it was her, before gathering himself and arranging his face into a smile.

It was weird.

But anyway. The German was back. He was getting some. The vibe was restored.

Daniel had bought a synth. A shiny new one. And he'd diligently practised the riffs she'd taught him, counting himself in under his breath as the beat kicked in and he played, messing it up the first time, starting over twice, looking up at her when he finished like a puppy waiting for a pat on the head.

'That's great,' she said. 'Well done.'

'Thanks. I've been trying to do the first one and then go into the second one. Still working on that,' he said. 'I found this sick beat the other day. Listen to this.'

Daniel pressed some buttons and a kind of Euro-techno type beat kicked in that he bounced to enthusiastically.

'Do you reckon you could show me something to play over this?' he asked eagerly.

'Sure.' Tess shrugged.

He had positioned his synth perpendicular to his decks so that it created a right angle of equipment. She created a tune on the unweighted keys that he could pick up easily. She played it a few times over and then slowed it down so he could follow. It took a while, but eventually he'd picked it up enough for her to step back, edge towards the window, where she looked down at the garden. Sue sat there, her legs folded under her, a book in her hand, a cup of tea placed on the garden table. From above, she looked like an Impressionist painting, the gentle greens and browns of her matching the colours of the garden perfectly. As Daniel fumbled with the notes, Tess wondered what it would be like to have a mum like Sue. To walk out of the room, down the stairs and out through the French doors, to curl up beside her and sit in quiet company.

The music stopped. He joined her at the window, holding her from behind. He kissed her neck – that was nice – and her shoulder, and the side of her face, tenderly. That was the kind she liked. But inevitably, his breathing started to get faster, filling her ear noisily. He turned her shoulder gently and they made out, standing by the window. Each time he took it slow, each time it went on a bit longer. He moved it on a little further, his hands under her top touching her skin, her stomach, her bra, down between her legs over her jeans. That's when he'd start watching her, adjusting his hand every now and then, trying a different pace, rhythm. She'd smile encouragingly. After a while he would slow down, sigh. Pull her to him in a hug.

Today he held her at arm's length.

'So,' he said meaningfully. 'Jay's party.'

'Yep.'

'I know it seems like ages away.'

'Just the small issue of the most important exams of our lives to get through first.'

'Sure. And the first half of the summer holiday.' He smiled, then got serious again. 'I thought it could be a special moment for us, maybe. A milestone, like.'

Tess's chest constricted slightly.

'You missed out on the last party,' he continued. 'I know you said you felt left out, so ... I thought maybe ... this time could be special for you ... for us' Daniel watched her closely.

'It's neutral ground, there's plenty of private places, rooms. Maybe it could be our first time?'

Tess felt her cheeks flush a hot red. She'd been waiting for this moment. Knew it was inevitable. She'd been surprised, actually, how long she'd gotten away with it, relieved every week she got through still with a boyfriend. But he'd been so patient, it wasn't fair to hold out on him any longer. Maybe she'd get into it once they got all their clothes off and got down to it. Maybe she'd feel something. Everyone else in the entire world, including her wrinkly old dad did. So she must do too. Eventually. At some point. Maybe if they did enough of that nice kissing thing they did at the start, maybe then she'd relax enough for them to . . . for her to actually be able to . . . have sex.

'Yeah, okay,' Tess replied.

He looked like it was Christmas and his birthday all at once. His face flushed with relief and gratitude and joy. He kissed her hand solemnly.

And now Tess was walking home with the very real prospect of having sex for the first time in just a few weeks and not knowing why she didn't feel excited. Not even in the way she had been when the girls had come for a sleepover, or the day of the gig, or that night watching Goldie in the club with actual David Bowie right there, or when she and the girls were drawing up in Art, or even when Linton made ackee and saltfish stuffed dumplings. As she walked home, the list of things that she felt more excited about than having sex grew longer and longer. Frustration at her stupid, broken self grew and grew. This was it, the moment she'd been waiting for her whole life, and she didn't even care.

Tess's jaw set stubbornly. If Linton had taught her any-thing, it was that there was always a practical solution. She'd be ready.

Sex with the German was obviously working because Linton was almost his chirpy self again, playing a Mozart record this morning because the combination of chords and tempo were meant to optimize inspiration and brain activity. He was cooking her favourite because fish was brain food. It made her think of Arianna whose mum was also probably cooking something nutritious and smelly and fishy this very moment, a few neighbourhoods away.

Linton was all efficiency and practicality. It calmed her as he bustled about, checking she had everything and re-confirming the timings of her first week of exams for the hundredth time, even though he'd also written it up and stuck it on the kitchen wall. He threw extra fruit into her bag and hovered at the door for longer than usual as she headed out, she only heard the click as she turned the corner, out of his sight.

As they filed into the huge assembly hall, they were ushered to the rows of tables on the left. Daniel whispered her name and Tess turned to see him settling a few seats back and to the right. He waved. She smiled weakly and then turned to face forward, trying to block all thoughts of them having sex from her mind, tried to fill it with all the Brechtian techniques she could think of. But her head started to fill with images of little placards held up by mini actors which read 'Sex Sex Sex'. The supporting cast faced the audience, one finger looped in a circle, the other finger penetrating it over and over.

For fuck's sake.

Afterwards, they all stood outside the main entrance talking animatedly, comparing answers, lamenting the impossible questions, the lack of time, the luck of having the very subject they'd just revised come up, or not. She arrived home exhausted and relieved.

Bilbo was out; she had the flat to herself.

Tess looked through the bathroom cabinet, then in her bedroom drawers. Finally, she found the mini bottle of perfume Dana had given her for one of her birthdays. It was cylindrical and just the right width. She remembered the lewd comment Dana had made about it at the time. Tess took the bottle with her to bed. She held her breath, gritted her teeth and tried to insert it between her legs. She tried again, and again, but Tess barely managed more than a centimetre – just like when she'd tried to use a tampon. Eventually, she gave up and sighed with frustration. Four more weeks.

2001

CANDACE

Candace pulled her hood up over her face as the bus went by. Just in case. It was a good hour after Tess went to school, but she hovered outside the flats for another ten, watching the third floor, then she climbed the stairs.

Linton took her in with relief, checking her all over as if to make sure none of her was missing, then he ushered her in. It had been five or six days. She tried to mix it up a bit, make sure she didn't rely on him too much, get too soft, but he always seemed ready for her. They had a bit of a routine now. She'd take her shoes and jacket off but keep them close. He'd get a massive plate of food together and they'd sit at the table as he watched her eat, then he'd fill it again. He'd hand her a towel and she'd have a shower. Then she'd lie down on a mattress in the tiny spare room, surrounded by shelves stacked with books and manuscripts, piles of newspapers, political magazines and vinyl. Dusty, homely, safe. Today there was a black bin liner in the corner.

'It's a few bits of clothing I gathered that we don't need. Take a look,' he said.

He closed the door and headed back downstairs. She

pulled out jumpers and jeans, a bulky coat. She recognized a couple of Tess's tops, too small for her even now that she was so much thinner. But the man's coat she could use. The rest would slow her down. Candace spread her new coat over the duvet Linton had laid out on the mattress, and slept.

She woke up and stretched as she felt her stiff, weather-beaten body soften into the mattress. The patter of rain on the window was getting louder. She sighed, remembered the new coat and started to form a plan in her head about where to go to sit out the rain. She could hear the tap of a spoon on a pan downstairs, the clang of a lid, the gentle rhythm of a reggae tune. Candace folded the duvet, stuffed it into the other bin bag he kept in the corner, adding the pillow and the sheet. Then she donned her new coat and stepped out onto the landing.

Tess's bedroom door was ajar; the posters of all those crusty white dudes made her almost smile, almost cry. The glimpse of a violin, a bow, a sheet of music, even the bloody instrument case, was almost too much. It made her so proud. Today she found herself pressing the door a little more open, stepping inside, standing in the middle of her old friend's room and taking in the smell. The smell of Tess.

She'd chucked a top onto her bed. Candace imagined Tess trying it on, looking at herself with disappointment, taking it off and going for something else. Some sheet music was open on a stand, something complicated, brilliant. Tess's boots, well-worn now, lay discarded in a corner. Next to them, a roll of paper. Familiar paper. Grainy, thicker than writing paper.

Candace walked over and unravelled it. It was artwork. On Ms Gail's sheets. A sob erupted from her. And another. Candace stood and wailed silently at her friend's beautiful artwork. And her teacher's grainy paper.

'Please. Stay.'

Candace dropped the paper and wiped briskly at her hot face. He was standing outside the door, looking at her with sadness. She tried to walk out of the room. Linton held up both hands.

'Candace, please. Just stay. There's no need for you to go out there. We'll wait for Tess together. We can tell her you're staying a while. I don't see the problem.'

'Still no,' she answered coldly.

'But why?'

'I told you. She's got exams. It'll mess her up—'

'Do you know how worried she's been? How long she searched for you. We all did. I went to the school. I talked with Miss White, Ms Gail. All of them. You're a child—'

'I'm seventeen now—'

'You a *picknee*,' he insisted. 'You got no business out on the streets.'

'You don't know my business,' she warned.

'Candace, I cannot keep this from Tess any longer. That is not how this family functions.'

Anger welled up in her. What was he flaunting the word family at her for? Shoving it in her face while she had to beg a meal from someone else's dad while her own mum wouldn't pick up the phone to her? Dickhead.

'Whatever,' she said, and pushed past him.

'Candace,' he said suddenly, gripping her by the arm. 'It is raining outside. You cannot go out there—'

'Get your hands off me you fucking nonce.' Candace saw Linton's face crumple at the word. She yanked her arm from his grasp and stormed down the stairs and out of the house. She swore loudly as she realized she'd left her old jacket behind. She paused, turned back. Stopped again. Forced herself on, into the driving rain.

2022

ARIANNA

The officer's face hardened behind the reception desk when he recognized Arianna. He looked behind her to see who she was bringing in to report today, then he realized she was alone.

'Can I help?'

'I'm not here to ... I don't have anyone with me ... I'm here to speak to someone who ... Her name's Karla. She works here.'

'Karla ... ?'

'Karla Malik ... She's in Fraud.' Arianna held his gaze.

He stared at her a moment longer, then he picked up the phone.

Arianna couldn't bear to think about what this conversation might do to Karla, what it might unlock for her. It wasn't fair to spring this on her in the middle of work, but Arianna had to try anything she could think of to get Saffy back.

The officer replaced the handset.

'I'm afraid there's no Karla Malik on the fraud team here.'

Arianna's heart sank.

'But I spoke to her, in there, a few days ago ... She ... Is she freelance? Does she work as a consultant? Or ... Please, it's important—'

'I'm not able to share that information.'

Arianna gritted her teeth as tears of frustration threatened to burst. She nodded and turned towards the exit.

'—But if a consultant *was* assisting on certain investigations, then that individual would usually be in attendance for the afternoon briefing.'

Arianna turned back around, but the officer was now busy adjusting a poster about knife crime on the back wall.

She stood outside and to the left of the entrance for hours, unwilling to move or find somewhere warmer in case she missed her. At ten to one, she walked straight past.

Arianna grabbed her arm. Karla turned in alarm.

'Sorry. Hi. We met in there a few ... Could we grab a coffee?' Arianna said.

Karla studied her carefully, but she had already recognized her, and the desperation on her face. 'Sure,' she said.

They sat in a café nursing their drinks. Arianna forced herself to speak..

'I'm only coming to you with this because I have to try everything I can to get her back.'

Arianna faltered, trying to decide what the beginning of this story was, realizing in real time that, if her assumptions were right, it was actually Karla who was the beginning of the story. But that part was not for her to tell, so she started with school, with poetry and a charismatic teacher and Arianna used the words she had learned to name what he had done, the police case, the decision, and now the discovery of his reincarnation. And Saffy. And how it was her fault, how she'd made it easy for Dana to take her, and that she had to get Saffy back. Whether they could get him for something else, anything, that might lead to police intervention. Fraud maybe.

Karla listened, her beautiful features withdrawing, her deep brown eyes growing haunted at the mention of his name. But she held her tongue, and even when Arianna finished, she remained quiet.

'I'm sorry to hear you went through all that,' she said eventually. 'You're wrong. It wasn't your fault.'

A wave of long-held grief rushed through Arianna as Karla continued.

'But I don't think I can help.'

Arianna's stomach sank. 'She's just a girl,' she pleaded.

'I'm sorry.' Karla stood, reaching for her jacket. Her sleeves pulled back revealing for a moment a trail of scars up the inside of both forearms. Light horizontal cuts, healed now, but forming a permanent pattern on her skin.

Karla pulled at her sleeve, walked out of the café.

ARIANNA

She woke to the crowing of the neighbour's cockerel. Bright sunlight penetrated the thin curtains, highlighting the white walls, the framed photo of a teenage Militsa, the old-fashioned bedding and the crocheted doily. Arianna stretched already-bronzed limbs, breathed in the smell of hand-woven furnishing, the earthy, musky, citrusy air of her Yiayia's house.

And now the chatter of at least five women drifted to her, the gossip and the busy hands, the aroma of thick coffee being sipped along with the first cigarette of the day.

And the heat. It was still morning, but already the cicadas chirruped the promise of another scorcher. Arianna stared at the patch of chalky plaster that was crumbling slightly in the corner of the ceiling. Her Pappou's work. The walls built by his hands, room by room, at the end of his working day. Bricks dried in the sun by Yiayia's hands, ready to be laid and set by his. Until they had a home. This home. Where they raised their family and then sent them abroad to get an education only to have them return, multiplied, to eat and sleep and argue once more.

Arianna slipped on a T-shirt and shorts, wetted down her messy curls, and made herself presentable for the aunties.

There was a moment, as she descended the stairs, where she caught her mum sitting among the women, sifting through a tray of lentils. Her face was relaxed, the lines softer. Here, she was witty, easy to laughter. There was something girly about her, playful almost, sitting on the veranda in a loose circle around the coffee table, putting the world to rights and preparing lunch in the relative cool of the morning. They turned as Arianna descended, and the lines on Militsa's face deepened a fraction, her mouth tightened, her gaze hardened.

The aunties exclaimed at what a woman Arianna was becoming, asked with incredulity if this was really the little girl they'd seen only a few years ago. She kissed them all, twice on each cheek, felt their wet blessings on both sides of her face. One auntie spat at her to ward off the devil. Yiayia had already hauled herself out of her chair and was returning from inside with a plate of pastries fresh from the bakery early this morning, and a glass of chocolate milk for Arianna. As the women settled back into their work and talk, Arianna was content to listen to them, amused by their turns of phrase, the odd filth and swearword that punctuated their assessment of the world, the neighbourhood, the family. Their perfume and hairspray. The second cigarette. The aromatic coffee.

But quite suddenly, the mix of smells was a little too sharp, the chocolate milk her Yiayia had been serving her since she was a child seemed to coagulate in her throat. She managed only a few bites of her *dashinopitta*, even though it was her favourite, before she had to stop. Casually, Arianna stood up, sauntered into the kitchen and left the rest of her breakfast on the side.

She went back upstairs and leaned over the bathroom sink until the nausea passed. Then to her room where she pulled out the envelopes hidden under the clothes in her suitcase. He'd written one for each day she was away, a pile of letters she'd ferried here among her underwear. She unfolded the paper and read today's protestations of love and lust hungrily.

They spent the day on the beach, Theo throwing himself about in the waves, Lelia caught somewhere between the pull of wanting to join him and trying out the more serious business of tanning that Arianna was doing, adjusting straps, turning regularly, ensuring maximum bronzing with mini-mum lines. Arianna swam too, every day, and watched as the mix of good food, sun and exercise transformed her body. But her skin felt extra sensitive this year, and she squirmed under the glare of the Mediterranean sun.

By mid-afternoon, she was exhausted and collapsed in her bed, shutting the door on the clamour of the extended family and falling into a heavy sleep through the final hot hours of the day. She woke to longer shadows, the cicadas replaced by the cricket evensong. Her cousins arrived in noisy cars, hair slicked back, designer jeans belted tight, kissing Yiayia and snacking on leftovers straight from the fridge while they waited for Arianna. Then they all piled back into the car. The music and the air con turned high, aftershave and perfume wafting around the enclosed space, they zoomed along the motorway to Ayia Napa.

It was a Friday night, and the best of London's Garage DJs and MCs had made the pilgrimage to her island. Watery Sex-On-The-Beaches were consumed before they headed into the club.

When DJ Luck and MC Neat took to the stage, Arianna was in the toilets vomiting. She held her hair back carefully, squatted so her clothes didn't touch the dusty floor, wiped her face clean, rinsed her mouth out, and re-applied her lipstick. Then she walked back out and joined her cousins once more.

Militsa was waiting for her, sitting in the darkness, making Arianna jump. She put a hand to her mouth so she wouldn't wake the kids. The letters were spread out across the bed. Arianna froze.

'You're having sex with him,' her mum hissed.

'No I'm not.'

'Don't lie to me, Arianna. You're having sex with him. The things he is saying. It's disgusting.'

'You shouldn't have read that. It's none of your—'

Her mum jumped up suddenly, glaring at Arianna.

'I should call the police! It's disgusting what he's doing. What you are doing. *Achristi. Ximarismeni. Poutana.*' Each insult landed like a blow. Militsa's face contorted with revulsion and rage. Arianna felt tears well up and clenched her jaw to keep them down. 'You will get pregnant and ruin everything!'

She stormed out of the room. Arianna stood in shock, then slowly gathered the sheets of paper. It had been coming for a long time. Ever since the gig, when he had turned up, almost kissed her, waited for her outside. Nothing got past Militsa. Arianna was almost relieved. She realized she had been bracing herself for this confrontation for months. And now, at least, it was done.

In the morning she woke to the click of the door as her mum made her way downstairs for morning coffee. Arianna stumbled out of bed, rushed to the toilet, and threw up again.

2001

TESS

Sundays were the worst. Loneliness pressed down on her until she could hardly breathe. Tess cursed the morning for being so early, for spreading the entire day, hours and hours before her, with nothing to do and no one to be with, belong to. She'd heard the door click as he left for his morning meeting with the Cardiganed Socialists. The German would probably meet him there, which meant they'd linger after the meeting finished, maybe grab another coffee or even food. Which meant at least four hours of being completely alone in this dusty, pokey flat with only the prospect of her weird old dad coming home to look forward to.

Tess was tired. She needed a day off. And even if Daniel hadn't been in Corfu with his family, she'd probably have fobbed him off anyway. But at least that would have been an option. All last week she'd been at the Camp for Young, Gifted Musicians, all of yesterday at orchestra. She'd longed for a day where she didn't have anything to get up for, but now that it was here, she longed for it to end, for tomorrow to come, so she had someone, anyone, to talk to, to be with. She had things to practise, of course, there was always practise to do. But she couldn't help but think of everyone else, literally everyone, sunning themselves somewhere lovely and far away, eating ice cream for breakfast and growing tall, curvy, boobs expanding, muscles forming with every kick and stroke, while she festered in her bedroom as the rain washed out another summer's day in London.

Tess hauled herself up and stared across the room at the little bottle of perfume on the shelf: her nemesis. She'd been trying to muster the courage to try again, to inch the bottle a bit further into her, prepare her for the looming de-flowering, now only days away. But the sight of it alone made her tense up, solidify, until she felt like she was made of the same hard plastic and glass that she had been trying to push into her body.

What was wrong with her? It was getting embarrassing now. And the girls at school didn't even bother to lower their voices anymore when they pronounced her a Frigid Troll. Phoebe, in particular, seemed to have decided she was her permanent enemy for supposedly stealing Dan from her. It was all so exhausting. Such bollocks.

Bollocks.

Daniel's pink little balls appeared in her mind, swinging and jiggling between her legs as they Did It. He was so excited, had treated her like she was some kind of hallowed fairy-queen since she'd agreed. He'd fly back the day before and they would have their reunion at The Party. With the whole of the sixth form present for her big cherry-popping moment. She jumped up suddenly, trying to erase the image from her mind, and walked into the spare room, filled with her dad's endless collection of books and manuscripts. Maybe there she would find something that could help her understand what was going on with her.

It was musty in there, dusty and close. The spare mattress was propped up against one side of the small room, a black bin bag in front of it with a book lying on top of it, frayed around the edges, folded and stained. It took a moment for Tess to recognize it: Maya Angelou's poetry book. The one Candace had been fixated on.

Candace.

Tess picked the book up and an acrid smell wafted from it. Stale piss. She dropped it and it hit the black bag, nudging the top open enough for her to see the arm of a lime green puffer jacket she recognized immediately.

Tess waited for him downstairs, her heart and mind racing. She'd pulled out the jacket, made sure it was Candace's, even picked up the stinking book again, leafed through it, trying to make sense of what was going on. She'd left a message on Dana's pager again, even though Linton had forbidden her from calling the number after he'd received the last phone bill – twice as much as any other he'd ever paid.

Finally, she heard the key in the door and Linton appeared on the threshold.

'Samwise?' he called.

He looked at her and the smile morphed into concern. 'What is it?' he asked.

'Has Candace been here?'

He slumped. He almost seemed relieved. Then he straightened and faced her. 'She has,' he said.

'What the fuck? When?'

'I've been wanting to tell you for so long,' he said.

'What? How long? When did she come here? Why?'

He took a few steps towards her. 'The first time she turned up, she was in such a bad way—'

'The first time? How many times has she been here?'

'I . . . I don't know—'

'Candace has been coming here and you didn't tell me?'

'She wouldn't let me. She didn't want you to get upset or distracted while you—'

'Upset? Why would I get upset? It doesn't make sense.'

'I should have told you.'

'But you didn't.'

'No.'

She got up and rushed past him, up the stairs to her room. Tess pulled clothes out of her wardrobe and drawers and stuffed them into her rucksack with a toothbrush. Tess slung the backpack onto her shoulder and stomped back down the stairs. She shoved her boots on as Linton looked on. She opened the front door and turned to him. Tears welled in both their eyes. Then Tess stepped out and slammed the door shut.

2001

CANDACE

Candace sat on the fallen log, watching the daylight make silhouettes of the trees in front of her. She liked this spot the best because from here, you could look around and see only nature, not one sign of man or human hand. No telephone lines or concrete paths. No bins or cars or adverts. Soft earth under her feet. The smell of grass. Wind in the trees. Birds. Gentle. Quiet. The Heath was a short bus ride away from the flats, or half an hour's walk. This was where they'd come once a year for the Long-Distance Run. They'd taken it so seriously that first year at school, she and Dana had even gone jogging the week before in preparation. She'd come eighth, out of the whole Lower School.

She watched the light change, snug in her big new coat. She tilted her head up, letting the last bits of the waning sun blind her eyes, warm her skin, grateful it was still summer, that the days were long and the nights short. She had about half an hour before twilight. She'd have to be back near the road by then, because this was paradise by day; the perfect place to get murdered by night.

She made it back onto concrete in good time. Something

had occurred to her, an option she hadn't dared try. So she headed South, following the number 85 bus route. The high rises on the estate loomed in the distance, way before she arrived. She'd been there before, visiting a mate from school, and remembered that someone had pointed out the flat her brother was known to frequent. The place he went when he disappeared for days on end. She remembered the respect his name engendered. The fear. Once it was known she was his little sister, people looked at her differently, gave her a little more space.

She hovered nearby and thought she recognized the building: two in from the right. Candace found a bus stop with a good view of the entrance and sat. She became aware of the rows and rows of windows looking down on her. So many flats, so many people who could recognize her. She hunched her shoulders and waited, humming to herself quietly.

Her bum had turned numb, the chill of the night had seeped up through the bottom of the coat and her feet were getting cold through her shoes. Finally, she thought she saw the back of someone she recognized. She jumped up, stalked forward, trying to get to him before he got to the entrance of the building, before the doors closed behind him. She still wasn't completely sure it was him, but she took a punt.

'Warren,' she said.

He looked around, squinted, recognized her. He looked left and right then behind him at the flat as he approached her. 'Candace? That you?'

She nodded.

He took her in, and a look of sadness settled on his face. 'You okay?'

She nodded again.

'Where you been? You not at home?'

Candace shook her head.

'Where you staying?'

'I thought ... I remember you lot had a place. I didn't know if he ... was out ...'

'You wanna stay here?' Warren rubbed the back of his head nervously. 'Ah shit, man. He's back.'

Candace nodded. Turned away.

'Hold on. Hold on,' he called to her.

She paused. Warren shoved something into her hand and made her close it.

As she walked out of the estate, Candace began separating the money and hiding it on various parts of her person. She'd make it last as long as she could, until she could think of another plan. She didn't catch a bus or even buy herself something to eat, but she promised herself a double cheeseburger first thing. Strawberry milkshake. Large fries.

ARIANNA

'I've tried everyone I know.' Arianna sat facing Candace in her boathouse on the river. Her heart sank as she clocked Saffy's school timetable still pinned to the fridge door.

She had forced herself to return here. To face Candace once more. To witness the crazed relief on Candace's face when she told her she'd seen Saffy, then the horror when she had explained who she was with.

'The law, it's ... slippery,' she continued. 'You've got to have something concrete. As a complainant—'

Candace suddenly slammed her fist on the table, Arianna jumped. Candace started pacing around her tiny home.

'Where does that motherfucker live? Where is he?' she demanded. 'What are we waiting for? Come on! Let's go!'

'All I know is where they're gonna be tonight.'

'When? How long do we have to wait? Let's just get her.'

'You've got to be careful. Legally I'm not sure I ... And you don't want them to clock you before you can get to them ...'

'*Me*? Aren't you coming?'

Arianna knew that breaching the terms of her own

injunction order against Mr M could have legal consequences. But then she looked at Candace's desperate face.

'Course I am,' she said.

They resurfaced from the underground into the waning daylight, heading to the venue in the hotel once more. She looked at Candace and suddenly realized that it would be just the two of them. Her heart sank. Tess should be here. She should have told her. But pride and revenge had stopped her from calling. Arianna frantically retrieved her phone and called Tess's number. It rang and rang and went to voicemail. She tried again.

As she held her phone, a message came through.

Call me. Karla.

Adrenaline coursed through Arianna as she called. Karla answered after one ring.

'Hold on,' she said quietly. Arianna listened to Karla's chair scrape back, heard her walking through doors into street noises.

'So, it looks like there is an ongoing investigation into The Xanadu Foundation,' Karla said. Arianna stopped walking, Candace frowned at her. 'Reports of large sums of money invested by individuals for promises of services with no clear return, trails to possible offshore accounts, but nothing concrete enough to make a move. There seems to be a lack of evidence, something irrefutable.'

'Is there anything we can do to stop him?' Arianna said.

'We need evidence. Someone on the inside. Don't call this number unless I call first.'

Karla hung up.

ARIANNA

Arianna woke slowly, drowsily, her eyelids heavy. She was in a ward, blue curtains pulled around her. She shifted slightly and felt something between her legs. A large sanitary pad.

She'd had an abortion.

The last thing she remembered was the cheery surgeon asking her to count. Before that, she remembered arriving at the clinic with Mr M, his agitated face as he paced the waiting area, making her think of upbeat, funny things to say, to prove this was all okay, that she was taking it in her stride. It was a private clinic. She was so far gone it was the only option. And she had insisted on paying half. She was a feminist after all. It had cleaned out her savings because she'd actually paid for the whole thing and then he was going to give her the rest in cash, so there was no official trace, seeing as he'd just got a new job in a school and was probably still having checks done on him.

Arianna suddenly wanted her mum. But she was still in Cyprus with the kids. Arianna had flown back to London early because she'd begged to be allowed to come back for Jay's party. After two weeks of throwing up Yiayia's delicious

food. Two weeks of pretending to everyone she was absolutely fine.

Her dad had come to pick her up from the airport. But so
had Mr M. She had tried to explain to him that her dad was
somewhere in the airport waiting for her, but his eyes blazed
with sudden anger as he accused her of ruining his romantic
surprise. So she let him lead her away and then called her dad
an hour later, making up some story that she'd gone straight
to a friend's house to get ready for a party. He'd been worried
and angry and she'd felt so guilty.

The curtains were pulled back, a nurse entered. She said
something chirpy and offered to take her to the recovery
room where she could have tea and biscuits.

Mr M was waiting for her as she walked gingerly out of
the ward half an hour later. He looked tired and put out. She
realized he was angry with her. It wasn't part of the image
he was curating: playing guitar, writing poetry, songs. A free
spirit with a girl fifteen years younger than him by his side.
Arianna tried to walk straight, brush the whole thing off,
smile for him.

'Sorted,' she said.

'Right. Let's get you back home.'

They walked out of the clinic to a bus stop.

'I've written you something,' he said. 'But I'll wait till we're
home.'

Arianna stopped. 'I think I should go back to mine. I need
a change of clothes and underwear.'

'Don't be silly. You've got plenty of stuff at mine,' he said.

She desperately wanted her own bed. To sleep and sleep

surrounded by her things. Lie there for as long as she needed until her body felt normal again. Until this whole nightmare was over.

'Besides,' he added. 'We can't let your parents see you like this. You're probably still high on the drugs they gave you. You might go and spill the beans and get me arrested. And I've got the tattoo booked tomorrow. You said you'd come.'

TESS

She had rung and rung the bell, banged on the door and looked through the letterbox. She thought she'd have to resort to calling on the neighbour again. But then she saw something move in the window and knew Dagmar was home.

The usual threats worked.

Dagmar flung open the door and scanned her daughter's face, taking in the changes since they'd last seen each other. It was the closest thing to maternal care Tess would get.

'Hi Mum, it's me.'

Dagmar grunted, padded back into the house leaving the door open, muttering about a flight she had to catch soon.

The first night hadn't been too bad. Tess had cleared the spare room enough to get to the bed in the corner that was piled with clothes, bits of dried fruit, colourful bowls and shells. She'd dragged over a wooden box and turned it into a bedside table. It was quite a nice room underneath it all. Small, with wooden floorboards and a window that looked out onto the quieter back of the building. It had Dagmar's old paints and an easel. Large painted canvases, all with Dagmar's signature use of extreme contrasts of light and shadow, leaned on each other against the wall, thick with dust. But when Tess tried to sleep, the smell of white spirit and oil paint, the mustiness and dust, was too much. Dagmar was downstairs on the floor of the living room, propped up against the sofa, snoring. So Tess slept in Dagmar's bed that night, and the following one. But then she was woken in the night by her mum cackling with two deeper voices downstairs, loud folk music and bad singing. Tess was too scared to go downstairs so she lay awake. By dawn, she was exhausted.

It didn't take long to gather her things. She walked downstairs and was relieved to find it was just Dagmar, now lying on the floor, surrounded by glasses and cans and overflowing ashtrays. Tess made a cup of tea and put it on the table next to her unconscious mum.

Then she let herself out.

He was waiting at the corner of her road near the bus stop. He jumped with surprise when she arrived from the other direction. It was Saturday morning, the Saturday of the infamous party. Daniel was expecting to catch her as she left for orchestra practice, not coming back from a rough few days at her mum's.

He was tanned, his blond hair bleached almost white from the Mediterranean sun. Even from across the road she could tell he was fitter, more muscly, taller, morphing into the strapping man he would soon become, effortlessly, just from living well. His face lit up when he saw her.

'I thought I'd surprise you. I couldn't wait till tonight. It feels like it's been years,' he gushed.

Rage filled her. She stopped just out of his reach, knowing she looked exhausted, her brown skin pallid, a summer spent in London, a sleepless night doing her no favours. He was showing off. That was what he was doing. He couldn't wait to show her his tan and bleached hair and muscles. It was pathetic. Cruel even.

'Right, well. You've seen me now, so,' she shrugged, coldly.

His beaming face morphed into confusion. 'Er ... Shall we go for a walk? Or breakfast? I could wait with you at the bus stop.'

'I'm just getting home actually.'

'Right,' he said, confused, still sure there was some mistake and that all would be perfect again, because his life was perfect so she must also be perfectly perfect for him so he could carry on living his perfect life with his perfect mum and tan. 'Where ... have you been?'

'Out. I've been out all night, actually. Just getting in now.'

He laughed then. As if it was ridiculous that she would do something like that. Have a life of her own that carried on while he was away sunning himself. But he sobered when she didn't join in. 'Did you ... have fun?'

'Bit of a mad one, actually. Didn't get much sleep.'

Now concern edged its way into his features. For the first time he began to suspect that it wasn't all working out for him. Good.

'Oh. Well, maybe you could get some rest ...' he said, pathetically.

'That's the plan,' she threw back.

His face dropped. For a second, she almost felt sorry for him.

'Okay, well ... I hope you ... feel better ... and I'll see you ... later.'

'I doubt it,' she said coldly.

'Did I, did I do something?'

'Look,' she huffed. 'Just go have fun with everyone, okay? Don't worry about it. It's cool. Do your thing. I'll do mine.'

'What's wrong, Tess?'

'Nothing's wrong. I'm just telling you to have fun tonight.'

'Do you not want to come to the party?' he asked.

'Like I said. Bit of a mad one last night. Don't think I'll make it.'

'Is ... is this over?'

Tears prickled Tess's eyes. She fought them with everything she had.

'Yep. Yes,' she said through gritted teeth. He looked devastated. 'We're just really ... different, okay? It's not going to work.'

'Tess.'

'Sorry,' she said, and it came out huskier than she'd planned.

Tess stepped past Daniel and up to the flat.

Linton was in the living room, sitting in the armchair, worrying his grey beard. He stood as she walked in. She dropped her bag and ran to him.

2001

CANDACE

They had been dancing on the pool tables. Someone had cranked the volume up until they couldn't hear anything else. It was deafening. Dana was yelling at the top of her voice, singing along to the music, dancing with a snooker cue. Winding her waist sexily. Throwing her head back. Losing her balance for a moment. Someone reached out to her. That was it. A hand had reached out and pulled Dana down. Someone was pulling Candace down too. She fought them off. Freed her hand and threw it in the air as the song reached its noisy climax. But it was no fun now that Dana wasn't dancing next to her.

And suddenly, down at that level, it all changed. Someone was pushing his sour lips onto hers now. Forcing her to lie on the pool table. Hands were holding her down. Faces looking down on her and her friend. Familiar faces, now changed, warped. She thought she'd screamed. She tried to look for Dana but she couldn't move or turn. And then the song finished and there was a moment, a few seconds, between songs. Someone was singing 'Ebony and Ivory' as he watched.

They were left there, on the snooker table, until finally He returned and hauled them both up. One girl under each arm. Carried

*them up the stairs to the flat where she vomited. Then he took Dana
into the bedroom.*

A hand gripped her shoulder and she screamed as she jolted
awake, flailing her arms in front of her.

'You can't stay here,' someone said.

She fought, blindly. All of the hands on her again.

'Candace is it? It's okay love. You're okay. I'm Sandra. You
can't stay here love, okay? I'm going to take you somewhere
warm.'

As Candace ducked and weaved, the woman insisted
on eye contact which she eventually got, locking eyes with
Candace so that she woke properly from her nightmare,
breathing rapidly, recovering from the blind panic she was
in. Candace stared into the kind face. The clear brown eyes,
the neat braids with a few friendly shells hanging at the ends.
And then Candace let out a wail. She cried loud, hot tears and
Sandra crouched by her, let her cry.

Then Sandra gently touched Candace's elbow, helping her
up off the hard, cold floor. As they made their way down the
road, Candace glimpsed a familiar figure standing across
the road: Warren. He nodded, then retreated into the dawn
shadows.

2001

ARIANNA

'Wake up. Arianna, wake up.'

She had been in a sleep so deep, it had been dream-free. Mercifully, blissfully fathoms away. There was a sharp nudge to her shoulder followed by a burst of pain in her abdomen. She gasped and opened her eyes.

Mr M loomed over her. 'Why won't you wake up?'

'What time is it?'

'We've got to go soon,' he said sternly.

Arianna couldn't remember where she was meant to be going, but she was mortified at making him late. The drowsiness was so heavy, it pulled her back.

'I don't know what to wear.' He shoved her once more, then pulled open his wardrobe. She closed her eyes, began to drift off once more. Something hit her in the face. A T-shirt.

'What do you wear to a tattoo parlour? I have no idea.'

Arianna looked at the clock. It was 7 a.m. She needed so desperately to sleep.

'Will you wake up, for Christ's sake?'

She propped herself up on her elbows and felt another sharp pain in her stomach. He continued to throw clothes at her. Arianna suddenly remembered what had happened the day before. She had had an abortion. She clutched her belly as he grabbed her arm and yanked her up. She gasped as pain shot through her.

'What is wrong with you?' he glared at her. 'Why are you being so lazy? I'm doing this for you for fuck's sake. It's your present and you can't even get out of bed.'

She'd never seen him so angry before.

'Sorry,' she said quietly and gingerly pulled herself up, pausing for the pain to subside before trying to find a way to stand.

He was trying T-shirts on now. Yanking them off. Throwing another one on. Turning to her.

'What do you think?' he demanded.

She nodded. 'Yeah,' she managed.

He huffed angrily.

They made their way down the road, each step causing her pain. She was relieved when they reached the bus stop and sat down. She was panting slightly. He pulled out the tattoo design.

'I think my M should be a bit bolder. I might get him to do it more Māori or something.'

The hardness of the plastic bench was excruciating. She placed a hand on his arm.

'Do you think we could get a taxi?' she begged.

'What do you think teachers are paid?' he said incredulously.

Arianna promptly threw up all over the ground.

'Jesus, Arianna.'

He took a bottle of water from his jacket and poured it over her vomit.

The bus came. She wasn't sure she could get on, but he had her by the arm now. And then the bus moved. Stopped. Started again. It was hard to tell what was worse, the nausea or the stomach pain. She tried to close her eyes, but the bus jerked her awake again.

Eventually, he pulled her up and off the bus. They were outside a tattoo parlour somewhere in South London. He looked nervous. She opened her mouth to say some words of encouragement, but he was already stepping into the shop.

A huge, beefy man with tattoos over his arms and neck looked up from the back of the room where he was working on another customer. A buzzing stopped in his hands.

'Alright mate,' Mr M said, suddenly speaking in a cockney accent she'd never heard before. 'I got an appointment, like. Ten o'clock.'

The man looked briefly at her, gestured to some seats near the door.

'Cheers,' Mr M said in his new voice.

It was dim in there. The radio was playing and the machine in his hand buzzed again. Arianna tried to breathe slowly and deeply. Tried to take each minute at a time. Mr M was edgy. Picking up a magazine and throwing it back down, his knee bouncing up and down rapidly.

Waves of nausea kept coursing through her. She looked around for something to throw up in if needed. Every time she shifted the pain in her stomach took her breath away. It was getting worse. She desperately needed to lie down. She tried resting her head on his shoulder, but he looked at her like she was mad.

Finally, they seemed to be finishing up. The tattooist cleaned his equipment, wiped down the chair and then looked over.

Mr M jumped up. 'My go is it? Sweet as.' He sat in the chair and got out the tattoo design. 'I'm thinkin' this but more Māori, like.'

The man frowned but also nodded. Started a mock-up of a design. They discussed it. A wave of exhaustion made her lean sideways. She caught herself falling and jerked herself awake.

'She okay?'

She opened her eyes to see the tattooist looking at her with concern.

'Yeah, bit of a large one last night, that's all,' Mr M said. 'Know wha' I mean?'

The man looked from him back to her.

'Come here,' Mr M pulled a chair next to him.

Arianna shook her head.

'Come see what it takes for when it's your turn,' he insisted. Arianna blinked. Her turn?

Mr M turned to the tattooist. 'I'm doin' this for 'er. Romantic present. Get 'er initials and mine done. And the silly cow can't be bothered to stay awake.' He was talking loudly. She slunked over to the chair.

The machine was soon buzzing and Arianna saw him tense as it began to scrape the ink into his skin. But soon her body was falling again, failing again.

He'd almost forgotten she was there anyway. He'd been keeping up a one-way banter with the silent ink-stained tattooist as he drew the outline of the A, the M into his reddening skin.

'I'm just going to pop out,' she said. The buzzing stopped.

'Stay there. You can hardly keep upright.' He'd dropped his accent for a moment. Then he remembered himself, turned to the tattooist and shook his head. 'Honestly, the things you do for love. Cost me my job, this one did.'

The buzzing started up once more.

Arianna sat very still. Her heart was racing, her breathing too. Mr M said something, laughed.

And then the pain disappeared, the wooziness lifted just enough. Arianna stood. She walked forward towards the door, then out of the door and down the road. She caught the first bus that came, concentrating hard on each breath, stop by stop, until she made it, pulled herself up and off. Step by step. She put her key in the lock. Turned it. Pushed the door open.

'Oh, you've finally decided to come home, have you?' her dad's hurt voice called from the living room.

Arianna took the stairs one by one, got to her room, shed her coat, her clothes, carefully pulled on her pyjamas. She lifted the duvet, lowered herself into her bed, and curled up, holding her stomach.

PART FOUR

2022

ARIANNA

The queue was already forming outside. Arianna gripped Candace's arm and guided her into the lobby. Candace looked around wildly, Arianna clocked a volunteer unrolling the Xanadu sign by the same conference room. The receptionist was focused on a form that a guest was filling in and ignored Arianna and Candace. Beside her on the counter was a pile of lanyards. Arianna grabbed two, handed one to Candace.

They walked into the conference room Arianna had been in just a few days ago. A dozen volunteers talked animatedly as they set up the various stations at the edges of the room. The chairs and stage were already set.

She had no plan, but they kept walking, past the people setting up, across the large room and towards the door at the far left where she'd seen Alan, Mr M, Dana and Saffy enter and exit that day. Arianna pulled at the metal handle, but it didn't budge. She tried again, nothing.

'Excuse me.' Candace and Arianna spun around to find a young white woman with a clipboard approaching. Her face was smiling but also asking a question. 'Can I help?'

Arianna's mind went blank. She couldn't think of a thing

to say. The woman stood, patiently waiting. Candace cleared her throat and pointed to the door.

The woman glanced at Candace's lanyard. 'Ah, of course,' she said and stepped past them, tapping a code into the key-pad beside the door and yanking the handle open.

'If you could start with Dressing Room Three, that would be great,' she said in a louder, slower voice, holding the door open. 'That's the messiest I think.'

Arianna nodded as she and Candace walked through into a carpeted corridor. The door clicked shut behind them. They looked at each other.

'Did she think we were ...' Candace began, lifting her lanyard and looking at it.

'Don't,' Arianna pleaded. 'I can't right now.'

They checked in Dressing Room Three, Two and then One, all empty, then carried on down the corridor turning to the left and then through two more sets of doors, down two flights of stairs, and found themselves in the car park.

Arianna and Candace stood looking around them. Candace suddenly kicked at a can on the floor and sent it clattering into the darkness. Arianna flinched.

'Where the fuck is she?' Candace's voice echoed desperately.

Arianna took out her phone and stared at the screen, hoping for some last-minute intervention from Karla. There was nothing.

Candace typed feverishly into her phone, but the bars in the top right corner had disappeared. She waved the phone above her head and then swore, returned it to her pocket.

There was a hum. The crunch of tyres turning. The echo of a metal barrier clanging. The growl of an engine getting louder, closer.

Arianna pulled Candace behind a parked car, and they crouched as a black Range Rover pulled up by the entrance they had just come out of. Alan stepped out of the driver's seat, bright eyed, galvanized, ready for their final appearance. Arianna had read up on him too, learned that he had a huge, rambling private estate somewhere near Tunbridge Wells, an affluent, secretive part of the English countryside where, according to those who had spoken out about Xanadu, followers went for the long-weekend retreats that they paid thousands to attend in order to be initiated into the next stage of the notorious PX12 – Xanadu's very own 12-step programme. There were lectures and martial arts mornings and rituals designed to free you from your ego, mostly by humiliating you; there were baptisms in the big swimming pool, pledges of allegiance and extra offerings, mostly financial. And it was never encouraged openly, but the whole thing was steeped in sexual tension. Hedonistic and intimate and full of desperate souls, these clandestine weekends in the grounds of a pop star's mansion alongside his guru were a hive of sexual proclivity where anything was permissible in the name of shedding your engrained shame and liberating yourself. Arianna was about to walk right up to Alan and thump him upside his privileged, brainwashed head.

But then Alan walked to the passenger door and opened it. Mr M stepped out first, followed by Dana, then finally, Saffy.

2022

SAFFY

'Saff!' Candace's cry rang out as she rushed towards her daughter. 'Oh god, Saffy.'

They turned. Alan strode towards her and caught Candace firmly, stopping her in her tracks just a few metres away from her daughter.

Saffy looked around in confusion, trying to make sense of what was happening as Mr M stepped in front of her and Dana, blocking Candace from their view.

'Get the fuck off me. That's my daughter!' Candace screamed.

'Mum?' Saffy exclaimed. Dana flinched at the word directed not at her, but at Candace. 'But I thought . . .'

Saffy looked wildly from Candace to Dana to Mr M and back.

'Get back in the car,' Mr M ordered the two of them firmly. But Dana remained frozen.

'Saffy come here!' Candace ordered. 'Get away from them.'

'But she told me you were waiting at the . . .' Saffy began. Then a lump of fear and confusion formed in her throat as she looked at the woman standing next to her, the woman with hair as golden as hers, skin as freckly, limbs and eyes and knees just like hers, and realized all at once that she was a complete stranger.

And a liar.

Saffiya Kali Crawford, also known as Saffron McDonald, aka Saffy, renamed herself the day after her twelfth birthday, almost exactly ten years after she'd arrived at Candace's house. One of the few times she'd been allowed to stay at home alone while her mum went on a rare date with her girlfriend, Saffy had gathered the incense, crystals, effigies, feathers and leaves her yoga-obsessed mum had dotted around the house, lit a candle and improvised a simple, magical ceremony all for herself. Candace had come back half an hour later and told her off for the ash spilled on the floor. They'd had a blazing row. Doors were slammed. And for the hundredth time, Saffy lay on her bed plotting her escape from that highly-strung cow who hadn't stopped long enough to hear that Saffy had just taken her surname out of respect and gratitude, before laying into her about a bit of poxy ash on the floor. And as always, Saffy's mind drifted guiltily to where she would go when she escaped from this cramped little floating prison, who she would stay with, and there she was again, that ethereal other mum she had no real memory of, but whom she could picture nonetheless. Blonde and beautiful and smiling and winsome, who would take her in and let her do/eat/try all the things her overprotective mum wouldn't let her do/ eat/try.

And then a year later, there she was, standing like a living dream on the bank beside their boat, so real, so similar to Saffy that it took her breath away. And from then on it was like she was living the recurring dream she'd had all her life. In a stupor, she had listened to Dana explain that she was there to collect her, that Candace would join them in a few days, somewhere special, in the countryside. That Saffy needed to pack a bag quickly and then they'd go somewhere where they could finally catch up, get to know each other, make up for lost time, meet some of Dana's friends, while they waited for Candace who deserved a few days to herself. Saffy knew, even then, that Candace would never have agreed to this without communicating with Saffy first, clearly and in person, but all Saffy wanted in that moment was to believe what Dana was saying was true. So she did.

What followed had been confusing but wonderful because she was with Dana, finally. And they'd talked and giggled and slept in the same room, and if Saffy was honest, the other people Dana introduced her to were a bit weird and kept interrupting her time with her real mum, but Saffy ignored these thoughts and feelings because being in the presence of Dana was like a massive final chunk of the puzzle that made up her self finally fitting into place.

As it got closer to the time to leave for the mansion in the countryside where Candace would meet them, things started to get busier, and Saffy found it harder to ignore the fear that something wasn't right. She had woken in the night, wanting her phone, and realized she didn't know where it was. Dana slept soundly beside her and Saffy didn't dare move. So she lay there, wide awake and desperate for Candace.

She tried not to think about how much she didn't like the people Dana had brought her to, the house they were staying in and those strange shows they had to sit through, the people Dana seemed so impressed with. She lay looking at the woman lying next to her and started to note each feature in minute detail, each eyelash and lip and curve of nostril that was so similar to her own, until she fell into sleep once more.

But.

She was now Saffiya Kali Crawford. The ceremony had been done. And Saffiya Kali Crawford was Candace Crawford's daughter. And she had been raised to be no one's fool. And no one's victim.

Standing in the dark underground car park, Saffy felt a wave of relief when she saw Candace run towards her. It took only one glance at her face to know something was very wrong. That this situation and these people were not what and who they said they were. That they were in fact the very baddies her paranoid mum had worried about this whole time.

She watched with rising terror as the man called Alan, who Dana had said was an old school friend from when she was the same age as Saffy, pushed her mum further away from her reach. As the creepy old guy who had Stranger Danger written all over him tried to block her from sight. As the lovely, fairytale of a birth mum standing right beside her was exposed as the two-faced liar she really was: there was no plan to meet Candace in the countryside, because Candace was screaming for her a few metres away, and Saffy needed to get to her ASAP.

'I said get in the car. Now,' the man called Mr Marlon growled over his shoulder.

Saffy looked desperately at Dana, but she remained frozen, her face pale. So Saffy broke into a run. She pelted towards Candace, only to find herself yanked back violently as Mr Marlon grabbed at her arm. She yelped at the shock of this grown man's touch, gripping her arm so hard it hurt.

'Get off me!' she shouted, kicking at his shins, trying to bite wherever she could as she felt him begin to pull her towards the car.

Candace was screaming. Then through the noise, another voice boomed off the concrete walls.

'No. Not again. Never again.'

A woman with messy black curls and a face full of glittering rage emerged from between two cars, phone held aloft, camera and light directed at them. She strode towards them and both Saffy and the man holding her recognized her at the same time: Saffy, as one of the two women who had visited her mum that day: the man, as his student. And lover.

'This is all being recorded. Let go of that little girl. She's a child. Just like I was. You don't get to hurt anyone ever again,' she said in a low, steady voice as she continued to stride forward.

He paused only a moment, an ironic smile beginning to form on his face. Then he suddenly lunged for the handle and hauled Saffron towards the open car door.

'Stop him for fuck's sake!' Arianna screamed at Dana, who stood looking with horror at the events unfolding before her, doing nothing, rooted to the spot. 'You're hurting her,' she whimpered to him, but remained frozen.

Candace fought against Alan, and Saffy screamed and kicked and bit. But Mr M was twice her size and an expert in women's self-defence, because he ran the classes and taught every single one of Saffy's techniques. And he knew how to counter each one.

Then a loud crack ricocheted off the concrete walls. And another.

Gunshots.

2022

Mr M threw Saffy and Dana in front of him, forming a human shield of them as he ducked. Two men strode into the car park from the other direction, one holding a rifle.

'Touch my sister again, I dare ya,' Candace heard her brother yell. She saw the violent blaze in his eyes once more. He headed straight towards Alan and nutted him square in the nose. Alan crumpled, holding his face as blood gushed from it. Warren appeared close behind and kicked Alan twice in the stomach for good measure, forcing him further away from Candace.

Saffy found herself finally free and rushed to Candace who held her tight, checking every inch of her, sobbing with relief.

Nathan aimed the air gun squarely at Mr M's head.

'You like pickin' on little girls, do ya?' he growled at the crouching man. 'I heard it's not the first time either, you fuckin' nonce. 'Cept this time, you messed with my family.'

He cocked the rifle and focused.

'Nathan. No!'

He paused but didn't take his eye off the man.

'Don't do it, Nathan.'

'He's a fuckin' nonce, Candace.'

'They've got money Nath. And lawyers an' that.'

'Exactly. That means he'll get away with it.'

'But *you* won't. You'll go back to prison. And that's that. He's not worth it, Nathan. But you are. You haven't hurt him. He's got nothing on you. Step back now. Cos we need you, Nath. We need you.' Candace pleaded, holding tightly to her daughter.

Nathan held his position, and looked into the eyes of the teacher who had hurt goodness knows how many girls. Then he loosened his grip and began to lower the rifle.

The man took his chance and leaped into the car, Alan with his busted nose had already crawled in the other side.

Dana rushed forward as the car began to move, tapping at the window as it sped away, leaving her behind. She turned back around and looked at the others, took a few steps towards them. 'Candace. I ...'

'GET THE FUCK AWAY FROM ME,' Candace spat. She led Saffy away, held between her and her uncle Nathan.

Dana turned to Arianna as she too started to leave. 'Riri ... I didn't know ... Please—'

'No. Just no.' Arianna glared at her. 'Not this time, Dana. You used me. You took Saffy from Candace and you took her to that monster. Do you know what he did to me? And now he's fucked off somewhere safe so he can do it all again. Because of you. You don't get another pass from me. I'm out.'

DANA

Dana Marie McDonald had always had a brilliant mind. Only a handful of people in her lifetime had cared about that. Dana Marie McDonald had stopped counting things in her head a long time ago just for the pure joy of it, had stopped taking account of things because they were too painful, too shameful and mostly unfathomable. She just kept on keeping on – from one place to another, from one bed to the next – terrified that some day soon, her luck and looks would run out.

So, when she'd found him and went to his meetings and he'd singled her out and made her feel special, after almost a year of isolation, after he told her what a brilliant mind she had and how much he needed her on his team, in his intimate circle of trust, Dana felt like she had been given a ninth life. And as she worked the programme – his programme – and finally revealed everything to him, so that she could be cleansed and reborn just like the others, the deep guilt she felt for abandoning her daughter, as he spoke to her one-on-one a few weeks later, suggesting that they bring the girl in, so that they could be a family, Dana felt like this could finally be her happy ending.

And now she saw him for what he was. Saw his promises and compliments and poems for what they were. And now she realized with horror what he had planned to do. How he had implicated her in the most awful thing. Made her work for him for next to nothing so that she could afford their courses and workshops, so that she had somewhere to stay, to pay off her debt, which only seemed to increase the longer she stayed. And that he had taken everything from her. And because there was so little left, it didn't take long to take account this time, to take stock, however heartbreaking it was.

Dana Marie McDonald had been left with nothing.

Almost.

Because Dana, used and abused, manipulated and gaslit and brainwashed and coerced, and friendless and daughterless and penniless as she was, *still* had a brilliant mind. A mathematical mind.

Which was why they had put her in charge of the accounts.

2022

ARIANNA

Arianna awoke from a fitful, exhausted sleep. She switched on her phone and scrolled through messages and emails. The first one, sent in the middle of the night from an unfamiliar address, caught her eye. The subject matter was a single X.

Arianna opened a couple of the many attachments and scrolled through. It took a while for her to realize that these were figures, spreadsheets, account details and more, all pertaining to the Xanadu Foundation, also known as several other names – for financial purposes – and all associated, directly or indirectly, with a Mr Marlon Bysshe Blake, and printed beside this on all documents, his birth name.

Arianna rushed to her laptop and took a closer look. Then she forwarded it all on to another email address.

2022

CANDACE

Candace lay beside Saffy, stroking her hair and kissing her as the morning river waves made a glinting pattern on the ceiling of her daughter's bedroom. Saffy was too old for this stuff now. She'd been so affectionate when she'd been little, but then she'd turned eleven going on nineteen and the arguments started, and with them the end of most affection between them. But last night they had slept curled up in each other's arms, Saffy clinging onto her like she was a lifebelt.

A knock at the door made Candace start. She disentangled herself from her daughter and went to the front door where a delivery man handed her a large envelope.

Candace took the package to the kitchen counter and opened it. She pulled out pages of documents. On the final two pages, a signature with a name printed below it. Dana's name. Relinquishing Saffy and consenting to her being adopted.

KARLA

The day Karla Malik had turned sixteen, she'd been plied with poems and cards and gifts from her teacher, and soon Karla found herself in her first ever relationship. Until an uncle who was really a family friend had seen the man pushing Karla up against a wall off the high street and called her parents. She was grounded for a year, moved to a different school, driven there and back every day, kept under close surveillance until she finished her studies and was finally able to move out. As she got older, she began to feel a sense of hurt, of having been used, of power and responsibility having been exploited. Of injustice.

She also couldn't bring herself to read poems anymore.

Fraud. A supposedly victimless crime. A way to beat the system that was so unfair anyway. A way to rebel against a faceless entity, exploit a loophole. But also a way to manipulate and gaslight, to control and confuse and isolate. Karla started in an organization that reported to the police and worked her way up until she became a consultant. She was diligent, good with detail and hungry for Justice.

Karla quietly passed the evidence that nailed Xanadu over

to a trusted detective. She watched from a distance as it was checked and verified, as arrests were authorized, as the case moved forward.

5 a.m. is the preferred time for a dawn raid. For suspects to be apprehended and for devices and paperwork to be seized.

Police cars surrounded the grounds of the large estate in the depths of Tunbridge Wells, then the team and their dogs descended. By 5:23 two men had been arrested.

Neither Arianna nor Karla attended the court case. Though every cell in Arianna's body wanted to see that man sentenced in a proper court of law, she couldn't be seen to be involved in any way, to jeopardize the case.

So, she waited and waited until finally the text came through, forwarded on through Karla from the colleague in attendance.

Guilty.

Of Fraud.

By Abuse of Power.

Epilogue

Tess comes in first, playing with signature precision the notes that seem not to make sense until her cellist joins her four bars in, followed by the pianist, the bassist and the singer. Each musician adding another layer of notes, all Tess's creation, that weave a melody, a harmony, a rhythm that is rich and complex and only complete when all instruments have joined. Then, one by one, they drop out until it's just Tess once more.

Silence, then applause, exclamations from the audience that Tess can't quite see because of the bright lights in the Union Chapel, East London. She beams at her band – real people, playing *her* music. Music that for a year she played alone, on an old loop pedal she'd found the first weekend she was child-free. Bereft and at a loss of what to do with herself, Tess had walked around her empty home until she'd found herself in Callum's old studio, where he created music, while she looked after their daughter. And now it was empty apart from a music stand and few old instruments she'd kept from the old flat. And a loop pedal. Gifted to her by Mr Tamworth on her last day of school. It still worked. And for the best part of 48 hours, Tess sat in that room and worked out arrangements to her own songs, becoming her own band, because with a loop pedal, she could be every instrument she needed.

And then she recorded it, released it, pulled in some favours so it didn't get lost in the mountain of offerings coming from this city every day. And it turned out there was an audience for it, a hunger for music played on musical instruments by musicians, for the resonance of string on wood, breath through brass, human voice. And she was offered gigs, and she rocked up with her instruments and loop pedal and voice, and she got standing ovations, and more bookings, and a tour. And then she found other musicians, brilliant women, who should have been famous, who'd had some kids and were hungry to play again.

And now she has a band of brilliant multi-instrumentalists who are also multi-tasking mums and they play her music in venues that she was previously only allowed in when she was playing other peoples' stuff, mostly white men's, many of them long dead.

Candace lets herself be pulled onto the dancefloor. She feels a bit silly, a bit old to be throwing shapes. Can't quite remember how to move her body the right way. But Asha does. She weaves and pouts and winds her hips and looks at Candace in a way that makes her remember. And Saff is watching the Lionesses on the telly back on the boat with Uncle Nath and Uncle Warren and they swore they wouldn't let her back in until tomorrow morning so she might as well have some fun for once. Might as well make the most of one of the few spaces for queer women left in this city.

Someone knocks her shoulder. She turns as the other woman raises a placatory hand. And they both frown, then their mouths drop open in unison. The ponytail and fringe have been replaced with a crewcut, a lip piercing and several tattoos, but the laugh is just the same.

'I knew it! I fucking knew it!' Bernie cackles as she disappears into the crowd of lesbians.

Arianna stretches in her bed, turns over, smiles. Today she can lie in. And tomorrow if she likes. Because Arianna has handed in her notice. She is done. She has passed the baton to another and saved enough money to take a few months off, signed up to a writing course, and started gathering those pieces together, bridging them, merging them into something bigger, more ambitious. A book.

The sound of her key in the door, the groan as it opens. The smell of fresh coffee and croissants reach her before he does: she messaged. Finally. On the dating app. And after a dignified few days, he replied. And they'd called. Then met. Then he'd stayed over last weekend. And it was so good, she'd invited him back. As his smiling beardy face – the same face that had made her swipe right all those months ago – hands her her breakfast, she notices her body respond, recalls her surprise at the level of pleasure her body was capable of, the tears of relief she'd managed to hide that first time together, the wonder at the way her little cocoon of a flat has been transformed into a playground of exploration and pleasure. And she wonders if she's done walking away from things and people now, if now it's time to start walking *towards*.

Because who knew kindness could be so hot? Who knew she was capable of so much intimacy, so much silliness, so much goddam pleasure, if she just felt safe?

Dana looks up at the fifth floor of the high-rise and sees the same net curtains from twenty years ago. She's been abroad, for the first time in her life, because Eileen didn't believe in going to foreign countries. She overheard a customer in the café she briefly worked at telling their mate how much less you could live on outside of Europe. So that's what Dana did. She went to India, then Kenya. The two places that make up Candace's heritage. She learned some things, figured out some other things, made peace with spicy food. And now she's back and starting from scratch and this time she's gonna do it right. Get some help, get some qualifications, start living right. But that takes time and money.

She's kept the key all this time. Dana steps onto the same pristine carpet, down the same hallway to the living room where Eileen sits smoking on the sofa alone, a little frailer, the TV on.

She looks at Dana, takes her in. 'Oh,' she says. 'Alright?'

'Yeah. You?'

'Yeah. You stopping?'

'Yeah.'

'Put the kettle on then.'

They've stayed friends, online at least. Every now and then one of them will Like a post, a photo, send a Heart or a Thumbs Up. And then, one day, one of them posts a picture of the original Scary Spice from all those years ago, teeth bared, curls and highlights and mini-buns, animal print and midriff and attitude. And three middle-aged friends in three different places log on at three different times, and see it, and giggle. Like schoolgirls.

ACKNOWLEDGEMENTS

To my editor Judith Long whose work to help hone this sprawling, many-headed story into something coherent has been invaluable – thank you. To Aneesha Angris, Melanie Hayes and all the team at Simon & Schuster UK, thank you.

To Hannah Weatherill for your advocacy, insight, sensitivity and level-headed support – thank you.

Thank you to Martin McGuigan and Darren John Travers for all the meetups and notes.

Thank you to my parents for my cultural and political education and for supporting my creative endeavours.

To the many individuals who gave me so much of their time to share their lived experience and expertise on issues and subjects ranging from Section 28, Domestic Violence, Sexual Violence, Law, Fraud, The Criminal Justice System, Homelessness, Asexuality, Sex Ed, Social Services, Adoption, Fostering, Sexuality, Cultural and Racial Identity – Nicole Latchana, Jade Swaby, Elizabeth Rose, Sorcha Fhionntain, Saffron Burley, Rob Brooker, Alex Limia, John Dorney – thank you.

To Jo, Emma and Leah for your friendship in those formative years and for trusting me with your, our, stories.

To my creative peers who have become such an important source of support, sanity and community – thank you.

To Kaash, my partner, ally, champion and now husband. You are such a consistent source of support, love and kindness which brings out the best in me and keeps me flourishing – thank you.

To my chosen family for being there through the darkest and the brightest – thank you.

GODDESSES

Ayesha is just about finding her feet on the London stand-up scene, but when her response to a sexist heckler goes viral, she finds herself drawn into an exclusive group of activists: a sacred circle of change makers, each woman with a specific gift to contribute to the cause.

The circle draws in her friend Yaz too and they are both invited to an intimate hen do, except it's not a hen do – it's a *Goddess Retreat*. While Ayesha, longing to find her tribe, tries to fit herself into a shape that the women will accept, Yaz treats the entire 'itinerary' with open disdain. But the Goddess Retreat is no laughing matter. As the weekend descends into chaos, they'll need to stick together if they want to get out alive.

AVAILABLE IN PAPERBACK AND EBOOK NOW